THE BILLIONAIRE'S CHRISTMAS BRIDE

L. STEELE

1

"I am just a girl standing in front of a salad, asking it to be a doughnut."
-From Amelie's diary

Amelie

"Aww, they clearly like each other," the radio show host exclaims.

"They hated each other, couldn't stop trading insults —" the male announcer interrupts her.

"Only it was all build-up, OMG…" the first announcer cuts in. "The feels, the emotions.. They wanted to stab each other, but turned out, it was a different kind of stabby that they had for each other."

"Is that what they're calling it these days, Ivy?" The man snickers, "Good thing this is a late-night chat show."

"I can always count on you to keep me in line, Wolfgang," Ivy quips.

"Call me Wolf," the male announcer drawls.

"Right, well," Ivy clears her throat. " For everyone listening on this blustery night in the lead up to Christmas…" She pauses to take a breath, "The question I'd like to pose is, is it rude to interrupt someone mid-sentence by uh! distracting them? Email us, text us, call in and tell us after the break. This is Smile FM..."

I snort aloud, then switch off the radio tuned into the local radio station. The talk show hosts seem to be living in la-la land, or is it the Christmas spirit that's affecting them? More likely, it's the chemistry, between them, which not even the airwaves could disguise. Must be nice, to have that kind of sizzling attraction, huh?

The kind that makes you want to slap the man, punch him in the nuts, maybe; right before you jump on him, wrap your legs around him, and—

That...had been the kind of no-holds-barred romance I'd hoped for when I had met my ex. He'd done everything right, hadn't attempted to kiss me until our third date. In short, he'd been a gentleman...of the double-crossing kind.

Bastard had dumped me after three weeks.

He'd seen my name connected to all the notoriety that had followed my friend Victoria and her now-husband Saint's wedding... His mother hadn't been happy about it, and as he'd rushed to inform me, he couldn't go against his mama's word... So, I'd been dropped.

On the other hand, my fledgling pastry business had taken off.

Everyone wanted the desserts that had been featured prominently in the publicity accompanying the marriage... I had more orders than I could fulfill. I had worked around the clock in the lead up to Christmas. I'd fulfilled my last booking this morning and handed over the reins of the company to my assistant—yep, I made enough money in the last month to finally hire the intern who had worked with me since I'd started the business.

I can trust her to keep the business going, while I take some time off over Christmas and New Year's. A few days of no work, no waking up in the early hours to bake... Not unless I want to do it for pleasure; and damn, if I am not going to bake the hell out of some new recipes that I want to try out.

I am going to use the next week to unwind, to reconnect with the girl I'd once been—carefree, happy, with hope in her eyes and a spring in her step—before business worries had taken over my life. I hunch my shoulders. At twenty-five, I am not that old... Except for the fact that I've never met a man with whom I've managed to hold a relationship down for more than uh—three months.

Well, to hell with that.

I am going to make the most of what I have. To start, I'll rejuvenate over the festive season, then bounce back into London all bright-eyed and ready to take the New Year by storm. Yeah! I turn off the highway, down the narrow road that leads me deeper into the countryside. My sturdy Volkswagen eats up the miles, until I get to a turn-off. I glance at the GPS... Yup, this is the road. Well, what the hell? I turn down the unpaved path. I'd wanted solitude. Guess I am getting it, one way or the other. I drive another mile, turn another corner...and drive up to massive gates.

I roll down my window, pull up the security app I'd installed on my phone, then reach out and wave my phone over the keypad in the wall.

The gates swing open. Awesome, and on the first try!

I continue down the driveway to a single-story bungalow, with a porch running around it, then park the car. I switch off the engine and listen. There... I can hear it... The silence. I can't stop the smile that lifts my cheeks. Most people don't like to be alone... Me? I thrive on it. As long as I can bake during the day, then curl up with my book-boyfriend in the evenings, with a glass of my favorite bubbly—champagne only, I'm strict like that—and surrounded by bubbles in a bathtub... Oh yeah, that would be a bonus. I push the door open, then walk around to retrieve my two suitcases. Don't judge. I like to have the comforts of home with me when I travel. So, what if I am only a few hours away from home? I need my favorite set of PJs, my bath bombs, my wine...and this. I walk around to the front of the car, open the door to the passenger side, and retrieve my most prized possession, the tools of my trade—my pastry chef bag, without which, I never go anywhere.

Sliding the strap of my baking toolkit across my chest, my handbag over one shoulder, I begin to drag one of the suitcases... which promptly gets stuck in the muddy ground. I haul at it, there's a cracking sound, then the valise dips to one side. Shit, did I break it already? To be fair, it had been a surprisingly cheap buy from the charity shop. I should have known better than to buy it, even though it had been marked down by about 70%. I wipe the sweat from my forehead. I straighten, take a step back, and instantly lose my footing. I hit the ground on my butt.

Bloody hell, this is all going tits over arse. A whistling sound emerges from the trees.

Goosebumps flare on my skin. Shit, is there someone…or something out there? It's all well and good to want to be alone… But in the countryside? I hadn't considered how…spooky it could all be. A low humming sounds in the distance. Is that a bird? A plane? Crap, there is no Superman around here to rescue me. I am on my own. *Better get your arse in gear, woman.* I jump up to my feet. Best get indoors, turn on some lights, then I can come back for my luggage.

A breeze blows and I hunch my shoulders. *Damn it, how can I be warm and cold at the same time?*

I take another step, trip over some rocks. *Hell, I need lights, and fast. Okay, hold on, I've got this.*

I grab my phone from my handbag, switch on the flashlight. A beam of light illuminates the way. I walk toward the patio, take the steps up to the front door, shove my hand into my handbag and scrounge around for the key. Where is it? Where the hell is it? There! I pull out the key and insert it into the lock. The door unlocks. Woo!

I push against the door, walk into a spacious living room. Switching off the light, I drop the phone into my handbag. Then I take stock.

There's an unlit fireplace in the center, a settee beyond that, facing the door, complete with a rug in front of it. To my right are big French windows, to my left is a bookcase, with floor to ceiling shelves, filled with books. Yay, that's another point for this place. Next to it is a small table with liquor bottles.

I walk to it, place my handbag on the bar counter, next to a wall clock that's turned face down. I turn it face up; realize it's stopped. Huh? Guess it ran out of batteries. I replace it on the counter, turn around. That's when I hear the low sound of whistling again. I gulp. Guess I hadn't imagined it then?

It's a whistling, and of the human variety. This is not from an animal or a bird. The hell? I glance around the comfortable space. Everything looks undisturbed, though how would I know? I hear the sound of something sloshing from the direction of the back door… What the—? Did the intruder decide to take a bath?

Is there a hot tub of some kind on the patio at the back?

I take a step forward, then stop. I need a weapon. I am not going out there alone. Shit, why had I thought it was a good idea to come here on my own, remind me again? I hadn't been running away, I hadn't… Yeah, right. I'd needed to take myself away from all of those shiny, happy, faces celebrating bloody Christmas, which honestly, I do love… I do… Just not this year. This year, I need to catch a break… And hell, if I haven't caught something, alright. A burglar, more like it. I unclasp my satchel of baking tools, reach in and remove a—spatula? The humming sound increases in pitch, then a full-blown song reaches me. The hell? I squeeze my fingers around my weapon… Don't laugh; a spatula can do plenty of damage when it connects with someone's balls.

I lower my chef's satchel to the ground, then unbutton my coat and shrug it off. I stalk toward the door at the far end.

The sounds of water splashing reaches me through the patio door. Huh? Maybe there is a hot tub out there…

Then a male voice breaks into a rendition of *Nothing Else Matters* by Metallica. What the—? There's someone out there, all right, and the singing's not bad, actually. My thief, has a thing for classic rock, and can carry a tune. I hum the lyrics in sync with him… *The hell?* I pause, draw in another breath. *Now or never. Do it, Amelie. Go for it. Whoever it is, he has no right to be here. Shit, should I have called the cops?*

The singing stops abruptly. *What the—? Did he hear me approaching?*

I half angle my body, turn to leave; the door to the patio flies open.

I pivot around, raise my weapon, and find I am confronted with a wall of muscle. Naked chest, water running in rivulets down those sculpted abs that narrow into a concave belly which points to his thick, long—

"My face is up here," he drawls.

Heat flushes my cheeks; I jerk my gaze up. Grey eyes clash with mine—stormy clouds that boil in a sky which hints at oncoming snow. Sleet. Hail. An uncompromising will to get his way, no matter what. A shiver runs down my spine and moisture pools between my legs.

The skin between his eyebrows crinkles and his nostrils flare. *No way.* He can't smell my arousal, can he?

That mean upper lip thins further. His pouty lower lip juts out above a chin that wears days' old growth of beard. Thick dark hair covers his jaw. *How would it feel to have him draw those rough whiskers across my inner thighs? Right before he dips his head, darts out his tongue, and licks my innermost secret place.* Goosebumps dot my skin. *Shit, what's wrong with me? Why did my mind go there? You know why... Because this handsome piece of 100% male goodness is, quite simply, the most wickedly delicious piece of dessert I've ever laid my eyes on.* My throat dries. Also, I happen to know him.

"You?" my voice comes out breathless.

"What are you doing here?" he snaps at the same time.

"What are *you* doing here?" I retort. "And in a hot tub, on the patio of this house, no less?"

"I am not in the habit of answering queries posited by women who look like they've been dragged in from a storm."

"What?" My jaw drops. I am gaping, and it's not only because the words complete the image of the man I've loathed from the moment I first saw him at the wedding of one of my best friends. "Dr. f'ing Weston," I snarl.

"That's Doc Kincaid to you." He yawns.

Of course, his surname would have to have the word kink in it in some form. "And are you?" I scowl.

"What?"

"A real doctor?"

He raises his hand, stabs the air with a cigar I only now realize he holds between his fingers. "Do you want to find out?" He looks me up and down, waggles his eyebrows. "I could give you a thorough examination." His gaze settles on my breasts, slides down to my core. "Make sure everything is in working order." He snickers.

Heat fizzes low in my belly. Hell, with that kind of hotness, this man could clearly get my cake batter to rise in seconds… *Wait, did I just think that?*

I make a gagging noise in my throat, "Does that line actually work?"

"You'd be surprised." His lips curl.

Oh, that smirk. My stomach seems to bottom out… Or maybe that's because I haven't eaten since breakfast.

He draws on his cigar, cheeks hollowing for an instant, before he puffs out smoke. Cherries, cloves…cinnamon. Yum. My mouth waters, "How would it be to bake a cigar dessert?"

"What?" He frowns.

Shit, did I just say that aloud?

"Nothing," I mumble, "and you haven't answered my question."

His voice lowers to a hush, "I'll answer yours if you answer mine." Another shiver ladders up my spine. How *did he manage to make that seem like an innuendo?*

"Is everything a trade to you?"

"You should try it." He smiles, a full-blown grin that highlights the laughter lines that stretch from the corners of his eyes. I mean, could this guy be any more perfect? I allow my gaze to take in the breadth of his shoulders, that gorgeous neck, the swell of those hard biceps, the smattering of hair on those forearms—*No, do not look lower; don't do it*—to the splint that he sports around middle finger of his right hand.

"What happened to you?" I scowl.

"This?" He raises his middle finger to show me the bird by default, "I fractured my middle finger in a car accident."

"How convenient," I scoff. "You can announce your jerk-face nature without speaking a word."

He chuckles, "You always this nice to injured men?"

"You always go around flashing women?"

"You enjoyed the view." He raises that goddam cigar again to his mouth, wraps those beautiful lips around the smoke stick.

And I'd love to get my mouth around his fat, juicy cigar too.

No, no. Enough with the terrible metaphors. But, hello, can you blame me?

I am only a woman standing in front of a man—a naked, gorgeous-as-hell, stud muffin of a male who pulls the cigar from his mouth, and blows out a cloud of fragrant smoke from between pursed lips.

Moisture melts my core. My toes curl.

Jesus, there should be a law against him using his mouth like that. Of course, I could find other uses for that mouth of his too… *No, no no. Why are you insisting on going back down that route?*

"Nothing I haven't seen," I toss my head.

"Unlikely." He lowers his right hand—the one with the splint and the default flip-me-off-bird to his crotch.

What the—? Don't look there, bitch— Don't bloody watch him grasp himself and squeeze.

I gulp, the sound audible in the small space. And damn him, but I can't take my gaze off of that gorgeous part of his anatomy.

He moves his arm to his side, "I rest my case."

Hell, but a certain part of him is far from being in resting position. Gulp. *Did I just word play on his dick play?* Clearly, his proximity is rubbing off if all I can think of are these poor jokes.

"By the way," his tone is conversational, "you planning on defending yourself with that?" He jerks his chin.

I tighten my grasp around the spatula and raise it. "This has been known to strike fear in the heart of burglars and those who've tried to break in on me before," I snap.

"You were burgled?" His jaw hardens.

"None of your business."

"Answer the bloody question." He takes a step forward. I scoot back. My leg brushes something warm and furry, which moves.

"Whoa!" I struggle to find my balance then, for the second time in ten minutes, the world tilts, and I find myself falling… Falling.

The spatula slips from my grasp. I squeeze my eyes shut, waiting for my butt to connect with the hard ground, only I'm yanked upright. Heat envelops me and my breasts flatten against something unyielding. I don't need to open my eyelids to know it's his chest, the one with the cut planes, the eight-pack abs. I slap my palm against that wall of muscles which coil, move, and writhe under my finger-tips. I gulp and my legs threaten to give way under me, but his hold around my shoulders tightens. I spot the smoldering smoke stick of his on the ground.

"Your…cigar," I stutter.

"You noticed," he quips.

I grimace, then nod my head toward the floor. "I meant that one."

"Forget that." His breath feathers over my hair and liquid lust shoots through my veins. The scent of pine and cloves mixes with that edgy darkness that is purely Weston. Speaking of — something hard stabs into my waist — the aforementioned "cigar." A groan boils up my throat. Not fair — this crazy attraction to someone I've barely met a couple of times. Why does he have to smell so delicious? Bet if I licked his chest, he'd taste more decadent than the chocolate mud pie cake recipe I've been wanting to bake. I'll lick the frosting off his cupcake any time. *Nooooo.* Not again. Enough with comparing his unmentionables with my favorite stuffed goodies. OMG, how would it feel to have him stuff his goodies in my cannoli? *Wait, did that even make sense?*

His voice dips, "You haven't answered my question."

"What?" I blink.

"Someone broke in on you?" He enunciates his words at a slow pace as if I am slow of mind… Which, I admit, at the moment, I seem to be. His larger-than-life charisma has turned my brain cells to mush. "Tell me," he coaxes. Is he using the same tone he'd use with the puppy to make him obey? Well, hell, if it isn't working on me as well.

"Y…yes." My stomach clenches. "But I fought off the thief…." I force out the words.

His muscles coil; tension radiates off of his body. "You confronted the man?" he snaps.

"Yeah," I hunch my shoulders, "It happened a week ago… No biggie." I swallow as my heart begins to race. It hadn't been pleasant, that almost encounter. I had been alone in the kitchen of my bakery at 4 am… Hell, it had been horrible, actually. The guy had thrown a fright into me and I had thrown this spatula at him. "I chased him off. Yay. See? I'm fine, still alive." And bloody shaken, but I'm not going to tell him that.

His grip tightens, "Did he hurt you?" His jaw tics.

I stare up into his tight features. You'd think Mr. Jerkass here is all concerned about my safety.

"Did he?" his voice snaps through the noise in my head.

"N…no," I shake my head.

"No, what?"

No, I will not give in to this insane chemistry between us. I didn't come all this way to run slap-bang into a man who is, surely, far worse than the one who recently broke my heart. "No, he didn't do any harm. He ran off before I could use the spatula on him." I tip up my chin. "Though I can't promise the same to you."

He chuckles, "I love a good fight, don't you?"

Jackass.

A whine sounds behind me.

I shoot a sideways glance to spot a puppy plant his behind on the ground…exactly the kind of position I'd have been in, if 'Mr. Overbearing Brute' here hadn't grabbed me first. Oh, so that's what I'd brushed against earlier and almost fallen over.

"Max," Weston talks to the dog, "you hungry, buddy?"

The puppy whines again.

"I'll be right there, little fella." His voice takes on a cajoling tone, and damn him, but my ovaries seem to spasm. *The hell is he doing to me?* Before this, I've never thought about kids… Hell, I've barely managed to embark on a halfway decent career, and I've never thought of myself as someone who'd want a family. But Weston, with his smoldering glare, his hard face, his harder—um—body, and that coaxing manner with which he talks to Max… I can see him with a child tucked under one arm, and me under his other… Heck, I can see me under him, period. My mouth waters. My panties dampen further. *Get your mind out of the gutter, you slut.*

"Isn't he Sinclair and Summer's pet?" I frown. My friend Summer had married Sinclair Sterling, one of the seven billionaire co-owners of 7A investments. The media had labelled them the Seven and, Dr Douche here is one of them.

"Summer and Sinclair are away on an extended honeymoon," Weston grunts.

"Aww. So you decided to puppy-sit?" A warm glowing ball lights up inside of me.

He glowers, "Don't gush any sweet icky stuff now—uh, what's your name again?"

Poof—that warm feeling I mentioned? Forget about it. The hell is wrong with this man? "You know my name all right, you ass." I stab my finger in his chest, "So why are you pretending otherwise?"

"Me?" He blinks, "Do I?" He tilts his head, pretending to think, "Is it Lily?"

A slow burn starts up my spine.

"No... No." He cracks his neck, "It will come to me, it will... It's Malia, right?"

Anger laces the edges of my vision. I draw in a breath, then another. *Stay calm, he can only get so much more obnoxious, right?*

"Wait, let me try, one more time..." He pats his temple with the palm of his injured hand. "It's...something French, isn't it? Like... Valerie, Malory, maybe? No, I have it." He snaps his fingers, "It's Celine. I got that right, didn't I?" He chuckles.

I clench my fists, then raise my hand toward his face.

He catches my wrist. "Tsk, tsk," he clicks his tongue. "What a temper you have, little one."

"Don't 'little one' me... You... You wanker."

"Finally," his eyes gleam, "here kitty, kitty, show me your claws."

"I'll do better than that," I hiss, "I'll show you how it is to see the sun at night time."

I bring up my knee, aim for his groin.

2

Weston

What the hell? I know what she intends to do, a second before she moves. I step aside and her knee grazes the outside of my thigh. I release her shoulders only to grab the nape of her neck. "Stop that," I scold her, "or you'll hurt yourself."

"The only one who's gonna be hurt here, buster, is you." She swings out with her fist.

As if this tiny thing could do anything to injure me? Oh wait, I'd done that on my own, when someone had run my car off the road a few days ago.

I angle my body, but I'm not fast enough. Her fist grazes my side; a burn of heat trickles down my spine. She didn't hurt me. Instead, my body is responding to her in a manner that leaves no doubt of the fact that certain parts of me would very much prefer to be in more intimate contact with her.

"Stop," I growl.

She makes a noise deep in her throat, "You uncouth, obnoxious, horrible, man." She swings with her other hand, the shot too wide to do any harm. But it causes her to lose her balance, and she topples over, crashing into me.

Softness, curves, the weight of her breasts, even through the layers she is wearing, is a thing of beauty against my chest. I release her nape, only to wrap my hand about her shoulders and haul her close.

"Let me go," she chokes.

"No." I say all casual-like, hoping she'll take the bait. Whaddya know? The little thing hits out with her fist again, this time catching me on the wrist of my injured hand. Pain flashes up my arm and sparks of brightness dot my vision. Shit, she hadn't been kidding about her threat.

I grit out the words through clenched teeth, "Stop it before I do something I regret."

"Ha," she scoffs. "I am not scared of bullies like you."

I draw in a deep breath. "Don't threaten me."

"Don't underestimate me." She raises her fists.

Ooh, I am so scared. I stifle the chuckle that crowds my throat. Max whines again, I glare at him from over her shoulder. He wags his tail, mouth open, tongue lolling. Of course, I could get my staff in the hospital to behave with that look, but it has little effect on the little rascal. I frown at Max. He pants back, then turns and runs off in the direction of the kitchen. That buys me, maybe, a minute before he'll be back. Best make full use of it. I train my glare on the handful of woman who glowers up at me. She barely comes to chest level… And that hair? Is she actually sporting streaks of purple? And there is so much of it… Her hair, I mean. It flows like spun gold around her shoulders, catching the light that filters in from the patio behind her.

"Hey," she snaps her fingers, "what are you staring at?"

"Your hair." I reach out with my bandaged hand to touch the shining strands. I bring it up to my nose and sniff it.

She stiffens. "What are you doing?"

"What's that smell?"

"What?" She tips up her perky little nose, sniffs the air.

"That." I grasp a handful of her hair, bury my nose in it, and draw in a deep breath. "Vanilla, sugar, apples...butter." The mix of scents go straight to my head. "Why the hell do you smell of dessert?" I frown.

"Ah, maybe because I'm a pastry chef?" She scowls. "What the hell do you think you're doing anyway?"

"Speaking of." I let the hair slide out from between my fingers-...*Why do I miss its softness already?* "I'm not letting you stay here. You do realize that?"

"What?" She blinks. "What did you say?"

"I was here first."

"Excuse me?"

The light in her blue eyes intensifies and little creases appear on her forehead. Oh, this is going to be good. "Here, at the cabin." I smirk. "I am staying here until New Year's."

"*I'm* staying here until New Year's," she says through clenched teeth.

"Nope," I emphasize the word with a popping sound, and practically see the smoke pour out of her tiny ears. Beautiful, shell shaped ears, that I'd like to curl my tongue around, suck on those pretty earlobes before easing it into that hole. My groin hardens. Hell... there are other parts of her which I'd like to push into as well... Lick her up, suck on the melting flesh between her thighs, nip on her lower lips, before I thrust my tongue inside her soaking channel and bring her to the edge.

"I am too." She props her hands on her hips, her curvy, deliciously rounded hips, which is one of the first things I'd noticed about her too. She's so different from the women I normally encounter... Hell, she's not my type at all. Soft, sassy, perfectly shaped for my hands. My fingers tingle. *I will not touch her, will not.* I tilt my head. "From where I am, you are...on your way out."

"What?" She blinks. "I am standing right here."

"That can be easily changed."

I take a step forward, and honestly, I'd totally expected her to retreat. To shuffle back, maybe even turn and run out of the house... I should have known better, after how she'd threatened me with that spatula earlier, for she doesn't move. She stands her ground, so my feet bump hers. I lean into her; she tips her chin up.

I lower my face toward hers, closer, closer. "You can't win this, Buttercup."

"Buttercup?" She scrunches up her forehead. "Why the hell are you calling me after the Princess Bride?"

"It was after a Powerpuff Girl, actually," I chuckle.

"Powerpuff?" She grimaces.

I nod, "You're small, annoying, and too headstrong for your own good."

"How do you even know about those cartoons?"

"I may have watched them with my little niece."

"Awww." Her gaze widens; her eyes go all sparkly as fuck. *Ah, hell!*

My neck heats. "Don't make it out to be anything more than what it is," I grunt.

"Which is?"

"That I babysit on occasion," I mutter.

"You also babysit?" Her features take on the expression I have seen on the faces of the women who have fallen for some of my friends. Specifically, Jace, Sinner and that mofo Saint. All of them ended up married, and shackled, and buying townhouses, and planning extended honeymoons, and baby showers... *Argh!* A shiver of trepidation runs up my spine. *Shit, no, no, no, I am not going there.* These kinds of entanglements, and all the bloody relationship fuck-ups that come with it? Not for me. So not my tumbler of whiskey — you didn't think I'd say cup of tea, now, would you?

Besides, what the hell am I doing, sharing that piece of information about myself? She'd gotten past my guard, obviously. It's the only reason I'd let that slip. More to the point, why the hell are we still talking, here in the house I co-own?

The hair on my nape prickles.

"How the hell did you get here?" I frown.

"I drove, of course." She sniffs, "What about you?"

"I was driven here by my chauffeur," I grumble.

"That's why there's no car parked outside." She nods. "How do you plan to get around for the time you are here?"

"I don't."

"Guess you can't drive with that finger, huh?"

"I can bloody drive, if I want." I scowl, "I choose not to; besides, every time I want to head out, I'll message my driver."

She opens and shuts her mouth, "Let me get this right. Every time you want to go out, you'll message your chauffeur who'll come in from where? London?"

I glare at her, "Don't be daft. He's staying in the nearest town. It takes him, maybe, 45 minutes to get here."

"To take you back into the village, and return."

"Umm, yeah." I raise my shoulders, "That's why he's called a driver. He drives me around," I snicker.

"I could do that."

"What?"

"Drive you around."

"Why should I want that?"

"Since we are going to be sharing this house —"

"Nope, we're not. I own this place with the rest of the Seven."

"Saint offered it to me for the duration of the holidays." She scowls, "Pretty sure he loaned the space to me first."

"I am one of the Seven. I take precedence," I declare.

She gapes at me and… Damn… Every time she opens her mouth, I want to shut her up with my tongue, or other parts of me that would very happily nestle into that warmth. Why the fuck does she turn me on, when she's the type of complication I can do without?

"Out," I snarl.

"What the hell is wrong with you?" She sniffs, "Why can't we work this out like adults?"

"Like adults, huh?" I smirk. "Trust me, the kind of things I want to do with you right now would definitely be classified as 'adult.'"

She reddens. "Can't you speak a sentence without coming across all lecherous?"

"I haven't even started," I smirk, "and PS, it's you who can't take a hint. Do you want me to spell it out for you?"

"You're a jerk, you know that?"

I yawn. "Get out of the house or I'll throw you out bodily."

"You wouldn't."

"Try me."

She raises her fist and I move. I grab her around the waist, haul her over my shoulder.

She yelps, "Let go of me, you oaf."

"You sure about that, Buttercup?"

"Stop calling me that."

"Not gonna oblige you. Next?"

She makes a huffing sound and the warmth of her breath sears my back. She wriggles her body, tries to scramble off. I place my arm across the back of her thighs.

She brings her fists down on my back, rains blows. How cute. As if that's gonna make a difference. From where I am, it's more like a massage. Don't tell her that, though. I stalk forward, and Max chooses that time to dart out.

Blame it on the fact I was distracted by her wriggling arse positioned so close to my face. Or the fact that I was having too much fun. Or that a part of me was bloody angry with that turd Saint, for having put me in this situation.

Clearly, he'd double booked me and this little puff pastry of a woman… whatever the fuck he'd been thinking, he is mistaken. I have no interest in her; none whatsoever... especially when she's proving to be such a distraction that I barely manage to sidestep Max.

My bare feet slip from under me. The world tilts.

The woman across my shoulder shrieks. I tighten my grip on her, as the ceiling recedes further. I manage to find my balance, lurch back a couple of steps, through the door. I must have spilled something earlier. My legs slip out from under me a second time.

I arc back through the air…and still holding her, hit the hot tub and tumble into the water.

"Woman," I growl, "you're going to rupture my eardrums."

"I'll do more than that, you…you horrible man. You…you Fruit Salad."

I blink, "Did you compare me to a dessert?"

"I'm not done you…you Carrot Cake." She rears up so quickly, I loosen my grip. She pulls away, and over…smashes straight into my injured finger. Bright lights flash behind my eyes… Jesus F… She hadn't been kidding when she'd said she'd show me the sun in the night time… Hold on. What the hell am I thinking? My brain seems to freeze, then pain ratchets up my spine, through my skull… A growl rips from me, "The hell are you doing?"

"You started this." She lurches up to her feet, stands over me, with my torso in between her legs.

Her wet blouse stretches across her chest, highlighting every gorgeous curve of that magnificent bust.

My cock twitches; my mouth dries. I can only stare at the nipples that salute me, the water that drips down the fabric outlining her flat stomach, the indentation of her bellybutton, down to the valley between her thighs, where her jeans have ridden up to kiss the cleft between her lower lips. What I wouldn't give to be able to place my lips there… I swallow. My dick lengthens.

Shit, bet if she looks down, she'll see exactly which parts of me are excited by this little rough play… Which it isn't… Foreplay, that is. It is an accident, that's all.

"Why the hell couldn't you watch where you were going?" She glowers.

"Me…?" I scowl. "I am as steady on my feet as I am with my fingers… Speaking of," I raise my throbbing hand, and glare at the offending digit, "You probably fractured it again, thanks to your clumsiness."

"It was already broken, you idiot."

"Heard about multiple fractures?" I growl. "And don't call me an idiot."

"Oh, pfft. I'll call you anything I want, you reprobate."

"Mind your tongue, Buttercup."

"Oh, stuff it." She swings one leg over. "And for the record, I'm the one who's staying, not you."

"Oh, no, you're not." I grab for her leg. She squeaks, evades me and jumps up and out of the tub. There's a howl… "Max." I turn to find her squatting down. She rubs the puppy's head. "Oooh, little fellow, did I hurt you? I didn't, did I?" Max whines again.

"Oh, I'm sorry, I'm sorry," she coos, makes kissing noises at the mutt, who whines. No wonder he's making the most of having her attention.

She plops onto her butt, cross-legged, pulls the puppy into her lap. The dog, lifts his head, licks her face, her mouth. Hmm. He whines again, she strokes him, and lifts him to her chest. The little bugger cuddles against her breasts. *What the—?* I glower. *How does he get to do that and not me? Wait, hold on? Am I seriously jealous of a canine?* I shake my head.

"Enough of this nonsense," my voice rings around the space.

The puppy shivers, snuggles his body tighter against her chest.

"Put him aside," I scowl.

She peers up at me, "Shh."

"What?"

"You're scaring the baby," she admonishes me.

"Baby?" I growl.

Max moans… No, really. That dog has definitely been taking acting classes, for he bleats out another piteous little whine that has her cuddling him, rocking him side to side. "There, there, little fella. Did Daddy's heavy voice make your heart go pitter-patter?" She lifts him up, and the dog plays along. He licks her lips…right on the mouth.

"Hey!" I growl.

I push up to standing in the hot tub, water flowing from me like I turned on the shower. The water splashes out onto the dog and the woman, who bows her head to shield him. "Stop that, you're making him wet." She huffs.

"Oh, yeah?" I scowl down at her bent head, the way she croons to the pet, hair flowing in a blonde waterfall about her shoulders, her dripping clothes that outline the curve of her shoulder…and that… The sight of the perfectly turned swell of a what should not be a seductive part of anyone's body… But on Buttercup… It's a bloody turn on. The blood rushes to my groin and my head spins. Must be the fact that I hit my hand. That's why I am feeling lightheaded. No other reason. It's why I step up and out of the sunken hot tub, to loom over her.

More water pours over her, drenching both woman and dog. He yelps, cowers into her further.

"What are you doing?" She tries to protect him with her body. "You're an insensitive dog parent."

"I'm not a parent, this is not a child, and you...are completely insane."

She peers up at me, from under her spiky eyelashes. Her gaze runs up my thighs, my crotch, getting an eyeful of my rather spectacular appendage — yeah, I'm well hung, deal with it — up my impressive eight pack — it is eight, I know, I've seen myself in the mirror — to my mouth. She gulps; her cheeks turn a fiery red. "You... you..." She swallows, "Why are you flashing the little mite?" She props her palm over Max's eyes. "You could have stunted his growth, with that exhibition," she huffs. "I mean just because you are ... Uh, massive... You don't need to go around shocking little doggies with your penchant for running around naked."

And that's when something inside of me snaps. My vision tunnels and the blood thunders at my temples — anger...and frustration... and jealousy... Yeah, bloody hell, I am living with rage that she's giving all of her attention to that...that... Usurper... I am going to teach her a lesson about ignoring me — one she won't forget in a hurry. I bend over, grab the nape of her neck with my unhurt hand, and haul her up to her feet, with just enough force for her gaze to widen.

"What did you say?'

"Th...that you're scaring him."

"After that."

"That you're running around naked."

"Before that."

She blinks rapidly, the dog wriggles in her hold. "M...max," she stutters.

I click my tongue, "Not the word that you are looking for."

"M…massive?" she wheezes.

"You noticed, huh?"

"Kinda….h…hard not to…" she swallows, tips up her chin, "considering…"

"Considering." I drop my head, thrust my face into hers. "Considering?" I lower my voice. "Complete the sentence, Buttercup."

She gulps, "Considering you've been waving that in my face since —"

I lower my head, close my mouth over hers.

3

Amelie

Finally, finally, finally he's kissing me… He's… Oh! Warmth, heat, the taste of him pours through my veins, fills my senses. Hot, lush, complex and fiery, notes of ginger, cardamom, bitter orange and sumptuous creamy champagne. Oh, my…he tastes like my very personal favorite dessert… If I had to bottle this taste, make it into a dessert, it would be called... Kinky Banana Split? No, Kinky Pavlova, maybe… Kinky Almond and Chocolate cookies with pomegranate seeds and a splash of brandy… Oh, my, my. I'd totally dive into that concoction headfirst; after I'd scooped up the cream from the dark surface, licked it up, and my fingers... Then rub the mixture all over that delicious torso, down to his impressive bon-bons and — Wait, did I just call his balls bon-bons? Does that make his very impressive dick a…rhubarb and chocolate cock pop?

A giggle boils up my throat. Above me, he freezes, leans back until his mouth is poised just above mine. "What's so funny?" he rasps.

"N…nothing." I'd lick his shaft like a penis cake — I choke.

"Are you laughing at me?"

"N…no," I gasp.

"What are you thinking?" He frowns down at me. An expression of genuine frustration on his face. My stomach flutters. Jesus, if that isn't the hottest thing I have seen… This alpha male, all flummoxed… Not to mention, still wet and naked, and holding my nape like I am a kitten.

Max whines in my arms. I glance down. "I think he's cold; I need to get him inside the house."

"He can wait."

"You'd allow a baby to freeze?" I scowl.

"He's a dog…"

"A pet."

"A mutt."

"A child." I frown.

"Fine."

"Fine what?"

"We'll take him to the other room, but first, 'fess up."

"What?" I blink rapidly.

"What made you chuckle earlier?"

"Nothing."

"It's something." He glares at me and a shiver runs down my spine.

"Maybe," I finally say.

"So, you were lying to me?"

"No," I stutter.

"I hate liars."

"Trust me, you don't want to hear this," I mumble.

"Trust me," he lowers his thick brows, "I do."

"You won't like it."

"Let me decide that."

Like hell, I will. I snicker to myself. *If you think I am going to tell you my X-rated thoughts, you have another think coming.*

"Fine," I grumble just as Max whines again, "Can I set him down first?"

He peers into my face, then nods.

"Let go of me," I demand.

"No."

I stare, "You serious?"

"Always."

Tell me about it. This grumpy-pants a-hole needs to be shown how to laugh a little more, in life.

"Fine," I mutter, then bend down. He bends with me, not taking his palm off of the nape of my neck. *Don't look at his crotch, don't.* I stare at his turgid cock that springs from a nest of dark hair as I lower myself, place the puppy on the ground. Max shoots off toward the kitchen.

He hauls me up. "Tell me now," he threatens, his voice hard.

"But… I need to go with him and—"

He glowers at me, and that familiar melting sensation crawls in my gut.

"P…penis-shaped cake," I blurt out.

"What?" His glare intensifies.

"It…it's a thing…" I assure him. "There's this town in Portugal where penis-shaped cakes are gifted to women as fertility charms." Not that I need any such help with this man. Just being this close to him is enough for me to get pregnant… *Eeeugh! What am I thinking?* I pull back, but his large hand on my nape tightens.

"And you know this, how?"

"It…it's ah, based on research I came across."

"Research, huh?" He bends his knees, so his face is more at eye-level with mine. "Why do I have this sneaking suspicion that is not true?"

"It is…" I lie, casting about in my head for something…anything to tell him. "Uh, I am writing a book."

"A book?"

"A cook…cookbook...for desserts that are aphrodisiacs…"

"And this… Uh, cock cake—" He frowns.

"A chocolate cock pop," I correct him.

"Chocolate cock pop…is an aphrodisiac, hmm?" His lips twitch.

"Don't mock it till you try it," I mumble.

"Hmm." He tilts his head, "You have a point there." He applies pressure on my neck—not enough to hurt, just sufficient for my knees to tremble.

"Wh…what are you doing?"

"What do you think?"

He peels back his lips and his teeth flash against his tanned skin. He eases me down and I drop to my knees.

Hell, he handles my body like I am made of room-temperature butter… Would he lick me like I am a toffee-topped crumpet too? That large rough tongue of his would lave my flesh, dig into the nooks and crannies of my sensitive core, strum on my pussy lips, nibble on my cream and sugar… *No.. No… No.* "No," I shake my head.

"Don't mock it till you try it," he growls.

I'm eye level with that part of him that has taunted me since I walked into this house. No, even before that… Since I first saw him, across a crowded room at my friend Summer's wedding, when he'd prowled toward the bar, leaned against the barrier, stance wide, reached for a tumbler for whiskey and I'd seen the tendons of his throat stretch as he'd swallowed it down.

"Open," he growls.

I tip up my chin. "You're no dessert," I huff.

"No, I'm better."

He releases me, only to grab his dick and—what the—? I stare. I can't help it. I mean, I shouldn't. I should look away, spring to my feet and follow Max into the kitchen, then keep going until I reach my car and get out of here. I could do it, too. He's not holding me back. I should get away from him; away from this insane start to what was supposed to have been a quiet time, of reflection, and experimentation, of coming up with ideas for new desserts that I could use to differentiate my business from the rest… Which is exactly what I have been doing since I walked in here.

Hold on a second… Is being with him sparking off brainwaves of the culinary, and face it, the lustful kind? And hell, if the two don't go together. Desserts and orgasms, puddings and sex, cupcakes and clit stimulators…

Whoa. Hold on. Back up there. That idea I'd pulled out of my arse earlier, of writing a book about desserts that are stimulants… Well, it's not a bad idea at all… In fact, it could inspire an entire range of recipes…that I could use for my occasions-themed menu — valentines, anniversaries, birthdays, weddings… Hmm. I chew on my lower lip, watch as he squeezes himself from root to swollen head of his fat dick. My mouth waters and my belly clenches… Hell, what am I thinking? I'm not seriously considering…

He squeezes his cock, so it stands straight out, staring at me in the face, with precum oozing from the slit, and hell… I'm only a woman kneeling in front of a beautiful dick, wanting to lick it.

"Do it," he insists. "Open up, Buttercup."

"Did you just rhyme your words with my so-called pet name — ?"

He shoves his dick in between my lips… He's not tender or gentle, by any means… He takes it like it's his right, to have his shaft in my mouth, filling me, bumping up over my tongue. "Swallow," he growls.

What the hell? How dare he think he can command me and I'll obey? How can he take me for granted…? Because I haven't left yet, have followed his directions so far, allowed him to maneuver me into this place of supplication, where I peer up at him, watch the sweat bead his forehead,

"Now." He glares at me, and heat flares in my belly; a shudder runs down my spine and my thighs spasm, I resist the urge to squeeze them together. I will not show him that his dominance is turning me on, that his complete arrogance in assuming I'll do what he asks is…a bloody turnoff.

"Amelie." His voice lowers to a hush.

So, he remembers my name, huh?

His jaw tics, "Take me down your throat."

And his tone brooks no argument. I tip my chin up, open my mouth further — wide enough for his cock to slip in, ease down my gullet. I cough and tears squeeze out of my eyes. I swallow and a groan rips out of him. His massive thighs on either side of my face ripple as if unseen currents grip him, the same ones that writhe down my legs, to my toes. My fingers tingle and my scalp itches. I raise my hands, grip the outside of each of his legs.

"Fuck," he rasps, "you have no idea what you're doing to me."

Oh, trust me, I do. Question is, why the hell am I still here?

"You want to leave?" His voice cuts through my mind. *Huh?* Has he been reading my thoughts? "Do you, Buttercup?" he asks.

Is it the fact that his nickname is growing on me—because it belonged to my childhood heroine…the one I'd wanted to be when I grew up? Or because the strain in his tone is evident? Because he doesn't touch me anywhere… Well, except for the most intimate part of him in one of my orifices. I swipe my tongue up the bottom of his cock over the throbbing vein, to the rim of his swollen head. I circle it, and another growl rips out of him. The heat pours off of him, and down on me. The strength of his dominance seems to grow, coiling around me, pinning me in place. Moisture pools between my thighs. Hell, what is he doing to me? What am I going to do to ensure that he doesn't take me for granted again? That he doesn't simply put me down as another of the women who've succumbed to his charms… Okay, so I am as guilty, but hell, if I am going to walk away from this encounter without making an impression. Yeah, did I mention I am bloody competitive by nature? It's been my downfall… The reason I'm here, about to spend Christmas on my own… I should take him up on the out he's extended to me and scram… I should.

"You scared you won't be able to finish what you started?"

He snickers. The bastard snickers—with his dick in my mouth. *Sheesh, men!* They can be so naïve. So full of their own ego, they can't see the truth when it stares them in the face. That I am going to make him regret every little insult he's thrown my way since I walked in there.

"You make up your mind yet, Buttercup? Either get out so I can complete this on my own or—"

I cup his balls and squeeze.

His big body freezes. I bring up my other palm, begin to knead that gorgeous well-hung part of him. His dick thickens and the muscles under his belly coil, ripple like there's some kind of internal struggle that holds his guts hostage.

"Are you sure, you want to do this?" His voice is so low, so harsh, a tremor courses through my veins and my toes curl. I lean in just a millimeter more, enough for his shaft to slip further down my throat. A growl rips out of him, "Last chance, Amelie." His voice is strained.

I peer up into his features. His jaw tics; a vein pops at his temple. The pulse between my legs beats in tandem. I lean back on my haunches, so his shaft slides out to the edge of my mouth. Then wrap my lips around his head, squeeze his balls at the same time.

"Jesus, fuck," he swears.

A thrill runs down my spine.

I knead his balls and the muscles in his stomach jump.

"You've done it now." He digs the fingers of his uninjured hand into my hair, and tugs. Pinpricks of pleasure race across my scalp. "I am going to fuck your face."

4

————

Weston

The hell am I doing? I'd meant to haul her to her feet and throw her out of the house, so I could get on with the quiet time I'd hoped to have over the holidays. Instead, I can't stop myself from tugging down on her hair. She flinches, raises her head, and the sight of those pink lips wrapped around my cock—bloody fuck—lust spirals through my veins hot and hard. Fuck. "I am going to do this my way, Buttercup. You understand that, hmm?"

She stares up at me, pupils blown, the green of her irises a slim circle around the black. Bloody hell, she's aroused, and so hot. I ease her head forward, and my dick disappears inside her mouth. My vision narrows and my scalp tightens, "Bloody fuck, I can't stop." I tighten my fingers in her hair; she winces. Lust spirals down my spine. The thought of bringing her to the edge, of hurting her just enough to give her the kind of pain which will heighten her pleasure…hell. My breathing grows ragged and my chest heaves. "Nod if you understand," I snarl.

Her eyebrows knit and her tiny hands massage my balls.

Pinpricks of heat race up my back. "Amelie," I warn her.

Her gaze widens and her movements become more frantic.

She leans into me until her elbows are positioned on my thighs, her head tipped up, her entire body tiny enough to fit exactly between my legs. She releases me, only to whisper her fingers up the back of my butt, into the crease between my arse cheeks…and that's when I snap. I drag her back a few inches…enough for her to pull back her hand. She draws in a breath, her cheeks hollow, and fuck, if I don't feel the suction all the way to my head. This woman, where did she learn to blow me like this? If I give her free rein, she'll suck my brains through my dick. A chuckle flicks up my throat, and anger…a slow burn of an emotion that's very much like jealousy. *What the—?* Am I jealous of whoever she was with before me? I've never had a problem with that before. All of my partners have been seasoned, experienced enough… Jaded and cynical. Happy to fuck and walk away… And her… I am going to fuck her, all right… And then what? I'll have to let her go. My guts twist. Why the hell is that an issue? This entire encounter has had the touch of surreal to it from the moment I'd opened the door of the hot tub area and seen this pixie of a woman.

Fuck her mouth, show her I'll take no quarter, make sure she understands that all of those dreams she carries around in her head —babies and puppies and all things nice? That's *not* what she's going to get from me. What she can expect is a man who knows what he wants, who goes after it and claims it…who takes no prisoners, as I am about to show her. "I need to see you nod your assent," I reiterate.

She pauses…a beat, another, then she jerks her chin.

Thank fuck. I haul her forward and my dick slides down her throat. Hot, moist, so fucking good that I almost come on the spot. I bring my other hand to the base of my cock, squeeze it to stop myself. Then I begin to use her mouth. I pull her back and forward, and again. Each time, my cock slips in between her gorgeous lips. Once more and her teeth graze the skin of my shaft. Ripples of pleasure flood my skin, my balls harden, my groin tightens, and I can't remember the last time I came this close, this quickly. I haul her close; this time her lips fasten around the girth of my cock, and when

I pull her back, she curls her tongue around my swollen head. Goosebumps pop on my skin, my thigh muscles bunch, and the tension in my belly grows, becomes enormous. *Fuck.* "I am going to come."

She stares up, holds my gaze.

"You're going to take all of me, you understand?"

She nods.

"Every single last drop."

She brings her hand back up to cup my balls again and I explode. Hot gusts of cum pour out of me, and she swallows, not breaking eye contact, and damn her, but it's the hottest, most erotic thing I have seen ever. Liquid spills down her chin, onto her top, but she doesn't pause. She continues to suck on me, swallowing until I swear there's nothing left in me to come. I step back; my cock drops from her lips with a wet plop. The hair on the back of my nape rises. I haul her to her feet, peer into her features. "You're something else, you know that?"

She opens her mouth, and damn her, but I don't want to hear her speak. No explanations. No need to dissect what just happened. So I do the only thing I can, considering the circumstances. I drop my head, place my lips over hers.

Mistake… Mistake… All of my senses jangle. A shudder of electricity screams up my spine and my dick instantly perks up… *The fuck?* I just came. It's a record, even for me. *Why the hell is she having this effect on me?* I pull back, but she rises on tip toe, throws her arms around me… Or as much of me as she can reach which, considering she comes to chest level, means she winds herself about my upper arms. She tilts her head, follows me. She parts her lips, swings her leg about my thigh. Only when my palm cups her butt, do I realize I've hoisted her up. She locks her ankles around my waist, licks my mouth. Heat flushes my cheeks; blood thunders at my temples. A growl rips from me, and I tighten my hold under her butt.

The scent of her, that sweet pastry essence, fills my senses, goes to my head. I can't stop myself; I kiss her back. Then yank her close enough for her breasts to flatten against my chest; for me to feel the hard buds of her nipples bite into my flesh.

A moan whines from her. She loops her fingers around my neck, digs her fingers into my hair and strains in my hold. Her melting core cocoons my hardness. My dick nestles against the crotch of her jeans, which I am happy to report is soaked right through. She wriggles around, trying to get closer. A chuckle rips from me. So impatient, this little thing is. I drag a hand up her spine, to lock my palm about her nape. She stills; a sigh trembles from her lips.

Hmm, she likes a firm hand, huh? Happy to oblige. I swipe my tongue over her teeth, down the seam of her lower lip. She groans; her body trembles. She pushes her core into my cock, which happily nestles into her. Fuck. This willing, quivering mass of woman is too enticing, too seductive…too much everything. If I continue to kiss her, I'll have to take her, and one time won't be enough. I'll have to fuck whatever it is between us out of my system, which could take… days… Hell, weeks… Probably all of the time that I'd allowed myself here… And how is that going to work out, hmm?

I lessen the intensity of the kiss. She whines, coils herself into me, as if she wants to crawl under my skin… Fuck, if she hasn't already, in some way. *Which is not too bad, hmm? What the—what am I thinking?* I don't want a woman in my life. Not now. Not when I'm trying to heal myself. I need to rest up, ensure my mind and body are rested and ready to go. It is my career at stake, if I don't mend. As a surgeon, the operations I perform demand that my faculties be more than a 100% when I perform procedures. It's the one thing that makes my life worthwhile—being able to save others. Perhaps because when I am in surgery, I am in control. It is in my hands to take charge, to see the operation through, ensure I do my best, snatch people back from the jaws of death and restore them back to their lives.

Something I could only hope for during the time I had been kidnapped and held hostage. Is that why I like to play God? Or as close to it as it gets, when I hold someone's heart in my palms...like she held my balls in hers. Her touch, her kisses, the flow of her hair about her shoulders, the pulse of her blood at the base of her neck, at her chest, between her thighs… Why do I want to acquaint myself with every goddam nook and crevasse of her body? I tear my mouth from hers.

Her chin wobbles, she blinks, and a whine spills from her lips. "Weston," she mumbles.

My name from her mouth, her tongue drawing out the vowels, her every part reaching, aching, wanting me… Fuck… I can't do this. Can't allow myself to feel whatever it is that connects us. I am not ready for this… Will never be ready for whatever it is that she wants from me—the kind of commitment not spoken, but voiced with her actions, her reactions to me, since she had entered.

"Weston?" She peers up at me, "Hey..." She cups my cheek, and her touch sinks into my blood. My pulse rate ratchets up and my cock—that needy part of me—instantly stands to attention. Fucking fuck, I gotta get out of here. Max chooses that moment to come tearing back into the space. Thank fuck. He parks his little body next to my leg, then paws at my ankle.

"The puppy," I say, "he needs to be fed."

She swallows; the brightness dulls in her eyes. My heart stutters. It fucking stutters at that. Why the hell is she affecting me like this? I can't let her get to me. Not now. Not ever.

"So you know, I am not sorry."

"Huh?" Her eyebrows knit, "What are you talking about—?" Her gaze widens as I grip her under her armpits and hold her away from my body. The cold instantly infiltrates my chest. Fuck… Now I am getting melodramatic, or perhaps, I've simply been standing around without clothes for too long.

"Don't you dare, Wes—"

I release her.

She plops into the hot tub and water splashes over the sides.

"You asshole," she splutters. "How dare you?"

"Oh, I dare, alright. In fact, I'm just getting started. I am taking over the house for the holidays. You'll have to find yourself other accommodations."

"Weston— You motherfucker," her screech follows me. "Come back right now, or else…"

I pause, glance at her over my shoulder, "Or else?"

"Or else…you'll never find out about the proposal I have in mind for you."

5

____

Amelie

"Proposal, huh?" He arches an eyebrow.

"Yeah." I nod. *What the hell am I doing? And after I'd blown him… Willingly, I might add… What the hell was that all about?*

Not that I have anything against giving a blowjob, but honestly, it's not something I've done before with a man I don't know well… And that is the problem. With Weston, there had been this instant reaction to him, from the time I'd first seen him. I'd wanted to slap that smirk off his face, then hit him in the dick, right before I pulled him close and smooched the hell out of him. Shit, this…push-pull reaction I am having to him is insane. From the time he'd walked through the patio door, he'd been mean to me. He'd been pushing my buttons, all right, trying to get a reaction out of me. And you know what? I am not going to let him win this David and Goliath game we have going on here. I'd been promised I could have this space over the holidays and I intend to make sure I do.

If it means sharing with this a-hole of a man… This hot and sexy, ripped, 100% macho maleness of a billionaire, doctor… Gulp. Then so be it. I am not going to let him crowd me into corner, or overpower me with his status…. Okay, so maybe I am a little over-whelmed by his uh, larger than life assets…but come on, who wouldn't be? And that kiss at the end? When I'd flung myself at him…because, well, I am a slut… Fine, fine, so berate me, but I swear, there had been something about the power I'd been able to wield over him, when I had taken him in my mouth, and his body had responded to mine.

Whatever his issues with me… Physically, the signals he's been broadcasting are clear—he wants me. And let me tell you, there's something very satisfying in that, in knowing that this powerful man is helpless in the face of whatever it is that our bodies are communi-cating with each other. And face it…sharing a space with him would be no…hardship… Except for that horrible attitude of his, of course. I'm willing to give him a chance though… Who wouldn't? Not when he'd kissed me back… He had. He had pulled me to him, closed that big sexy mouth of his over mine and kissed the hell out of me… Enough for my knees to go weak, for my pussy to clench, and my panties to dampen all over again, like I'd just run into the Thames. Okay, so maybe not the last comparison, considering the Thames is grimy as hell, but you get what I mean, huh?

"I… I am not leaving," I say.

"Yes, you are," he reiterates.

"Nope."

"Yes."

He leans a hip against the door, and damn him, couldn't he have, at least, put on some clothes? I mean, this entire encounter? He's been butt-naked, and it's a mighty fine butt, and massively corded thighs, and that eight pack…and… Hell, not going down that path right now.

"You'll want me to stay, I promise you."

"Huh?" He folds his arms over his chest. Those biceps bulge, his shoulders fill the doorway, and it's not because its narrow. The entrance, I mean.

"I'll be your housekeeper—cook your food, clean…" I wave a hand in the air, "Considering you're laid up with that…uh, injury, you'll need someone to take care of your needs."

"Needs, huh?"

Shit, I hadn't meant to word it that way, but whatever, at least he's listening to me.

"You bet." I swing one leg up over the lip of the hot tub, then scramble up and straighten. "You hadn't thought about how you were going to manage over the holidays without being able to use your hand."

"Hmm." He raises his injured palm, then scratches at his jaw. "You offering to help?"

"Do you want me to help?"

"You want to keep house for me?" He smirks.

I frown. Asshole, of course he'd twist my words around to suit his needs.

"I'd cook and clean the house…" I mutter, " You'd have to pick up after yourself. I am not picking up your dirty laundry."

"What else?"

"What do you mean?" I frown.

"What else can you do for me?" he drawls.

"I could…uh, drive you around, like I already said."

"And?" His lips curl and his eyes gleam.

Oh, no, no, he's not getting at that. "Whatever it is you're thinking, you can forget about it," I huff.

"How do you know what I am thinking?"

"A man like you has only one thing on your mind."

"As opposed to a woman like you?"

"I'm not the one walking around naked."

"Does it bother you?"

"Of course, it bothers me." I swipe my hair over my shoulders. "How would it feel if I were to walk around without clothes?"

"Are you offering?" He smirks.

I throw up my hands, "Oh, forget I said anything. Clearly, this entire discussion is going nowhere… Meanwhile —" A whine sounds from beyond him, "Don't keep Max waiting. Feed the poor thing, will you?"

He scowls, "Don't tell me what to do."

"Oh, my God." I plant my hands on my hips, grimace when that dislodges more water from my clothes. "You're bloody impossible."

"And you're staying out here."

He walks inside, slams the door behind him. *The hell?* I race forward, try the door. It's locked. Of course, it is. I bang on it. "Weston, you asshole, let me in."

No answer, not that I expected one… But how dare he simply… lock me out? I kick at the door. Pain shoots up my leg. I groan, then glance around the patio. There are heaters out here around the hot tub, so I'm not cold. The wind blows, and I shiver… Okay, scratch that. I won't freeze, but damn, if I am standing around here waiting for that bastard to come back and get me.

I stalk past the tub, jump down onto the grass. I walk around the side. Ha, he's going to keep me out the house, is he? Not if I can help it. I break into a sprint, jog up the field surrounding the house, around to the front. Reaching the door, I find it…closed. *Bugger.* I try the door handle, and it's locked. I throw up my fists, ready to punch my way through…? As if that would help… Think… Think… What can I do…? I walk down the steps, get back into the car…search for my phone. Shit. My handbag — I left it inside the bloody house, along with my chef's satchel. *Argh!*

I slam my palm on the steering wheel, and the horn blares. Hell. I press down on the horn a little longer. I'd left the keys in the ignition… So, at least, I am mobile, but without my phone and my wallet… Hell, even if I went out into the village… which is a 45-minute drive away, I couldn't do much. Damn it, I can't even call anyone for help.

Ugh! I grip the steering wheel, take a deep breath, then another. *Don't lose it. You can think it through.* He isn't going to leave me out… Nah! He wouldn't…would he? Damn it. It would be just like that reprobate who has chocolate tarts for brains to do something exactly so…assholish. *Argh!* Anger ladders up my spine. I swipe my wet hair out of my eyes… Great. Here I am, soaking wet, with no dry clothes in sight… Uhm, no, I do have my suitcase where I left it outside. There's a distinct boom, then drops of water drizzle down. Shit. That doesn't help. No way am I going to get soaked all over again. I snatch up the keys, step out of the car and lock it. Then run over to my suitcase… I drag it up the steps to the front entryway, and place it against the wall.

Then retrace my path down the steps, then around to the back porch.

The wind blows. I shiver and step closer to the warmth emanating from the tub. Hmm. Should I? I glance around for the controls, spot a switch. When I throw it, the bubbles begin to churn in the tub. I dip my hand, and yep, the water's warm. I turn the dial further toward the red. With the rain smattering outside and the floor patio heaters going full force… Well, it is not too bad. But that doesn't get me inside the cabin. I hear scratching at the door—Max trying to get out again.

Okay, I'm not going to stand around here, as if waiting for him… I am going to… I grab the hem of my blouse, pull it off. I hear Weston talking to Max, then the sound of the door being unlocked. I strip out of my jeans. The door begins to open. I race toward the tub, jump inside, unhooking my bra at the same time.

6

———————

Weston

What the—? What the hell is she up to now?

I walk out of the door and onto the patio in time to watch her sink into the hot tub. There's a flash of pink, then she holds up her bra… something slinky and made of scraps of nylon. My jaw drops and my belly hardens. She can't be doing what I think she is. She can't be undressed…and turning the tables on me…can she?

I'd fed the mutt…then proceeded to take a cold shower…before pulling out clothes. When I could delay no longer, I'd walked out. Okay, also because I was curious. The last thing I'd expected was for her to reverse engineer the scene I'd played out for her earlier.

I stalk forward and my foot brushes something wet. I glance down to find her abandoned blouse…then her jeans… I follow a trail of clothes strewn across the patio that leads me to stand over her.

"What are you up to?"

"What do you think?" She tosses her bra at me and I catch it. Damn her, but I want to smell it. Would it have her scent…of sugar and spices and everything nice? *Argh!* I really have to stop reading to

Birdie, my niece. Now I am thinking in nursery rhymes? Or is it simply her nearness going to my head?

She scoops up some of the hot water, pours it over her shoulders. The bubbles cover her up to the swell of her breasts, but she's naked below it... Is she? Did she take off her panties? I glance around, can't see the abandoned lingerie...so she must have it on... Would the cloth be transparent enough for me to see through it to that melting center of her, that I desperately want to get my hands on? My cock throbs and blood thunders at my temples. "Get out of there."

"No."

"If you don't step out..."

"What? You'll step in?"

Oh, I'm tempted to, but considering I spent the last few hours in there already, I'll pass. Doesn't mean I am going to let her get away with this little tease-filled antic, either.

I toss her bra aside then reach over to grab her shoulder. She twists her body and water splashes onto my shirt. "Oops." She giggles in a voice that seems to imply she's not sorry at all.

"Why you little —" I scowl, then straighten. "Stand up," I snarl.

"Make me."

"You don't want me coming in there. Trust me."

"Oh?" She tilts her head, "We'll see, shall we?" She slaps the water; more of it splashes onto me. *What the —?* I fold my arms over my chest, lower my voice to a hush, "Up." I growl.

She swallows.

"Do it."

"You sure?" she asks.

"I won't repeat myself."

"Fine." She juts out her chin.

"Fine?" I frown. Why is she agreeing so readily? She's up to no good, for sure, she — She rises to her feet. Water pours from her slim frame down the jut of her hips, in between her legs...and fuck, I was wrong. She doesn't have her panties on.

The water slides down her flat stomach, down to the triangle between her legs. And I can only watch as a drop clings to her pussy lips, begging me to go closer, closer. My knees bump into the side of the hot water tub. I blink.

"My face is up here," she drawls.

I can't stop the chuckle that rumbles up my throat. "Very good." I tilt my head. "Clearly, you've been paying attention to our conversation, and PS," I make air quotes with my fingers, "you ain't got nothin' that I haven't seen already."

She blinks, then gapes at me, "I was wrong about you."

"Oh?"

"You're not just an asshole, but a bloody, egoistical brute with no manners."

A grin threatens to split my face. I swallow it with a cough. "I'll give you one thing though; you got my attention."

"Hallelujah." She raises her arms skyward and tilts her head back. Her tits jiggle with the action. My cock instantly springs to attention. Fuck. It's not like I haven't seen better-looking women—certainly, those with bigger tits, slimmer waists…curvier hips… But the complete package of the woman who stands knee-deep in bubbles, with her hair sticking to her forehead…the flushed cheeks, the pink lips… Yeah, the ones between her legs as well... All of it comes together in an amalgamation that is uniquely her… Something I want to get to know better… To own and to understand, to pull apart and piece together until she makes more sense… Until I get her out of my system, that's all. Perhaps that's reason to keep her around a little longer?

I jerk my chin, "Come on."

"Huh?" She frowns.

"Out of there. Chop, chop." I clap my hand. "You've got a lot of work to do."

Turning, I head for the doorway leading back to the house.

"Wait," she calls out.

I reach the door, step inside.

"Does this mean you accept my proposition?"

"It means," I turn to glance at her, "you'd better get inside before I change my mind."

She stares back, spine straight, shoulders hitched back. She props a hand on her hip, breasts thrust up, nipples pebbled — Hell, if she isn't as aroused as I am feeling. This is going to be interesting. I start to close the door. She springs into action, clambers over the side of the tub. "Wait," she screeches.

My lips twitch as I try to keep the smile off of my face. "You have one minute to get your arse in here," I drawl.

"Bastard," she huffs.

I yawn, "You're getting repetitive, Buttercup."

"Aargh." She makes a sound deep in her throat, "I hate that ridiculous name."

"Prefer Blossom? Or Bubbles, maybe?"

"No," she scoffs, "all three of the Powerpuff girls are dumb."

"Hey," I lower my chin, "you did not just say that."

"Yes, I did." She grabs her blouse, pulls it on and it falls to mid-thigh.

My gaze, of course, goes there, to the curved flesh that jiggles as she moves. The women I've dated before have been emaciated, by comparison. None of them had that lustrous skin that I itch to mark, the delicate turn of ankles that invites me to run my tongue up the hollow, scooping the water droplets that are sure to be nestled there, up her calf and her inner leg, to that object of my obsession — her beautiful gorgeous core. *Fuck*.

"Just for that, your first punishment is watching the cartoon characters on loop."

"Punishment?" She grabs her boots and her socks; one of her shoes slips from her hold and hits the ground. "Crummy apple crumble," she swears,

"Did you use a dessert as a swear word?" I chuckle.

She rescues her footwear. "You could help, instead of ogling my body," she grumbles.

"Oh, if I were ogling, you'd know it, sweet thing."

She straightens, her cheeks rosier than they had been a few moments ago, "You're a chauvinist."

"You're a submissive."

She stiffens, "How dare you say that?"

"You want to be taken without being given a choice. Somewhere deep inside, you want to be dominated. At your core, you prefer to have all options taken from you, so you can relax into your true self."

She scoffs, "The hell you mean?"

"Right now, as we speak, you want me to bend you over the nearest chair, then part your legs, strum your clit, finger your pussy and make you come, right before I sink my hard, throbbing… aching…length into your melting center."

She draws in a breath, stares at me. Even through the darkness, her blue irises shine… The light in my darkness, the silvery fucking lining to my black cloud of a bloody life… And I am waxing poetic, all right, and all because this woman here has crawled under my skin. I want to grab her and pull her close and kiss her… Right after I turn her over my lap and spank all that impudence out of her. Speaking of... "Okay, I'm shutting the door." I let the barrier swing.

"W-a-i-t!" She scampers forward, then slips through the crack between the door and the frame. The door snicks shut. Silence, a beat, then another. This close, the scent of her—that vanilla and apples essence of her, laced with that sugary-tart sweetness that lingers on my tongue like a memory of that smell...when you go to the mall and you walk past the candy shop and smell the sugar? That smell intensifies. My mouth waters as my cock lengthens. I curl my fingers at my sides.

"Go on," I jerk my chin, temporarily capable of little more than monosyllabic words and spastic movements.

She scowls, "So you can stare at my arse?"

"If you'd rather ogle my butt instead…" I shrug, which has the added benefit of relieving some of the tension I'm feeling.

She snatches up her satchel, wears it across her chest, then bends to pick up her coat. Her toolkit jostles forward and smacks the back of her head. "Ow." She straightens, and her coat slips down to trail on the floor. "Shit," she swears aloud, "I am a mess."

"And I'd love to mess up my bed with you in it," I cough.

"What did you say?" she sputters as she scoops up her coat again.

"Just that you are pretty in your disarray."

She stares. "Somehow, I don't believe you."

"Somehow, I don't think I care."

"Is this some kind of NLP technique?" She frowns.

"No idea what you are talking about." I turn away.

"This entire mirroring my words thing you have happening."

"The only mirroring I want to do is of the 69 kind," I snicker.

"That's it," she snarls, "I've changed my mind."

"Hmm."

"I thought we could find a way to get through the holiday season, but clearly, if I spend any time with you, it's going to drive me insane."

"Goes both ways, sugar," I retort. The patter of paws on the wooden floor announces the arrival of Max. He jumps up, places his paws on my legs, as if he hasn't seen me in years, instead of minutes ago when I'd fed him. "Hey Buddy, whatcha doin', hmm?" I scratch at his head behind his ears and he makes a low, rumbling sound in his throat. He attempts to jump up again, but this time I oblige. I snatch him up, cuddle him, turn to watch her watching me.

I tilt my head, "What?"

"Every time I think you're a horrible monster, Max saves the day."

"Should I be thankful?" I smirk, digging my fingertips into Max's skin. He makes a deep groaning sound.

"Did he just…?" She blinks.

"Max is every bit as expressive as you," I snicker.

"Thanks." She tosses her head, "Doesn't get you off the hook. I'm still leaving." She marches past me, snatches up her handbag from where she'd placed it on the bar counter.

She heads for the door, then pauses, to rifle around in her purse.

Wait for it.

Wait for it.

Wait for—

"You asshole." She turns on me.

"Alphahole." I correct her.

"You took my phone."

I lower Max to the floor and he darts off toward the kitchen. I follow him, shut the door that leads from the living room, then lean against it.

"You did, didn't you?" she grumbles.

"If you mean that piece of shit technology that went out of date…"

"Hey, don't insult Hedwig."

"Hedwig?"

"My phone, you idiot."

"Who gives a phone a name? Wait, you named your phone after the owl in Harry Potter?"

"Wow." She swallows, "You placed that?"

She stares at me, her gaze taking on that familiar googly-eyed look.

I hold my hands out in front of me. "Don't go reading anything into it. And for the record, owl post wouldn't work, in real life," I mutter.

"What do you mean?"

"It's a scientifically-proven fact that owls can't stay in flight while carrying packages."

"Just because it isn't supported by science, doesn't mean it doesn't work."

"What do you mean?" I frown.

"Magic, remember?"

"Which is what you believe in, of course? Stars and unicorns and all that girlie shit."

Her face heats, "You could do with believing in a little of that yourself."

"When you're kidnapped and starved for days, and tortured to within an inch of your life, you lose faith in all that stupid stuff very quickly," I snap.

Her features scrunch up, "I'm so sorry for what happened to you and the Seven."

"I'm not. If it weren't for that incident, I'd still be naive —"

"Like me, you mean?"

"You said it." I let my lips curl.

She frowns, "Why am I debating this with you?" She holds out her hand, "Give Hedwig back to me."

"Sorry, I can't."

"What do you mean?"

"I can't remember where I put it." I grimace.

"What?"

"If you find it, you can keep it." I raise my shoulders.

"He belonged to me in the first place."

"He..." I shake my head, "It...the phone's mine now."

"No, it's not."

"Alas, poor Hedwig, he's going to have to spend Christmas without you, I'm afraid."

Her features contort, and I am sure she's going to stamp her foot and rage, and have a full-on tantrum. This should be interesting. I head to the armchair by the fireplace, drop into it, then pick up my novel.

"The hell are you doing?" she squawks.

"Reading."

She makes a snarling sound at the back of her throat. I hear the thump of her toolkit satchel hitting the floor, then a softer crash — that's her handbag — followed by the soft sound of her wet clothes hitting the wooden floor. Good. Footsteps approach; the next second she grabs the book from my hand.

"Hey, you only had to ask."

"I did, for my phone. Remember?"

"I mean the book." I lean back in the chair, fold one leg over the other.

She peruses the cover of the book, then blinks. "Harry Potter? You're reading Harry Potter?"

She glances at me, with...stars in her eyes, once more.

Oh, no, no, damn it. "Why do you think I recognized your reference, which I can tell you, is way too obvious. You need to up your game, Buttercup."

Her features tighten.

Bloody fuck, I shouldn't have insulted her...but what the hell? I need to live up to my reputation as someone who doesn't give a damn about anyone else... Besides, that strange gooey expression of hers... It scares the shit out of me. Har, har. Ask me to perform a complicated bypass, I am there. Ask me to try to figure out why I have this strange push-pull reaction to her, and hell, if it doesn't flummox me. Time to set this right and lay down the rules. We'll see then, how she copes. Fuck that hint of hopefulness I've spotted on her face throughout the evening. It is time to show her what I am actually made of.

"Don't let the fact that I am reading the Potter fool you."

"God forbid," she mutters.

"It's only so I can keep up with my older niece."

"How many nieces do you have?"

"Two…and I am not answering any more questions."

"Like I care."

"I think you do, actually. And I have to warn you right now."

"What?"

"Don't fall in love with me, Buttercup. You'll only have your heart broken."

7

———————

Amelie

My jaw drops. Again. The arrogance of the man. "I wouldn't fall for you, if you were the last man on earth.

"I'll hold you to that."

"What is that supposed to mean?" My heart begins to race.

"You know," he replies, his tone hard.

Sweat beads my palms, and it's not because the inside of the room is warmer than it was before… When had he lit the fireplace? Probably when I was outside. The light from the flames flickers over his face, throwing his features into relief, deepening the shadows under his cheekbones, hollowing out the spaces under his eyes. His dark hair appears almost blue, and those grey eyes seem almost colorless. Deep and fathomless. What would I find if I looked into those depths? A soul that would take, a male who'd possess, who'd pleasure me in the way no one else ever has. A dominant man who'd push aside all of my doubts and teach me how it is to be claimed. A shiver runs down my spine. *Is that what I want? Is that why I haven't left?* Hell, it could be just the two of us in this house—a faint scratching comes from the direction of the kitchen—and the puppy.

Not another living soul for miles around; no business demands on either of us. He'd come to heal and I had come to find…something… That spark inside of me that had vanished…and which I had been hoping to recapture. That leap of faith that had pushed me to start my own business… That makes me take a step forward…close the distance between us.

He watches me as I move closer. He lowers his feet to the floor, parts his thighs. I step in between them. He tips his chin up. It feels…different this way. Me looking down on him. The angle intensifies that brooding edge that coils under the surface. I want to find out what makes him tick. Why he blows hot and cold; why he'd decided to spend the holidays alone…when he could have been with any woman… Instead, he's gotten me. I frown.

He shakes his head.

I scowl.

"You have no idea what you're letting yourself in for," he mutters, half to himself.

"And you do?"

"I've been around the block many more times than you."

"You sure?"

"Have you?" he shoots back.

"Maybe not as much as you," I concede, "but I've had my share of boyfriends."

"How many?"

"What's it to you?" I snap.

"If we're going to get through our time together, then there are some ground rules you need to follow."

"*You?*" I scowl.

He tilts his head.

"You meant *we* need to follow, surely?" I elaborate.

He stares at me with those almost-colorless eyes and another shiver of electricity runs up my spine. *Shit, he doesn't even need to speak to me and I know what he means. Is it because I am that tuned into him?* More likely, I know exactly the kind of obnoxious, merciless man he is. My toes curl. *Why the hell does that turn me on?* It shouldn't be so appealing. I shouldn't be this attracted to him… It's precisely the fact that he wouldn't care about my needs, that he'd simply take what he wants from me, that I find…refreshing. There would be no pretensions with this man. It would be all give… At least, there would be no surprises, huh? So, I won't be disappointed. Is that how low my expectations have fallen?

"You shouldn't overanalyze everything," he remarks.

"You shouldn't take everyone around you for granted."

"Now you're doing that NLP shit…" he points out.

I half laugh, "You going to explain exactly what this is about?"

"This?" He looks perplexed.

I point to the space between us, "This."

"Ah." He steeples his fingers together. "It's simple. I am willing to let you stay here for the holiday season."

I frown.

"But?"

"Did I say a 'but'?"

"There's always a 'but' with people like you."

"People like me?"

"Overindulgent, spoilt, rich pricks who think they own the world."

"That's because I do."

I snort; I can't help it. "Why am I not surprised that you said that?"

He raises his shoulders, "It's a fact."

"Whatever," I mutter.

"What was that?"

"I said, 'What-fucking-ever,'" I say, with more aggression that I am feeling.

"Hmm, you have spirit. That's good."

"Oh, stop talking in riddles."

"That's Saint," he chuckles.

"What?"

"Doesn't matter." He draws in a breath, then straightens his shoulders, "Enough beating around the bush. It's six days to Christmas. We spend it together. You do everything I ask of you in that time."

"What does that mean?" I stare.

"Exactly what it sounds like. Nothing hidden."

"Does it mean…uh…?"

"What?"

"You know."

"No, I don't." He smirks.

Oh, spit it out already, why the hell am I being coy? "Sexual favors," I burst out.

"Only if you want it to," he replies.

I blink. "You mean…"

He nods.

"So, if I decided I didn't want to blow you again…"

"You'd be missing out," he rolls his shoulders, "but your call."

"You sure?"

"Would I lie?"

"Wouldn't you?"

He grins. "I love this little sparring thing we have going on…"

I purse my lips together, "It's not 'little' anything."

"That's true," he chuckles.

"Oh, my God!" I throw up my hands. "We get on each other's nerves. That's all it is."

"Hmm," he scratches his jaw, "you may be right there. We'll have to tone it down though, when we're seen in public."

"Public?"

He nods, "I have to go to visit my family sometime before Christmas and you'll come along, of course."

I stare at him. Has he gone mad? Why is he jumping around topics like that? "Wh...what do you mean?"

"You'll come with me, as my date, to visit with my family in the lead up to Christmas." He speaks slower this time, as if I didn't understand him the first time around. I still don't.

"No, I won't."

"Yes, you will."

I blink. He's so bloody confident, it borders on delusional. *I hadn't mistakenly agreed to this earlier, had I? No, of course not.* "Why the hell would I do that?" I scoff.

"Because you wanted a place to spend the holiday season, and this is the only space available."

"No, it isn't." I shuffle my feet.

"Ever tried finding a place to stay over the holiday season? It's either sold out, or so expensive, it would be out of your price range.

"How do you know what my price range is?"

"Whatever it is, I can afford it." He smirks.

My jaw drops. Again. Shit, I've been doing a lot of that since I got here… But this…this…wanker… He's got his head up his arse. No doubt, he thinks the sun shines out of it too. I snicker.

He frowns. "Also, you can't do that while you are here," he drawls.

"What?"

"Think impertinent thoughts."

I blink, then laugh, "Man, you're something else, you know?"

"As you are going to find out."

I open and shut my mouth, I mean… Why am I standing here arguing with him? I should just march out of here, figure out alternate arrangements across the new year.

"Giving up so soon?" he drawls.

"What do you mean?"

"Guess you know that you can't last the next six days without falling for my charms."

"What charms?" I look him and down, "You're a douchebag, is all."

"Exactly what you find so attractive, hmm?"

"You have no idea what I like, or not."

"Oh, trust me," He sits forward in the chair, "I have a very good idea what you…want…. Question is," he lowers his voice to that hushed tone that sinks into my skin. My blood heats; moisture laces my core. *How the hell does he draw that reaction from me without trying too hard?*

"Do you, Buttercup?"

I swallow, "I have no idea what you're talking about."

"We'll have to work on that too."

"What?"

"This entire self-denial thing you have going on... It's cute..." he tilts his head, "but it can get wearying after a while, for both of us."

I stare, trying to keep pace with his thoughts.

"It is?"

He nods, "And we don't want that."

My head spins; my skin heats further. *Why the hell is it so warm inside?*

"I... I think I need to go."

I turn to leave, reach the door, when he calls out.

"A million pounds."

I pause, then turn, "Excuse me?"

He's standing in front of the chair. "You heard me." He props his palms on his hips. "I know how much in debt you are."

"My business is doing well." My heart begins to race; sweat dampens my palms. *Dammit, why the hell does this guy make me nervous?* "In fact, that's why I am here, to recuperate from the stress —"

"No doubt, caused by the college loans you carry. Not to mention, the ones you took out to finance your fledgling little business."

Argh, did he just call my thriving enterprise 'little,' which it is, but what the hell gives him the right to come across all condescending like that? "And you know all this...how?"

"Do you deny it?" he asks.

Do it. Don't give him the satisfaction of finding out how right he is. I open my mouth, shut it again. Damn it, but I can't tell a white lie. Not even to save my arse. Which might be more literal than I realize. A giggle bubbles up.

He frowns. "If you did make a success of your business —"

I open my mouth to protest.

He holds up his hand to stop me, "—which is dependent on your business acumen as much as on your ability to be a cook —"

"I'm a pastry chef, you knob."

"Cook." He closes the distance between us, "Even then, you'll be paying off your loans for the next twenty years."

My pulse rate ratchets up. *Shit,* those numbers... Not that I wasn't aware of them. I prefer not to think about it, that's all. I mean, sure, I could look on the negative and the fact that I'll be paying off the loans forever… But I've been confident I could turn the corner at some point. What's the other option? Not take risks, work a nine-to-five… Nothing wrong with that. It's not for me, that's all.

"So?" I sniff.

"So, you'll work back-breaking, long hours, behind a stove —"

"An oven, you prick."

"If you keep alluding to that part of me, I'll have to assume you've been thinking of it."

"No, I haven't."

He grins. *Bastard.* My cheeks heat. So, fine, I've been thinking about that particular attribute of his nonstop since I sucked on him, like my own private lollypop. *Gah!* So? Hey, it was a bloody good blowjob too, thank you very much.

"As I was saying," he drums his fingers on his chest, "you'll waste away your best years, working non-stop, trying to pay off the loans. Before you know it, you'll be forty and single, not having had the time to find a man —"

"I don't need one," I snarl.

He laughs, "Meanwhile, the debt is going to stop you from expanding your business further… And that, you do want, hmm?"

I scowl. He's got me there. I have plans. I want to grow my business to set up a store front… Then a chain, not only in England, but abroad. And while I'm sure I won't let debt stop me, not with the help of expert advice on how to structure my business holdings… Still, nothing like cash in hand to inspire confidence, especially from future creditors.

"One million, huh?"

His eyes gleam.

I frown. Damn it, have I walked into a trap? I shouldn't have shown interest in his offer, but I'm human, okay? I mean… No, I won't sell my principles for money… But this is an awful lot of money. Not something to sneer at, get me? Besides, what principles is he really trying to pay me to betray? It's not like he's offering to pay me for sex. I chew on my lower lip; his gaze drops there. The tendons of his throat move as he swallows. Huh? He's affected by me as well? I mean, I know he wants me... That entire blowjob thing between us... It had confirmed he wants to get in my pants... But this... His hooded eyelids, the way he watches me with single-minded focus... My scalp tingles. A bead of sweat trickles down my spine.

I clear my throat.

He jerks his chin up, "Per day."

"What the—?" I gape. "You didn't... Why would you—?" I rake my fingers through my hair. "This entire thing is bizarre."

"It's a little out of your comfort zone, I understand." He shoves his hand in the pocket of his jeans, "But opportunities like this don't come often."

"You're telling me," I laugh. The sound comes out weak. Shit, I sound uncertain. And I am not. Not about my answer... Just his intention. "Why?" I frown. "Why are you so keen on ensuring that I stay?"

"You said it." He tilts his head, "I am not much use with this—" He holds up his finger in the splint. "Until you pointed it out, I hadn't realized it." He nods.

Nice one. Blame it on me that he'd come up with this insane idea, huh.?

"You could get a housekeeper...or something."

"Not over the holiday season. Besides, why would I look for a stranger when I want you?"

"Umm, because you don't know me well either?"

His gaze drops to my mouth.

"That...that was a one off." I redden. "It doesn't mean you know me as a person."

He raises his shoulders, "You're a friend of Summer and Victoria's, women who are trusted by the Seven."

"Right," I draw in a breath.

"So?" He tilts his head.

"So?" I shuffle my weight from foot to foot. *What do I say?* I twist my fingers together. "One million for every day makes it..."

"Six million pounds." He nods.

"S... six?" I squeak.

"It'll set you up for any kind of expansion you want to finance for your business."

I narrow my gaze. How could he have intuited my plans? "How do you know that?"

"You're ambitious, I get it." He stares back, "Not that much of a stretch, to know that you'd be planning to grow your enterprise.

"Right." I scowl at him. "I guess that makes sense. I mean, you weren't stalking me or anything, before I came here to find out this information, were you? Although, it does beg the question, how did you know about my debt?"

He chuckles, "Don't flatter yourself, babe. We check into anyone who enters our orbit. Can't be too careful, you know?"

"Hmm." I fold my arms around my waist. "It's what Sinclair and then Saint did before they proposed to my friends," I say, referring to the now-husbands of Summer and Victoria, respectively.

His lips quirk, "You think that's what this is about? My sneaky way of trying to form some kind of fake marriage proposal with you?"

Hmm, when he puts it like that, it sounds pretty far-fetched, but still, "You did ask me to accompany you to see your family."

"Just a way to get them off my back," he grumbles. "You're going to be hanging about here. I may as well as put your time to good use."

"Jeez, you have a foolproof way of charming women," I mutter.

"Right?" His smile broadens and his features light up. He is taking the piss, isn't he? I mean, no one could mistake his attitude to be anything but self-satisfying, egoistical, narcissistic —*gah*—I'm running out of adjectives.

"Well then, you'd best get your luggage in…"

"Hold on, hold on." I blow out a breath, "Nothing's settled."

"Of course, it is."

Gah! I almost cross my eyes at the sheer lunacy of this situation. Six days with an egomaniac, who is going to make every moment a living hell. Would it be worth the money? Six million freakin' quid! *Ohmigod!* That's what's at stake here. How many zeros are there in that number anyway? I pout, "You sure…uh…this isn't another way to—"

"Get in your knickers?" He raises an eyebrow, scans my features. "Face it, Buttercup. If I wanted," his voice lowers to that seductive hush, "I could take you now, and you wouldn't say 'no.'" His lips curl in that hotter-than-bubbling-custard-sauce smirk. *OMG, how could I compare him to one of the food dishes that I am famous for?*

He closes the remaining distance between us and that scent of his —pine and cloves and an edgy depth that coils around me—pins me in place. I can't move, can't think, can only watch as he looks down on me from his superior height.

"N…no," I stutter.

He pauses inches in front of me, "Did I ask a question?" His lips twitch. What a stupid idea this was. Damn…but six million. Six freakin' million pounds. Hell, I'd do anything for that. Even put up with his alphaholeness for a limited period of time. I mean, this is only for a short period of time, right? It has an end, after all, this time with him.

"Fine," I mutter and my stomach flip-flops. *Shit, what am I getting myself into?*

"The arrangement is dependent on one thing."

Knew it. I scowl, "Now what?"

"You can't sleep with me during our time together."

I blink. "So, you'll pay me a million pounds a day, to be your glorified housekeeper, and sex is not part of the bargain?" I pause. "And if I sleep with you?"

"Then the deal is off."

Huh? I peruse his features. Is he for real? Is this…weird-ass bargain as good as it sounds?

"So…" I try to give voice to my thoughts, "Everything but sex?"

"Not gonna repeat myself." His lips quirk.

What's the catch, huh? What is it?

I stare at him; a low smoldering burn begins to curl in my belly, "So…" I gulp. "Wh…what's not off limits, then?" *Why is my voice shaking?*

"You sure you want to know?"

No.

No.

"Yes." I clear my throat, "I need to know before I sign on the dotted line, right?"

"Hmm." His eyes gleam. He bends his knees, thrusts his face into mine, "What's not off limits includes, but is not limited to, squeezing, fondling, strumming, stuffing, kneading, massaging, pinching, spanking, hurting you, tying you up, making you scream, cry, beg, plead, howl—"

"Stop," I gasp.

He nods. "That's another thing you need to learn—to not tell me to stop when you don't mean it."

"Of course, I do."

His lips curl. He swoops out his hand to cup my pussy through the blouse that covers me to mid-thigh.

I squeak, grab at his wrist. He digs the heel of his palm into my core, and the strength of his touch, presses up through the soft fabric of my blouse into my clit. Sparks of heat, of lust, and streaks of emptiness slam into my gut. I shudder, "Oh, my God."

He rotates his palm in circles. Pinpricks of need swirl up my spine, my thighs spasm, my toes curl, my scalp tingles, and damn him, but he's barely touched me. How could my body betray me like this? Is this what I want?

He releases me, retracts his palm, and I jerk my pelvis forward. *What the hell?*

He tilts his head, brings his palm to his nose and sniffs, "That's what I thought. You are so aroused, if I had continued my ministrations, you'd have come."

"Not," I sniff.

"Fine then. " He smirks, straightens, turns to leave.

"Stop," I burst out.

He keeps going. *Asshole.*

"Don't," I call out, then bite on the inside of my cheek. "Please," I mumble.

"What was that?" he asks.

"Please," I half snarl, "don't go."

He pauses, then shoots me a glance over his shoulders "Admit it first."

"What?"

"That you want me."

I swallow.

He glares at me.

All of my nerve endings pop; a delicious edge of anticipation crackles up my legs, my back. I nod.

"Say it." He lowers his chin, "Tell me you wanted me to caress your pussy, shove my fingers into your cunt, make you wet, drag the moisture around your slit, and bring you to the edge."

My breathing grows shallow and my chest heaves.

"Well?"

"Yes," I sputter. "Yes." Jesus, now I sound like I am about to orgasm and he isn't even touching me. And everything he'd said… It was filthy, and erotic, and no holds barred…and I want it. *Gah!* Maybe that last breakup had gone to my head? On the flip side, I haven't thought about my ex since I got here, huh? Perhaps that's what I need—a firm hand to keep me under control, a jerk-ass to occupy my thoughts and keep them off of my past, and his dick… Admit it. Since seeing that gorgeous cock… All you can think of is how it would feel inside of you—pulling, stretching, filling, bumping up against your innermost walls, driving you higher, higher. My knees seem to buckle. I push my heels into the floor to steady myself.

"You're right," I manage to force out the words. "What you said turned me on."

"That's a start." He draws himself up to his full height, walks back toward me. "Believe me, it's good for you to speak what's on your mind."

"Oh?"

"You have no idea what it does to keep your innermost desires bottled up inside."

"Is that your prognosis?" I mumble.

"That's my advice, as your doctor." His eyes gleam. "Don't hide your needs. Bring them out. Live them, revel in them. It's good for your mind, and of course, your heart." He leans forward places his palm over the skin above my left breast, "Let go of your inhibitions. Put yourself in my hands for this interval of time. I promise, I'll take care of you, Princess Buttercup."

I stare at him. He meets my gaze, unblinking. His features are composed, even sincere. And my soufflé rises every time I make it. Not.

I shuffle my feet. "Well…" I blink rapidly. *It seems too good to be true. Is there a catch? There has to be a catch. An egomaniac like this wouldn't suggest this unless there was something in it to trip me up. But the money, OMG, what I couldn't do with it.*

"You'll stick to your part of the bargain?" I scowl.

His eyes gleam. He holds out his hand, "You have my word."

I glance down at his palm, then back at his face, "Hmm."

"Go on," he cajoles, "I promise, I'll keep my end of the agreement."

"Will you?"

"Try me." His lips curl. Bastard. He's challenging me. Bet he thinks I'll turn tail and run out screaming about now. Which I should, but I won't. Because... Yeah I'm stubborn that way. I haven't come this far by backing down at the first sign of trouble, and no dominant, macho, sexy as fuck, obnoxious prat is going to deprive me of my much-needed holiday, not to mention the opportunity to get a head start on my career...my life. My bloody future beckons. All I have to do is embrace it.

"Fine." I place my hand in his.

His wide palm engulfs mine, warmth from his skin sizzles up my arm. Electricity zings up my spine. *Whoa. The hell was that?* I try to pull back my hand, he holds on.

"You good, Princess?"

No.

No.

"Of course," I stutter. "Why would you think otherwise?"

He surveys my features, "You seem pale."

My guts twist. *Bloody hell, this is happening. This is really, really happening.* My stomach flips and my heart thumps in my chest. *Damn… What the hell am I doing?*

"You not going to faint or anything, are you?" he asks.

I stiffen; my head instantly clears. "Of course not," I huff.

He nods, "Also…you're welcome."

I blink. *No, no, don't react. Don't say anything to this obnoxious bonehead.* He pauses a few inches from me. Sweat breaks out on my forehand. "For what?" I force out the words, knowing I shouldn't, but wanting to know what twisted notion his very clever mind has thought up.

"For accepting my invitation to the most exclusive private New Year's Eve party in London."

I open my mouth to refuse, but he shakes his head, "Think before you say anything. Trust me, you want to be there. The kind of contacts you'll make there will give you a lead over your nearest competitor."

I firm my lips together, mind racing.

"The list of guests is a who's who of the well-connected from around the world. It's perfect to build contacts, invaluable for a fledgling business like yours."

I peer into his face. Is he making fun of me? Trying to undermine my efforts as a business person? But his features take on a sincere expression. Hmph. Not that I am buying it, but he has a point. It won't hurt to be there. Invitations to those kinds of events…are like gold dust. Of course, I could work hard…but being at the right place, at the right time… Well, that's when things get interesting.

"I…guess…that makes sense," I venture.

He nods. "If we last until then." He smirks.

"Is that a challenge?"

"No, it's a fact. Do you think you can get through our time together without walking out in a huff?

8

---

5 mins later

Weston

"OMG, you're such an ass."

She marches out of the house, slamming the door behind her. The crash reverberates through the living room. Max whines and runs to the exit. He scratches at the door, then barks and jumps up onto it.

"Hey buddy." I amble toward the puppy and scoop him up. He stares up at me with soulful eyes; a small whine catches in his throat.

"What?" I growl. "Why are you making those moony faces at me?"

What the—? Am I talking in some kind of puppy lingo with him? I mean, seriously. I scowl at him. "Don't go thinking you can soften my heart or anything." I frown.

He blinks at me.

I angle my head.

He tips up his head and licks my face, my mouth…

"Hey—" I arch my neck, but am no match for the little guy's persistent slobbering. A chuckle rumbles up my throat. Who'd have thought I'd be giving in to a mutt, of all things?

"You want me to go get her, huh?"

He licks his chops, and I swear, he jerks his little head.

"What the—?" I frown, "You can't understand me, can you?"

He pops his head on my shoulder, gazes at me with those soulful brown eyes, pleading, asking… Something hot stabs at my chest. *That…is probably my ego having a cardiac. The fuck am I thinking? And I am supposed to be a heart surgeon. Duh.* If anyone knows the ins and outs of that particular organ, it's me, and here I am, imagining all kinds of ridiculous things. Blame it on the pup. Blame it on that sassy, little Buttercup, who had taken one look at the bedroom…and the queen-sized bed in there, and had thrown up her hands in disgust. She'd marched right out—still holding onto her handbag and that infernal satchel-like bag over her back, and banged the door shut.

"It's not my fault. You know that, right?" I address the puppy. "She should have asked if there was a second bedroom. Hell, she could have asked to inspect the premises before agreeing." I frown. "Why hadn't she?" I muse. "Why had she agreed so easily to the arrangement? I mean, sure, six mil is a lot… " I glower at the little dog, who stares back, unblinking. Had I wanted her to turn it down? Show me that she was different from the other women I'd dated so far? And what? I'd expected her to throw it in my face and walk out? I raise my shoulders.

Well, my conscience is clear, at least. I am more than compensating her for her time... Which begs the question, "What the hell had I been thinking when I'd asked her to stay? And accompany me for the Christmas visit to my family…?" I ask the mutt. It had seemed like a brilliant idea—two birds, one stone, and all that. And the little fact that we'd have to share the bed? Hell, I hadn't thought of it until she'd walked into the room, but it's going to make things entertaining, for sure, huh?

The puppy yawns.

"Thanks." My lips twist. "You sure know how to handle me, little bugger, huh?"

He licks my mouth again.

I wince. "Okay, not sure how I feel about that."

He whines again, wriggles in my hold. I put him down and he runs to the exit. I follow him, shove open the door, and he races down the steps to the parked car. He leaps on the door. She opens it, careful not to hurt him… He jumps inside. Through the darkness, I make out the two of them in the front seat.

I watch for a second longer. Is she wearing her coat? I don't think she took it with her. So that means she is wearing that skimpy blouse…in the biting cold. At least, she had her boots back on.

I march inside, shrug into my coat, grab hers, then stalk to the car. I reach the passenger side, try the handle. it's unlocked. *The hell?* I slip inside, drop the coat on the space between the seats, "You forgot this." I glare at her.

She pales, holds the puppy closer.

Max snuggles into her breasts, and stares at me.

His expression implies he's got something I don't. I scowl at him and he pants, tongue lolling. *Is the damn mutt laughing at me? And now I'm jealous of a bloody puppy? The hell? Do I still have my balls?*

I glare at her profile. "Why didn't you lock the bloody door?" my voice booms out in the space.

Max whines.

She frowns. "Do you have a thing for scaring helpless puppies?"

"Not as much as for ensuring that sassy women don't get themselves kidnapped."

"Who's going to kidnap me here?" She waves a hand in the air.

"Things are not as safe as they seem."

She huffs, "You're acting too dramatic."

"No, that's you."

She strokes Max's head and addresses him, "What are you doing here?"

"If you're going to stay in the car, you may as well turn on the heater."

"It's my car—"

"No mistaking that." I glance around the cramped space. My

knees are almost doubled up in front of me. I lean down, grab the lever to push the seat back.

"What are you doing—?"

The grip comes off in my hand. I stare at it.

"Yeah… I was going to warn you..." Her voice trails off.

"Does this thing even start up?" I reach for the car keys, but she grabs them first.

"Stop insulting KITT."

I stare. "You named your car after—"

"Knight Rider." She nods, then brightens. "You know about the series?"

"This isn't anything like that KITT," I growl.

"Shh," she pats the dash, "you'll upset her."

"Of course, your car had to be female." A headache begins to drum behind my eyes.

"Why not? KITT isn't the prerogative for a male name."

"What-fucking-ever." I massage my temples.

"You're a sore loser."

"The only thing getting sore here are my knees."

"I know you're getting along in your years…but maybe you need to get that looked at."

I scowl.

Her lips kick up and her entire face brightens. Damn, when she smiles, her features resemble those of an angel… *No. What?* Hello, bloody Christmas spirit must be getting to me.

"I'm not old."

"You're older than me."

"You're what, twenty-five?" I snicker.

"If you wanted to know my age, you only had to ask."

"Like I bloody care?"

She purses her lips, "Don't swear in front of the baby."

That's when something inside of me snaps. *Of all the annoying, getting-on-my-nerves, blonde-haired bombshells in the world… This…tiny, pint-sized, sassy-as-fuck, with the sexiest tits-that-I-want-to-suck-on-like-cotton-candy woman walks into my house… Yeah, my place… Mine. Hold on. The fuck am I calling mine? Her? The cabin … Yeah, that's what I'm refer-*

ring to. That's all it is. It's not about her… Not at all. Naw. Hold on… Did I compare her breasts to a treat…? Cotton candy? What the fuck? I reach forward, grab her shoulder.

She squeaks.

Max growls in his throat.

I shoot him a dirty look. Fucker changed camps, deserted me so easily... Wait until he comes looking for treats. *Guess who wears the pants around here, you mutt!*

Max whines.

"Hey," she hunches her shoulders over the puppy, "back off, you big bully."

"Not happening." I firm my grip on her. She winces but doesn't back down. *Hmm.* This woman has a backbone, all right. I am going to take so much pleasure in breaking her down. "Get out of the car," I growl.

"No." She firms her lips.

"You have until I count to five."

"Whatever." She continues to pat the puppy's head.

"Four." I set my jaw.

"Count faster." She rubs behind Max's ears and the mutt makes a contented sound. *Hell. How dare she ignore me…for a…a dog?* She is fucking with my head, all right.

"Three." I lower my chin.

"Guess he knows his numbers, huh?" she sing-songs to the puppy.

My pulse begins to race.

"Two." I move in closer.

"I am soo scared," she simpers

Adrenaline spikes my blood. My pulse thuds at my temples, behind my eyelids, even in my fucking balls. "Don't say I didn't warn you," I lower my voice to a hush. She pales, a visible shudder running up her spine. *Good.*

"One." I apply just enough pressure so she turns to me.

"What are you doin—?" Her gaze widens.

I yank her toward me, puppy and all, lower my lips to her taunting mouth.

9

"I could give up chocolate, but I am not a quitter."
-From Amelie's diary

Amelie

Warmth, heat, the hardness of his chest digging into my breasts...
But his lips…his lips… They're soft and coaxing…and completely
not what I expected. Not after how he'd grasped my shoulder…
Certainly not, after how he'd kissed me that first time…all
demanding and dominating… Oh, he's still ruthless, hellbent on
taking from me… But with his mouth, he seduces me. He nibbles on
my lower lip and I part them. He swipes his tongue across the seam
of my mouth, and a moan trembles up my throat. He releases my
shoulder, only to cup my cheek. His warm breath mixes with mine
and I draw of his in greedy gulps. I want to bottle that essence of his,
roll around in it, absorb in it, bathe in it, let it tease my core, slink up

my channel… *Argh!* Everything in me wants him to lick me down there with as much finesse as he's demonstrating with his very able mouth. "Wes," I hear myself plead with him… *Did I say that aloud or was I simply thinking it in my mind?* He tilts his head, easing his tongue over mine. A ripple of pleasure darts up my spine. All thoughts drain from my head. I move in closer, strain against his chest. Bring my arms around his—a whine cuts through the air.

I pull away, but he holds me in place. "Ignore him."

"But…"

"The pooch will survive."

"He's getting restless," I insist. "Did you take him out earlier?""

"Open the door and let him out."

"No." I stare at him. "Out here?"

"It's a gated property," he replies.

I turn down my lips and he glares at me. A frisson of something —nervousness, fear, something I can't quite identify—quivers in my stomach. I lick my lips and his gaze drops there. Those colorless eyes seem to turn into mirrors—cold, hard. He could cut me, and hurt me, rip me apart, and I'd enjoy it all. I gulp, the sound audible. He jerks his chin up, then draws in a breath. "Fuck," he growls, "you owe me."

"What—?

He reaches across me and I shudder, then almost cry out when he straightens. He cuddles the puppy against his chest, "Stay," he growls.

Is he talking to me? Before I can respond, he's shoved open the door, and stalked toward the house. What the hell is he up to?

He pushes open the door, squats down to lower the puppy to the floor, then pats him. Even now, when he's angry with me, he can't resist making sure the puppy is comfortable, huh? The man may disagree, but it's clear to me that he has a soft spot for the pet… Which, surely, shows that he isn't all that alphaholish as he makes himself out to be, huh?

He rises to his feet.

Which doesn't mean I am going to stay out here and wait for him to come back. And what? Finish what he started? The way he'd kissed me earlier… Softly, gently, revealing that part of him I'd sensed under those layers of brutishness… If he did it again, I know I'd give in to him… And hell, if I am going to let that happen. At the very least, I am not going to give in to him that easily.

He turns.

I shove open my car door and race out.

"Hey," his voice follows me.

I pick up speed.

"Stop. Where are you going?"

Good question. If I'd wanted to get away, all I'd have had to do was turn the keys, start the car, and drive away; I'd have had to wait while the gates opened, but I'd have managed to leave. Which I hadn't.

And it's not like I can leave the property, considering I have no way of opening the gates now.

So, what is this? A dash for freedom, to show him that I don't mean to obey him? Do I want him to chase me? Either way, I'm not going to give in so easily.

"Amelie," his voice whips through the still night… My name from his lips…? Ohmigod! A thrill runs down my spine. Moisture laces my core. I increase my pace.

If he wants me, he has to come and get me.

I pound down the driveway.

"Princess." He's so close. Adrenaline laces my blood; a giggle catches in my throat. *What the hell am I doing? What's wrong with me? Am I toying with him? With myself? Doesn't matter.* This is one race I plan to win. I plan to… Something—someone—his big arms catch me around my waist. I scream as the ground comes up to meet me. The next second, I am hauled up and around, and against that firm chest. Heat from his body surrounds me, envelops me; my thighs clench; my scalp tingles. A burst of excitement ignites in my veins. "Let me go," I squeak.

"No."

He drops my coat—he'd picked it up from the car?—and yanks me up to my toes, thrusts his face into mine, "Where the hell do you think you are going?"

"Somewhere… Anywhere… To get away from you."

"What if I don't let you leave?"

"Do you want me to stay?" I jut my chin, daring him. *Say it, do it. Just one word... Anything to show you're as affected with this...chemistry between us.*

He looks me up and down, "I don't care either way."

Jerk. My insides twist; anger sputters up my spine. He releases me so suddenly, that I stumble. Then right myself. *Goddamn him.*

I stand there and watch that snickerdoodle of a man bend to pick my coat.

He straightens and his shoulders once more block my line of sight. I take in how his waist tapers down to meet his powerful thighs. My mouth waters. My fingers itch. I want to reach out and trace the cut abs outlined by his shirt.

His lips kick up. Heat flushes my cheeks. Of course he is well aware of the effect of his nearness on me.

He tilts his head, "Have you decided?"

I peer up into his face, rake my gaze across his strong features, that mean upper lip, his broad jaw. My nipples pucker and my toes curl. What would happen if I stayed? And if I leave? Will I always wonder how it would have been to spend a few days with him?

"Amelie?" His voice is impatient.

"I.... I...am not sure," I stutter.

He peruses my features. "Turn around," he orders.

I do. I sense him close the distance between us, then he drops the coat over my shoulders. I shove my hands through the sleeves, and he pivots me to face him. I stare at that broad chest that's going to haunt my dreams for a long time. *Hell.*

He places his knuckles under my chin, applies pressure so I have to tilt my head up. I meet his gaze.

"You can leave now," his voice is harsh, "or you can come into the warmth."

"Come into the parlor, said the spider to the fly," I mumble.

"Oh, you're no fly, Buttercup." He grunts, "More of an annoying, pesky mosquito."

"And you're what...an octopus?"

"I can certainly wrap my arms and legs around you in a similar fashion." He chuckles. "To keep you warm, of course."

"Of course." I draw in a breath, "Fine, I'll stay."

"Good."

"On one condition."

"You don't make the rules, babe." His voice is soft, almost playful. His eyes take on that flinty look I'm coming to anticipate, and hate. My toes curl.

"But I'll let you have your say," he adds, "this time."

"You…you'll sleep on the couch," I state.

"No."

"Fine, I'll sleep on the couch." I tip up my chin.

"You think I'd let you do that?"

"Why not?" I scowl.

"A deal is a deal." His grin widens, "Six days—same house, *same bed.* You'll cook and clean and do everything I ask of you. Every day you complete, I deposit one million pounds in your account."

I gulp. OMG, I'm going to do this. I am. I can't turn this down. I tried. I went so far as trying to run away, but who am I kidding?

I can never turn down a challenge; and I admit, a tiny part of me is curious about whether I can actually resist him. I have to, of course. Otherwise, I'll lose any measure of self-confidence I have in myself.

I pull back; his hands drop away. I tug the coat closed, then turn and walk around him toward the house. I reach the porch steps, then turn around, "Coming?"

He scowls. My insides knot. Guess he's not happy I took the lead. Too bad. I don't care that he's pissed-off. That seems to be his perpetual state of mind. But why does he have to be so hot when he glowers at me? I reach the door, then turn again. "Would you bring in my remaining luggage, while you're at it?" I suppress a giggle as I walk into the cabin.

10

Weston

"What the fuck do you have in them, stones?" I'd hauled her bag over the threshold of the house, and into the bedroom.

"Did you pack for a month?" I glower.

"I believe in traveling with everything I need."

"Clearly," I mutter.

Grabbing a bottle of beer from the kitchen, I return and prop myself on the bed.

"What are you doing?" She drags her second suitcase into the bedroom.

"What does it look like?"

She dumps the bag in the middle of the floor of the room, "Why don't you drink in the living room?"

"My house."

"It's not yours," she huffs. "You co-own it with the Seven."

"Semantics," I grumble. "It's more mine than yours, at any rate."

She opens her mouth.

I shake my head. "What made you decide to become a pastry chef?"

She blinks. "Why do you want to know?"

Good question. Why the hell do I care? Except I am intrigued... Fine, I want to understand what makes this bundle of energy tick.

"I don't care either way," I take a healthy swig of the beer, "but it's the kind of conversation you women seem to love."

She opens and shuts her mouth, then straightens, "So this is your idea of being polite?"

"Nope," I finish off the beer, place the bottle on the sideboard, "but this is." I yank my shirt over my head, toss it aside.

"What are you doing?" she squeaks.

"What do you think?" I rise to my feet, drop my pants, along with my boxers.

Her indrawn breath fills the space. I don't stop the grin that tugs at my lips. Buttercup can deny it all she wants, but the attraction between us is alive and kicking. It's making this entire exercise a hell of a lot more interesting. It's definitely the reason I'm allowing her to stay. If nothing else, to see how far I can go before I stop resisting her. I get back into bed, pull the covers up to my waist, then switch off the lamp on my side, leaving the room in darkness.

Silence for a beat, then another.

"How is this polite?" her voice cracks. She clears her throat, "Seriously, can you enlighten me here?"

"I'm sleeping on my side of the bed, aren't I?"

"Gah." She makes a sound deep in her throat.

A chuckle rumbles up my throat. I swallow it. "You're welcome."

I hear her moving around, then, "Why is this clock not working?"

I glance up to find her holding the digital timepiece in her hands. She turns it over, fiddles with the little compartment at the back, "Huh, it has no batteries." She turns to me, "Did you do that?" She frowns.

My heartbeat begins to race. "I don't know what you're talking about." I sink back into my pillow, close my eyes.

"The clock in the living room, too, had been dismantled."

What the hell does she want to know? Why can't she leave it alone already?

"Do you have something against clocks or something? Maybe you don't like the idea of time running out?" She chuckles.

I turn my back on her.

I hear her open the drawers, "Okay I found the batteries. I am going to—"

"Put it back." I snap.

"What?"

"Put the bloody clock back where you found it."

There's a pause.

"If you don't do it, I swear I'll come there and make you do it."

She huffs. There's a click as she places the timepiece back on the table.

"I've returned the batteries to the drawer," she mutters. "So don't get your dander up about it."

The breath I'd not been aware of holding rushes out.

Shit, the hell is wrong with me? Why the hell am I getting worked up over this little thing? It is a clock—a functioning clock. Doesn't mean anything. *Why the hell can't I bear the thought of it counting down the time as I sleep?*

The numbers mounting, the hands moving, the tick-tock-tick-tock of the countdown as he'd watched me closely, peered into my face, searched for a reaction, anything to show I was afraid, that I'd give in and break, ask for help. Ask it, do it. My heart thunders in my chest. Close your eyes. Count down the time.

Twelve o'clock.

Eleven o'clock—

I hear the sound of something connecting with that massive suitcase. Then a howl, "Bloody hell!"

I switch on the light. "What are you doing?"

She sits on the ground, nursing one booted foot. "Taking out my frustration, you oaf." Her hair flows about her shoulders. Her cheeks are pink. From anger? From embarrassment at seeing me naked? Considering she's already had her mouth on my dick... Well, isn't that cute.

"There are better ways of dealing with it." I lower my gaze to her heaving breasts.

"Aargh, stop that." She yanks off one boot, then the other. "Turn away."

"Why?"

"I want to undress, you… you neanderthal."

I laugh, "Running out of insults?"

"Oh, I have plenty where that came from." She pulls off her other boot, then rises to her feet. "Some privacy please?"

"Not happening." I lean back against the headboard, fold an arm behind my neck. Her gaze darts to my biceps; she swallows. I scratch my chest and her breasts heave. A glimmer of sweat gleams over her upper lip. "Is it too hot in here for you?" I grin.

She huffs, then undoes the button of her coat and pushes it off her shoulder. She glances around, then walks to the closet and pulls it open. She surveys the contents, then hangs it up. "You didn't bring too many clothes, did you?" she grumbles.

"Worried about me?" I smirk.

She throws up her hands, then steps back and slams the closet doors shut, "It's pointless making any conversation with you."

"You were the one who declined to answer my question."

"Whatever." She pulls off her jeans, giving me a flash of pink underwear. My groin instantly tightens. *Fuck.* She is more modestly dressed than women wearing skimpy bikinis on the beach… So why does she seem so much more alluring, so attractive…? So fucking gorgeous, as she folds her jeans then places them on the chair near the bed. She lifts a corner of the cover, then slips inside. She stays on the far end… Right at the end. "Any further and you'll slip off."

"I'll manage."

"I won't bite."

"Ha," she snorts, "famous last words."

"Unless you want me to?"

She stills. Tension pours off of her to fill the space between us on the bed. I switch off the light, then fold my arms over my chest. "If you stay that stiff, I'll have to tickle you."

"Wh…what?" she squeaks.

"Not good for your muscles to be so bunched up. You'll have a headache when you wake up."

"Like you care?"

"A deal is a deal, Buttercup."

"I wish you wouldn't call me that."

"I wish you'd relax a little."

If anything, she tenses further. I turn away from her, close my eyes. The stress that rolls off of her slams into my back. My shoulders bunch, My muscles coil, ready to spring... *Fuck.* I turn back to her, scoot over.

Her gaze widens, "What are you—?"

"Hush." I pull her to me, so her back is pressed into my chest, then I spoon her.

She makes a noise of alarm.

I tighten my arm around her waist. "Raise your head."

"What?"

"Do it, woman," I snap.

She does as I ask. *Fuck, finally.* I slip my arm under her neck, throw my leg over hers.

She doesn't say a word. Nothing. Her entire body goes stiff... As hard as my dick, which instantly lengthens. It nestles against the curve of her hip. Well, someone's happy, at least. I tuck her head under my chin.

"Weston," she whispers.

I sigh, "Now what?"

"What is it with you and clocks? Do you have a phobia or something?"

Or something. Not that I am going to tell her about it. I'd already given away enough with that half-arsed fit I'd thrown. Shit, do I have my balls about me or what?

"Weston—"

"Goodnight, Princess."

She huffs, but stay's silent.

Thank fuck.

I close my eyes, count back the time on the hands of a clock. Restart the stopwatch.

Twelve o' clock.

Eleven o'clock.

Her shoulder muscles relax.

Ten o'clock.

Nine o'clock.

Her breathing grows more uniform.

Eight o'clock.

Seven o'clock.

She wriggles her butt. The blood rushes to my groin.

Six o'clock.

She thrusts her feet in between my legs. The coldness from her toes shivers over my skin. I swear aloud, "Did you dip your feet in ice?"

"Sorry," she mutters.

Five o'clock.

Four o' clock.

She pushes her body into mine. My cock lengthens, stabs into the valley between her butt cheeks.

Three o'clock.

She rubs her cheek against the pillow. Then digs her toes into my calf. "The hell are you doing?" I grouse.

"Can't sleep," she mumbles.

I turn her over to face me. *Mistake.* The moonlight floods in from the open window, highlighting her baby blues. Her hair clings to her forehead; her nose turns up above those gorgeous pink lips. My heart stutters. It fucking stutters. The fuck? "What is it?" I grumble.

"I forgot the chocolate."

"Chocolate?"

"And I need fresh eggs, cinnamon, butter—"

"You've lost me."

"To make breakfast."

I shudder and mime throwing up in my mouth. "Who has chocolate for breakfast?"

She laughs. "Chocolate pancakes, dummy." Then she adds, "What do you like to eat in the morning?"

"Anything but chocolate." I grumble.

"Wh-a-a-t?" Her eyes go all round, "You don't like chocolate?"

"Why settle for chocolate, when," I drag my gaze down her body, "there are other things that make for a tastier breakfast."

She gapes, "Do you only think of sex?"

"Do you only think of desserts?"

"What else is there?" her voice cracks.

I scan her pink-tinged features. "Are you blushing?"

"Of course, not." Her face grows fiery.

"What are you thinking?"

"Nothing."

Oh, it was something all right. "Go on, you can tell me."

She shakes her head.

I glare at her, lower my voice to a hush, "Say it."

She trembles. "I… I was thinking how much I'd like for you to eat me out."

Amelie

What the hell am I doing? Why did I blurt that out? I'd honestly not realized that it was what I had in mind, until he'd commanded me to speak… And hell, when he assumes that voice, that hushed tone which whips through my mind, I can't stop myself. I have to obey him. *But did I have to tell him the truth? Couldn't I have deflected?*

His nostrils flare and his grip on my waist tightens. "Say that again," he rasps.

"I… I…" My throat closes. How can I repeat what had come out in a moment of utter lunacy?

"Complete your sentence," his hot breath sears my lips. My panties instantly dampen. My thighs clench and I can't stop the small whine that spills from my mouth.

"Ask…and you shall receive." His lips curl. An answering quiver thrums at my center. *OMFG! I can't even… This man… How can I refuse him anything? Why the hell had I agreed to stay…? Is that why I hadn't wanted to leave?* I blink; all thoughts empty from my mind.

"Please," I breathe out. "Eat me."

Even before the words are out of my mouth, he's flipped me on my back, "With pleasure, Alice." He smirks from above me.

"A…are you my white rabbit?"

"You'll have to let me know."

I blink, then heat sears my cheeks. Is he alluding to my favorite vibrator? "That's not what I—" My breath hitches as he slides down my body.

His hard chest presses down on my breasts, my belly, then his head is between my thighs. He shoulders apart my legs, places one of my hands on his ear, then the other on the other side. "Hold on." His eyes glitter.

"What the—"?" I gasp, then tighten my fingers around his ears, for he's buried his face in my pussy.

He nuzzles my flesh.

I whimper.

He blows on my throbbing core, and hell, but I almost come right then.

"Not yet, Buttercup." I sense his lips curve against my center.

"Don't…don't stop," I gasp.

"Hmm," he makes an appreciative sound deep in his throat.

All of my nerve endings seem to explode.

"Which dessert should I sample first, you think?"

"Wait," I gasp.

He peers up at me.

"The arrangement."

"What of it?"

"You said no sex."

"So?"

"Does this count as sex?"

"I thought we already covered this, Buttercup."

"As long as you don't…uh…you don't—"

"Sink my dick into your pussy?"

My cheeks flush, "Yeah, no penetration, in the traditional fashion, equals no sex, right?"

"Sure, if that's how you want to see it."

"I…"

He drags his fingers up my pussy lips.

I huff.

"So?" He smirks.

"Yes…" I force out the word.

He stares back.

"Yes, that's the definition, for the…uh, the arrangement." I clarify, "As long as you don't uh, penetrate my puss—eee" The word comes out on a whine for he's replaced his finger with his mouth. OMG. OMG. A moan trembles from my lips.

"My, my, Buttercup," he mutters against my core, " is this how greedy you are when you bake?"

What the—? I blink. Why is he still talking? Didn't his mom teach him not to talk when his mouth is full? Why can't he—?

He raises his head. Cool air envelops the heated, melting triangle between my legs, right before he slaps my pussy. Right on it, across my swollen core, which erupts in a miasma of sparks, that travels out from the contact, up my spine, and explodes behind my eyes. The room tilts. *Ohmigod.* Sweat beads my brow. The pain fades, leaving behind an ache that swallows me up from the center. "What was that for?" I shudder.

"Answer the question, doll."

"Wh…which one?"

"Should I taste you here?" He dips his head, slips his tongue inside my backhole.

My entire body snaps to attention. All of my pores pop. My chest rises and falls.

"Or here?" He drags his wicked tongue up my slit.

I moan.

"Maybe I should be as greedy as you and not wait?" He fixes that instrument of torture-pleasure, aka his mouth, around my throbbing bud, and I shoot upfrom the bed.

"Wes!" I howl.

He releases my pussy. "You still haven't answered the question," he rumbles.

"Wh…what?"

"Last chance, babe."

He leans back, and I thrust up with my pelvis, trying to recapture that earlier feeling, honing in on his tongue.

"Well?" he asks. "You need to ask for what you want, darlin'."

Maybe it's that endearment that makes me crack my eyes open. "All of it," I gasp. "Please lick me, suck on me, thrust your tongue inside my—" I huff, for he's done just that.

He twists his tongue inside of me and goosebumps flare on my skin. He slides his big arms under my legs, pushes up my knees on either side of my body, then he swipes his tongue in and out of me, and again. He slurps his way down to my backhole and up to my cunt again and again. I cry out, but he doesn't stop. He slips his tongue in between my pussy lips, samples me like I am the tastiest puff pastry. He bites down on my clit and I scream, dig my fingers into the space behind his ears and yank.

A growl rumbles up his chest and the vibrations swell my core, pour over me like the sound waves from a fucking dinner gong— *Wait, why am I thinking with this bizarre metaphor?* Except, hell, if I am not ready, I'm going to…

"Come," he growls into my hot, melting core, and I explode.

My climax crashes over me, shoves me up…up…up. Maybe I black out. I force myself to open my eyelids, look down to where he's still between my legs, my knees splayed out. "Wow," I breathe.

He doesn't smile back. He stares at me. His gaze unwavering.

"What?" I croak.

"You ready, yet?"

"Huh?"

He drops his mouth, nuzzles my pussy.

I moan, "I can't."

"I haven't even started, babe."

"No…no."

He licks my lower lips and pleasure radiates out from my core.

"Oh, my God."

"Hold on," he says.

"What?"

He rises up, grabs my wrists and holds them over my head. He wraps my fingers around the wooden bars of the headboard. "Stay," he commands.

I stare at him. *As if I could move.*

One side of his lips kicks up; he presses a firm kiss to my lips, then slides down to position his face over my pussy. He grabs my knees, pries them further apart so I am splayed wide for him. I should blush or feel shy, for heaven's sake. Those are my most intimate parts, served up to him for display; but all I can think is, *please... please... please.*

"Lick or suck?" he asks.

"Anything, either... Both," I gasp out.

He glares at me.

I shiver... "Anything you want."

"Right answer."

He drops his head and thrust his tongue back inside my melting channel.

"Oh, my God," I whine. "More, please, don't stop...don't..." I push myself up and into his face, not caring what he thinks of me. Any restraint holding me back is gone. Poof. All he has to do is touch me and I'll do anything for him. Damn it, I should have known that... But I'm not sleeping with him.. Yet. I mean, technically this doesn't count. Like the blowjob... Anything other than full penetration... Yep, that's it; anything else is fine. It is. "Fuck me with your mouth, please," I plead.

He laughs, "One fuck-me-with-your-mouth, coming up." He releases my knees, only to grip my arsecheeks. He squeezes down and I whine. He pries them apart. *What the—?* He hauls me up, slips his tongue down and inside my arsehole. *Oh, my f'ing god.* It's like nothing I have experienced before. No one...has touched me there, and this man? He slides his tongue into that forbidden part of me... As if, as if... We are lovers. No, fuckbuddies... Not... Anything-but-fucking-buddies, that's what we are. A giggle wells up, turns into a scream, when he begins to fuck my backhole with his tongue. He thrusts in and out, in and out, brings his hand up to grind his heel against my clit, and that tightness inside of me snaps out, expands... "Wes..." I moan. "Weston..."

He doesn't answer. He can't, because his mouth is full of me.

"Wes. Wes. Wes," I chant. *Aloud, or in my mind?* No matter, if food is a religious experience for me, then his tongue-fucking me has to count as a close second. The orgasm screeches up my legs, up my spine.

He slides his tongue out, replaces it with his finger, another, then shoves his tongue inside my pussy.

"Weston," I scream.

He releases my other knee and grabs my breast, squeezes my nipple so hard, stars burst behind my eyes.

"Oh, my God, I am going to…going to…"

He slips his thumb inside my mouth, at the same time that he crooks his fingers inside my backhole, then tears his mouth from my pussy and growls, "Come."

11

———————

Weston

Her body bucks, her spine curves, she opens her mouth, but no sound emerges. Her eyes roll back in her head as she shatters. I tilt my head, lick up the cum from between her pussy lips. *So fucking sweet. Is she made of the sugar that she likes to bake with?* Her climax seems to go on and on. Her shoulders jerk, her head thrown back, and the arch of her throat beckons.

I crawl up her body, fit my mouth to hers. I slide my fingers inside her pussy, she moans, and I swallow it up. I swipe my tongue over hers, tasting our joined-up essences. I drag my other hand up the curve of her waist. She shivers. I cup her cheek, lean back and peer into her features, "Look at me."

Her eyelids flutter. Those blue eyes peek up at me, pupils blown, still high on the orgasm. Something hot stabs at my chest. I flip over on the bed, pulling her with me. I coil her over my chest. Another spasm runs up her spine. I tug her closer, wrap her up in my arms.

Fuck, fuck, fuck, what am I doing? I hadn't meant for it to get this… intense, this complicated. *Keep things light, stay away from all entanglements,* has always been my motto. And I've succeeded so far, haven't

I? I had asked her to stay…because I'd thought it would be entertaining. Okay so that's not the full truth. The last time I'd spoken to my mother, she'd asked me if I'd met anyone yet. It is the one thing —the only thing—she wants from me. For me, I guess. It had been a flash of instinct that had had me stipulating she come along to the Christmas dinner. My family… They'd pulled me out of the depression I had fallen into after the 'incident' when I had been kidnapped along with the rest of the Seven. They'd reassured me, never allowing me to falter.

The incident had turned everything upside down. The only people who had seemed to get me after that were the rest of the Seven, and not only because they were, each of them, mean motherfuckers, as unfeeling as me… It was the shared experience of the days that had changed our lives, scarred each of us in similar, yet unique, ways.

Still, my parents had been encouraging, supportive, taken me to therapy, tolerated my outbursts at them as I'd struggled to come to terms with what had happened. They had been stellar in their roles and duties toward me. It's not their fault I've turned out to be an asshole. Blame that on me… Maybe it's the way I was born.

So, it had been a spur of the moment decision that she accompany me to see my family for Christmas. *The hell had I been thinking?*

This pint-sized woman with the sassy attitude, honeyed mouth, and a cunt that tastes like all the forbidden delights she specializes in baking—has clearly addled my thought processes.

I drag my fingers down the waterfall of her golden hair. Softer than cookie dough— *What the fuck? I do not think in food metaphors.* Her proximity is definitely affecting me. I stay still, watch her eyeballs move behind her now-closed eyelids. She snuggles into me; her breathing deepens. I stay still until her body twitches. She's definitely out cold. Apparently, I tired her out. Too bad I can't say the same about me. My muscles coil and bunch, my mind racing. I need to figure out what the hell to do with her. My proposal stands, but the boundaries are blurring… Hell, I am still here, holding her, caressing her, watching her as she sleeps. The fuck is up with that? I ease her down onto the bed. She doesn't stir. Good.

I slide out of bed, pull the duvet over her. Turning, I crash into her suitcase, which plops over. I glance over to find she's still sleeping. I shake my head. What I wouldn't give to be able to switch off like that, huh? Since the incident… I've never slept for more than three, maybe four hours a night. Useful when you're at medical school and need to study before exams… A bitch at any other time. I pull on my jeans, a sweatshirt over my long-sleeved T, socks and boots.

Grabbing my phone from the side table, I walk through the living room, Max stirs from his rug near the fireplace, lifting his head. I go over, pat him on his flank. He licks my hand, then burrows into the special cushion I'd ordered for him. Hey, don't go all gooey-eyed. It was simply to ensure he'd be comfortable enough to not want to share my bed, okay?

I slip out onto the back porch. Early dawn lights up the horizon as I head toward the shed at the back of the property. I open the door and walk in, then head for the work bench. I switch on the desk lamp, and when my phone buzzes, I slide it out of my pocket, swipe the screen.

"Hey, motherfucker," Damian's image fills the space.

"Same to you, dickwad," I mutter.

"What's gotten into you?" He peers into the screen as if he's there in real life with me.

"What's gotten into you?" I growl. Now I'm doing the fucking NLP mirroring shit Buttercup had talked about. *Why the hell am I thinking about her, huh? Didn't I come here to get away from her? Huh? Had she actually pushed me out of my own space?* I scratch my jaw. Now, that would be the first.

"Uh-oh." Damian clicks his tongue, "I've seen that look before."

"What bloody look?" I frown.

"The one that says you're about to fall."

"Fall?"

"For her."

"Who?"

"The woman who's there in the country manor—"

"Cabin," I correct him.

"Whatever." He grins, "Admit it. You're attracted to her.'

"What shit are you talking about?" I grumble.

"You denying you hooked up with a woman in a difficult-to-reach place?"

"It's four hours away from London."

"My point exactly," he smirks.

"You city fox."

"So are you," he replies, "which is why, when Saint mentioned that you were going to be there, and not alone..."

"Hold on." I rub my temple, "Saint told you I was going to be here with a woman?'

"Aren't you?"

"That's not the point." I tilt my head, "How did he know that I was here...ah!" I stiffen. "That cunt," I growl. "He fucking played me, didn't he?"

"Hold on, I'm adding Arpad to the call," Damian says.

"What? No," I protest.

Too late. The screen blinks, then Arpad appears in another window. "Hey, bitches, you're chin-wagging like old ladies, I see."

"Hey, fuckface," I growl, "why aren't you in a boat in the middle of somewhere with no reception?"

"I have my own satellite, dickwad."

"Of course, you do." I rake my fingers through my hair. "Why are you guys calling me, anyway?"

"Checking in, ol' chap." Damian chuckles, "Making sure you're still alive after that face-off."

What face-off?

"You and Amelie...?" Damian prompts.

"What is it with you guys?" I crack my jaw from side to side, "Can't you give a man space?"

"Space?" Arpad cackles, "Did he just say what I think he did?"

"Aww, cho chweet," Damian makes kissing sounds.

Arpad cracks up laughing.

My face reddens. "That's it; I'm hanging up now."

"Hold on." Damian pretends to wipe the tears from his face, "You haven't told us what you intend to do with her?"

"What's it to you?" I growl, "And don't talk about her."

"So, it's like that, huh?" Arpad snickers. "You seeing what I'm seeing, Rockstar?" he asks Damian.

Damian stares at me, then shakes his head, "My, my, the doctor who had his arse splashed all over the internet for making a sex tape has met his match, huh?"

"It's a damn fine arse," I grumble, "and if you don't have a sex tape to your credit, you technically are persona non grata in the online world."

"But does she know about it?" Damian asks.

My neck heats and my heart begins to thud. "Why would it matter to her?"

"It would matter if you didn't tell her," Arpad points out, "Hold on, I'm adding the Father to our chinwag, so he doesn't feel left out."

"What the fuck?" I growl as Edward's face appears in another window on the screen.

"Hey Doc, how's it going?" Edward asks.

"It was going all fine and dandy until you lot decided to intrude."

"Sorry to cut in on your alone time with your lady—"

"Not my lady," I grumble.

Damian snickers.

Arpad chortles.

"What the fuck are you jokers laughing at?"

"You, arsehole, and how you've been played."

I scowl, "Fucking Saint."

Damian nods.

"He double-booked me with her. Wait until I get my hands on the dickwad; I'm going to throttle his neck.

"Victoria won't like you getting your hands on her husband."

"Man," I rub the back of my neck, "not that I begrudge them their happiness, not after everything they've been through... But he could have *not* intruded in my life," I grouse.

"Jace, then Sinner, and Saint," Damian drawls. "You'd think it was catching...all that happiness."

"Bull-fucking-shit." I sink into my chair, tip it back. "I'm not falling for whatever madness possessed those knobs to get hitched."

"Just make sure you give me enough notice," Edward pipes in.

"Notice?" I crack my neck, "The hell you going on about Father?"

"If you plan on getting hitched —"

The two front legs of the chair land on the ground with a thump, "Hitched? What the fuck are you talking about?"

"Your last-minute plan that you don't know about yet." Edward stabs a finger at me, "If you're planning on doing it, I need a little notice. I have a life too, you know. I can't always drop everything and put in an appearance to marry you guys, you know — ?

"Wait, what?" I run a finger under the collar of my shirt. "You lost me there."

"A million?" Arpad asks Damian.

"Money is beginning to lose its appeal," Damian grumbles.

"You wankers," I growl, "the fuck are you all betting on?"

"We need to up the odds," Arpad replies, as if he didn't hear me. What a tosser.

I grip my phone with such force that my fingers hurt. "Shut the fuck up, you bitches."

"It's happening, all right. You see how he's losing his shit, huh?" Arpad continues.

"What do you suggest?" Damian talks over me, "Wanna play with something a little more personal?"

"What do you have in mind?" Arpad rubs his jaw. "Property? Shares..." He snaps his fingers, "I have it."

"What you thinking of, dipshit?" Damian drawls.

"If he gets married, accept the gift I send you."

"Ooh, thanks darling, for thinking of me," Damian deadpans.

Arpad grimaces, "Cut that shit out. You won't be laughing when you see what is it."

"A woman?" He waggles his eyebrows, "A hot honey, no doubt. Why would I refuse it, huh?"

"You on then?" Arpad asks.

"And if he doesn't?" Damian jerks his chin at me.

"I'm here, you bitches."

"Oh, he will." Arpad smirks, "I present to you exhibit A... Also known as, the man who has no idea that he's counting his last few days of freedom."

"Newsflash, you toffs, I ain't planning on giving up my bachelor status anytime soon, and PS," I growl, "you can't go around placing bets involving the lives of others."

Damian's gaze widens, "Since when has Mr. Obnoxious here, developed a conscience?"

"Since he's the one about whom such bets are being placed?" Edward offers.

"Since he decided to shack up with her?" Arpad replies.

"I am not shacking up with her, you reprobates," I snarl.

"The two of you...in a cabin...in the middle of nowhere…" Arpad waggles his eyebrows.

"It's four hours from London," I remind them again.

"Wait until it snows," Edward chimes in… "I am not marrying you in a remote ceremony."

"For the final time," I jump up from my chair so fast, it crashes back, "I'm not getting married. She just happens to be here, and I'm putting the time with her to good use."

"No doubt," Damian says with a straight face. "If that's the story you're going with."

"I am taking her home to meet my family."

Silence, then Damian addresses Arpad, "Shit, can I take back that bet I agreed to?"

"Too late, old sport." Arpad chuckles, "Told ya, he won't last the holidays, but wow." He scowls at me, "You've only been with her since yesterday. Isn't that a little too soon…?"

"What are you talking about?" Clearly I am being slow on the uptake here. "And how do all of you know about her—?" Realization dawns. "That fucker—Saint." Anger sweeps my blood, "He let you all in on his dumbass plan?" I roll my shoulders, "Don't you have anything better to do than trade gossip?"

"Aw, he's no longer any more fun," Arpad shakes his head.

"Wankers gone for a toss." Damian grins, "Does that make him a tossing wanker or a wanking tosser?"

"Guys, go easy on him." Edward grins, "He's one dropkick away from having his heart broken."

I raise my phone and bring it down, intent on smashing it, then stop myself. Fuck, if I don't need the bloody device right now. Not that I can't replace it, but if what the Father said is true and snow is on its way... Then hell, all the money in the world couldn't deliver me an alternative mode of communication. Maybe I should have insisted on having the helicopter parked on the helipad in the field. Damn, missed opportunity.

"For the last time, there's nothing between us," I growl. *Why the fuck am I even explaining it to these douchebags, huh?* Maybe it's because they are the closest I have to non-blood family; though right now, I'm not sure if they are my friends or my enemies.

"You don't have to convince us," Arpad nods.

"Right, I don't care about your personal uh—relations. Of course, I care about your state of mind, which at the moment, seems rather frayed at the edges," Edward points out.

"As I was saying," I draw in a breath, "she happens to be here; so am I. We've come to an agreement, and that includes taking her home to get my mother off my back."

"Right, you keep fooling yourself, ol' sport." Damian grins. "Not that I'm not rooting for you. I mean, I want you to get through the holiday season without getting hitched." He scratches his chin, "Although, if you did get married, I'd still win, in a matter of speaking, so—"

"Fuck you, motherfuckers." I hang up. *What the fuck was that all about?*

The hair on the back of my neck rises and I hear a sound behind me. All of my senses go on alert; I pivot, fists raised.

12

Amelie

"It's me; it's only me," I squeak.

His chest heaves, his color pale. He glares at me as if he's seen a ghost.

"Weston?" I prompt.

His gaze fixes on my face. His jaw tics. The tendons of his throat move. The skin across his knuckles stretches tight. If his control had been less than perfect, I have no doubt, I'd be on the ground, with his fist buried in my face. Hell, I wouldn't mind other parts of him buried inside of me, given what had transpired between us earlier. It's clear that we are as compatible as cheese and biscuits. *WTF?* Enough with the cheesy comparisons… *Noooo, now I am punning on my own poor jokes? Gah!*

"Wes?" I take a step forward; he watches me. I raise a hand; his gaze stays on mine. I reach up on tip toe and cup his cheek. "You okay?"

He blinks, lowers his fists.

A breath I hadn't realized I was holding whooshes out. At the same time, he draws his in.

"Wes?" I step close enough for my boots to kiss his. His gaze intensifies. Those colorless eyes seem to mirror every emotion, every confusion, every screwed-up, mixed-up thought that I feel inside.

"Everything okay?" I ask.

"Why wouldn't it be?" He steps back from me and the heat of his big body recedes.

A hollow feeling coils low in my belly. *What had I been expecting?* That after the way he'd made me orgasm earlier, he'd...be more tender toward me? Maybe throw me down and decide to forget about our 'arrangement' and make love to me? *Hell, I want him to fuck me... There, I've said it out loud. Well, not really out loud, thank God.* I'd settle for him having me any which way—frontways, sideways, bent over, with my arse up in the air for him... My cheeks heat. *Jesus H, something about this man brings out the filthy girl hidden inside of me.* The one who wanted to hold onto more than his ears as I rode him off into the sunset. Huh? That picture... It's hot... And all wrong.

"What are you doing here?" He frowns.

"I, uh, woke up and you were gone—"

He looks me up and down, "Is that a... What are you wearing?"

I glance down at my pullover. "What?"

"Is that a reindeer with glitter on his nose?"

"Oh, you mean my Christmas jumper?"

His features take on an expression best described as loathing.

"Let me guess." I push a finger into my cheek, "You hate Christmas-themed sweaters."

He grunts, "And reindeer, and Christmas carols, and mulled wine..."

"What?" I stare at him. "You're joking."

"Nope." He rolls his shoulders, "Can do without that shit, and anything to do with the festive season."

"But it's the silly season." I stare at him, horrified. I mean, Mr. Grumpy McDick here is surely just trying his best to scare me off. "It's not working."

"Huh?"

"This entire, alphaholish, man-about-town, who sacrifices baby goats to the devil and screams at little kids—"

"And kicks kittens," he adds, "don't forget that."

"That's what I mean," I slap my palms on my hips. "You'd never do that."

"Because you've seen me tolerate Max?"

"More than tolerate." I scowl, "Why are you so intent on putting yourself down?"

"Why are you so intent on believing I am something I am not?"

"And what are you? Billionaire—"

"Gazillionaire."

"Doctor."

"Surgeon," he corrects me.

"Someone who's hiding away from the world because he has some deep-rooted hurt."

He laughs—a fake, hard noise that prickles over my skin. My stomach clenches. *Shit,* this is not the man who had pulled me on top of him and stroked my hair until I'd fallen asleep. This is not the generous lover, who'd dived into my pussy and eaten it out like it was creme brûlée.

"What happened?" I frown. "Why are you like a chef with a hangover."

"Maybe because I don't like the look of your face this morning?"

My heart cracks a little; it fucking splinters. *Asshole, jerk, clod.* I glare at him, "Oh, you seemed to like me well enough last night."

"I was proving a point."

"What?" My heart begins to race and sweat beads my palms. It can't be... He can't be this...arrogant and mean, this ready to hurt me... Not after how he'd kissed me and touched me like I belonged to him. *Does he do this to every woman he' takes to bed? Does he make them all feel that special?* Maybe, whichever female he's with for the moment is made to feel like the center of his universe. "What point?" I insist, "Tell me."

"That you won't get through the holiday period without sleeping with me. That all I have to do is look at you and you'll open your legs for me. That you're so needy, you'll do anything for a touch, a kiss, little bit of attention, to make you feel special—you—"

My hand connects with his cheek before the thought has time to form in my brain. Pain shoots up my arm and my palm stings. I lower my arm, my breath coming in pants like I've run a mile to get here... When I'd walked over to the shed in search of him, and overheard the last of the conversation... I don't mean anything to him. Fine. I'm a transaction. That's all right too. But this... Insulting me just out of spite... No, this is unacceptable.

I step back, "The deal's off, you horrible man. All the money in the world isn't worth putting up with the lies that pour out of your mouth."

He tilts his head as the outline of my fingerprints blooms on his cheek. "Leave then," he drawls.

"You think I can't?"

"Do it. See if I stop you." His features close; those colorless eyes seem to grow darker. *Is he hurt? Why should he be hurt? He provoked me. What did he expect?* That I'd simply take it...because...of this attraction to him...that I'd hope would deepen into something else? Ha! How stupid could I be. Or maybe, he thought I'd stay because of the money. Think again, asshole.

I pivot to walk away, and that's when the world seems to explode. I slap my hands to my ears as a clanging sound overpowers the space. *What the hell? What is that?* All of my brain cells seem to knock together at once. I turn... "What's happening—?" That's when I notice the wall... No walls, plural, of clocks. Every single available space across the walls of the room is chockablock with clocks. Old clocks, antiques, made of steel, of wood, newer models made of glass and chrome... And every single one of them is mechanical. Their alarms clang out in different tones to indicate it's nine in the morning. I blink...turn around in a circle, taking in the sheer variety of time-keeping devices. "Wow." I turn to face him as the last of the sound dies away. "Holy shit," I breathe. "What is this...place?"

"It's mine," he says simply.

"But the cabin... I mean, that palatial house which you guys refer to as the cabin." I mutter, "It belongs to Saint?"

"It belongs to all of the Seven."

"Oh."

"The last person who had access to it was Saint. When I injured my finger, I told them I needed to borrow it for the duration of the season."

"Right, so he sent me here…"

"Knowing I was here already."

"Why would he do that?"

"To fuck with me?" His lips twist.

"But this place…" I glance around the walls again, "This is yours?"

"I built it in the backyard."

"You constructed it by yourself?"

"I employed an architect. And a builder."

"Of course." I walk up to a clock on my left. In the center is a horse, hind legs reared up in the air, its white mane caught as if in mid-jump. "And these clocks?"

"I collect them."

"Are they valuable…?"

"What do you think?"

I hear the humor in his voice, turn around to find him seated at the desk pushed up against the wall. I walk over, lean over his shoulder to find him looking through a magnifying glass at the guts of a clock.

"You repair them?"

He picks up what seems to be forceps, and which seem too delicate for his thick fingers to hold, and begins to tinker with the parts of the clock.

"You're an uh, horologist?"

"I like to repair clocks. It's a way to unwind."

I snicker, "Ha, you can be funny sometimes."

"Yeah, that's me—a hoot," he says in a voice that signifies something to the contrary.

I stare at his bent head. His dark hair falls to about his shoulders, and is mussed on top. Has he been running his fingers through them? The locks had been surprisingly silky to touch yesterday when I'd held onto those ears and… I shift my weight from foot to foot.

"But you disabled the clocks in the cabin."

"They came with the house. I hadn't acquired them."

"So, because you found—" I wave my hand in the air, "all these, and fixed them, you're fine with them?"

"I put them together; I know what they are made of. I can trust them to be accurate."

"Unlike the ones back there."

"Yep."

"So, you are fine surrounded by these..." I turn a circle, "time pieces on the wall, just not the ones you didn't acquire yourself."

"Sounds about right."

"You know how weird you sound?"

He shoots me a glance, "Says the woman who calls her phone Hedwig, and who uses the names of desserts as swearwords."

"So, what's wrong with that?" I frown.

He snickers, "My point exactly." He focusses on his work.

I shuffle my feet, wind a strand of hair through my fingers.

"I haven't forgiven you yet," I mutter.

"You can leave at any time."

But I don't want to, and therein lies the problem. What the hell is keeping me here? Him? This chemistry between us that I have to explore? What happens if I do explore it further? Will I survive the time we spend together?

And what if I did walk away?

Would I forever wonder how it could have been between us? What if he was...the one? Ha, me and my romantic notions. But this is Christmas; I'm allowed to indulge myself, right?

I lean around him and stare at the contents of the clock's insides on the table.

He continues tinkering away...or whatever it is he's doing there.

The pieces of the machinery seem to be disjointed, yet they come together to form a certain symmetry, to dance together and make music. Like us.

If he were to only give us a chance. Do I want to give him a chance? "Weston, you're not a douche, you know."

He grunts.

I resist the urge to roll my eyes. "Why do you have to be this macho?"

"Why are you still here?" he growls.

"Because I cooked bloody breakfast and came here to call you. Then, you had to go and pull that…"

He straightens, "What?"

"That…" I wave a hand in the air. "That…obnoxious McFuck act of yours."

He swivels around to face me, "What was that? What did you call me?"

"Obnoxious?"

"After that."

"Mc…McFuck?"

"What does it mean?"

I raise my shoulders, "Dunno, it just, uh, seemed appropriate."

He chuckles, "You're a funny one, Buttercup."

I groan, "I am not sure I like that name yet."

"I am not sure I like you either." He looks me up and down, his tone serious, "But hell, if I don't want you to stay."

"Is that an apology?"

"For what?" He glares.

"For being horrible to me."

"Was I?"

I huff, "Fine. Whatever. And," I tuck my elbows into my sides, "I'm sorry too."

"For what."

I jerk my chin toward the reddened skin of his cheek.

"I deserved it," he replies.

I open and shut my mouth, "You…you did?"

"You should know though, that it turns me on when you get physical with me."

I squeeze my eyes shut. *Do not lose it; do not.* I draw in a breath, "I'll ignore that."

Turning, I stalk to the door.

"Where are you going?"

"I made breakfast." I pause, then turn to scowl at him, "Aren't you coming?"

. . .

Fifteen minutes later he pushes back the plate with a sigh. I'd made chocolate pancakes for me, regular ones for him. Why had I bothered…? Good question. Perhaps because, as much as I hate him, I hate seeing him starve. Food is sacred. It's how we nourish not just our bodies, but our souls, and if there is a soul that needs some sustenance… It is this alphahole's. A slurping sound fills the space. I glance sideways as Max licks the bottom of his bowl. He raises his head, then patters over to push his nose into my lap. "Hey boy, you still hungry?"

"Don't feed him more," Weston warns.

I frown, "I wasn't going to."

"Yes, you were too." He grins, "When you twitch your nose, it means you're thinking something sappy in your head."

"Am not." I set my jaw.

"Yep, you were." He chuckles, "And PS, you're welcome."

I frown up at him, "For what?"

"For the compliment I'm about to give you."

I shake my head. Jeez, this man… I mean, he can't be real. He can't be this incorrigible, can he? He stares at me; I meet his gaze.

His lips curl, and of course, my heart does that little flip-flop it always does when he goes all bad boy on me. "Fine. I give in." I huff, "What compliment?"

"You're not a bad cook." He smirks.

I open and close my mouth. "That was a delicious breakfast," I half-snarl.

"My, but you like your own cooking, huh?"

My lips turn down, "You can tell, huh?"

His brow furrows. "What's that supposed to mean?"

"I know I'm not svelte and long-limbed, like some of the women you date."

He frowns, then looks me up and down, "Firstly, let's get something straight. You look incredible."

Wait, was that a compliment? It was a compliment. Wasn't it?

"And secondly," his eyes gleam, "have you been keeping tabs on me?"

"Of course not." I huff.

"You've been keeping tabs," he concludes, looking way too self-satisfied.

"Hardly."

"It's okay, you can admit it." He smirks, "It's only natural to want to follow what I have been up to. Some of us have the kind of irresistible charisma that attracts attention."

Oh, that compliment thing I said earlier, forget it.

"You're so full of yourself," I scoff. "Seriously, how can someone say what you do and keep a straight face?"

He stares at me.

I fidget in my seat opposite him. "And yeah, maybe I tracked your exploits in the media, a little." I admit.

He arches an eyebrow.

I throw up my hands. "Oh, all right, so I did read up about you."

His grin widens.

"I was curious how you looked in your scrubs, okay?" My cheeks flush.

He blinks, "In my scrubs?"

I nod, "I have a thing for men in uniform."

His grey eyes grow stormy, "I could wear them for you, if you ask nicely."

I gulp, chafe my thighs together to relieve that gnawing emptiness that's been building since I woke up this morning. Then he had to go and spoil it all with his rudeness.

His features tighten. "I'm sorry," he offers.

I stare. "For which part?" I ask. "For being horrible to me from the moment I walked in here or is it for a specific insult?"

He tips back his chair until it rests on the back legs, "On second thought..." He scratches his chin, "What can I say? That's me. It's not my fault."

"No?" I frown.

"It's the way I was born."

"That's your excuse, huh?"

"At least, I don't lie. My life is an open book." He winces as he says it.

"What?" I ask.

"Maybe too open, on occasion."

"What do you mean?"

He rolls his shoulders, a dead giveaway that he's uncomfortable. Less than 48 hours with him, and I'm interpreting his actions. What is that about anyway?

"Tell me."

He folds his arms over his chest, "For the record, I like your curves."

Heat sears my cheeks. "You're kidding me."

He shakes his head, "I like that you have a healthy appetite. There's something sexy about a woman who enjoys cooking and eating."

"Thank you, and it's baking."

"You cooked breakfast," he points out.

"Yeah." I shift in my seat. Hell, I'm terrible with taking compliments. "And you are deflecting."

He barks out a laugh, "You caught me there."

"What is it?" I ask, genuinely curious. What could make this confident, dominant man, this uncomfortable?

"I may have a…uh, sex video to my name."

"Sex video." I blink.

"My ex—" He raises his shoulders, "She got hissy when I dumped her. Took it out by leaking a video."

"Oh," I swallow. My guts twist and something bubbles up my throat—something hot and angry and twisted. Something like jealous. *Holy shit, why the hell do I care who he slept with? Except, I do, for some reason.* Not like I have a claim on him or anything, but hell, for some reason, I've been trying to not think of the women in his past. I mean, if I don't acknowledge them, then they don't exist, right?

"A sex video, huh?" I clear my throat, "Is it uh—explicit?"

He glares at me.

Right. "Of course, it is," I mutter. Something hot presses down at my temples. *Shit, okay. This isn't good. What does it matter to me what he did?* He's paying me. It's the only reason I'm here, right? Not. I stare back at him, and therein lies the issue. I've been falling for this obnoxious, alphahole from the time I'd first laid eyes on him. A ripple of something claws down my spine. *Don't fall in love with him; don't.* He'd warned me about that already. Apparently, he knows me better than I know myself. I push away from the table so fast that Max yelps. "Sorry, buddy," I mutter, then walk past the table.

"Where are you going?" he asks

"None of your concern."

"You haven't finished your breakfast."

"So?"

"So, you'll need your strength."

"Oh, to hell with you. Don't pretend to care about me when you clearly don't, and—" He swoops out his arm, snags my wrist.

"Let go," I say through clenched teeth.

He doesn't answer. Instead, he tugs on me, with just enough force that I am pulled toward him. He turns his chair, then lifts me up by my waist and props me on his lap.

"What are you doing?" I mumble. My cheeks heat. Not that his lap isn't comfortable, and hell, if the entire maneuver wasn't hot. I mean, he'd handled my body like I'm made of candy floss. Do I taste as sweet to him? "Let me go." I dig my elbow into his chest.

He huffs, "Stop wriggling." There's a hint of a smile in his voice.

"And if I don't?" I twist around to face him. The curve of my waist bumps against the hard length of him in his pants. "Oh."

He grins. "See what you do to me?"

"Did you say that to *Ms. Sex Video* woman?"

His features shudder. *Damn it, why did I have to go there?*

"Sorry, none of my business."

"I didn't." His tone is clipped, "I never told her that. Nor did I ever seat her in my lap like this or…" he leans around me, grabs my plate and pulls it over, "…feed her breakfast." He scoops up some of my chocolate pancake, then holds the fork up to my lips.

"Open," his voice is husky.

A shiver runs down my spine. He's only giving me food, so why does it have to feel this…erotic?

"I'll eat it if you do," I whisper.

"Hmm." He glances from me to the piece of food on the fork, then back at me. "I have a better idea."

He brings the fork to his mouth, closes his lips around the chocolate crepe. He chews, swallows, then leans in and places his lips on mine. I gasp, and he darts his tongue inside my mouth. The taste of chocolate, of dark edginess and hot sex...the unique flavor that is Weston-fucking-Kincaid fills my mouth, coats my tongue, overwhelms my senses. My head spins. My toes curl. He pulls away and I lean forward. I hear a sound of protest. Hell, is that me?

I crack open my eyelids—when had I shut them?—to find he's scooping up another forkful of the breakfast that I will always associate with him. *Gah!* I did not think that, did not allow myself to indulge in such utter sentimental crap.

"Did you like that?" I whisper.

"Let's say that I may have underestimated the merits of dessert for breakfast."

"Are we talking about the same thing?" I frown.

"I was talking about your chocolate pancake," he snickers, "which you should eat." He raises the fork, "You need your nourishment."

I part my lips and he slides the food into my mouth.

I chew then lick my lips.

His gaze drops to my mouth, "My, my, what beautiful lips you have, little Red." His eyes gleam.

"All the better to kiss you with," I murmur.

His gaze intensifies. The heat from his body seems to deepen. A bead of sweat slides down my spine.

He picks up another forkful of the crepe, holds it up. "Finish it," his voice lowers to a hush, and I'm instantly wet. My nerve endings pop; my brain cells seem to melt all at once.

I close my mouth around the fork, wipe the tines clean, chew, then swallow.

"What a gorgeous throat you have, little Red," his voice is hard. As is the evidence of his arousal that stabs into the valley between my butt cheeks.

"All the better to take you in my mouth," the words tumble from my lips. *What am I doing?* Indulging this man's love for nursery rhymes and children's fairy tales is one thing, but taking it to the extent where the story of Little Red Riding Hood comes to mean something else completely? Not to mention, what was that thing with the rabbit? Had he actually compared himself to my favorite vibrator?

He scoops up the last morsel of food from the plate, holds it up to my lips. "You have a choice," he says.

"I do?" *Do I even want to know?*

He nods, "You can have your last bite before, or after."

"After?" I gulp, "After what?"

"After Christmas shopping."

13

Weston

I watch as she peruses the range of baking produce on the shelf in the only grocery store in the nearest village.

A woman walks behind me, "Excuse me," she says stiffly. I move aside. Hell, the aisles of this place are so narrow I have to flatten my back against the shelf to ensure I am not blocking the route. And the ride in the car over here? Why the hell had I agreed to that torture? Probably because, by the time I'd realized that the only means of transportation available to get to the village was in her dinky car—a bloody Volkswagen—it was too late. When was the last time I'd been a passenger in anything other than my chauffeur driven car…? I don't even remember.

So why had I done it now?

Why had I told her that I'd take her out shopping?

When what I'd wanted to do was eat her out right there on the dining table…for breakfast; and if I had my way, for lunch and dinner too. One taste of her sweet cunt had not been enough. The blood rushes to my groin.

Is that why I'd brought her here…? Because I'd wanted to get away from the cabin and the intimate atmosphere that seemed to be building between us. I lean a hip against the shelf. My shoulder brushes the stocked cans; one falls off of the top shelf, bumps me on the head. I throw my arm out, catch the can before it hits the ground, even as stars flash behind my eyes.

The fuck? From the time I'd met her I seem to be getting rather well acquainted with heavenly bodies, especially hers… Jesus, what's wrong with me? Next, I'll be spouting poetry, comparing her to a summer's day… No, not Shakespeare now. I'd loved poetry in school, had not hidden my love for the Bard, even acted in school plays. Then the incident had taken place. I'd been enroute home from a rehearsal for a play. And that had changed my proclivity to take part in extracurricular activities. Other than hanging out with the Seven… Not that we'd spoken much. We'd preferred to take our frustrations out on each other… You could say we'd spent a lot of that post-incident time beating each other up. It had been our own personal coping mechanism.

I wonder, have I channeled my love for the spoken word into the nursery rhymes I recite with my nieces? Is that why the fairy tales I read to them have etched themselves into my subconscious mind?

It had been hot though… That entire series of events at the breakfast table… I'd wanted to take her right then. Tempt her into spreading her legs open for me, so I could bury myself inside her sweet cunt. Would she have resisted me? Was the money so important to her that she'd continue to deny herself the release that came from only the most intimate act, of my cock enveloped within her wet channel? Is that why I can't stop myself from tempting her to cross the line? Is that why I'd set such an impossible-to-uphold term to the agreement?

Does she really think she is going to get through the next six days without giving in to me? And if I want her to fail, why hadn't I moved in when I had her ready and willing this morning? Fuck. I drag my fingers through my hair. She is not the only one getting in too deep. The difference is, I know how to turn the tide so it won't drown me. Hopefully.

I stare at the can — it's chocolate. Figures. The one thing in the world I hate more than the thought of losing her. *Hold on… Hold on… I meant losing to her. Yep, that's what it is. Bloody fuck.* I rub at the rapidly forming bump on my head. Did the run-in with the can knock my brains out of whack too?

I prowl up the aisle to where she stands in front of a display of frozen treats.

"How much longer will you take?" I growl

She squeaks, then shoots me a sideways glance. "You startled me," she mutters, then turns her attention back to the display. I follow her gaze to the Sticky Toffee Pudding she's salivating over. I reach for it, but she grabs my arm. "What are you doing?" she scolds.

"You want this?"

"Of course, not."

"Why do you deny yourself?"

"I'm going to be baking enough, as it is. If I also buy these goodies, I'll turn into a Christmas butter ball," she mutters.

"Don't you mean buttercup ball?" I chuckle.

She shoots me a sideways glance. "Knew I could count on you," she snarls, then turns and pushes her loaded shopping cart forward.

"Hold on."

She doesn't stop. No matter. I catch up with her, drop the tin of chocolate onto the heap of shopping. "You sure you have enough there?"

She frowns. "You mind your own business."

"But you are my business."

"Whatever." She speeds up, turns the corner and crashes her cart into a man. Some of the items fall out.

"Oh, I'm sorry." She bends at the same time that the man she'd run into says, "Excuse me." The stranger grabs a can of chocolate — motherfucker, it's the same can I'd placed there earlier. I scowl. He snatches up a few of the other items, then straightens at the same time as her. Their heads bump. Something explodes inside of my chest. My vision narrows. I stalk forward.

He places the items in her shopping cart. "I'm Hunter," he holds out his hand.

"I'm Amelie." She raises her arm, and I plant myself between them.

"And she was just leaving." I thrust my hand in his, squeeze the motherfucker's palm.

The expression on his face doesn't change; he doesn't flinch. I scowl at him.

He glances from me to Amelie. "Uh, a pleasure to meet you," he says.

"Can't say the same," I grunt.

Amelie huffs, "Don't mind him." She grumbles, "He was born with a lemon in his mouth."

I frown, "What does that mean?"

"It means that you have a terrible attitude and you are the most impolite person I know."

"Good," I mutter. "You done here?"

Hunter chuckles, "How long you guys been together?"

"We're not—" Amelie starts.

"Long enough." I thrust out my chin at Hunter. "What kind of a bloody name is that anyway?"

His expression hardens, then he barks out a laugh. "You're refreshingly candid."

"That's not all I'll be if you don't get out of my face," I shoot back.

He holds up his hands, "Not intruding on your patch, buddy." He glances around me, "Bye Amelie."

"Bye," she choruses back.

The man squeezes past me; my shoulder bumps his. He shoots me a narrowed gaze over his shoulder.

I glare back at him.

He frowns.

I glower.

His shoulders tense, then he jerks his chin.

Good, he got the message.

He pivots, walks away.

"What the hell was that?" Amelie huffs.

"None of your bloody business."

"Why are you so angry?"

"Why were you talking to him?" I snap.

She gapes, "What do you mean? He helped me pick up the groceries. What did you expect me to do? Ignore him?"

"Yes."

She shakes her head, "You've lost it." She pushes the cart forward, muttering, "Of all the crazy, asinine things you could do, this one takes the cake."

I stare after her. *The hell is wrong with me?* So maybe I did overreact, but hell, when he'd bumped into her, all I could think was, mine. *She's mine…* For the next few days, at least.

She struggles with the shopping cart, and I stalk forward, grab at it. "Gimme that."

"Fine." She raises her hands. "For being such a crazy-ass jealous man—"

"I'm not jealous."

She rolls her eyes, then snorts, "No, I forget that's your CRGPF."

I frown. "Excuse me?"

"Your chronic resting grumpy pants face," she clarifies.

Only when I'm around you. She does something to me. Yeah, she confuses me… I blow out a breath. Jesus, now I am going all googly-eyed over some chick who'd dropped in on my life and turned it upside down. *You can't let her get to you; no way.*

I jerk my chin.

She frowns.

I glare at her.

She pales, then juts out her chin and walks forward and out of the shop. I join the queue. When it's my turn, the woman at the checkout counter opens her mouth.

"Don't—" I growl.

"But, Sir—"

Bloody fuck, is the entire population of this village out to get me? I pull out my wallet, then separate a large stack of bills…and prop them on the counter. "Keep the change."

Her gaze widens, then she proceeds to check out the items.

Thank fuck. So, this is how it is to shop for yourself? What a nightmare. I pull out my phone, depress the buttons on the keypad. When my driver comes on the line I tell him, "I need a few things delivered to the cabin." I give him the list.

Arms full of shopping bags — I had to leave the shopping cart behind at the store — I step out and stalk toward the Volkswagen. Of course, she's nowhere to be seen. *Where the fuck is she?*

I place the bags next to the car, look around. A familiar figure in tight jeans, coat buttoned to show off those curves, catches my eye. She's talking to the man from the store — Hunter. *What the fuck!* My feet eat up the distance between us.

She reaches up, pats him on the shoulder, and a hot sensation stabs in my chest. I lengthen my strides, reach them. "Get away from her."

Hunter looks between us and frowns. "I didn't mean any harm."

"Of course, you didn't," she interjects.

I glare at her.

She pales.

"Go to the car."

She frowns.

"Now."

"But," she pouts, "I was only…"

I bend my knees, thrust my face into hers. "Do it," I command.

She opens her mouth, then seems to change her mind. Turning, she stalks off.

Thank fuck.

Can't let her out of my sight; got to keep her safe from anything untoward, and that includes strange men sniffing about her.

Hunter glances after her, "Everything okay?" He frowns.

"Shut the fuck up." I growl at him.

He turns to me, "You're Weston?"

I stiffen.

"Dr Weston Kincaid, I presume?"

"How the fuck do you know my name?"

"I'm a friend of Damian's."

"Hmph," I glare at him. "And you know him, how?"

"Our fathers are good friends."

"What are you doing here?"

"The same thing as you, I assume."

I frown.

He chuckles, "I am home for the holidays. I am also the MP for the area."

"Right." I roll my shoulders, "That why you were here? Campaigning?"

"Among other things." He smiles, "Anything you need." He holds out his hand, I ignore it.

"Stay away from her."

"You got it." He keeps his hand extended, "Take it, you never know when you might need help."

I ignore his hand while I stare at his face and something clicks, "You're Hunter Whittington?"

He tilts his head.

"You're standing for the upcoming elections."

A genuine smile splits his face, "Whew." He mock mops his brow. "My PR isn't that bad then."

I jerk my chin. So, he's a well-known politician, albeit one who's being tipped to be the next Prime Minister. *We'll see.*

I turn to leave.

"Make sure you stock up for the next few days."

"Why's that?" I ask.

"The weather," he says. "There's a cold spell coming on."

14

Amelie

"Cold spell, is that what they're calling it? More like, the Beast from the East," I grumble.

The wind whistles through the gaps in the shutters. I shiver, pull the shawl around my shoulders tighter. I'm sprawled out on a cushion, near the fireplace. Sir Grumpy Dickface here, had hauled in wood from the woodshed… Yep, this place has a freakin' designated space where the wood blocks are stocked. All chopped by minions before the onset of winter. To my surprise, Alphahole here, had hauled enough wood in on his own—broken finger notwithstanding—and without protest. Okay, so maybe that's unfair.

He'd helped me with my luggage, hadn't balked about carrying the bags of groceries to the car and then to the house… He'd even ridden, without complaint, in the cramped passenger seat. Unlike the journey through the grocery shop, which had been interesting. In fact, I'd been half-expecting that he'd have called his own driver to ferry us to the village, but he hadn't. Huh?

I shoot a sideways glance at the stony-faced man reading Harry Potter, Max at his feet. His hair is tousled—a perpetual just-rolled-out-of-bed look, which suits him too bloody well. He'd changed into a Henley and jeans, with soft moccasins on his feet, when we'd gotten home. Dinner had been…without incident… Actually, he hadn't said a word. And that had been…a relief…or not. Maybe I prefer his alphaholish behavior…to this lack of communication which…seems uncharacteristic.

I clear my throat, then glance toward him. His head is bent over the book. He raises his cigar to take a puff. The scent of cloves and pinewood deepens.

I'd wanted to buy a Christmas Tree but I hadn't raised it with him… Well, given how he'd blown his fuse at my talking with Hunter… It had been cute, actually, that fit of jealousy he'd exhibited. Not that he'd admit to it. He had nothing to be jealous of, of course, but it had been refreshing to see him show some semblance of human emotion, after that rather brutish start to our relationship. Relationship? Are we in a relationship? Nah.

He blows out another puff of cigar smoke, that almost-Christmassy scent deepening. My mouth waters and I rise to my feet. "Do you have another?"

"What?" He replies without looking up. Huh?

I pause in front of him. His eyes stay glued to the page.

So, Mr. Potter is worthy of a lot of attention, but darn it, this once, I wish he'd prioritize me over the adventures of the boy wizard.

He raises the damned cigar to his lips and this time I snatch it from him.

He frowns.

I raise my shoulders, "I asked."

He watches as I lift the smoke stick, purse my mouth around the end wet from his. A shiver runs down my spine. It seems intimate to do this. I draw on the cigar, choke a little. A slight burn races down my throat. I blow out the smoke. My head spins. "Whoa," I giggle, "This is good."

"Don't inhale," he cautions me.

"I know how to smoke a cigar."

"How to puff a cigar," he corrects me.

"That's what I said." I scowl down at the smoke stick, then raise it to my lips, I take a long drag. The smoke swirls down my throat, fills my lungs. I blow it out without coughing. A buzz works its way down my limbs. My fingers tingle; my toes curl. "Hmm." I stare at the cigar, "Why is it that smoking a cigar kissed by you is almost as good as kissing you?"

"You sure about that?" His voice is tinged with humor.

I glance up, "Oh, what?"

"You want to test out that theory?"

I blink, then heat sears my cheeks. "Damn." I drag my fingers through my hair. "I didn't just say that aloud, did I?"

"You sure did." He sets the book aside on the side table, then leans back in his chair. The firelight glows off of his beautiful face, highlighting the shadows under his cheekbones. The dark blonde strands of his days-old beard glint. He resembles a pirate, an old-world marauder, someone who'd swoop in and take and ravish. A melting sensation flares to life between my legs. Oh, hell… This man, he's bloody potent.

His eyelids grow hooded; he watches me as I take a final puff from the cigar. The smoke lingers between us, framing those gleaming colorless eyes that survey me with more than a modicum of interest, and questions. Damn, he has so many questions in his eyes. As do I.

"Why did you tell me about the sex tape?" I blurt out.

The expression on his face doesn't change. He doesn't speak immediately. The silence grows, a beat, another. At his feet Max sighs. He springs up to his feet, looks at me, then at Weston, before pattering away toward the kitchen.

I glance back at Weston to find he's staring at my face.

"What?" I tilt my head. "Shouldn't I have asked that?"

He shakes his head, "Truth is, I am not sure why I mentioned it."

He rolls his shoulders, then settles deeper into the chair, "It felt like it was best to be upfront with you, considering —"

"Considering?" I prompt.

"You're coming home to meet my family, and if it did come up in conversation, I didn't want you to be surprised."

"Your family knows about it?"

He stares back.

"My mother is aware, yes..."

"Oh." I swallow, "And your father?"

"He died when I was sixteen."

Right.

"Heart attack."

My throat closes. Why is he sharing his past with me? What does it mean? *Nothing.* It means nothing at all. We're having a conversation, that's all it is. "Is that why you became a heart-surgeon?"

"Among other things." His features close.

Right. That sharing part? Guess I spoke too soon.

"My parents are retired and in Spain." I shuffle my feet. "I'd visit them more often, but they are happy in each other's company. They had me late, you see. I don't think they were prepared for how a child would turn their lives upside down. I mean, they never shirked their duties. Just... I think they were happy when I left home."

He scowls, "You miss them?"

"Sometimes." I raise my shoulders.

"You don't want to spend Christmas with them?"

"They uh, don't care either way, and this year... Well, I wanted some downtime, know what I mean?" I peer up into his face.

"You're spending Christmas with my family, so you won't be alone," he declares.

I frown. Am I that transparent that he'd guessed that I didn't particularly want to be alone through Christmas?

"Careful," I warn him, "or I'll begin to think that you are being nice to me."

"And what? Is it Christmas?" He smirks.

I stare, "You made a joke? Wow!" I clutch my chest, "It's a Christmas miracle."

"Don't get your hopes up." He firms his lips, "My family isn't the easiest to get along with."

"What family is?" I pull my hair over my shoulder.

"Now who's being nice?" He chuckles.

"Not me." I tip up my chin.

"Liar." His gaze grows intense.

I swallow, glance away. Shit, this is...getting... Uh, more emotional than I'd expected. "Your family," I prompt. "What did they say when they found out about your, uh, escapades?" *No, I don't want to talk about his sex tape, but damn if I don't want to know more about him.*

He frowns, then rolls his shoulders, "They were...disappointed."

"No!" I blink. "You Mr. Billionaire, money bags, surgeon of all he surveys."

"Yeah," he blows out a breath. "Impressing the world is so much easier than impressing your own blood."

"Tell me about it." I glance around for an ashtray to drop the cigar in, then spot it on the side table.

I lean toward it, when he reaches for the stub, "Don't."

"Don't what?"

"Don't snub it out." He takes the stub from my fingers, lays it to rest on the ashtray. "If you do, the cigar oils flow out and burn, and it causes an unpleasant smell."

"So cigars are another of your passions huh?"

"It's a thing that unites us Seven."

"All of you smoke? I mean," I make air quotes, "puff?"

"I like to occasionally indulge."

"Is it bad for you?"

"You mean because I am a surgeon?"

I nod.

"Most things that you have a weakness for are bad for you." He looks me up and down.

"And you?" I meet his gaze, "What about you?"

"I am the worst, of course."

I take a step forward. He widens his stance, and I step in the 'V' between his legs. *What am I doing? Why can't I stay away from him? As long as I don't sleep with him, it's fine, right?* The arrangement still stands.

"The papers?" I lower my chin. "From your lawyers, I mean. When will they arrive?"

"I'll have them for you by tomorrow."

His phone vibrates from the side table, "In fact, that must be it."

He makes no move no reach for it.

"So…" I swallow.

"So?" He runs a finger up the side of my arm. Goosebumps flare in the wake of his touch. A slow burn begins to hum, creeping, swirling up toward my heart. It would be so easy to lose myself in his presence, to forget the outside world exists. Just him and me, locked away in this cabin and—the lights blink off just then. "Oh." I glance up toward the bulbs set in the rustic settings in the ceiling.

"The wind must have gotten to the power supply."

Right. I glance down to find him watching me from under hooded eyes. If he'd been handsome before, lit by the firelight and nothing else, he's devastating now. My throat dries, my belly twists, and moisture laces the secret area between my legs.

"Weston." I whisper, "I—"

Barking sounds from outside.

15

Weston

"Did you hear that?" I stiffen.

She freezes and her gaze widens. "Was that—?"

"Max." I'm already moving. I grab her by the waist, lift her and set her aside.

She squeaks. I jump to my feet, race toward the back door. I grab the handle and the door swings open. "I swear I shut it."

Footsteps sound behind me. I turn. "Stay inside," I stab my finger at her.

"Like hell, I am." She pauses, chest heaving. Her beautiful tits rise and fall. I glance at them and my belly hardens. *Shit, not the time to get distracted.*

"Get back in," I growl.

"No way." She folds her arms over her chest.

More barking, this time farther away. "Fuck." I pivot, race down the steps. She follows. "Stay behind me," I growl at her over my shoulder.

Amelie juts out her chin, then nods. *Thank Fuck.* If she'd tried to disobey me, I'd have bodily hauled her inside and tied her up. I shake my head, dislodging the image. Hell, if she doesn't bring out the caveman in me. I turn, then bolt across the back garden. The light from the patio streams out. I race toward the shed, the direction from which I'd heard the barking. It's silent now. *Fuck, fuck, fuck.* My heart begins to race and my pulse rate ratchets up. I slow down as I near the shed. I hear movement behind me, then she pulls abreast. "Is there someone in the shed?" she whispers.

I train my gaze on the darkened shed. The hair on the back of my neck prickles. The knot in my stomach grows. I reach the side of the shed, press myself against the wall. Amelie follows my lead. I turn, place a finger to my lips. She swallows. I hold up my hand. *Don't move,* I mouth the words.

She bites the inside of her cheek, then nods. I point to myself then at the door of the shed; she jerks her chin. I turn back toward the door. *Shit, wish I had some kind of weapon.* I bite back a laugh as I think of her spatula. I bunch my left fist at my side. Of course, the finger on my right hand is hurt, so I won't be much use if there is, indeed, someone inside. A whine sounds from inside the shed so I move toward it. *Wait, wait.* There's no other sound inside. If there's someone in there... Well, I'll have to deal with it. I slip in through the crack between the door and the frame. There's a shuffling sound, then a low bark. "Max." I feel my way across the wall, hit the switch. The lights blaze in the space. I glance around, draw in a breath.

"Oh, my God," Amelie breathes next to me.

"I told you to stay outside," I remind her.

She ignores me, takes a step forward. "Wes... Your... your clocks."

My stomach knots and a hardness winds itself around my chest. "Fuck, bloody, fuck." Almost every clock in the place has been smashed. I move forward and my loafers crunch on the glass. Shit, should have changed into my boots before I rushed out, but fuck that. I stalk forward to my table. A shuffling sounds from underneath it. I pull back the chhair and a growl rips out of me.

"What happened? Where's Max?" Amelia rushes forward. I plant my body in between her and the dog, but she's already there. "Oh, no," she cries out, "Max."

I sink down to my haunches, reach for Max. He whines, shrinks away. *Fuck.* "Something—more likely, someone—scared him."

The poor pup is shaking. My gut tightens and my pulse pounds behind my eyes. "I am not going to let him get away with this," I swear.

"Who? Who could do this?" Amelie's voice is low.

"I don't know, but you can bet your ass, I am going to find out." I lean forward, lay my hand on the side of Max's head, "Shh, it's okay, little guy. I'm here now. We'll take care of you, hmm?"

Max whines, folds further into himself.

"Fuck," I swear aloud and he flinches.

"You're frightening him."

"Don't be silly," I growl.

Amelie squats down next to me, loses her balance and grabs at my thigh to right herself. Pinpricks of heat vibrate out from her touch. I glance at her hand, which seems too delicate, too fragile against the broadness of my leg. She leans forward, on her knees, holds out her hand. "You okay, baby?" she croons.

Max blinks up at her, then whines. *Is he playing it up for her? No, he's hurt, but why the hell did he back away from me? And why is he shuffling forward toward her?* She caresses the side of his face, rubs her palm over his flank. He whimpers, then crawls toward her. She lifts him up, carefully, and cradles him. "You poor thing, are you hurt? Don't worry, we'll take care of you now." She turns to me, "We need to take him to the vet."

I place my hand in front of the mutt's mouth. He blinks, then licks my fingers. "Let's go." I rise to my feet. She follows, cuddling the dog close to her chest. His little body trembles. *Why the hell didn't he want to come to me?* I frown, looking from the dog to the tiny woman who rocks him, making soothing noises in her throat. A strange feeling coils in my chest. Jealousy? A little… That the dog preferred her over me… Not that I blame him. Given a choice I'd have laid my head on her breast…and done more than just cuddle, of course. *Enough, motherfucker.* Best get them both out of the shed, at least. I step over the glass. "Watch out," I caution her. She glances down at the glass, places a foot between the shards. "You're in your socks?" I swear.

"Yeah… I didn't have time to get my shoes."

More glass shards crunch under her feet. I growl, "Fuck that." I turn and sweep up both woman and dog into my arms. She squeaks, "Put…me down." Max continues to shake.

"Not a chance"

"But you're hurt."

"And you'll be hurting on parts other than the soles of your feet if you don't shut up."

"Oh," she draws in a breath. "I can walk," she mumbles.

"You're not wearing shoes." I stalk forward. "How could you be stupid enough to come out without your shoes?"

"Excuse me for caring enough about little Max," she huffs.

"You should have stayed inside, like I told you to."

"Why the hell are you angry now?" She frowns.

"You don't want to know." I stalk toward the cabin. "It's enough that I have to take care of the mutt, add you to the mix and—"

"You don't have to take care of me."

"Right," I mutter. "Tell that to the thief who decided to break in."

"Not my fault that the lock to the cabin was weak."

"There's a security system for both the cabin and the shed… And one that runs around the perimeter of the property that—"

"The cabin," we both say in unison.

I jerk my gaze down to hers.

Her face whitens. "You don't think he went to the—"

"Only one way to find out."

I tighten my arms around her, "You should stay here while I go check out the cabin."

The lights flicker then go out.

"Oh, no," Amelie squeaks. "Do you think the intruder had anything to do with this?"

I frown, not wanting to answer her.

She draws in a sharp breath, coils in closer to my chest. Hmm... this is not too bad, huh?

"Are we safe here?" She gulps, "Maybe you should call your driver and we should leave here?"

What, and miss this opportunity to find out how much more she can take before I break her? No fucking way.

"Relax." I infuse a tone of reassurance into my voice. "It's probably the incoming storm."

"You... you sure?" She peers up at me.

"Positive." I glance down at her upturned face. The starlight brings out the silver in her blue eyes, turns the blonde hair about her shoulders to spun gold. *Spun gold?* What the fuck? Clearly, I've been reading too many fairytales to my younger niece. Jesus, do I still have my balls or what?

"Oh, look." She raises her chin.

I glance up as the first flakes of snow hit my nose. "That's all we need," I grumble. "Fucking snow."

"It's beautiful, isn't it?" Her voice is dreamy.

I glance down to find her sticking out her tongue to catch a flake.

"It's polluted water," I warn her.

She scowls, "No one can accuse you of being a romantic."

"No one can accuse you of being practical."

"If I were, I never would have left home at eighteen to go to culinary school, against my parents' wishes."

"Where did you study?"

"At Le Cordon Bleu, Paris."

"Funny, I can't see you at a snooty French course like that."

She frowns up at me. "You're right," she replies, "I hated it. The course taught me a lot, gave me the basics, but... I couldn't wait to get out of there and into the real world."

"You don't like rules, huh?"

"I like to be free."

"Do you?" I allow my lips to twist.

"Of course." She scowls, "Why do you ask?"

"I think you'd like to be tied down. In fact, I am positive you'd love to test your limits; to find out how much you could take before you break down and beg for your release."

She gulps; her pupils dilate.
"You… You're wrong." She whispers.
"Are you sure?"

16

Amelie

"Of course, I am." I squeeze my thighs together. Damn it, stop imagining the scene he's laid out.

He doesn't know me or my needs or my likes. He has no idea how close he came to hitting on a certain forbidden dream I've harbored… One that I won't give in to, no matter that it is being laid out by the meanest, sexiest toad-in-the-hole ever. And that would be an insult to toad-in-the-hole's everywhere. I blow out a breath. I totally have to stop with these weird food-related metaphors that I seem to come up with when I am around him.

"How do you know if you haven't tried it?" He lowers his voice and studies me, "Have you tried it?"

I bite down on my lower lip. *Damn it, why can't I lie to him? Say it; do it* . "Uh... Not really," I venture.

His eyes gleam, "I think you might be surprised."

"The only surprise would be if there isn't an intruder in the cabin," I mutter.

He walks up the patio, past the now-silent hot tub. He stops at the entrance. "I need to go in and check the place first," he grumbles.

"I'm coming with you."

"It's safer here."

"It's colder." The snowflakes intensify, more of the white, powdery stuff sticking to my lips. I lick them off. His nostrils flare. Did that turn him on? Why is he so attuned to me? Is that why he'd laid out that stupid condition that I can't sleep with him if I want the money? Maybe it was to give me a way out of having sex with him... Except damn it, now I want to shag him. OMG!

Do I want the money so badly that I'll do everything but allow him to fuck me? Okay, don't answer that. It isn't fair, putting this big ol' hunk of chocolate slab on one side and my future on the other. *Would you give up his spotted dick for the chance at realizing your dreams?* Not that his dick is spotted...but it has a certain rhyme to it, know what I mean?

He bends as if to lower me to the floor.

"No, no, please no." I pout, "Don't do this. Don't leave me out here alone." Max whines to punctuate my words. *Good boy.*

He glares at me. His shoulders seem to swell. The full force of his dominance seems to weigh down on my shoulders.

I gulp, "We...Weston?" *Crap, why is my voice trembling?*

"You owe me, Buttercup." His voice is low, hushed.

"Can... can we go in?" I shiver.

He frowns, then jerks his gaze away and in front. Whew. The breath shudders out of me. I glance forward as he steps inside the house. He walks into the living room. It's silent, the space lit by the flames from the fire.

He glances around the space, his muscles tensed. I look up at the jut of his jaw. The hair covering his face seems thicker. Jeez. Do his whiskers multiply by the hour or something? Isn't that a sign of virility? At this rate, he's gonna have a Santa Claus beard by the time it's Christmas Day. And he can take me across his knee anytime. I snicker, and he looks down at me, catching me off guard. Heat sears my cheeks.

"What were you thinking?" he growls.

"N...nothing."

"Don't try that. I know exactly when your thoughts turn X-rated."

"Huh?"

Max grumbles in his throat.

"I think you can put us down now," I manage to say.

He stares at me a second longer, then stalks over to the cushion in front of the fire. He lowers me down to it. Max wriggles in my hold. I place him on the floor and he stretches, yawns, then patters off toward the kitchen.

"Well, he seems okay." I clear my throat, the adrenaline fades away and my limbs tremble.

"Hmm."

"Should we take him to the vet?"

Weston straightens. "Let's watch him tonight, and if he shows any signs of trauma tomorrow, we can take him then. I think he just had a fright."

"That's a plan." I yawn so hard, my jaw cracks. My eyelids seem heavy all of a sudden. "Sorry," I mumble. "It hit me all at once, I think."

He peels off the socks from my feet. His fingers brush my ankle. I shiver. He runs his fingers up the heels of one foot, then the other. Goosebumps pop on my skin. "What are you doing?" I say, breathless.

"Making sure you didn't cut yourself."

"I'm not hurt," I insist. I tug on my foot and he releases me.

"You should take off your loafers." I say.

"Excuse me?"

I glance down at his feet, "Uh, you're dragging in the snow from outside, not to mention the glass pieces from the shed."

He frowns, then retraces his steps to the door, toes off his shoes. I stare at his beautiful feet... beautiful naked large feet. My throat closes. My belly flutters.

I had no idea I had a foot fetish, until I met Dr Grumpy Pants Kincaid. Hell I had no idea I had a fetish for other male parts either... Not *all* male parts... Only *his* male parts. My belly flutters. My throat closes. Bloody hell. Clearly, I am obsessed.

"Why don't you wait here?" His voice cuts through my thoughts. I tip my head up to meet his gaze, and warmth laces my cheeks.

"You okay?" He frowns.

No, of course not.

"Of course I am." I fold my hands in my lap.

He looks at me intently until I nod, then straightens. "I'll check the cabin and lockup, to ensure we're safe. Then we can go to bed." He grabs a log and heads toward the bedroom.

My eyes widen, but before I can worry too much, that dumb voice inside of my head chimes in. *We. Gah!* He used the *'We'* word. I stare up in his direction. *Doesn't signify anything, bitch.* Wait, does he mean go to bed to sleep or go to bed for something else? And omigosh, isn't that all cozy? So domestic. Would it be like this if we were together…? Maybe married, with kids… *What the f—?*

"Bedroom's clear," he says as he stalks toward the other end of the house.

I shake my head, push myself up to my feet. Clearly, I am delusional, or the Christmas season is affecting me, or the way he'd swept me up in his arms like I didn't weigh anything at all, and proceeded to carry me in here had made a huge impact on me. No one had ever done that before. No one. *Shit.* I am this…close to doing something stupid. *Gah!* Like giving up the money and giving in to him. *No, no, no.* I need advice. Need to talk with someone.

I march to the bedroom, which is illuminated by the moonlight coming in from the window, then reach for my handbag; my fingers brush my phone. Huh?

So he decided to return it to me? When had he put it back? Why would he do that? Is this his way of making up for the douche he's been thus far? My head spins. Talk about being complex. The alphahole is certainly the most complicated man I've ever met; and the most intriguing… Don't forget gorgeous. Why does he have to be this difficult though? It sure makes this entire relationship hard work… And unique… No wonder I can't stop thinking of him. And no… Our relationship is strictly professional. *Yea, keep telling yourself that, bitch.* Regardless, I am going to take every break I get… Like this phone. He returned it; now I can use it.

I grab the phone, glance around.

Where can I speak without him hearing me? I walk into the ensuite bathroom, lock the door behind me. *Shit, it's dark.* I switch on the light on my phone, walk over to the bath candle at the head of the tub. I grab it, rummage around in the drawers under the sink, until I find a lighter. I light the candle, place it on the counter next to the sink.

Then, for good measure, I crawl into the bathtub.

I swipe the phone screen, notice a text message. It's from Julia, one of my oldest friends. She'd left high school, gone to Australia for her gap year and stayed on as a nanny for a family there. Last I heard, she'd planned to stay on for another year. I peruse her text:

Hey Amelie, change of plans. I'm returning to London. Should be there just after Christmas. Can I stay with you until I find a place of my own?

Oh, yay!

It's going to be awesome to have her back, especially considering Summer is on her honeymoon. Victoria is still in that early stars and sunshine phase in her relationship with Saint. Karma… Well, she seems to have forgotten about us, since discovering her hottie on her extended Sicilian sojourn—a hottie she is still hiding from us. So that leaves me and Isla—the only other single woman in our clique, and Julia, when she returns.

I text her back:

Awesome news.

Can't wait to see you! Of course you can stay with me. Come over when you land.

• • •

I press send, then call Isla. She picks up on the third ring.

"Hey," her voice is breathless.

"Did I disturb you?" I keep my voice low.

"Nope. Just me and my Hitachi getting all cuddly." She snickers. "If I were to fall pregnant now, I'd give birth to batteries."

"What the—?" I snort, then swallow down the wrong way and start coughing. "That was such a bad joke, it was good." I clear my throat. "At least someone's having fun." I bite down on my lower lip.

The silence stretches, then, "Amelie?"

"Yeah."

"You okay?"

"Of course."

"Why are you whispering?"

"Because I don't want to be heard?"

"Aren't you at the cabin?"

"Yep."

"So why the secrecy thing?"

"What secrecy thing?"

"You're still whispering, babe."

"Right."

"Amelie?" she asks, worry in her voice. "Everything okay there?"

"There was a break-in at the cabin."

"What?" I hear the sheets rustle, then the click of a lamp, "Are you okay? What happened."

The line buzzes and I glance at the screen. She's asking for access to video mode. I decline.

"What the hell?" She demands. "Why aren't you on video?"

"Uh, because, I'm hiding in the bath tub."

"What the—?" Her voice sharpens, "Why are you hiding? Did the intruder hurt you—"

"I'm fine," I mumble.

Why'd I have to go and blurt that out to her? Maybe I needed someone to empathize with me, huh? Not that Weston hadn't. He had taken care of me, even if it was grudgingly… Still, I needed to hear a familiar voice, someone unthreatening with whom I don't need to pretend.

"Then why are you still whispering?" Her voice sharpens, "Is the intruder still there?"

"No, no. I think Wes scared him off."

"Weston?"

"Yeah."

"He's there with you?"

I draw in a breath. "I walked in on him, completely naked, as he was wrapping up his hot tub session."

Silence, then she chuckles, "You found him naked?"

"Yeah."

"In the hot tub?"

"He'd just been in...yeah, and he didn't have a stitch of clothing on and he had a cigar."

"Hot damn." She laughs, "Talk about phallic symbols, hmm?"

That's true. He'd been all but sending me subconscious signals... Okay, seeing his massive dick upfront? Not that subtle...but you have to give the man full marks for making an impression.

"That's not all," I add.

"You mean there's something to top off that picture?" She chuckles.

I frown, "Wipe that image from your mind, please."

Silence again. "Did you just ask me to refrain from imagining the hot doctor naked?"

"Yeah." *Shit, I know how that sounds...* But I really don't want her going there... Nowhere near that very male, very gorgeous naked ass...or dick, of said doctor...because...well I am...

"Are you jealous?"

Of course, I am. "No, no, nothing like that..." I bite my lips.

"It's fine; I understand." I can hear the grin in her voice.

"Nothing to understand."

"You're holed up with him over the festive season, huh? Planning a hot and dirty week, eh?"

"No, no," I hasten to clarify, "nothing like that."

"Oh?" Her voice is credulous.

"No, seriously, uh... He wants me to meet his family over Christmas."

The silence stretches this time. A beat, another.

"Family? Christmas?" Her voice sounds strangled. "Isn't that uh, premature?"

"It's part of the deal."

"The deal…? What deal? Amelie, what the hell is happening there?"

The phone vibrates again; I glance at the screen. She's asking for access to my video again. I huff out a breath, then agree.

Isla's face fills the screen. Her eyes are wide, concern writ across her features.

"Finally," she huffs. "The hell have you gotten yourself into?"

"Me?" I frown, "Why are you yelling at me, when it's that alpha-hole's fault that I am here in this bath tub?"

"Where is the doctor?"

"He's shutting down the house for the night."

She raises an eyebrow.

"What?"

She makes the motion of zipping her lips, "Nothing."

I scowl, "Out with it, bitch."

"It sounds like you two are playing house up there."

"Yeah, and Max is our child," I say, only half-joking.

"Sinclair and Summer's puppy?"

"Yeah, Weston's dog-sitting."

"He can't be that much of an asshole if he's dog sitting."

"He knows how to fool people, huh?" I mutter.

She peers up at me through the screen. "The deal," she prompts. "What's that all about?"

"He's paying me a million pounds a day for my time."

"A million?" she splutters. "You sure?"

"Yeah, we shook on it."

"Hmph." She purses her lips, "He's filthy rich. No doubt, he can afford it." Her forehead furrows, "And what does he want from you in return?"

"Uh, I'm going to have to housekeep for him, until we leave here."

She bursts out laughing. "You? Housekeeping?" Isla has been to my place.

"Shut up," I say, before giggling along with her.

She snickers, "So, what does that mean? *Housekeeping.*" She emphasizes the word, as if it has a hidden meaning.

My cheeks heat. "Well, uh..." I shift my body. *Why can't I get comfortable?* "It means I have to do everything he wants."

"Ooh," she perks up, "you mean kinky games?"

"Sort of…" I look up at the ceiling before continuing, "except, I'm not supposed to sleep with him."

"Excuse me?"

I hurry to explain. "As long as I don't have sex with him, I get the money."

She blinks rapidly. "That..." she frowns, "that makes no sense."

"Right?" *Glad I'm not the only one who thinks so.*

"I mean, shagging him would be almost as good as getting the money in your account."

I squeeze the bridge of my nose, "This entire thing is gonna go tits-up on me."

"So, he'll come through with the money. You're confident of that, right?"

"Right."

"And all you have to do is get through the next few days... Break bread with his fam..."

"Yeah," I nod.

"So, what's the problem?"

I stare at her.

"Oh." She tilts her head, "OHHHHH."

I turn down my lips, "Now you see?"

"You want to ride him horizontally?"

"Don't be crude." I laugh.

"You want to fuck him, get it on with him, shag him until you can't walk straight, until you're enveloped in a sex haze…?"

"Gee thanks," I mutter. "Thanks for laying it all out there."

"So, do it." She raises her shoulders.

"What?"

"You want him; take him. He won't say no. Shag him; live out your wildest dreams with the dirty doctor."

"And then?"

"Then go back to your life."

"My indebted-to-hell life," I complain.

"That does suck..." she taps a finger to her forehead, "unless."

"Uh-oh!" *Do I want to hear this?*

"You, change the terms of the deal."

"You think I could?"

"Sure. Revise it to include money *and* sex."

"Ah...But..."

"What?"

"Doesn't that make me a slut...in his eyes?"

"Aren't you already one?"

"N...no." I mean... "Maybe."

"Is it him or yourself you're worried about?"

"I don't understand."

"You want to keep your conscience clean—keep your skirts clean, so to speak. Do what he wants, on his terms, take the money, and run."

"Yeah."

"Think you can keep it that simple?"

"I..." I hang my head, "I'm not sure."

"So, call off the deal. Forget about the money. Go for the man."

"But... but, I need the cash."

"Then do as he says."

"I don't want to." I pout.

She throws up her hands, "Gah, you're making my head hurt."

"Tell me about it." I press my fingers to the bridge of my nose.

"So..." she scans my features, "What are you going to do?"

"I don't know."

There's a knock on the door. "Amelie?" Weston's voice reaches me. "You okay in there?"

"Shit, I gotta go."

"Let me know what you decide."

"Thanks, Iz."

"Bye, babe."

Weston bangs on the door again and raises his voice, "Amelie? Is everything okay?"

"Yes, coming." I walk over to the commode and flush it. Then check my appearance in the mirror over the sink. My hair is all over the place, skin flushed, no makeup, lips wiped bare. Ugh. And is that...? I lean in closer. Yep, there's dog hair on my sweater. "Damn it." I take off my sweater, glance around, then toss it into the laundry basket. My blouse is crumpled, but it'll have to do.

"Amelie?" Weston sounds pissed. "You coming out or do I need to come in there?"

"Hold onto your britches," I yell back, slide my phone into my pocket, then turn toward the mirror. I mean, it's not even a question anymore, is it? No sex. That's fine. I can still stick to that plan, but it would be nice to have a bit more fun with him at least, no? I grab the bottom of my blouse and whip it off.

"Amelie." Weston juggles the knob, "I'm coming in."

"Wait!" I toss aside the blouse and scamper for the door.

17

Weston

She opens the door, and I stare. Her tits... Her beautiful...gorgeous breasts, ensconced in her bra salute me. I glare at her chest, then at her face.

"Just," she swallows, "getting ready for bed."

I frown down at her. She walks forward. I don't move.

"Uh, excuse me?" She squeezes through the space between me and the door jamb.

She saunters over to the bed, walks past her suitcases propped up against the wall, to her side of the bed. She unzips her jeans, shoves them down, bends to take them off. Her heart shaped butt juts out. I clench the fingers of my right hand, wince when my injured finger protests. "Fuck," I growl.

"You, okay?" She tilts her head, shoots me a glance from her bent over stance.

I glare at her and she pales. Then straightens and kicks her jeans to the side.

I take a step forward.

She scrambles over to the bed, "Uh, I think I'll go to sleep." She slides in between the sheets, pulls the comforter up to her chin. She turns over on her side.

I'd lit candles on the side tables, and their light flickers across her delicate shoulder blades. Her creamy skin is perfectly smooth, perfectly soft, perfect to be marked by my fingerprints. I take a step toward her, then clench my fist at my side. *What the fuck? Is she playing with me?* And I'd started this goddamn game. What a bloody mistake. *Why the hell had I put the money between us? Why hadn't I flipped the agreement the other way? Asked her to sleep with me in exchange for the money? Fuck.* I reach the bed, stand over her.

Her shoulders quiver. So, she's aware I am here? Hmm.

Her fingers clench at the covering that flows over her shoulder. I reach for the fabric, tug. She shudders, then releases her grip on it. I draw the sheet down the curve of her waist, down the jut of her beautiful arse, until it pools about her ankles.

The swell of her butt catches the candlelight—gorgeous, beautiful, curved at just the right circumference, it'd fit so right into my palms.

My fingertips twitch. I sink to my knees by the bed, press a kiss to that point where her waist meets the swell of her hips.

She shudders. "Weston," she whispers.

"Shh." I nibble my way to the swell of the enticing flesh to the valley between her butt cheeks.

"Oh, my God." Her entire body quivers.

I am not a religious person—well, not unless you count the time I'd been kidnapped and had prayed to every power that might be to help me… And now, faced with the sheer gorgeousness, the beauty that is this woman unclothed— Yeah, I send up a prayer of thanks to that power that I am here. Is this why the cops had found me, still and lifeless, ready to give up? I had been hanging on by a thread, reaching for something in the distance, not within reach…a belief that I'd get through it. Can I get through these days with her? When, with every moment, she is sinking into my blood, wrapping herself up around my heart… *Heart? What? Fuck that.* I am not ready for that kind of entanglement.

Nothing and no one will undermine the lifestyle I've worked so hard to build. I'll never let another in… I fuck them and leave them. That's what I am good at. I'll never allow myself to lose control. Never put myself in a position where I am vulnerable.

I slip my tongue into the space between her arsecheeks. Her entire body jerks. "Wes," she moans, and my groin hardens.

"Do you want me, Princess?"

"Ah," she gulps, "I… You know I do."

I squeeze her arse, part the cheeks then nudge my tongue into her backhole.

"Jesus, Wes," she groans. "What are you…doing?"

"What do you think?"

"Why do you always answer my question with a question?"

"Because it's my prerogative to ask and yours to submit."

She huffs, "Where is that written?"

"In Doc Kincaid's manual of '100 ways to torture—I mean—pleasure a woman,'" I chuckle.

She stills, "Bet you have it written down too." She grumbles, "Methodical and detailed grumpy pants that you are."

"You think you know me, huh?" I nibble my way down to the apex between her legs, slip my tongue in to the sweet hollow of her pussy.

"OMG," she hisses, tries to pull her legs up.

I grip her thigh. "Don't move," I growl.

"But," she whines, "this is not fair."

"Good." Time she felt a little bit of the agony she's been putting me through. I lick the entrance to her channel and her entire body bucks. I slide my hand around to cup her pussy, slide my tongue in and out of her wet, melting core.

She groans, throws out her hand to clutch at a pillow.

I bring my other hand up to squeeze her breast and she cries out, "Why are you doing this?"

"Because… I can?" I murmur against her center. "Because you won't stop me?"

"Does this… Uh, count as—?"

"Breaking the arrangement?"

She nods.

"No," I slurp the moisture that trickles from her center, "but all you have to do is say the word and I'll put you out of your misery."

"Fuck," she hisses.

"Yeah, exactly." I allow my lips to curve into a smile, then press little kisses to the back of her thigh. I suck on the soft skin, and the taste of her goes to my head. I bite down on the tender flesh and she moans.

"Please, please, please," she pants.

"You know I can't." I smirk. "But say the word, and I can take you—" I drag my tongue up her thigh, retrace my way to her back-hole, "here."

"Oh," she gasps. "I… I...am not sure about that."

I raise my head, slip a finger back inside her puckered hole. "You mean this?"

She groans, "I… I think I hate you."

I twist my finger inside her, then slide two fingers inside her pussy.

Her body jerks, goosebumps pop on her skin, a quiver works its way up her legs, her thighs, she clenches her butt around my intrusion, and her pussy clamps down on my finger.

"Oh, my God, Weston, I am going to—"

I pull my finger out from her butthole, from her channel, then rise to my feet.

She stills, "What the fuck?"

She turns on her back, then springs up.

"What are you doing?"

I yawn, "I'm tired."

She gapes, tracks my progress around the bed to my side. I grab my sweatshirt and peel it off, along with the vest I have on underneath. I reach for my pants.

She squeaks, "You're undressing?"

"It happens." I smirk, "I have been known to do so when I want to get into bed."

I shove down my pants and boxers. I kick them aside and straighten. I turn to face her. Her gaze widens as she takes in my full-frontal nudity, rakes her gaze down my stomach to where my dick stands to attention. *I'm aroused — of course, I am. And that's too fucking bad. I don't intend to do anything about it. Guess I am going to suffer along with her… Uh, who am I punishing here? Her or me? Both of us. Right, whose idea had this entire fucked-up arrangement been?*

I climb between the covers, then fold my hands behind my head.

Next to me, she stays perfectly still, muscles vibrating with tension. The nervous energy vibrates off of her, reaches out to me. My shoulders bunch. I close my eyes, begin to count down.

Twelve o'clock.

Eleven o'clock.

Ten o'clock.

She shifts position.

Nine o'clock.

Eight o'clock.

She turns over on her side, facing away from me.

Seven o'clock.

She mutters under her breath.

Six o —

She sighs aloud.

That's it. "What's wrong?" I snap.

Silence from her.

I close my eyes again.

Six o —

She jerks on the cover, pulls it off of me.

"What the fuck?" I turn to her, "What's wrong?"

"I'm…c…cold." Her teeth chatter.

I frown. The temperature had dropped and the heating hasn't come on yet.

She shivers again.

I turn, scoot over, then drag her to me.

She squeaks, "What are you doing?"

"Making the fuck sure that I can get some shut-eye."

I tuck her head under my chin, lock my arm around her waist, and pull her close enough for my dick to nestle between her arsecheeks.

She wriggles her hips, "You're… Uh, you're hard."

"Deal the fuck with it," I growl.

"But, I can't—"

I close my palm over her mouth, "Sleep, Princess."

She draws in a breath, another, then licks my palm. My cock instantly lengthens. "Don't do that, not unless you want to be brought to the edge of climax again…and left unfulfilled."

"You won't," her voice is muffled against my hand.

"Try me." I snuggle her closer, throw my leg over her thigh. She stills, muscles wound up. I close my eyes, start my countdown.

Six o-clock.

Five o'clock.

Her chest rises and falls.

Four o'clock.

Her breathing deepens.

Three o'clock.

Her shoulder muscles loosen; her body twitches.

Two o'clock.

I lower my palm to cup her breast. Not intentionally, of course. It's a logical resting place. Besides, the shape is a perfect fit for my palm. Sleep overcomes me.

Something cold nudges my face, a wet tongue licks my mouth, "Seriously, Buttercup, we need to talk about your morning breath." I crack open my eyelids. Max gazes soulfully at me. I am on my back; Max rides my chest. He flicks out his tongue, I turn my head to the side, then stiffen. The bed is empty. *Where the hell is she?*

I set Max aside, swing my legs over the side, and head out of the room. A crash reaches me from the kitchen, then a scream. *The fuck?* "Princess?" I race toward the commotion.

18

———————

Amelie

"Aw… Hell… Butterfingers." I glance down at the mixing bowl I had overturned. I'd woken up early, determined to try a new recipe for chocolate banana muffins…and managed to drop the bowl.

No wonder he calls me Buttercup. But I admit, I prefer Princess. There's a thud of footsteps, the sound of barking. I glance up as Weston barrels through the door and into the room, Max on his heels.

"What's wrong?" He stalks into the room, "I heard you —"

His shoulders block out the rest of the room. The planes of his chest are hard. I rake my gaze down his concave stomach, to where his cock juts out between those powerful legs and those gorgeous feet that he's currently about to place in a puddle of chocolate sauce.

"Watch out —"

His feet slip on the gooey streak on the floor and his big body tilts back. Shit, I leap forward, reach for him… I mean, what the hell am I trying to do? It's not like I could stop him from falling, and hello, he isn't wearing any clothes, so I couldn't exactly grab onto anything, except...Well... You know. A-n-d nope, I don't want to risk hurting that part of him. I stumble aside.

Too late, I realize I am about to step on a banana peel. Yes, really, a banana peel. Can my life get any more cartoonish? I twist my body, lose my balance anyway, and pitch forward. "Oh, no, no, no," I wail, throw up my hands, squeeze my eyes shut and connect nose first with a hard barrier. Shock waves ricochet through my head, down my spine. The breath whooshes out of me. "Ugh!" I flail around, and my arms are caught and twisted behind me.

"The hell is wrong with you?"

His voice rumbles below my ear and that's when I realize I am sprawled over his body. His very naked body. My cheek is smooshed against that delectable chest, my breasts flattened against that eight pack, my pelvis positioned right over that hard, gorgeous part of him that stabs into the cleft between my pussy lips.

Max dances around us, barking near my ear. "Max, stop," I pant, then try to pull back from the annoying man I am currently draped over.

He scissors his legs around mine, "Stop struggling."

I tip my chin-up, "What are you trying to do?" I scowl.

The light shining through the window brings out the gold flecks in his eyes. Huh? So his eyes aren't completely grey? Imagine that.

"I heard you scream." He glowers up at me, "I was convinced there was an intruder in here."

"No, it's just me," I huff. Gosh, he's grumpy first thing in the morning, huh? Is it because he hasn't had his way with me yet? Would stabbing his dick inside of me put him in a better mood? My thighs clench. My nipples tighten.

He tilts his head, his lips taking on that curl that I hate… And love. *Oh, my God, stop acting like a sex-crazed slut—but hello, can you blame me?* That mussed up hair, that broad chest, over which I am sprawled. That warmth of his that rises up from his big body, to coil around me, sink into my blood, and travel straight to that emptiness in my center. *Gah, stop that.*

I push back; his grasp tightens. That hard length of his pushes up and into my very eager center. I gulp. *Okay, don't panic; don't.* Pretend it's normal. Just a conversation, that's all this is. I tip up my chin. "I, uh, had a little accident," I mutter.

"I can see that." He pushes back my hair that's come lose from its bun on top of my head, then rubs at a spot on my cheek. He brings it to his mouth, sucks on his digit. "Chocolate." He grimaces, "Of course, it's chocolate."

"Is there any other kind of ingredient worth waking up early for?"

"There are other reasons worth losing sleep over," he smirks.

I scoff, push at his chest, "Let me go."

"No."

Max shoves his face between us, aims his tongue at Weston's mouth. Wes groans, turns his face the other way.

Max barks, wags his tail, turns to me instead. I crane my head away, "Chocolate isn't good for you, Max," I scold.

Max pants, then shoves his nose into my throat. "Ooh, it's cold." I giggle. He licks my throat, then proceeds to place his paw on my breast.

"Hey," Weston releases my arm, grabs Max by the scruff of his neck and places him aside. Max barks. The moment Wes lets him go, he jumps forward toward me, shoves his nose down my blouse.

I laugh, "Max, no, that tickles."

"Bloody hell," Weston swears. He releases both of my arms, then grabs Max. I roll away from him. Weston jumps to his feet, stalks across the kitchen and places Max in the hallway. He points a finger at the puppy. "Chocolate on the floor, buddy. I don't want you getting into that." Max groans.

I swear, that dog can speak.

The mutt blinks up at Weston who shakes his head. "Nice try little fella, but you can't come in here right now." He closes the door.

I spring up to my feet, and slip again, on the gooey dough this time, slide forward, tilt back, grab hold of a chair which tips over. *Gah!* The world tilts again; I squeak, throw out a hand, which is grasped. I am pulled upright.

"Steady." There's amusement in his voice.

"Thank you." I tug on my palm, but his grip tightens around my wrist. He tugs, I careen forward, and he grabs me and swings me up. I wind my legs around his waist.

"Hello, there." He waggles his eyebrows.

"What are you doing?" My voice is breathless. Bloody hell. His dark, edgy, masculine scent entwines with the chocolate-banana notes of the muffin mixture. My mouth waters and it's not for the muffins. My head spins and I dig my fingers into his shoulders.

He walks to the other side of the table, then plops me on it. He keeps his fingers on my hips. "That's better."

"For…for what?" I clear my throat.

"For breakfast, of course." He grins, then steps back. He leans around me, grabs the chocolate sauce we bought.

I frown, "I was going to use that to cook."

"I have a better idea." He holds it upside down, squirts. I glance down to find it dripping into the valley between my breasts.

"Wh…what are you doing?" I gulp.

His lips curl, he drops his head, and licks the sauce from the top of my cleavage toward the hollow of my throat.

"Oh," I stutter.

He sucks on the delicate skin at the base of my neck and I feel the tug all the way down to my core. My pussy spasms and my thighs clench. "W…Weston," I plead.

He pauses, "Do you want me to stop?" He leans back, "Should I leave?" He takes a step back.

I throw out a hand and grab his hip, "Wait."

He tilts his head, "What do you want?"

I want you inside me; I want you to fuck me right here. I blink, "I… I want to complete the recipe I set out to cook."

He frowns, "You want to make breakfast?"

"Y...yeah," I nod, "it's a new recipe I'm trying out for—"

He scratches his chest and my gaze drops to those cut abs. Not that I hadn't noticed them before… I mean, I'd managed to look away though, so he wouldn't catch me staring, but now that he's drawing attention to it, well… I can't help but stare. "For a doctor you sure have a great physique."

"For a chef, you sure haven't figured out the obvious."

I frown. "What do you mean?"

"You were making… What was it you were going to create?"

"Muffins." I frown, "Banana chocolate muffins."

"The oven," he jerks his chin over my shoulder, "the electricity's not back."

"Oh!"

"And the refrigerator isn't working either," he adds. "Or didn't you notice?"

"I... I didn't," I confess, and I had opened the refrigerator to pull out the ingredients I needed. Hell! I drag my fingers through my hair. "How can I be such a ditz?"

"Maybe your mind was otherwise occupied?" He chuckles.

"How do you mean?"

"Want me to spell it out?" He takes a step forward.

I shake my head, "No, no, it's fine. You're right, I was, uh, thinking of other things."

"Oh?" He smirks, "Did it involve me in anyway?"

"Ah, your family actually. When, uh, when do we set off to see them?"

"In four days."

"Four days." I gulp, glance around the room. Four days, during which I still have to resist him. *How the hell am I going to get through this?*

"What should I do about breakfast?" I pout.

"I have an idea." His grin widens, "Why don't I make my special instead?"

Twenty minutes, later I sit across the table from him. He'd, thankfully, changed into sweats and a long sleeved T-shirt, which damn, it only set off his broad shoulders even more. I mean, the only thing to beat the sight of this man unclothed is him sitting across the table, with Max at his feet. I'd cleaned up the kitchen by the time Weston had returned with the little guy in tow. I'd topped off Max's bowl, which he'd wolfed down in minutes, before taking up his position by the table.

Now, he watches as Weston pours the cereal into the bowls. He tops his off with milk, offers it to me. I refuse. Yeah, for a chef, I don't like milk. Not in my tea, nor in anything else.

"This?" I mutter, "This is your idea of cooking?"

"Hey, don't mock it until you've tried it."

He uses his uninjured hand to dip his spoon into his bowl, and begins to eat.

"It's not chocolate," I whine.

"Precisely." He scoops up more of the stuff.

I frown, "How the hell am I going to get through the days without cooking?"

"You could clean."

"Yeah, well." I shuffle in my seat. I absolutely hate household chores. Yeah, a tiny detail I'd left out. I know.

I glance down at my bowl, begin to scoop up the mixture. I eye it, then force some of it into my mouth. The flavors explode on my tongue. I crunch down, swallow it, reach for more.

"Not bad, huh?"

I raise a shoulder, "It's all right." I eat some more. "I couldn't use firewood to fire up the oven, could I?"

He stares across the table, "Probably not."

"Can I call someone to come and take a look?"

"I already called for service, but they won't come until the storm blows over."

I frown, glance out the window. Snow comes down in heavy flakes. It does look bad, and if people are being careful before venturing out... "Maybe the roads will be blocked and we won't be able to get there?"

"The storm's supposed to blow itself out in 48 hours."

Right.

"Maybe the roads will be too slippery?"

"I've asked my driver to come by to take us there."

"Your driver?"

"He's on standby in the village."

Of course. My shoulders droop. And I'd been hoping to put the time to good use by trying out new recipes, huh?

"Perhaps," he rolls his neck, "I could take a look at the generator."

"You would do that?" I cry.

"Hmm." He looks me up and down, "How badly do you want it?"

I frown, "What is that supposed to mean?"

He leans forward, "I mean, how far would you go to get the generator working, I wonder?"

I swallow, wriggle around in my seat, "How far do you want me to go?"

"I want you to beg."

"Excuse me?"

"Beg me to do it."

"No," I scowl.

"Fine then." He pushes back from the table, pivots to leave.

I frown, watch him as he prowls toward the door. I train my gaze back on the man, or rather on that fine piece of ass of his, those power thighs that undulate as he puts more distance between me… And the muffins I so very much want to bake. Is there not one thing in your life that you can complete? Not a relationship? Just about hold onto a business that if you don't comply with his wishes… You'll lose the money to ensure that it survives. Ugh, why do I always find myself stuck between a rock and a hard place? And no, I am not talking about certain parts of his anatomy that would give granite a run for its money.

He steps out of the kitchen and I call out, "Wait." I spring up and my chair careens back. "I beg you," I call out, "please fix the generator."

He shoots me a look over his shoulder, "Get on your knees, and ask like you mean it"

"Wh…what?"

"You heard me."

I scowl. *If he thinks I am getting down on the floor — I confess, I didn't do a great job of cleaning up earlier and there are crumbs everywhere. Ugh! Note to self: make sure to be more detailed in all parts of your life, so it doesn't come to bite you in the arse — or in the pussy —* My thighs tremble.

"Do it," he tilts his head, "or our deal is off."

"Fine, fine, whatever," I huff, then swing my leg onto the table.

19

Weston

"What are you up to?" I frown as she scrambles up onto the table, on her knees.

She looks at me with wide eyes, "What? I'm doing what you ordered me to do."

I growl.

"You didn't specify where." She flutters her eyelashes at me.

I scowl. Of course, I didn't, but then, I hadn't expected her to kneel on the table either. This woman... Every time I think I have her pegged, she throws me a surprise. *Goddam it.* I pause at the door. Max whines, and I bend down to pat him. He pushes his nose into my hand, then drops back on his hind legs.

"Stay there." I growl, then straighten, and shut the door in his face.

"Why...why did you do that?" she squeaks, her tone so close to panting that a chuckle grips my throat. I swallow it down, then turn and crack my knuckles. "Why do you think?" I growl.

She gulps. Fear and excitement wafts off of her. Fuck! My dick thickens. She watches me as I prowl toward her, closer, closer. I pause in front of her; her spine straightens.

I roll my neck; she winces.

I glare at her and color fades from her face. "What…what are you going to do?" she whispers, all wide eyed, and my groin tightens.

I put my finger to my lips.

She swallows. Her eyebrows knit as I circle around the table to stand behind her.

"You misinterpreted what I said," I chide.

"What?"

"I told you to kneel."

"I'm kneeling."

True. I scratch my chin, "Sassy and impertinent. You don't know how to follow orders, huh?"

"I'm not one of your patients," she scoffs.

"No, our relationship could never be that…professional." I place my palms on either side of her body, bend toward her, forcing her upper body forward until she puts her palms on the table.

She shivers. Does she feel the heat from my body? Does she realize how much I want her right now?

"Weston," her breath hitches, "what are you doing?"

I palm her butt. The silence stretches a beat, another.

She shudders. "You… Are you…" She arches her back, and I flatten my palm onto the center.

"Am I?" I prompt her.

"Are you going to punish me?" her voice cracks.

"Should I?" My lips curl. I apply pressure and she curves her spine, juts out her arse.

I release her, step back. Hmm, perfect. I raise my left hand, "Beg for it." I take aim.

"For what?" She turns to glance at me over her shoulder, her gaze wide, lips parted.

Blood rushes to my groin. Hell, I haven't started, and already, I am so close to losing control. One glance at her upturned nose, that sweet mouth, and all my promises to myself go out of the window.

"Eyes forward," I growl.

She gulps, then obliges, turns her face to look ahead. *Thank fuck.* Any more sass from her, and I swear I'd have turned her over my knee... And that would have been too easy...for her...for me... Yeah, this is more arousing—the anticipation, the build-up, the sweet ache as she waits...waits.

"Say it," I snap.

"Please," the words tumble from her lips, "slap me, spank me, treat me like I'm your..."

"My—?"

"Your property, your uh—Christmas present."

"That the best you can do, Princess?"

"Like you're Santa and I'm a naughty child." She swallows.

"And have you been a bad girl?" I lower my voice to a hush, "Tell me, Princess."

"Yes," she breathes, "I have been terrible. I disobeyed you. I willfully misinterpreted your directive, I—"

My palm connects with her butt.

"Ow," she howls, "What are you—?"

I raise my hand, bring it down on her arse with enough force that her entire body jolts.

"Ah!" she cries out.

Crack, crack, crack. I slap her on alternate arse cheeks.

"Argh." She throws her head back, her shoulders shudder, she squirms, and tries to pull away.

I grip her hip. "Stay," I command.

A ripple shivers up her spine. She tenses, clenches her thighs together.

"Or you can go."

She draws in a breath.

So do I.

Will she go? Will she take this opportunity I am giving her to get away?

"Nothing standing in your way, Princess," I remind her. "You can leave right now. Walk away, and I won't stop you."

"The money," her voice is low, but I hear her. Of course, it comes down to that.

"I'll pay you for the two nights you spent here."

"You…you would?" She half turns, then changes her mind and positions her head to stare forward. "You'd do that?"

"Of course," I mutter. "I'm a jerk, not a cheat."

"And I'm not leaving."

"Say that again."

She gulps, the sound loud in the silence of the room.

"I… I want to stay."

"You want to see this through?"

She nods.

"Why?"

"You're not the only one who wants to fulfill your side of the bargain."

"Good." I slap her arse.

"Hey," she snarls, "I told you I wasn't leaving."

"And I am not letting up."

She lowers her chin, "And when you're done, you'll take a look at the generator?"

"You bet."

"Fine," she tosses her head, "have at it —"

I step back, walk around her to drop into my seat, and resume eating.

"What are you doing?"

I crunch down more cereal.

"I'm talking to you," she scowls.

"I'm not."

She stares at me as I shovel more of the disgusting stuff into my mouth. Cold breakfasts have never been my thing. And since when have I wanted to taste chocolate-laced savories in the morning, huh? Come to think of it, when had I begun to stop hating chocolate? Bloody hell, this woman is changing me and she isn't even trying.

I push back, stand, "I'll check out the generator now."

I turn to leave and there's a sound behind me. I hold up my hand. "What do you think you're doing?" I ask without turning around.

"Uh, I'm going to finish my cereal?"

"No."

"What?"

I pivot to glare at her over my shoulder, "You stay right there, Princess."

"Bu…but," she blinks rapidly, "you're leaving."

"And I haven't given you permission to move."

She gapes, "So you want me to stay right here, on the table, on all fours?"

"You can get naked if you want," I chuckle, "or not. Up to you."

"You're a prick," she mumbles, "a sadistic, jerk-face, wanker."

"And you're going to obey me," I inform her.

She glowers at me, "I hate you."

"And I love that wrinkle you get between your eyebrows when you're angry." I blink. *Did I just say that? I didn't say that. And the worst thing? It's the truth.* I frown at her.

She stares back.

"Stay." I stab a finger in her direction, because well, I need to reinforce my rich prick status. Then turn and leave.

I make a detour to collect my phone from the bedroom, then step out, past the silent hot tub. At some point in the night the snow had turned to rain. Now as I stalk across the lawns they glisten from the overnight storms.

When I reach the shed at the back, I hesitate, draw in a breath, and walk in. The glass from the broken clocks glitters on the floor. I stare at it, my life's work—a fortune in antique clocks that I'd bought and fixed myself. I walk to the nearest one, pick it up. Its face is cracked, but the mechanism works. I could piece it together once more. I glance around the space… Hell, I am going to reassemble every single one of these pieces. That's not the problem, though. I stalk forward, toward the table at the far end. Fact is, someone was here… They intruded on my privacy… Which I don't give a fuck about… But her… She was here. So was Max. They'd frightened the dog and it could have easily been her. They could have hurt her… My belly knots. Fuck, if I am going to let that happen again. And it's only because I am responsible for her, until Christmas… Perhaps until the New Year, if I have my way. I cannot put her at risk again. Whoever targeted me, won't hesitate to come for her either.

I have to find a way to protect her…for as long as she is here… And later? I cannot allow them to get to her.

I pull out my phone. My first call is to the company that manages the services to the cabin and the shed.

I give them the go-ahead to switch on the electricity to the kitchen, and only to the kitchen. With the fancy bucks we pay to the private supplier, anything is possible. As for the water supply? I ask them to ensure there's only enough for two days—nothing like water running out to test the mettle of a person, huh? As for the power cut? I orchestrated that too. Just a test, a way to exert complete control over the situation, and on her. Only I hadn't counted on a goddam intruder, violating my personal space. If something had happened to her—! My shoulders bunch. Goddam it, I have to find out who was behind the break-in.

Then I dial Damian's number.

"What?" he grumbles.

"Did I disturb you?" I ask.

"Yes." He yawns. "You woke me up, you knob."

"Good." I roll my shoulders, "We have a problem."

"Not we," he mutters, "you." He yawns again, so loudly, I hear the sound of his jaw cracking over the phone. "Don't pull me into your personal shitstorm, motherfucker," he warns.

"The shed was broken into last night."

There's silence, then, "What do you mean 'broken into'?"

"Exactly that." I begin to pace. "Someone got in, then got to my collection of clocks."

There's a pause. "Didn't know you still collect and repair them."

"I never stopped."

I also don't talk about this affliction of mine with the Seven.

"I had Karina check on the security for both the cabin and the shed, so whoever managed to break in—"

"Was no ordinary burglar," he completes my thought.

I stay quiet and the silence extends.

"The Mafia." I blow out a breath. "They were behind this," I growl. "I should have known that they wouldn't stop coming after those close to us."

"And is she?" Damian asks.

"What?"

"Is she close to you?"

"We are sharing the same cabin," I snap.

"That's not what I meant."

"That's all you're getting," I retort.

Damian doesn't respond.

"If the Mafia thinks this is going to scare us off, they are wrong." I snarl.

"We won't stop until we find out who among the Mafia was behind our kidnapping," Damian agrees.

"If they're breaking in and entering now, they must be getting desperate," I mutter.

"We must be getting close to a breakthrough." Damian grunts, "Have you heard anything from Saint or Sinner about the latest on the investigations?"

"Not since they found their lady loves," I gripe. "Not that I begrudge them their happiness, but clearly, it's time we take things into our own hands."

"The New Year's eve party," Damian replies. "We'll all be there."

"Everyone except Baron." I say, referring to one of the Seven who prefers to stay clear of us and conduct his business remotely.

"Except fucking Baron," Damian agrees. "The rest of us will be there. We are bound to get an update then."

"Right." I pinch the bridge of my nose, "Meanwhile, I need to up the security here at the cabin."

"You going to ask Karina for help, again?" Damian asks.

"Why wouldn't I?"

"You know how upset Arpad's going to be about that?" he replies.

"Whatever is between her and Arpad is not my problem," I bite out. "Her investigative and security services are the best in the business and—"

"You can't trust anyone else when it concerns the safety of those you care about?"

"Right," I nod.

He chuckles.

I frown, then straighten. "I mean, no," I growl. "I mean, yes, I can't trust anyone else with securing the space and no, I don't care about her."

"Man, you're delusional," he scoffs.

"What is that supposed to mean, you piece of shit?"

He laughs, "When you get repetitive in your insults, I know you're not thinking straight."

"Fuck that." I frown, "Are you helping me or not?"

"Do I have a choice?" he replies.

"Nope," I bark, then move the phone to my right hand. "I'm stuck here with this bloody broken finger, with my woman…"

"Did you say *your* woman?"

"A slip of the tongue." I grunt, "I'm here with her and Max, and it's my responsibility to keep them both safe."

"That's all this is about, huh?"

"Of course, what else would it be?"

"You tell me." I hear the grin in his voice.

"Once you're done indulging your asinine sense of humor — maybe you could sober enough to hear me out?"

"Aren't you forgetting to say something?" he drawls.

I stay silent.

"A word beginning with 'p'?" he prompts.

"Piss off." I oblige him.

He chuckles, "Good to know you have some game left in you yet."

"That was me being polite, you tosser," I growl. "If you don't help me out, I'm going to release the video I have of you making out with your harem."

"Harem?" his voice is cautious.

"You don't think that what takes place in Vegas actually stays in Vegas."

"You recorded me?" his tone is flat

"Don't pretend you didn't do the same." It was a trip the two of us had taken, a few years ago. The rest of the Seven hadn't been available that year over the Christmas break and I had flown into LA to join Damian. We'd taken his private jet to Las Vegas… And the rest, well…as they say, it's recorded for posteriority. His, not mine.

"What do you take me for?" Damian laughs, "Of course, I have a stockpile of pics and videos on each of the Seven, including you." His voice is pleasant. "Perhaps I should upload the video of you…" his voice trails off.

"Yeah," I quip, "I jerked off to you and your three women, which face it, is nowhere as interesting as what I have on you. Not that it doesn't make you look good… I mean, they were all over you, and your face can only be seen in one frame." Which would be more than enough for him to capture the headlines of the media that day. "It's slow over Christmas, and you have a big single coming out. No doubt, it would ensure that happy families everywhere would want to look you up to find out what the fuss is all about." Not. It would effectively cost him his reputation… Oh, he'd recover from it all right, but not before the Christmas single tanked… Probably.

"Whose idea was it to release a Christmas song anyway, huh?" I snicker. "Isn't that what reality show winners and washed-up rock stars go for… Oh, wait." I laugh, "That's what you are, someone who's yesterdays' news."

"Fuck off," he growls.

"With pleasure, after you've promised to help me."

"After that incredible selling job, how can I refuse?"

"Aww," I coo, "did I hurt your itty-bitty wittle feewings, Mr. Rock Star?"

"Sometimes I am not sure why the Seven of us keep in touch," he grumbles. "It's not like there's much love lost between us."

"Maybe it's something deeper," I muse, "a shared moment—a few days in time that changed the course of our future."

"There is that." He sighs, "I could, of course, release your video anyway and see how it plays with your little girlfriend, huh?"

"Not my girlfriend, and PS, I told her about the sex tape already, so—"

"You told her?" He coughs. "Isn't that unusual for you?"

"What?" I frown, "Just making sure she understood that she

can't underestimate my sex god status." I brush an imaginary speck from my sweater, as if he can see me.

"You being upfront with a woman?" I sense him shake his head. "So, it's that serious, huh?"

"Of course, not."

"Just for that, I'll do this for you."

"For what?" I crack my neck.

"To see you fall. Fuck, it must be something in the air…" He continues, "It started with Sinner, then Saint, and now you."

I move the phone away from my ear, and stare at it before switching to speakerphone, "I have no idea what you're talking about." I frown.

"Of course, not." His voice is calm, "You have no idea, do you?"

I grit my teeth, "You're getting on my balls, Savage." I growl, "One click and your video gets uploaded."

"No, you won't do it," he retorts.

"Wanna test me?"

There's silence, then he sighs, "The fuck do you want from me?"

"Listen," I speak into the phone.

20

"There is no we in chocolate."
-From Amelie's diary

Amelie

The overhead light flickers and comes on. I blink. Guess the alphahole kept his word. He managed to fix the power supply to the kitchen, which means I can bake. Yay. I bite down on the inside of my cheek, glance around the space. Why does everything seem so bright? The place is bigger than I realized. The candles I had lit earlier appear weak. Too bad the attraction I feel for him shows no similar signs of waning. Dark or light, morning or night… It's a constant source of irritation that gnaws at my gut, forces me to act out of character. Like now. Why am I still on my hands and knees, on the bloody kitchen table, waiting for him?

I had said that I would obey him, but surely, this is out of bounds, even for someone like him. I mean, leaving me stationed here like I am his...possession? Am I his? Do I belong to him...? What hold does he have on me that I'd rushed to do his bidding? What would have happened if I'd gone against his decree? Hello... What am I thinking? Decree, huh? I snort. Like he is the master of all he surveys and I am his... *Don't think it; don't think it. Slave!*

Noooo, I can't allow myself to think that.

I can't allow him to have this hold on me.

But the money...the bloody millions that he holds over me? Well, he said he'd deposit the money for the nights I've already spent here...and Weston wouldn't go back on his word. Well neither would I, and I am still here, right? I'm not leaving.

I am simply, a woman standing in front of the most dominant, hot-as-fuck, alpha male she's ever met, wanting to ask him to fuck her.

There you have it—the story of my life. That ol' perception-reality thingummy... The one I can't hide from when I face the mirror.

Guess there had been more comfort in the gloom of the morning light. Everything had seemed so much more intimate. Now—I glance down at myself—I see myself through his eyes. A stupid woman, who'd allowed this obnoxious, mean-ass to manipulate me... To use his money to seduce me, to coerce me to do his bidding. *Where's your pride, Amelie? Where's that strength of character, that streak of obstinacy, that blind confidence in yourself that had you taking risks...and loans...and putting everything you have into this venture? Turning your passion into a livelihood?* My bloody foot. What a pipe dream. I'd sailed along blissfully in my little boat, even though I was fighting against the current... Until Weston bloody Kincaid had unleashed a storm that threatened to engulf my teacup. *He can dip his teabag in my hot water anytime.* I giggle, then shake my head. That's it. I am losing it, completely.

I straighten, scramble back, then off the table. My knees creak and my thighs spasm. Jesus, am I out of shape or what? I stalk over to the shelves by the oven, lean down and rummage around. There! I snatch up another large bowl—not a mixing bowl, but it could work. Thank God, we bought enough flour and chocolate and bananas to last me another round. I grab my provisions, measure out the flour on the old-fashioned scale. Seriously, it has weights and everything, I snort again. Lifestyles of the rich and famous, huh? They have all the time in the world… No, they have servants; that's what it is.

I pour the flour into the mixing bowl, break the eggs, then begin to beat it together. When it's smooth enough, I reach for the ripe bananas, peel the remaining three and drop them in. I mix them in too, then pour in the milk.

I hum to myself, shimmy my hips, taste some of the concoction. Yum.

Footsteps sound behind me, "What are you doing, Princess?"

His voice is all casual, nothing threatening about it, and that makes it worse. I straighten, reach for the pack of chocolate chips.

"You're only making it worse by not answering."

His voice is right behind and above me. I yelp, lose my grip on the packet and the entire thing tips in. "Gah!" I place the half-empty pack to the side, then whirl on him, "Look what you made me do."

"I give you one thing to do." He holds a finger right in front of my face, "One, and you disobey."

"You were gone a long time."

"Less than half an hour."

I throw up my hands, "Exactly. How long did you think I'd stay in that ridiculous position for you?"

He bends his knees, then peers into my face, "Until I gave you permission to move."

I toss my hair back from my face, "I couldn't wait, I wanted to get back to the baking."

"Is that right?" His voice lowers to a hush and my nerve endings spark, "So eager to make your crumpets—"

"Muffins." I correct him.

"Same thing." He shrugs.

"It's not." I gape at him, "Why do you constantly try to get on my nerves?"

"Because I can?" He looks me up and down and my belly quivers. He raises his gaze to my face, "Because you are mine for the next four days—mine to command, to order about, to play with as I see fit."

"I'm not your…fuck toy."

His eyes gleam, "Don't bet on it."

I purse my lips, then tilt my chin-up, "You're beginning to annoy me. You're illogical as hell, full of yourself, totally obnoxious, and cannot decide what you want."

"Oh?" He peels back his lips and his teeth shine against his tanned skin.

"If it wasn't for your…your…broken finger…I'd…"

"You'd…"

"Teach you a lesson."

"Go on," he drawls, "try me."

"Don't say I didn't warn you," I mumble.

"I'm soooo afraid." He holds up his hands, as if to ward off an attack. "Princess Buttercup and her idle threats. Has no one warned you not to play with the big bad wolf?"

"Your references are all mixed up," I snarl.

"And that disgusting mixture in that bowl… Is that the best you can do for breakfast?"

That's it, I am letting him have it. He can say anything about me, but my cooking? No fucking way. I am bloody good at what I do, and no one, definitely not a neanderthal, alpha billionaire can take that away from me. I make a noise deep in my throat.

His features brighten, "Ooh, did I hurt your feelings? Does the princess want to be saved from herself, yet?"

"Newsflash, alphahole." I shove my hand behind me, search for the mixing bowl. "This Princess can save herself."

My fingers brush the smooth surface, I snatch the vessel, fling its contents at him.

21

____

Weston

"Oops." Her lips quiver and her chin wobbles. She drops her gaze to my chest.

I glance down to find splotches of the brown gooey mixture sticking to my pullover. "That item of clothing costs £7000," my voice is calm. No hint of the anger that bubbles up inside... Along with something else—frustration. 48 hours... I've tried to teach her to obey. I've ordered her to obey me, told her to follow my directions. I've walked naked in front of her, slept with my body coiled around hers. I've raced toward her when I thought she was in danger... Been on the phone making sure I could find a way to protect her... And what does she do? She greets me with this...this goop? A low growl rumbles up my chest.

She blinks, "Did you just...did you?"

"What?"

"You, ah, sounded like Max when he's frustrated."

I glower, "Did you compare me to a bloody mutt?"

A snort spills from her throat.

The fuck? "Are you laughing at me?"

"Me?" She bites down on her lower lip. Her cheeks redden. She lowers the bowl—her hand trembles… Is it from my proximity or from the weight of the vessel? Maybe it's fear of how I'll react. Good. The blasted container dips. I grab hold of it.

"Ah, thanks," her voice is strangled.

"Don't thank me." I reach past her, lower the bowl to the counter.

"Wait," she bursts out.

"What?" I frown.

She angles her body, scoops up some of the mixture. She glances from it to me, "It, uh, has chocolate."

"So?"

"I missed a spot."

"Excuse me?" I glare at her.

She bites her lips and her eyes gleam.

"Don't you fucking dare, Princess, I—"

She tosses the stuff at my face. It hits my cheek, and some of it drips down my chin, onto my chest.

"There," she angles her head to the side, "much better."

"That's it," I growl, "you're going to pay for that."

She squeaks, tries to duck around me. I plant my injured hand on the other side of her, caging her in.

"Apologize," I growl.

"No."

"Say you're sorry."

She sticks out her tongue, "You can go and dunk your swollen head in that stupid hot tub."

"I have a better idea." I reach for the mixture in the bowl, scoop up a palmful.

"No, no, no." She angles her body, takes in what I am doing. "You won't," she breathes.

"Oh, you bet I will." I smash the gooey stuff in her face.

She screams, wriggles around. I thrust my hips into her, to hold her in place, then rub the mix into her face, down her neck, across her chest… over the fabric of her blouse that encloses her breasts, and draw circles around her erect nipples. The blood rushes to my groin. My dick lengthens, nestles happily into the valley between her legs.

"Wes… Weston," she gulps.

"Shh!"

I glare at those peaked delights. I reach behind her to gather more of the goop and trail it over one breast, then the other. The mixture dribbles down from each mound. "Beautiful." I lower my head, close my mouth around one.

"Ah," a moan leaves her mouth. "Wes… Please."

I glare up at her. "Stay still," I command. "Don't say a word."

She purses her lips, draws down her eyebrows. She opens her mouth.

I click my tongue. "Don't," I growl, "Nothing; nada."

"But—"

"Another word and I'll stuff this mix in your mouth, and I promise you, that would be a waste, cause I plan to use every drop of your muffin mix to draw out your pleasure."

She swallows, then presses her lips together.

"Excellent."

She stares at me.

"Should I reward you for that little bit of compliance, hmm?"

She nods.

"All right then." I reach behind her, snatch up some of the mix. I hold my fingers to her lips, "Open."

"But—"

I plop my fingers inside her mouth. She bites down with her teeth and I feel the tug all the way to the tip of my dick. My cock thickens, pushes up into her.

Her gaze widens.

"Feel that, Buttercup?"

I bring my other hand to massage her breast, then press my hips forward with enough pressure that her pelvis cradles every throbbing inch of my very aroused shaft.

She swallows, and the suction on my fingers, sends a shudder of heat racing down my spine.

"Fuck." My breathing grows shallow. I ease my finger out from between her lips, and bring it to my own. I lick my glistening fingertips.

She moans, "Jesus." She gulps.

"Nothing to do with the man above," I mutter, "but if I don't have you right now, the one between my legs is going to hate me for a long time."

She chuckles. "You're so corny." She grins up at me, her features alight, with so much mischief, so much life, that fuck, my cock thickens even more.

I frown. "Silence," I snap.

She winces, then pouts.

Fucking adorable. I shake my head. The fuck am I doing, thinking about her in those cutesy adjectives? And cutesy—? What the fuck? How did that even get in my vocabulary. I frown down at her and she stares back.

"I'm corny, hmm?" I reach behind her, grab the bowl with both hands, then upturn it over her head.

She gasps.

The mixture flows down her face, her neck, her chest, down to where our bodies are joined. "That's better." I place it down behind her, then straighten. I step back, rub the mix down her front, across her stomach, to the valley between her thighs.

Her breath hitches.

I pat the mix into the apex of her thighs, onto her jeans.

"Ah," she trembles. I sink down to my knees, then thrust my face into her sweet, core. I bite down on the fabric that covers the crotch of her jeans and her entire body bucks. She grabs at my hair and tugs. The pain rams straight down my spine, to my cock. I grip her thighs, pry them apart, then dig my teeth into the now-damp cloth that stretches across her pussy.

She screams. "Oh, my God, ohmigod…oh…my…"

I rise to my feet, bringing her up with me, and hoist her onto the counter and straight onto the bowl I'd placed behind her, which tips sending more of the gooey mess to pool around her. She shivers, tips her chin up.

"I need to be inside of you."

She nods. She opens and closes her mouth, her gaze pleading with me. But she doesn't speak. About time. "You worried about our arrangement?"

She jerks her chin.

"So maybe I should…" I step back.

She scissors her legs around my waist.

"Don't want me to go, huh?" I study her face. "Want me to fuck you?"

She frowns back.

"Where?"

She purses her lips.

"In your mouth?"

She shakes her head.

"Your pussy?"

She nods.

"I have a better idea." I lean in until our breaths mingle, "How about I take your arse?"

She swallows; her pupils dilate.

"You want that, huh?"

She bites down on her lower lip and her little teeth worry the tender skin.

I rub my thumb over the swollen skin and she gulps. "Maybe I'll save that for later, huh?"

Her shoulders rise and fall.

"Maybe I shove my fingers in your arse, while I tear into your pussy with my dick, while I stick my tongue down your throat?"

She nods, then shakes her head, then throws her hands up.

I know the feeling. "Decisions, decisions." I chuckle.

She digs her thighs into my hips, uses it to leverage herself up, then smashes her lips to mine.

22

Amelie

I press my mouth to his, fold my arms about his shoulders, and proceed to climb him, like he's a massive tree… Or hell, like he's Santa fucking Claus, come to grant me all of my wishes. Is it Christmas yet? Gah! Almost…though it sure seems like all of my dreams have come true. This man… He drives me mad, he makes me want to slap him and kiss him. Love him and hate him… Throw myself at his feet and beg him to put an end to this growing, yearning, emptiness inside. I cling to his big frame, bite down on that full, pouty lower lip of his that's hypnotized me since the first time I saw him. I slip my tongue inside his mouth, suck on him, pour all of myself into that kiss. My head spins, my pussy clenches, and my nipples hurt. I lose my hold and begin to slip down, the muffin mixture sloshing and giving with each contact of my clothes against his. Shit, I scramble to hold on, and he places his broad palm against the seat of my butt.

Heat instantly flushes up my spine. I shudder.

He wraps his other palm around the back of my neck, and holds me there.

I release his lips, lean back —well, put as much distance between us as his firm grip allows, which is about uh —an inch…maybe a little more. Our noses bump; his long eyelashes graze my forehead. Hell, how can a man have such feminine lashes?

"So greedy," he mutters, "so damn sexy. Such a tiny package, but so much potency packed into those curves."

Shut up and fuck me already, is what I want to say. Instead, I hold his gaze, look deeply into those grey eyes, past the colorless, mirror-like surface, to that darkness that pools inside, the flecks of gold that intersperse their depths. Contradictions, such complexity he holds within himself.

"You can trust me." I whisper.

He blinks and his features open with the surprise.

"I won't hurt you," I add.

Where is this coming from? If anything, he's the one who can break me. His dominance could crush me, his strength could render me powerless, as his lips tease me, taunt me, his fingers dig into the curve of my hips, and his dick throbs against my aching center…
"Please," I mumble. *What do I want from him? Why is it that this push-pull between us makes it so difficult to bare myself to him?* I cup his cheek, "Take me. Use me. Fill me up with your cum, bury yourself inside of me, and fuck your past out of me."

Wait, did that even make sense…? "I mean —"

"Shh…" He rubs his nose against mine, the gesture tender and gentle and so unlike any other emotion he's shown toward me. A pressure builds behind my eyes. Shit. A little bit of affection, and I'm ready to bawl my eyes out.

He rakes his gaze down my features, then he brushes his lips across mine, once, twice. He lowers me back onto the countertop. "You on birth control?"

I blink.

"Are you?" He frowns.

I nod. "Yes," I clear my throat, "I'm just coming off a relationship so…"

He glares at me and I feel the blood drain to my core. How the hell does my body recognize his intentions before my mind has fully digested what he wants from me?

The sound of a zipper being lowered reaches me. Air hits my swollen center. "Up," he growls.

I wind my arms about his shoulder, raise my butt. He shoves down at my jeans which move an inch, then get stuck around my hips. "Umm."

He shakes his head and I stop talking. He glances around, notices my chef's satchel on the table. He hauls me up by the waist, turns and takes a step, then plants me on the table. I'm not light, I have curves—Hey, don't begrudge me my chocolate—and of course, he's a powerhouse of muscles, but the way he maneuvers my body… Well… My knees turn to jelly. Bloody hell, this guy is machismo personified, and I am putty in his hands. And now—he whips out a pair of kitchen scissors. Then steps back, holds up my leg and proceeds to cut the fabric up one side.

What the—?

He does the same for the fabric on my other leg and it falls away, then cuts my blouse at each shoulder.

"Weston—"

He shakes his head.

"You can trust me," his lips quirk as he repeats my words back at me.

Can I though?

I frown.

He locks his gaze with mine, then raises the scissors. He glances down, then I feel the give of my bra straps. My breasts spring free. His nostrils flare. He bends, licks a nipple, before sucking on it.

Goosebumps flare on my skin.

"So fucking sweet, you're one melting mass of chocolate, Buttercup."

Jeez, he makes me sound like a dessert…which is flattering, I suppose.

He pulls back, I hear the snap of the blades cutting through the fabric of my blouse. The garment falls off. Air hits my skin, goosebumps pop along my forearms, and my nipples harden.

He straightens, places the tip of the scissors to the center of my chest, without cutting the skin. I shiver. He drags the blade up over the mound of one breasts, circles the nipple, which instantly pebbles further. Down to my belly button. I swallow. He glances down and his breathing grows labored, "Fuck me," he growls. "I can't hold out any longer."

He tosses the scissors aside, reaches for his zipper and lowers it. His cock springs forward—big, throbbing. I've seen it before…but somehow, he seems bigger. More aroused. The swollen tip is almost purple with need, and drops of precum bead the slit. Saliva pools in my mouth; my chest rises and falls.

I reach for him, but he grabs my wrist. "If you touch me, I won't last," he growls.

I frown, implore him with my eyes.

His gaze intensifies, then his lips quirk. "Later," he promises. "For now, I am going to take your cunt." He swoops down, grabs my thighs under my knees, pulls my legs up and apart so they're at my ears and I fall back to my elbows. He glares down directly at my sex.

OMFG! My head spins. I am open and displayed for him, my arousal so strong I can smell myself. Is that gross? His nostrils flare… Uh, guess he can scent me too?

"Look at yourself." His grip tightens, "You're so wet, so ready. You want me, Princess?"

Gah, is that even a question? "I…" I open my mouth and his lips curl.

Trick question, huh? I pout again, thrust my pelvis up and against his hold.

His smile widens. "Hold yourself open for me," he commands.

I blink. He can't be serious.

"Do it," he snaps.

I don't even realize I've rushed to obey him until I feel my fingers brush my cunt. Damn him, is there anything this man can't get me to do? I pry open my pussy lips, and his gaze intensifies. "Fuck me," he mutters, "I am going to drink from you."

Yes. Yes.

"Scoop up your cum and offer it to me."

Wh-a-a-t? My vision narrows. Black spots dot my line of sight. My heart begins to pound so hard, I am sure it's going to break out of my chest.

"Now."

His hard voice whips through my head, erasing every other thought. I am a vessel, an empty canvas which he'll paint with his cum. No, what? *Don't think. Don't react. Do what he asks.* I slip one finger, then a second into my channel. My chest heaves. His throat moves as he swallows. He's as affected by this connection... This, whatever it is that he's doing to me, is arousing him just as much. I curl my fingers inside of myself and a moan rises up. It's nowhere close to what I need, but the way he watches me... How he follows my movements with his heavy-lidded gaze...is as erotic as looking on while he fucks me... Okay, I lie... Not the same... But it is hot nevertheless. Know what I mean? I hold up my glistening fingers, and he closes his mouth around my digits, drags his tongue over the skin. My sex clenches and more moisture pools in my core.

"How the hell do you taste so sweet?" He licks his lips, "Of chocolate and the most tempting honey."

"You hate chocolate," I mutter.

"That's true." He tilts his head, "But, it tastes different on you."

"It does?"

He nods. "It tastes like sin when I lick it off your lips."

"Oh." My belly quivers. That was almost poetic. *Gah!* Who'd have thought the brute could actually string words together until they sound erotic.

"In fact," he peers into my features, "I am convinced you have desserts for all three meals." He stares at me, "You do, don't you?"

"What do you think?"

"I bet you sneak that black gold in between, too." He lowers his gaze back to the triangle between my thighs, "Makes me wonder if you taste as incredible there as you did the last time..."

Why don't you try it for yourself; why don't you —? I gasp as he does just that—drops his head, licks me from arsehole to cunt, and again. He stabs his tongue inside my channel, and begins to drink from me. He slurps on me, licks my swollen nub, lavishes attention on it, then bites on it. Goosebumps flare on my skin; I arch my back off the table, push myself up and into his face. More, more. My fingers tingle. I itch to take my hands off my pussy, to grab hold of his hair and tug him to me, to force him to fuck me with his tongue until I come.

"Don't you dare."

I blink, to find him leaning above me.

"I'm not done yet."

What's he talking about? I'm done, more than done. I'm on the verge of exploding like a pie that's been left too long in the oven. Ugh, these comparisons are terrible, and my brain cells have turned to mush.

"Eyes on me," he commands.

I watch him as he lowers his chin, his unshaven whisker-edged visage, and rubs it up my pussy.

"Ah!" My entire body bucks. I writhe under his touch, thrash my head from side to side, "Oh, my God, oh, my God." He does it again and I see stars. The climax rushes up from my toes, screams up my spine, and threatens to explode. I can't stop, I can't.

The next second he straightens over me, positions his dick at my entrance. "Condom," he growls, then reaches into the back pocket of his pants, pulls out a wrapper.

Does he walk around with one all the time? Was he that confident that he was going to fuck me…? When the agreement was for us to do everything but? Will this change things between us? What will become of the money? Could I allow him to pay me after this…? Wouldn't that reduce everything between us to something it wasn't? What is it anyway, what —?

"Stop."

He frowns down into my face.

I draw in a breath. Am I that transparent? Or is he that perceptive? Does he have a sixth sense that he can focus on simultaneously wrapping his dick and reading my expression? What the hell am I thinking? Why am I tying myself up in such knots? I glance around... What the hell am I doing here, with him, holding my pussy open to him like a sex-crazed pervert? I withdraw my fingers from my cunt, open my mouth to speak. He leans in and presses his lips to mine. He swipes his tongue inside my mouth, across my teeth, draws from me, shares my breath so absolutely. I stutter.

He pulls back, peers into my face, "Do you want me to stop?"

Do I?

"Once I take you, there's no going back."

Uhhh?

"If you want to leave, I won't stop you."

Won't he?

"But if you stay..." he glares at me, "if you stay, you're mine."

23

Weston

"Mine to protect. Mine to possess and break. Mine to fuck so hard you won't walk straight for days, and when you do, you'll sense my cock in your deepest most intimate of places. I plan to not stop, not until we've fucked whatever is between us into the open, until my skin fuses with yours and I have invaded your secrets, gleaned your fears, and infused your innermost thoughts with my presence."

Her pupils dilate, and her face pales.

This is it then; she's going to refuse me. I've bared myself to her, told her what I am thinking about and she'll decide it's not for her. She's going to turn away from me, tell me she doesn't want me or my money. She's going to— She reaches out her hand, tugs at the condom I hold. She rips open the wrapper, then reaches down between us. She eases the condom over the swollen head of my cock, struggles with it. The condom slides over the rim and she smooths it down. I glance up to find her forehead furrowed in concentration. That line between her eyebrows crinkles. I lean down and press my lips to it. She positions my shaft at the entrance to her pussy.

"I want you," I mutter against her forehead. I press my lips to her eyelids, one after the other, to the tip of her nose, then press my mouth to hers, " I want to kiss you until your mouth can't ask for more." I nip on her chin. "Every part of you tastes of a different dessert."

She giggles and the sound is so light, so beautiful. My throat closes. I pull back enough to take in her features, watch her gaze widen as I kick my hips forward and impale her. Her mouth parts, a soundless scream that only I can hear. I wait for her pussy to adjust to my girth, for her channel to grip my dick, flow, melt, tug on my shaft. The tension builds at the base of my spine. Shit, I've never been so close to coming, so quickly before. The taste of her swirls on my tongue; the scent of her envelops my senses. I grip the backs of her thighs, drag my hand up one, then the other, urge her legs over my shoulders. "Hold on."

She nods, locks her ankles around my neck. I press my elbows to the table on either side of her head, then push in further. Her entire body seems to thrum; her eyelids flicker. She brings a hand up to my face. I turn my head and kiss her palm, then grip her wrist and twist her hand over her head. Her gaze widens and her breathing grows ragged. Fuck, if my little show of dominance didn't turn her on even more. I bring her other hand up, shackle both of her wrists with my uninjured hand.

I pull back, then thrust into her with enough force that the entire table jostles. Something—one of the plates, or both—crashes to the floor. I begin to fuck her in earnest. Pull back, push forward, back, forward again. With every plunge, her body moves up the table. I wrap my fingers around her neck, lean some of my weight on her to hold her in place. Her pupils dilate further, the blue so light, the color of her eyes seems to mirror mine. I see my reflection in them, sense the climax building inside of her. I squeeze my fingers around her neck, and she gasps. Her chest heaves. She digs her heels into my back, tugs her hands in my grasp. I pull back, all the way back to the edge of her channel, then tilt my hips and impale her with such force that her eyelids flutter, she throws her head back, arches her spine, and the trembling shudders up her body, her chest. "Come." I loosen my grasp and she shatters. Her pussy clamps around my dick and moisture bathes my shaft. Her orgasm seems to go on and on, and when her shoulders slump, sweat beads her forehead, her upper lip. I bend down, lick it off. She stirs.

"Eyes on me," I demand.

She cracks her eyelids open, locks her gaze with mine, and I begin to move again, thrust into her, angle my hips and sink deep inside of her. Bury myself in her sweet melting cunt again and again. She reaches up, locks her lips with mine, her eyes still on mine. Something hot stabs at my chest, my balls draw up, the tension in my groin snaps and I come inside her.

Her eyelids flutter; her body twitches. I pull back, just enough for our breaths to mingle, then stay there and watch as her muscles uncoil, one by one. I watch her as her breathing deepens. A flush creeps up her cheeks. When I pull out of her, she stirs. "Don't move," I whisper. Her lips curve. I pull off the condom, tie it up, then leave it on the table. I'll have to come back for it later.

I scoop her up in my arms, kick the door to the kitchen closed behind me, and carry her to the ensuite in the bedroom. I lower her to the floor near the tub, take in her curves. "You're gorgeous." I lean in to kiss her, before placing her in the shower stall.

"Your splint," she murmurs, "you'll get it wet."

"It's waterproof." I reassure her.

She wraps her arms around me, presses her nose into the skin bared by the 'V' of my shirt collar. "You smell like chocolate." She giggles.

I lower my chin and kiss her head, "And you smell of me."

"Mmm." She nuzzles against me and my heart begins to race. A tightness coils in my chest. Shit... This... Tenderness... This whatever connection is there between us... It is the beginning of the end. If I continue down this path, it leads to a slippery slope. One I have no intention of traversing. Not for a long time. If ever.

I pry her arms from round me, and step back.

She frowns.

"Gonna look in on Max," I say. "Why don't you shower first, huh?"

She peers up into my face, then nods.

I pivot, shrug out of my sodden pullover and pants and dump the clothes in the laundry basket on the way out.

Once in the kitchen, I dispose of the used condom, along with the remnants of her clothes. I clean up any chocolate within reach of his short, little legs, then top off the food and water bowls for Max, who scrabbles in and attacks the food like he's been starving. Speaking of, I need more of her. Fuck, this is ridiculous. I drag my fingers through my hair.

I've been away from her for a few minutes, and already, I miss her.

That sensation when I was inside her...? Fuck. It was...different, yet familiar. Like coming home. Home? What the fuck? I shake my head. So, the sex had been intense—more intense than any experience I've ever had before—it means we're compatible in bed. So, I'll fuck her, give her pleasure, make her orgasm more than she has ever before. I'll ensure her time with me is the single most incredible experience of her life, that it spoils her for any man after.

The band around my chest tightens. Of course, there'll be men after me... She isn't mine...except for the length of this time that I've bargained from her. For the days that are left, I can make good on my promise. I can protect her, take care of her every need, treat her like the princess she is. And when we are done... I'll walk away without a second thought.

I clench my fist at my side. Why the hell does it matter to me what she does after that, huh? I'll use her for my needs, then leave. It's what I do best. No commitments. Nothing holding me back. It will be a great break. I glance down at my hand with the splint... And the sex will, surely, only help the healing, huh? My heart hammers in my chest. So why the fuck am I standing here in the middle of the kitchen, still naked?

I straighten, march toward the door, when a scream sounds from the direction of the bedroom. I race forward.

24

———

Amelie

I stare at the spider that crawls across the floor. My skin feels too tight, my stomach twists in knots.

Shit, I can face grown chefs having a tantrum, or irate clients. Hell, I'd even face an alphahole who wanted to force me to submit. But the creepy, crawly, eight-legged species…? Gross. I could do without them. My pulse races, my heart hammers, and adrenaline fills my blood. I glance around, then spot the towel and snatch it up. I hold it out in front of me, sidle toward the exit, when footsteps sound and Weston's massive figure fills the doorway.

"What's wrong?" His chest heaves, his gaze alert. He has the fingers of his uninjured hand curled into a fist. Huh?

"The hell?" He stalks inside.

I glance down and scream again.

He flinches, "Jesus, woman, why are you having a breakdown?" He pauses mid-step.

"That…" I point my towel at the floor in front of him.

He glances down, then lowers his foot…missing the spider by an inch. A breath whooshes out of me.

"It's… it's…" I gulp.

"A spider?"

"Eek." I sidle back from both of them… "Please, can you get rid of it?"

He glances down at the bug, which scuttles toward me.

I scream, then dance around it in a wide circle that places me directly in front of Weston. "I hate those things," I whine.

"All that sass and spirit… I thought you were a spitfire, then along came a spider and frightened little Miss Muffet away."

I blink a little. "Did you just compare me to another nursery rhyme?"

"Can't seem to make up my mind about you, huh?" His warm palms descend on my hips. He lifts me up—like literally snatches me up from the floor—and plants me at his side.

My belly and other parts of me flutter. Shucks, every time I try to hate him…he disarms me…shows a part of him that unnerves me.

He grabs a tissue, scoops up the insect then heads for the doorway.

"Wh…where are you going?"

"To get Miss Muffet's spider outside."

"Oh." My cheeks heat. "Won't you be, ah…?" I look his gorgeous, unclothed figure up and down, and all thoughts leave my mind. OMFG, he's…hot. I mean, I knew he was and yep, he's had his cock and tongue and fingers inside of me… But when he flaunts his eight pack and those powerful thighs and the—uh!—all of him in full-frontal, then… Well…Uh, what am I trying to say? I blink.

"I'm beginning to think you prefer the sight of my dick to my face."

I jerk my chin up, "Nothing like that… I mean," I wave my palm in front of me, "yeah, I do… I mean, I like both… I mean…"

His chuckles at my blathering response. "Get in the shower," he orders. "I'll be back."

I shiver. He turns and stalks off, and I admit, I watch that tight, glorious arse of his until he's out of sight. Hell, I'm in a sex haze. And I admit, it's almost as good as the endorphins brought on by a choco-late binge… Okay, better… Surely, it must be the most pleasurable way of losing calories. At this rate, by New Year's, hopefully, I'll have lost some weight. I snort… Likely story. I only have to look at desserts for the pounds to kiss my thighs… Not that he'd complained…

I turn and survey my figure in the mirror—flushed face, reddened patches on my neck and chest… My breasts seem almost too big for my narrow waist and my hips.

But hey, at least, I look like I sample my desserts. I mean, imagine if I were reed-thin. And a dessert chef? I toss my head. That would send out the wrong signal, completely. I love my curves, okay… Normally… When I'm not having sudden bouts of self-doubt. Doesn't everyone have them?

I hear him talking to Max in the kitchen.

Shit, better get into the shower as alphahole had commanded. I head in that direction, then stop. *The hell am I doing?* Because he'd ordered me to… Would I give in and do what he'd asked? So, we had an arrangement… But won't that be null and void, considering we've slept together? I blow out a breath…

Well, then… Guess I'd better kiss the money goodbye, huh? My guts twist. Okay, so it means I am back where I started—debts to pay off, a business to run… Correction—a business I have nurtured with sweat and passion… and chocolate. I chuckle. A business which I've enjoyed building up. So what, if sometimes, when I'm bone-weary tired, I've wished I had someone by my side to share the load?

I am good at what I do. I don't need some bloody man to help shoulder the burden. Certainly, not a mean-as-hell, epitome of masculinity whose bearded chin is a potent weapon that can rub me to orgasm like Alladin's lamp. I snort out a half-laugh. Those stupid fairy tales and nursery rhymes that he often speaks in… It's getting to me. It's as bad as my pudding fetish.

I hear his footstep thudding down the hallway, and head for the bathtub instead. It's a small act of defiance, but hey, it's the best I can do. I reach over, plug the drain, then flip on the taps.

I am about to step in, then pause. I race to the sink, rummage around in the cabinet underneath… Aha! Bath bombs, and chocolate-flavored, at that… OMG… Yes! Half running back to the tub, I drop them in.

"What are you — ?"

I hear his voice taper off as I climb into the tub and stretch out.

The hair on my forearms rises and I tip up my chin to find him watching me through hooded eyes.

I cup my breasts and squeeze; his nostrils flare.

I drag my palms down my waist, to the space between my thighs.

He shakes his head.

I pause, "What?"

"Who does your pussy belong to?"

I swallow.

"Tell me, Princess." He lowers his voice to a hush. My nerve endings pop. "Say it," he insists. "Who owns your sweet cunt?"

"You," I swallow, "you do."

"Damn right." His lips curl and he jerks his chin.

I lean back in the tub.

"Spread your legs," he commands.

I am instantly wet, and it's not from the bath water, I assure you. Hell, he could ask me to eat strawberries instead of chocolate and I would… No… Not that. Anything but that. Honestly, I don't have anything against those fruits, but nothing comes between me and my chocolate, except… I peer up at him from under my eyelashes, "Why is it that only you get to tell me what to do?"

"Because, I can," he growls. "Because you promised to do everything I asked of you," he adds.

"And what about the fact that we already slept together?" I ask. "Doesn't that mean the agreement is void?"

"Fuck the agreement. I propose something new."

"You… you do?"

He nods.

"I'll pay you what I promised, as long as you let me fuck you."

25

Weston

Shut up, shut up. What the fuck are you saying? Why did you have to take everything that happened between the two of you and make it into something twisted?

Because I can? I tense my shoulders.

Because that last time I'd taken her, the way I had kissed her had been…different. *It had meant something… Don't ask me what… I have to figure that shit out, but holy fuck, that had gone beyond fucking…* It's the kind of experience you don't forget, which is why I am back here, watching as her gaze narrows. As she tightens her lips, as the color fades from her cheeks. As she swallows, then folds her arms around herself. "Excuse me?" Her voice is low but firm, "What did you say?"

"You heard me." I fold my arms over my chest, mirroring her… Because she's right, that NLP shit works… Why the hell am I echoing her words? I widen my stance, glance down at her, "I'll pay for the remaining time I bought from you, as long as I can —"

"Fuck me?"

I tilt my head. "I am not going to repeat myself."

She swallows, "So, this is it?" She hunches into herself, "That's all this is to you? A transaction?"

"I told you from the beginning, that's all it was." I lower my chin. "Wrong place, wrong time… Although, perhaps it was the right occasion for you, huh?" I drag my gaze down her body, pausing at her breasts, then at the gorgeous flesh between her legs. My dick throbs and my balls harden. Of course, I still want her. That hasn't changed. I'll have to do my best to get her out my system; there is no other way out. "Well?" I roll my shoulders, "What do you say?"

"Why are you doing this?" She stares. "Why are you suddenly conforming to your alphahole persona?"

"This is who I am." I raise my shoulders. "Deal with it."

"I don't believe it." The water rises up to over her breasts. "What happened in the last few seconds that you went from…?"

"Dominant?"

"With a heart…to an unfeeling brute who reduces everything to a transaction."

"If you thought everything that happened between us was anything but, you're wrong."

"I'm not." She brings up her knees, covering the sight of both her pussy and her breasts.

My fingertips tingle. *Lean over, pry those long thighs apart. Get in there with her, bury your face against her sweet cunt and bring her to orgasm. Make her forget everything that you said since you walked back in here.* I lock my thighs, dig my feet into the floor.

"What's different between how it was to what it is now?" I frown. "I was going to pay you. I am still paying you… Only now there's sex —the penetrative kind— thrown in for good measure." I shrug, like it means nothing to me.

She doesn't react. *Shit, that's not a good sign.* I'm not that blind; I know exactly how I affect her when I curl my lips and command her.

"Well?" I tap my toes, "You in or out?"

She swallows. "Don't do this," she whispers. "Don't reduce what we had into something it's not."

"You're the one who's making it out to be something different." I glare down at her. "Take it or leave it."

She pushes her forehead into her knees. "I… I can't do it."

My heart begins to thump. Sweat beads my forehead. *Shit, don't make her choose, you wanker. The hell are you doing pushing her away? You had it all…for a few seconds. You could have handled this differently, shown her exactly how much you care. You could have, for once in your fucked-up life, done the right thing.* Instead… I'd decided to go all billionaire alpha-hole on her… Because…face it, that's what I am. That's how I intend to stay, and no sassy, curvy, chocolate-scented, gorgeous woman like her is going to reveal the feelings that churn under the surface.

"Fine, then." I turn and stalk to the door, then pause. "I'll pay you for the two days you spent with me, and we leave tomorrow."

I pivot, move forward.

Wait for it. Wait for it.

"Hey," she calls out. "What did you mean? Where are we going?"

I turn, glance over my shoulder, "To meet my family of course."

"It's not yet Christmas." She rises to her feet and the water flows from her shoulders down her waist, to splash onto the almost-filled bath tub. Her blonde hair curls over her forehead, sticks to her shoulders. The scent of…chocolate — of course, what else — laced with something honeyed and spicy swirls through the air.

"It's almost Christmas." I raise a shoulder.

"It's not the same," she scowls.

"It is now," I curl my lips, "because I say so."

She swallows, "And if I say no?"

"Are you saying no?" I glare at her.

She pales, opens her mouth.

I shake my head.

She purses her lips shut.

"Well?" I snap.

"No," she replies.

"What?" I growl.

"No, I'm not saying no." She winces, "I mean, yes, I'll come with you to meet your family. But that New Year's Eve thing? You can forget that."

I glower at her.

She juts out her chin, snaps back her shoulders, and doesn't blink.

Bloody hell, that sass of hers is back, thank fuck. Damn, if I don't hate it when her spirit is cowed.

"Fine."

"Fine." She tosses her head.

I turn.

She calls out again, "But the roads, the storm..."

I can't stop the grin that splits my face.

I wipe it off of my face, turn, "What storm?"

"Uh, the one that caused the roads to close and the electricity —"

The overhead lights come on and she blinks. The brightness pours over us, envelops us, cuts the space between us as if it's a barrier. How strange. Apparently, this time, the darkness had been kinder.

"Oh, and Princess?"

She angles her head.

"Shut off the tap, will you?"

26

"Life is uncertain; eat dessert first."
-From Amelie's diary

Amelie

I stare through the window from the backseat of the luxurious SUV. We'd left early this morning, heading toward the outskirts of Durham, where Weston's family home is.

Max whines from the back. I turn around and pat his head. Weston has his faults, but he hasn't stinted when it comes to Max. The car has a specially fitted pet booster seat in the rear, complete with a tether attached to his harness to keep him safe. Max licks my hand, then turns to glance out of the window. I swear, the puppy is more human than many of the two-legged variety of animals I've met… Present company included, of course. I shoot a sideways glance at the man in the seat next to me. His hair brushes against his collar, his beard seemingly fuller than what it was a few hours ago... Is he sprouting hair by the minute? Does it mean when he drags those whiskers across my pussy it will feel more intense than before? Ha, not possible. Whoever had said that once you go beard, you don't go back, was bloody right.

He raises his hand and drags his fingers through that hair on his chin. I gulp, then squeeze my thighs together. *Come on, you can't be turned on by that simple act.* I wriggle around in my seat. *Get a life, woman. He misled you, remember? Made you think there was a storm outside that kept you marooned in the cabin, without electricity, when there was nothing of the kind taking place.*

"What else did you lie to me about?" I mumble.

After that break-up in the bathroom... Could it be qualified as a break-up when we were never really together? Sure, in the carnal sense, I mean, but there was never any relationship between us, was there...?

Well, after the end of that relationship that never was and which shall never again be referred to by me, I'd stood there dumbstruck and naked and in the bath tub. The water had spilt over the sides and I had scrambled to shut off the tap. Of course, the alphahole had had the last say there, as well. Damn, but I hate the man. Hate his superiority complex, hate how, without even trying, he'd managed to turn my life upside down.

"What do you mean?" his voice rumbles over me. His presence thrums in that enclosed space. His larger-than-life persona pushes down on my shoulders, keeps me pinned to my side of the back seat.

"The storm," I mutter, "you lied to me."

"Not my fault you didn't check the weather."

"My phone didn't have a signal..." I bite the inside of my cheek. I could have tried harder. I could have checked online when I'd called Isla from the bathtub. Bloody bath tub; I hate bath tubs.

I'd clambered over the side of the tub, almost slipped and fallen, dried myself off, wrapped a towel around myself.

For the rest of the day we'd ignored each other. I'd made grilled sandwiches for lunch and we'd eaten them separately. I'd spent the rest of the day avoiding him... Cleaning the house... Or at least, trying to.

Dinner had been soup and a pasta dish, the ingredients available, thanks to our trip to the supermarket. We'd eaten together at the dining table in the kitchen. He'd offered to help load up the dishwasher. I'd refused. And he'd headed outdoors with Max. I was reading in the living room, when he'd come in. He'd ignored me, headed off to the bedroom.

By the time I'd gone to bed, jerkface was under the covers…on his side of the bed, the white sheets pulled up to his waist, his sculpted chest all angles and planes, his biceps bulging from where he'd folded his arm behind his neck.

I'd almost crawled into bed right then, and cuddled up next to him… Not. Thankfully, I'd managed to retrieve my clothes from my bag, marched back into the bathroom to change. Dressed in pajamas and socks, I'd slipped between the sheets, after building a virtual fort between us with pillows and cushions. I'd fallen asleep almost at once… At least the sex had worn me out… Fringe benefits. I snort aloud.

"Care to share your thoughts?" he drawls. That voice… Dark and edgy and with an hint of mystery that had entranced me from the beginning, ripples down my spine. My nipples harden and my toes curl. I clutch my handbag to my chest. Hopefully, it will hide exactly how turned on I am. *Gah!* This is so not fair.

I rub at my temples, shake my head. "It's nothing," I respond.

"It's something." I sense him turn to me and tip my head so my heavy hair falls over my face. Anything to hide from him.

"Nothing of consequence," I insist.

"Whatever is in that bag, seems to be of consequence though."

I blink, shift the bag into a more comfortable position. "It's—"

"Don't say nothing," he growls.

"Cookies."

"Huh?" His forehead furrows.

"I baked cookies," I explain.

"Cookies?" He seems taken aback, "You made cookies?"

"We are going to see your family. I am a baker…" I raise my shoulders.

"That's why you were up early this morning?"

I nod. I'd remembered to charge my phone, and set an alarm, and woken up a few minutes before it had gone off. Guess those years of getting up before dawn and heading off to get my baking done for the day had come in handy. I'd switched off the alarm, crawled out of bed and out from under the weight of his arm.

He'd shoved aside the pillows at some point in the night and had pulled my body against his, and spooned me... No wonder I had slept well. I had turned and seen his features relaxed in sleep. His beard had seemed thicker, his pecs closer to a work of art, and that beautiful throat...that gorgeous throat... I'd moved in to inhale his scent at the base of his neck, where it would be the most potent. He'd stirred. I'd frozen. His muscles had relaxed and I'd scrambled off the bed. Lucky escape...

Was it, though? If he'd woken up then, would he have...taken me over his lap and spanked me? My sex clenches. I squeeze my thighs shut. Dip into my bag and pull out the tin—I'd emptied out the contents and repurposed it. I pop the lid and the scent of vanilla and chocolate, and the touch of cinnamon I'd sprinkled on at the end, fills the space.

He reaches for one; I slap the lid on his fingers.

"Ow." He pulls back, shakes out his hand, "Do you want to break a finger in my good hand?"

"Did I succeed?" I bare my teeth.

"It'll take more than a batch of your cookies to bring me down," he retorts.

"Don't bet on it," I scoff.

"Hmm," he glares at the tin, then at my face, "my mother doesn't expect gifts."

"It's Christmas."

"My presence is gift enough."

My jaw drops, "Do you seriously believe that?"

"It's what she insists, every time."

"Of course, she'd say that. She's your mom, after all. Doesn't mean you shouldn't get them anything. Besides..." I peer up at him.

"Besides...?" he prompts.

"Besides, after spending time with you, I can vouch that your presence is less a gift and more of an unwelcome surprise." I snicker.

"Har har." He scowls. "Feeling cheeky this morning, are we?"

"Feeling grumpy, as always, I see?" I shake my head, "You could collapse soufflé, just by your proximity."

He stares at me. "What-fucking-ever."

"That so eloquent. Impressive go-to-word for Mr A-holasaurus." I snort.

"Woman, your metaphors are —"

"Stupid?"

"Creative." He nods, "I'll give you this round."

"Ooh." I hold up my fist.

He glares at me.

"Fist bump. Come on, come on," I coax him.

"Nope." He holds up his right hand, with the upright middle finger, "Injured, remember?"

"Aww." I deflate like the bloody soufflé I'd mentioned, and crap, now I'm hungry.

"Coming back to the topic at hand," he continues. "You could have bought my mother something on the way. We could have stopped at one of the stores in town."

"I believe in the personal touch," I retort. "Unlike you."

"Oh, trust me, when it comes to you, my touch is as personal as it gets." He smirks.

I draw in a breath. Patience, patience. Don't react. *He's being this…overt to get a rise out of you. Don't stoop to his level… Can I be at eye-level with his crotch-candy though?… Eeeeagh, I did not think that.*

I lower my chin, hiding behind my thick fall of hair. "Has your family always lived in Durham?"

He sighs loudly, then leans back.

Whew! Dodged that one. After how he'd pulled that cheap stunt of lying about the storm, I should seriously have been angrier… But for some reason…I'm not. Maybe I'm flattered that he lied to ensure I'd comply with his plan. But…what else did he lie about? I chew on my lower lip.

"My mother moved there after my siblings and I left home. I grew up in London," he explains. "After the incident..." he pauses.

I hold my breath. *Is he going to tell me about himself? Is he going to share a little more of what goes on behind those colorless eyes of his?* Weston doesn't come across as closed off... But his demeanor...that hard outlook of his hides so many secrets. I turn to him, "The kidnapping you mean?"

He nods, then rotates his neck from side to side, "I was one of the lucky ones. My parents rallied around me. Even my asshole of an older brother became protective for a period of time. And my younger sister? Well... She sensed something was amiss. She'd crawl into bed every night and comfort me while I sobbed myself to sleep."

"You...cried every night?"

"I was twelve." His lips twist. "The incident forced me grow up fast... But at night, when I couldn't hide from myself anymore, the demons would come out to play. I don't think I have slept properly since ... Until..." He trails off, then turns to me, a strange look on his face.

My throat dries. "Until?" I prompt.

"Until that first night in the cabin, when I spooned you in bed."

My cheeks flush. I turn, crack open the window, and the outside air rushes in. "Why are you telling me this now?"

"No reason," his voice is emotionless.

I turn to find he's staring ahead.

"Not long now," he says in that same colorless tone.

Right, guess that's me being put in my place, huh?

"Did they hurt you?"

"Who?"

I frown, "The...men who kidnapped you with the rest of the Seven."

"Are you really interested in finding out about it?"

I open my mouth, then shut it. "Guess not." I turn away once more, ball my fingers into fists, "I'm trying to be polite, that's all."

"Don't be."

I swallow, "We're going to see your family. We should, at least, put on a veneer of politeness."

"My mother would prefer it if we were to speak our minds; she can spot something fake from a mile off."

I turn on him, "And you think we can get away with…" I point between us, "this?"

His lips stretch in a smile that is not one at all, "Why do you think I asked you and not someone else?"

"I don't understand."

He turns, trains the full force of those grey-silver eyes on me, "There's enough chemistry between us to pull this off."

I open my mouth.

He raises his hand, "Don't deny it. We may not be able to stand each other, but you know what they say?"

"What?"

"There's a thin line between hate and a connection."

What a condescending jerk.

"From where I am, it's a 100% loathing," I force out the words.

"Good."

"Eh?"

"It'll seem realistic, after all. Nothing like make-up sex to cement a relationship, huh?"

27

Weston

*Make-up sex? What the fuck am I talking about? Clearly this entire idea —
which I'd pulled out of my arse, by the way — is a bad one.*

The SUV crawls up the driveway of the Victorian house on the
outskirts of Durham where my mother lives. The ivy covers most of
the west wing, the leaves a burned red this time of the year.

The vehicle stops in front of the steps leading up to the house.

Before my driver can come around, she's pushed open the door
and is hopping out. She opens the passenger door, hauls Max into
her arms.

"I have his leash." I frown.

"I'm going to carry the little fella."

Right.

She hauls him closer to her face, "Hey baby, missed me, boy?"

Max licks her nose, her chin.

She laughs.

I scowl.

How dare another male intrude on my territory?

I growl deep in my throat.

Both Max and Amelie turn to me.

"Did you just growl?"

"So?" I glare at her.

She bites her lips, "Uh, you don't have to be jealous of Max." She tips her nose up.

"Me?" I laugh, "Woman, you are delusional."

"Now who's lying?" she scoffs.

"You seriously need to stop being obsessed with me."

She gapes at me, "You know what? This conversation is pointless." She straightens and stalks around the car, heading for the stairs. The dress she's wearing flies up and exposes a flash of her creamy thigh. She takes the steps, and I notice the dark line running up the back of her stockings. My dick twitches, my groin hardens, and this is so, not the fucking time. I don't want to walk into my family's home sporting a hard on.

I adjust myself, then duck out of the car.

Peter—Sinclair's chauffeur who's working with me since Sinclair is away, and because my finger's still bloody busted—walks around to pop open the lid of the trunk.

I turn and stalk her as she walks up the steps to the front door.

"She keeps you on your toes, huh?" Peter asks.

I tilt my head.

"The two of you remind me of how it was with Mr. Sterling and Ms. Summer before they got together."

"You're mistaken." I scowl, "There's nothing like that."

He places both of Amelie's suitcases, and a considerably smaller suitcase —i.e. mine—on the ground; he slaps the trunk shut.

I frown down at Amelie's pink frothy wardrobe on wheels. "You'd think she were packing for a month instead of two nights."

He chuckles, then reaches for the suitcase, but I shake my head, "I'll carry her load."

He peers up at me, "You do that, Sir."

I frown, open my mouth to ask what he means, but he's already walked off, with the rest of the luggage.

What-fucking-ever. My brain cells are, clearly, not functioning at full force, which is why I'd read between the lines. He didn't mean anything by that… He didn't. Did he?

I shake my head and follow Peter up the steps to where she stands, at an angle to the door.

I dump the bag, pause next to her, "Couldn't you have packed more sensibly?"

She turns to me, an expression of almost comical consternation on her face, "No. I need it all. I mean, you weren't helpful at all, gave me no pointers on what to wear, or what to expect, so I had to make sure I had all of my emergency clothes on hand."

"And that?" I point to the chef's toolkit that she has slung over her other shoulder.

She tucks it under her arm. "I don't go anywhere without this."

"Right." I drag my fingers through my hair, "Look, maybe this wasn't a good idea after all, I mean —"

The door opens. "Weston," my sister's voice calls out.

Next to me, Amelie stiffens. She swallows, clutches at her handbag. The skin stretches white across her knuckles. I should revel in her nervousness, in how out of her depth she seems. I mean, isn't that the point of this entire charade, to show her who is more superior in this relationship? *Is there a relationship between us? And who, exactly, is out of their depth? Her? Or me?*

I grip her shoulder. She peers up at me, and I hold her gaze before saying softly, "It will be fine." *What will be fine? Why the hell am I trying to put her at ease?*

She parts her lips, and fuck it, I can't resist. I lower my head and brush my mouth over hers. She draws in a breath and I deepen the kiss. Swipe my tongue inside to tangle with hers, draw of that chocolate and honey taste of hers. My head spins.

I break the kiss, survey her face. Flushed cheeks, dazed eyes. She blinks, sways. Good, that should take her mind off of the upcoming ordeal — I mean, the family stuff. Not that I don't want to spend time with them, but so many people all at once, can be a little overwhelming, especially since my family doesn't take shit from me.

There's a commotion behind me, then, "Unca Wes." Arms wrap around my legs. I glance down at my niece.

"Present... Christmas." The little imp smiles up at me. Well, one of us has our priorities right, at least.

"Phoenix," my sister calls out to her daughter, "let Uncle Wes and his friend inside the house, at least, and it's impolite to ask him what he's got for you. Speaking of," she turns to me, "I didn't realize you were bringing a guest." She looks between us.

Amelie's body goes even more rigid; she turns to me, "You didn't tell them?" Her gaze narrows on me and color flushes her cheeks.

Oh, this is going to be so much fun. That thing about keeping her off kilter? I intend to deliver on that.

"I like to be spontaneous," I allow my lips to curve.

Amelie makes a sound deep into her throat.

I train my gaze on my sister, "Kirsten this is Amelie. Amelie...this is my younger sister, Kirsten."

"Amelie," Kirsten's eyes bob between us. She shuffles her feet in that manner which is a dead giveaway that she's dying to quiz me... Not that I am going to allow that.

Max barks from his vantage point against Amelie's breasts. I seriously needed to have a man-to-man with that pooch.

Phoenix tugs on my hand. "Moosic..." she chants, "mooooosic."

"Hey, honey." I release my hold on Amelie, then bend to swing Phoenix up in my arms.

The little girl giggles, "Mooooosic."

"Music?" I turn to Kirsten for help.

"Yea, music," Kirsten sighs. "She's driving us mad with her music blocks."

"Moooosic bo-k-ssss," Phoenix warbles. "Unca Wezz."

I chuck her under her chin and she giggles. "Play...play... Unca Wezz."

Right.

I glance toward Amelie, who smiles at the little girl. "Hey, baby doll," she coos, "What's your name?"

Phoenix blinks at Amelie, then holds out her arms.

"Oh." Amelie looks at Phoenix, then at me.

I reach over, fasten Max's leash to his collar. "Told ya so," I whisper into her ear.

She scowls, lowers Max to the floor, and her handbag slides down her arm.

"Let me get that." I grab the bag before it hits the floor.

Then I straighten and hand Phoenix over to her. Amelie cuddles Phoenix, and her other bag—the chef's toolkit—bumps her back. I reach for it; Amelie frowns.

"You can trust me," I snicker.

She raises one eyebrow, "Can I?"

"Of course, Sweetheart." I raise one eyebrow.

She opens her mouth, to protest, no doubt. I lean down, press another kiss to her lips, and slide the bag off of her shoulder in the same move.

I step back, swinging her chef's satchel over my other shoulder.

"Smooth," Kirsten laughs.

"Doggy," Phoenix pants.

Max woofs, wags his tail, pawing at Amelie as he tries to get to the little girl.

"Wait...." Amelie protests. Phoenix pats her cheek. Amelie glances down at her and her face breaks into a smile. "Hey pumpkin, what's your name?"

"Phe," she grins, jumping a little in Amelie's arms.

Amelie props her on her hip, "Hey, Phe." Amelie's smile widens, "Whatcha wearing on your head."

Phoenix touches the unicorn shaped hairband, "Pepper."

"Good name." She leans in closer, "What about your friend behind you?"

Phoenix gazes at her wide-eyed, "You...can see him?" She gulps.

"Yep, I can. What's his name?"

"Jack." Phoenix bobs her head, "Jack. Jack."

"Jack?" I turn to Kirsten.

Kirsten nods. "He's imaginary," she says in a low voice.

"Ah." I glance back at the woman, who bends her glossy blonde head toward the dark blonde-haired kid. Something hot stabs at my chest.

"You want one of your own, huh?" Kirsten nudges me.

"What?" I turn to her, "Of course, not."

Kirsten tilts her head, "Hmm." She looks me up and down. Seeing...what? The bags over my shoulders, the dog straining at the leash, the other end of which I hold onto with my uninjured hand...

I scowl at her, "You have a weird look on your face."

"I am not the one who's changed." She grins, then reaches up to pat my cheek. "Finally," she titters, "I can't tell you how I was looking forward to this day."

"You are not making any sense," I grumble.

"It's normal—so much happening in so little time," she waggles her head, "but when it's right, it's right, you know?"

"No," I glower.

The fuck is wrong with my sister? Had I grown another head on my way here?

"Hey," a new voice mumbles. I glance up as my eleven year old niece ambles into the room.

"Skye." I hold out my fist. "Whassup?"

She walks over, ignores me, then frowns at Amelie, "Who're you?"

"Skye!" Kirsten exclaims. "You apologize right now to Amelie, you hear me?"

Skye rolls her eyes, then sighs, "Yeah, fine, whatever. Sorry... Amelie. Pleased to meet you, Amelie. Hey, Uncle Wes." She tosses her head. "There," she jerks her chin in Kirsten's direction. "Happy now?" She turns on her heel and flounces off.

"Whoa." I blink. "What happened there?"

"Sorry." Kirsten turns red. "She's already turning into a teenager. I shudder to think how she's going to be in a few years' time."

She crosses over to Amelie, "Let's get you inside." She holds out her arms to Phoenix, who jumps back into Kirsten's arms.

"Mommy!" Phoenix throws her arms around Kirsten's neck, then strains in her grasp to peer at Max, "Doggy, doggy, play...play."

Kirsten lowers the little girl to the ground, "Come on, let's go in." She hitches her arm through Amelie's, "Was the trip okay?"

The three of them walk in.

I stare after them, then down at Max, who whines, and strains at his leash. Amelie's bag slides down to the crook of my arm. How the hell did I get stuck with this? Brilliant surgeon? Check. Obnoxious billionaire? You bet. Carrying my girlfriend's luggage into my family home? Wh-a-t? Time for a reality check. Why the fuck did I think this was a good idea? Who suggested this? Oh, wait, that was me.

Peter walks out. He glances down at the pink suitcase then at me,

"Keep this the fuck to yourself," I mutter. "Not a word to the rest of the Seven."

He chuckles, then schools his expression into one of indifference. "Of course, Sir, you can trust my discretion."

What-fucking-ever. I stalk forward, my progress somewhat impeded by the blasted tank on wheels that I pull along.

"Oh, Sir?"

I turn.

"The pink brings out the blonde in your beard."

Peter walks off.

Blonde hairs in my beard? I don't have blonde hairs in my beard. The only blonde hair my beard has been close to...is her pussy hair. Those luscious lower lips of hers that had indicated that she was a natural blonde, and fuck me, if that hadn't been a turn-on. My dick twitches in agreement. I pause. Nope, not going there. The last thing I need is walking in with a chub the size of England in my pants. I shake my head, and follow Max into the house. Of course, the bloody pooch has to lead the way.

He barks, tugs on his leash, which slips from my hand, He darts forward.

"Max." I quicken my pace.

Footsteps approach down the curved stairwell.

"Weston," a woman's voice calls out.

I pause, turn toward the woman who walks down the steps, the first love of my life, the one woman who has my complete irrevocable devotion.

I smile up at her.

Her features light up, "You came."

28

Amelie

I hear the sound of barking, the patter of nails on the wooden floor. I turn as Max races toward me, his leash dragging behind. "Hey, you." I bend down to pet the little guy, who jumps up and licks my face as if he hadn't done the same thing not five minutes ago. "Down, boy," I laugh.

Phoenix squats down to rub the puppy's back, "Doggy," she squeals. "Love doggy." She holds out her arms to Max, who jumps on her; the two collapse on the floor in a flurry of arms and legs and doggy barks and little girl exclamations of delight. My smile widens so big that my cheeks hurt. Damn, I love this. What are little girls made of? Sugar and spice and puppy dog tails. Ha! Why should only little boys have the right to dogs, huh? Talk about my own spin on the ol' nursery rhyme.

The hair on the back of my neck prickles. I glance up to find Weston walking forward to greet a woman approaching him. She's wearing a beautiful peacock-green colored dress that flows to below her knee.

He bends and kisses her cheek, "Mother."

I straighten, holding onto Max's leash. So, this is his Mum? Guess alphaholes have parents too… I mean, of course they do; it's just difficult to imagine Weston as a small boy…vulnerable and innocent.

She reaches up to touch his face, "Why do you look different?"

He frowns down at her, "It's the beard, perhaps?"

She tilts her head, the gesture so similar to Weston's, my throat closes. There's no doubt about the blood relationship between the two.

"That's not it." She steps back, takes him in, "It's not the handbag you're carrying either." She giggles.

He shuffles his feet. I blink. I mean, I've never seen him this uncomfortable before. I stifle the giggle that rises up. Trust a mom to put her son in his place huh?

He straightens and turns to me.

I stiffen. Not that I am doing anything wrong, but I bet it seems like I was staring at him, which I wasn't. Okay, I was. I clutch Max's leash. He whines, pulls toward Weston. "Shh, Max," I whisper to him, "Not now."

Weston turns to me; he jerks his chin.

I shake my head.

He glares at me.

I pale.

He holds out his hand.

I sigh. Okay, hell, I'd been hoping to put off this meeting with his family… Not that they are my in-laws or anything, but authority figures of any kind? I run a mile. And not because my own Ma was a strict disciplinarian—okay, maybe it is that. It doesn't take a shrink to tell me my issues with not wanting to conform have to do with my home and the convent school I was educated in. Yeah, the nuns wouldn't be happy with how I've turned out. I purse my lips.

"Amelie," Weston's tone lowers to a hush. To anyone else, I'll bet it sounds normal, but damn, if I don't recognize the demand in it. Shit, I'd left home because I wanted to be independent, I thought… Until I met him, and the kind of disciplining Weston has in mind… Hell, if I don't respond to it from that place deep inside that had resisted being told what to do. My head spins. Is that why I want his kind of dominance? Because I had hankered for it... A structure that imposes boundaries within which I can be myself... Had I held onto the illusion of control until I met a man who I trusted enough to hand it over to? Is that man Weston? I gulp.

Weston frowns, "You okay?" I hear his voice across the short distance.

Max whines, brushes against my leg. I bend, scratch his ear, then straighten. Best to treat this like breaking an egg. Just aim for the center, tap it against the side of the bowl, do your best... Either way it's going to break, you just want to be around to catch the yolk. Me and my stupid metaphors. I walk forward, Max straining at the leash.

When I reach them, I pause. "I'm Amelie." I hold out my hand, "Pleased to meet you."

Weston's mother smiles. The lines etched around her eyes deepen. "What a pretty name."

She takes my hand between both of hers.

"That's very kind of you to say so," I reply, schooling my features into a neutral expression, "and thank you for having me."

Max yelps, she glances at him, and her face breaks into a broad grin. Her features brighten and those grey eyes sparkle. The resemblance between her and Weston becomes more pronounced. Strange, huh? Considering Mr Grumpy-grump's face rarely wears an expression that's not borderline angry.

"And who's this?"

"Max," I reply.

She releases my hand, bends down to pat the puppy. He wags his tail, jumps up at her.

"Is he yours?"

"Uh, he belongs to my friend Summer and her husband."

"Ah, the Sinclairs." She straightens, "Is that how the two of you met?"

"Yes," I say.

"No," Weston declares.

We stare at each other, for a beat, another. I scowl at him. This is what happens when you don't get your stories right. And jerkalope here, didn't want to talk about it before-hand.

I tuck my elbows into my side, open my eyes wide, stare at the alphahole. *He got us into this one, he can dig us out of it. This should be good.*

His mother chuckles, "Which is it, then?"

"I saw her shopping for groceries at my local supermarket. She was talking to herself as she decided which brand of chocolate to buy for baking, and that was it."

"Oh," I blink. *Damn, but he sounds so sincere. I almost believe it myself.*

"Ah." His mother nods. "Chocolate and sex—the unbeatable combination."

"Wha—?" I gape at her.

"Mother," Weston admonishes.

She laughs, "It's not like you were conceived through immaculate conception." She chuckles and looks at me, "I hope I didn't shock you."

"No…Yes." I chew the inside of my cheek, "I mean, it's not shocking, except it came from you, so…"

"Ah," she grins, "you mean from a woman in her fifties. We're supposed to know our place, take care of our grandkids, and leave the running of the world to our husbands and sons."

I hunch my shoulders. Shit, what is the right response here, "No, I think it's women, and especially those in the prime of their life, who have brought up children to face the world, and who have stood by their men, supported them while following their own passions, who wield the power."

She tilts her head, then laughs. "Good save." She chuckles, "Call me Rosie." She pulls me in for a hug.

I take it. "Rosie." I nod.

Phew! Guess I passed that test… Whatever that was.

She releases me, and steps back, "You can take him off the leash, dear."

I stare at her.

"Weston, I mean." Her eyes twinkle.

"Ah," I open and shut my mouth.

"Just messing with you," she chuckles, then glances at Max.

Right. Is that where Weston gets his warped sense of humor, not to mention his dominance?

I unhook the leash from Max's collar. Max bounds off, toward the living space at the far end of the hallway, following the sound of Phoenix's laughter.

I twist the leash around my palm, wondering what to do with it. Weston places his hand on mine; I look up. One side of his lips kicks up. Is that supposed to be reassuring? The warmth from his touch sinks into my blood. I draw in a breath and my heartbeat slows. How strange. This man... Who I am not sure how to react to... Who I am sure I hate... Who I have definite feelings for... When did his presence become so reassuring?

He twines his fingers with mine and the leash slips from my grasp. He catches it, glances around. A maid wearing a uniform materializes. Huh? Of course, they'd have staff. They are rich and the house... Well, it seems the kind that has been in their family for generations. "Master Weston?" The older woman smiles.

"Mary, how are you?" He hands the leash over to her.

"I'm very good, Sir." Her smile widens. "The luggage has been sent to your suite already," she adds.

"Excellent," he grins at her.

Wow. That's two smiles in as many minutes. Seems the alphahole can lose the obnoxiousness on occasion... Just not with me.

"How is Veronica?" he asks Mary.

"Grown up and at university. She has her own life now."

"You miss her, huh?"

Mary raises her shoulders, "Always. But I'm also glad to have her out of my hair." She chuckles.

She turns to Rosie, "Dinner is served Ma'am."

Rosie touches my arm, "Shall we?"

29

Weston

"You're not sleeping on the couch." I growl at her.

Dinner had been mercifully quiet. Kirsten had taken Phe and Skye up to get them ready for bed. Max had mercifully tagged along, not wanting to part from the girls.

Which means we are alone, in my room, and I intend to take full advantage of that.

"Excuse me?" She frowns up at me.

"You heard me," I drawl. "Get your sweet tush into bed." I jerk my thumb over my shoulder, pointing at the massive four-poster that occupies the center of the room.

"We are not together; this is all a farce." She glowers, "Have you forgotten that you wanted me to come here to put on a front with your family? I have done that, and now I want some privacy."

"No." I fold my arms over chest.

She gapes, "What…what do you mean?"

"Exactly that." I glance down my nose at her, "We need to keep up the pretense."

"In here?" She glances around the spacious suite that takes up the entire top floor of the house. It also comes equipped with its own kitchen, a fact I had pointed out to her earlier. Why was that? Why does it matter to me that she feels at home in this space? I shake my head, narrow my gaze on the woman who scowls up at me.

"No-one's going to come in here," she insists.

"You don't know that. One slip-up, and this entire charade will amount to nothing."

"That's all this is—a farce." She juts out a hip, props her hand on it, "So why the hell can't you allow me to sleep on my own?"

"Because..." *You're mine,* is what I want to say, but fuck that. I have no claim to her. I can't call her mine. I don't want to have any relationship with her, do I? So why the hell am I being this unreasonable? I crack my neck, draw in a breath, "As long as you are here, under my roof, you do as I say."

"It's not your roof," she growls.

"It belongs to my family," I retort.

"I don't care."

"You should, because in one second you are going to be breaking a record, one that you'll remember for the rest of your life."

She balks, "Wh...what do you mean?"

"Just try to walk out of that door, and I'll have you on your back and make you orgasm so fast, and so many times, that you'll forget all about the world outside this bedroom."

Her chest heaves, her face pales, she swallows hard, and clenches her fists by her sides, "You wouldn't dare."

"You know better than to challenge me, Princess."

"I'm not your princess."

"You're right," I look her up and down, "you're the woman I am paying to keep me company."

She falters, then pulls her shoulders back, "You forget that we no longer have an arrangement."

"So why are you here?"

She bites the inside of her cheek, "Because..."

"Because?"

"Uh, I didn't want you to let your family down."

"Bull-fucking-shit," my words crackle through the space.

She winces. "Keep your voice down," she hisses at me. "You may not care about your family hearing us, but I do."

"The walls of this suite are thick enough for you to scream all night long and no one would notice."

She swallows, twists her fingers together, "You're lying."

"Want to try it out, hmm?" I take a step toward her; she skitters back.

I tilt my head.

She holds my gaze.

I widen my stance.

She tips her chin, "You…you don't scare me."

"So you keep saying."

"We are here with your family; your sister and nieces are sleeping on the floor below. You won't try anything with them so close."

"You think I'll stop because of that?"

"I saw you with them, Weston." She narrows her gaze, "You respect your mother, you love your nieces, you'd do anything to protect your sister… You're not half as much of an unfeeling man as you make yourself out to be."

"You're right about that."

"I… I am?"

I nod, "I'm much worse." I lunge forward.

She screams, pivots, then makes a run for the door.

I swoop down toward her, grab her across the waist and throw her over my shoulder.

"Let me go, you oaf," she yells.

I stalk toward the bed.

She wriggles, brings her fists down on my back. The jolt travels down to my cock, which is already erect. Is it wrong that I am getting off on her struggle? On her curvy butt that wriggles so near my face. I tilt my head to nuzzle the side of her hips.

She stills. "Did you…" Her voice cracks, "Did you just do what I think, you did?"

I bring down my hand on her arse.

She howls, "What the fuck?"

"Language, Princess." I smirk, "And don't question me again."

Her body tenses, all of her of muscles coil, and tension rolls off of her in waves. *Wait for it. Wait for it.* She bucks her body, then digs her knee into my chest with enough force that my breath catches. She lowers her head, buries her teeth in my back. Pin pricks of pain race from the contact. My dick throbs and my groin hardens. I change direction and head for the ensuite bath.

"The hell are you doing?" she yells again.

"Not so worried about waking up the family now, huh?" I chuckle.

"You douche, how dare you use your strength against me?"

"Because I like to play dirty?" *Because I am losing my mind, that's why.* The thought of her walking out of here, never looking back… Hell no. My chest tightens. No way, am I letting that happen. And it's not my ego speaking… It's the fear that I'll never see her again. Never scent her gorgeous essence, never hold her curves, bury myself in her sweet cunt; never pit my will against hers. I stumble, then right myself.

The challenge… That's what attracted me to her. It's why I keep taunting her, trying to get a rise out of her, and why I can't let go of her either. What do I want to do with her? I want to get a rise out of her. Revel in her spirit, that fire inside of her that could burn through my past, rejuvenate me, give me a reason to move forward. I want to live fully, to feel for the first time in my life. I want her. Only her. I march into the bathroom, turn on the shower.

"Let go of me," her scream slices through my ear drum.

"Stop that," I growl.

"You stop what you're doing and release me this instant."

"Your wish is my command." I swing her around, plonk her down under the shower. She opens her mouth and the water pelts her face. Her scream is cut off in a series of unintelligible words.

"I can't hear you," I taunt.

She kicks out, I angle away, and she tips over.

I grasp her shoulder and keep her upright.

She swings at me, connects with the arm of my injured hand. Pain explodes behind my eyes.

"Fuck!"

I loosen my grip and she throws herself at me. Her weight connects with my chest. I stagger back, hit the wall of the shower cubicle. She hooks her leg around my waist, hauls herself up, and climbs me like she's a cat and I am her personal scratching post... Fuck. She lowers her head, digs her teeth into my neck, on the side of my injured finger.

"You little hellion!" I grab the back of her neck, tug. She doesn't let go. I apply pressure; she holds on. Pain shoots down my injured arm and my finger hurts. I squeeze down, her shoulders tremble, and her body arches. She gasps and her hold loosens. I pull her back, lower my face to hers, "I am going to teach you a lesson that you'll never forget."

30

Amelie

Water from the shower drums against me. His grey gaze clashes with mine. His features twist into an expression of rage…? Of arousal? His nostrils flare. "I am going to fuck you like you are mine."

Am I his?

Is he mine?

Do I want him to fuck me?

No.

No.

"Yes." I peel back my lips, "Finally."

He crashes his mouth into mine, thrusts his tongue inside, sucks on me, demands that I open myself to him, that I give in to him. *No, no. I can't. Yes, you can. Show him you won't back down, that you're not scared of what he does to you. That you will not turn and hide from the emotions he evokes in you.* I tip up my chin, wind my arms around his neck, dig my thighs into his waist, press my melting center to the hardness that tents his pants.

"Fuck me," his harsh whisper chafes my skin and my nerve

endings flare. My brain cells seem to evaporate. Poof, I am smoke. I am one melting, writhing mass of need in his arms.

Take me. Tear into me. Sink into me. Push all thoughts out of my head. I don't want to think, don't want to worry about the future, the past. All that matters is me, here, with him, clinging to him, holding on with every single strand of strength in my body. Him. I want him. Only him. I tear my mouth from his, "Fuck me."

Before the words are out of my mouth, he's flipped positions. My back presses into the wall. The weight of him pins me. His massive body cuts off the water. The blood drums in my ears; my pulse thuds against my neck, my wrists, at my ankles… The beat between my legs grows, louder, needier, angrier. "Now," I huff. "Do it."

His lips twist. He brings his hand up to curl his large fingers around my neck. I gulp. Shit, I'd asked… Demanded that he fuck me. Isn't that, like, against the rules of dominance with this man? Am I not supposed to ask for what I want?

His fingers meet around the diameter of my neck. He presses his thumb into the pulse that skitters at the base of my throat. "Aren't you forgetting something?"

I frown.

He tilts his head.

I lower my chin.

He glares at me and the blood drains from my face, straight to my cunt. My head spins. My throat closes. I flick out my tongue to touch my lips; his gaze drops to my mouth.

He growls and my stomach seems to bottom out. Oh, my God. This man… He's too hot, too much. Too everything.

"Do it," he barks.

I hesitate.

"Or not." He steps back.

I lose my grasp around his waist; my legs begin to slide down. *No, no, no. I want this. I do.* "Please," I gasp.

"Please what?" His fingers tighten around my neck and my airflow slows. I open my mouth, try to breathe. My lungs burn. I thrust my thighs into his, hold on. *Don't let go. He's testing you. Don't give in; not yet.*

"I… I…" I try to form the words, but my brain cells don't comply. "Wes… I…"

"Want me to help you?"

I nod.

"Want me to play with your pretty cunt?" He tilts his hips and his thick length stabs my sensitized core.

I moan. I'm not proud. I tried to resist, tried to hold onto the last shred of my dignity that lies in tatters around me now. "Yes," I beg. "Yes."

"Want me to squeeze your butt," he grips my arse, "before I cram my fingers into your arsehole?" He drags his fingers down the valley between my butt cheeks. His touch sinks through the sodden mess of my clothes, my panties, into that empty part of me inside, that curls in on itself, throbbing with a need that only Doc Grumpyface can fulfill.

"Don't stop," I whine.

"Want me to…" He brings his hand around, and grabs my pussy.

I wordlessly push my core forward, begin to fuck his palm like the out-of-my-head, sex-starved, stupid idiot that I am.

He hauls me up, his right hand around my neck—apparently, his injured finger does nothing to restrain his movements; with his other, he grips my pussy—pins me against the wall, and stares into my face.

My feet don't touch the ground, and I should be scared. This position implies exactly what we are—me at his disposal, at his mercy, his to do with as he pleases. His grasp is firm enough to prop me up, allowing enough air to reach my lungs that I don't suffocate, and yet… The lowered oxygen heightens my reactions, my sensitivity to his every move. I watch him watch me strain against that large hand at my core, and all of my nerve-endings seem to catch fire all at once.

He slides his palm under me so his fingers are flat against my butt. He presses his thumb through my tights and my panties into my swollen nub. Sparks explode behind my eyes. I throw my head back and pant. He rubs circles with his thumb around my clit. My pulse rate ratchets up.

"Look at me," his command whips through my thoughts.

I lower my face, crack my eyes open.

"Who do you belong to?"

"You."

"Who do you come for?"

"You."

"Who will you shatter for?"

"You," I groan, "Only you."

"Shatter for me, my Princess. Right fucking now."

He releases the hold on my neck and my climax explodes up my spine. Spots of white fold in to my line of sight. My pussy clenches; moisture floods between my legs. I hear the sound of someone wailing… Me? Is that me? My ears pop; my throat closes. A whine pours from me.

"Good, girl." He bends, licks my lips, "I am going to fuck you now."

Wh-a-a-t?

I blink as he lowers me to the floor. My knees give way; he holds me up with his fingers around my neck. My shoulders slump, I should say something… Do something…?

He reaches around to shut off the shower, then grabs the hem of my dress, pulls it over my head, and tosses it aside.

He glances down at the tights, reaches for the waistband with his injured hand. He pauses. I hook my fingers in the waistband of my tights and tug them down along with my panties. The lycra sticks around my thighs. Shit, and I'd worn them in the hope of seeming sophisticated. Go figure! I try to peel them off, but the damn thing resists. Shit! I yank it down further, manage to twist it around my knees. Another tug and I shove it down to my ankles, peel it off. Whew! I straighten, and with a low growling sound he's on me.

He lowers himself to his knees, pushes his face into my pussy and fastens his mouth on my melting core. "OMG." I yell, "Wes, Wes… Wes." I chant his name as he stabs his tongue inside my channel, swipes his tongue up from my backhole to my clit. He bites on my clit and I arch off the wall. OMFG! This man's tongue should be worshipped; also his mouth, and his dick, and his digits… Gah! He slides his finger inside my melting pussy and I shudder. My knees seem to give away. I begin to slide down the wall, dig my fingers into his hair for purchase and tug on it. He growls. My nerve endings spark. *Ooh, I like that.* A lot, actually. I yank at that luxurious hair on his head.

He peers up at me, "You know you'll have to pay for that, huh?"

"Promises, promises." I smack my lips.

His nostrils flare. He rises to his feet, and keeps rising. I mean, he is tall. I know that, but in that enclosed space he is larger than life. A lethal, vital, sex machine of a man. My sex clenches, heat coils low in my belly, emptiness gnaws deep inside. I need him. Want him... Yearn for him to fill me up and put me out of my misery. "Wes," I groan.

"Here baby, right here."

He plants his thigh between my legs.

"I am going to make this so fucking good for you, Princess." He thrusts his fingers…two…three inside my pussy.

I gasp; my knees buckle. One thing I can confirm. Weston-built-like Adonis-Kincaid, always delivers.

He wraps his fingers around my neck, holds me upright, even as he shoves the fingers of his other hand in and out of me. I moan, reach for his shoulders. He doesn't stop; he scissors his fingers inside of me. Goosebumps dot my skin; a trembling begins from the soles of my feet, inches upward. He releases his hold on my neck, then turns me around. *What the —?* I sense his hot breath on the curve of my hip a second before he pries my butt cheeks apart and rims his tongue around my backhole. *Oh, my God.* The trembling pulsates from where he slides his tongue in and out of me. He slips his palm between my hips and the shower wall, then grinds the heel of his hand against my pussy.

"Weston," his name is torn from my lips. I sense his lips curve against my arse… Is that even possible? Then he thrusts his fingers inside my pussy, and I explode. The orgasm sweeps up my thighs, my spine. I slap my palm against the shower wall, hold onto his forearm with my other hand. He continues to lick me, shove his fingers in and out of me, extending the climax, which seems to go on and on. He pulls away his hand, removes his tongue, and just like that, my orgasm fades. No way, he can't command my body with such…finesse, can he? My knees give way, for real this time. His arms come around me. He turns me toward him, pinches my chin, so I look up at him.

"Wow," I gasp, "that was…" I swallow, "It was…"

"Just the beginning."

"Huh?" My head spins. "I… I don't think I can…"

"You can."

He grins down at me, that toe curling, sex clenching, scalp tingling smirk that sends a surge of heat racing up my spine.

"Are you a sex god?" I mumble. *Hell, did I blurt that out?* Must be my sex-addled brain that's speaking. Not my fault. *Gah.*

"That's Dr Sex God to you." He laughs, "And you're welcome, again."

"Huh?" *Do I want to know why? Don't ask him; don't.* "For what?"

"For the third, fourth and fifth orgasm that you are going to experience."

"No." I blink.

"Yes." His lips curl. He reaches behind him, shuts off the shower, then steps back and rakes his gaze down my naked body. I will not cover myself, will not hide what he's already pinched and massaged and teased and licked and sucked and… I press my thighs together.

"Hmm," he smirks.

"You going to take off your clothes, or what?" I mutter.

He unbuttons his shirt, whips it off, then unfastens his belt. My gaze drops to his crotch. *Don't stare; look away, you slut.* He shoves down his pants and his boxers, kicks them aside. He straightens and I gulp. OMFG. I take in his cock that stands to attention against his stomach. It's thick and wide, and longer than I remember it to be. How had I managed to take him down my throat?

I must have made a strangled noise, for he chuckles. "It will fit," he assures me, "I'll make it."

That's what I'm afraid of.

I sidle away and toward the door of the shower cubicle.

"Where do you think you're going?" he drawls.

"Ah, I…uh… I need to pee."

"Will you pee on me?"

"What?" I stare at him, "Are you serious?"

He laughs, "No, but coming to think of it..." He scratches his chin, "Can I pee on you, instead?"

"No," I stutter. "Is that, like, your kink or something?"

He frowns, "Never thought of it before, but," he looks me up and down, "you have to admit, it's an effective way of marking my territory."

My jaw drops, "You're crazy."

He steps forward, plants himself in the doorway, "Crazy is what I feel every time Max insists on occupying your attention."

I frown, then stiffen, "Wow, you're jealous."

He frowns.

"You resent that Max prefers my company to yours."

He folds his arms over his broad chest, "You done?"

I plant my hands on my hips. "Come on," I wheedle, "at least, admit that you don't want Max anywhere near me."

"You're wrong."

"Oh?"

He nods. "I don't want any male—no man or animal of any kind —near you."

I swallow. My heart begins to race. I know he's dominant, and an alpha, and demanding… But this crazy possessive side of him? Wow, it's hot as fuck. We stare at each other. Water drips from the shower onto the ground. I swallow and the hair on the back of my neck rises. *Say something…anything to break the silence.* I lower my arms to my sides, "Do…do you mean that?" I ask.

He tilts his head, drums his fingers on his chest, then straightens, "Want me to show you?"

31

Weston

What the fuck am I playing at? Why are you allowing her to see how much she affects you? Peeing on her? Seriously? Fucking fuck, it's not something that had crossed my mind… Not before her. Is that how much I want to possess her? Is that how much I want to imprint myself on every cell of her body? My vision narrows. The hair on my forearms rises. This crazy-ass need to own her… It's new, it's different, it's real. I bend my knees, peer into her face.

Her pupils are blown; the blue in them has deepened to an almost purple. Her cheeks are flushed, her pulse skitters at the base of her neck. "Do you, Princess?"

"I…" She bites the inside of her cheek, then lowers her chin, "I do."

"I didn't hear you."

She draws in a breath, tips up her chin. She takes a step forward until her toes bump mine. "I want you to show how much you want me, what you'll do to possess me, how much you need to ensure that no one will have me like you do."

"Good." I step away from the entrance of the shower stall, jerk my chin, "After you."

She frowns, then walks past me. I follow her past the bath tub, out the door of the ensuite, into the bedroom. She approaches the foot of the bed.

"Stop," I call out.

She pauses, angles her body.

"Don't turn around."

She trembles, but obeys.

I stalk over to her, wrap the towel I'd snatched on my way out of the bathroom around her shoulders, drag it down her back, over the lush curves of her butt, her strong calves, about those shapely ankles —that I want locked around my neck, fast.

She gasps.

I straighten, then circle around to her front.

Her chest rises and falls.

I lower my gaze to her chest and her shoulders quiver. I pat the towel about her creamy breasts; her nipples pucker. I lower my head, bite down on the pebbled flesh. She moans.

A droplet of water slides down the valley between her breasts. I lick it up, then follow the trail of another down to her belly button. I curl my tongue into the indentation; she groans. Lower my face to her pussy and close my mouth around the delectable flesh. She gasps, and the sound of her pleasure percolates into my cells, filters through my blood, straight to my balls.

I straighten, peer into her face.

"Get on the bed—on your back, legs apart, pussy exposed, hands behind your neck, so you can't touch yourself," I growl.

Her muscles quiver.

"Do it," I snap.

She scrambles up on the bed, turns around, lies flat, spreads her knees, locks her fingers behind her neck.

I smile, "My, aren't you the obedient one today."

She glowers at me and I widen my stance. I draw the towel, now damp with the water from her body, down my chest, my stomach, my thighs. Her gaze follows my every move, her pupils dilated, breasts swollen. I toss aside the towel, lower my gaze to her pussy, to where the evidence of her arousal drips down her inner thigh. My dick throbs; my groin hardens.

I lean over, scoop up her cum, and suck on it.

She whines.

"Want some?"

She nods.

I tilt my head, arch an eyebrow. "Maybe later." I smirk, "If you've been good enough, that is."

She groans, mumbles something under her breath.

"What's that, Princess?"

She stares at me, then presses her lips together.

I laugh, "You're learning fast."

I fist my cock, swipe it from root to tip. She glances at it and her lips part.

"Want a taste of this?"

She pouts, doesn't reply.

"Damn, but you beat me at my own game, huh?"

She scowls.

I chuckle. Then walk around the bed to the side table, pull it open and get a condom.

I slip it on, walk back to the foot of the bed.

"Soft fuck or hard fuck?"

She purses her lips.

"Both?" I tilt my head, "Neither?"

She shakes her head.

"One after the other, maybe?"

She swallows; her chest rises and falls.

"Maybe I should decide, huh?" I tap a finger to my chin. "Perhaps I should surprise you?"

I lean over, grab her by her ankles.

She squeaks.

I pull her forward, until her hips are almost at the edge. I kneel on the bed, draw her legs over my shoulders, position my dick at her entrance.

Her belly quivers, her thighs spasm, and goosebumps flare on her skin. Good, I am not the only one who's not going to be able to walk away from this unaffected. "You ready, Princess?"

She tips her chin up, opens her mouth. I plunge inside her. Her entire body bucks. She flings out her arms, grabs hold of the sheets. I wait, wait for her to adjust to my size. Her eyelids flutter and a bead of sweat trickles down her temple. "Eyes on me," I order.

She looks up, holds my gaze. The pleasure and hunger, and that edge of desperation in them, mirrors the strange confluence of emotions inside of me. I grip her thighs and hold them further apart.

Her breathing grows shallow, but she jerks her head, and I begin to fuck her in earnest. I plunge into her again and again. The bed shudders with each thrust. The headboard slams into the wall, punctuated by her cries, her moans, her gasps, her whines, her wails. Each sound from her beautiful lips sinks into my blood, curls around my heart, hacks away at the walls I have built up against the world.

My God, this woman… She tears me apart. The scent of her, the taste of her, the sweet poison of her cunt...will be my death. I pull back, stay poised at the edge of her channel, move over her, until my face is close to hers. My lips above hers, breathing in her perfume, her essence. The very breath that we share ties us together.

I kick my hips forward, sink into her. "Come," I command, and she arches up and off the bed. I fit my mouth to hers, draw from her scream as she breaks apart under me. I sink in and out of her, drawing out the aftermath of her orgasm, reveling in her complete submission. My chest hurts, my temples throb, my balls draw up and I let myself come inside of her.

I collapse forward on my elbows. A bead of sweat trickles down my chin and plops on her cheek. Her eyeballs move behind her closed eyelids. I pull out of her, tie the condom, then walk over to the waste basket and toss it in. When I return to the bed, I pull the covers over her, slip in between the sheets and pull her to me.

I spoon her, our bodies in sync from throat to chest to hips. I throw my leg over hers and fall asleep.

When I wake up, I am on my own.

I glance at the dent in the pillows, the mussed-up sheets, the scent of sex, of chocolate and cinnamon, is heavy in the air. Her scent. My dick lengthens. Shit, haven't I had enough of her? My fingertips tingle. Why the hell do I want to touch her, pull her to me and hold her, then bury myself inside her again and again? I shake my head. The fuck is wrong with me?

I sit up, swing my legs over the side of the bed. I head for the walk-in closet, step in and pull on a pair of sweat pants. When I step out, I hear a sound from behind the door that leads to the kitchen. I head toward it and the scent of chocolate deepens. I wasn't dreaming then? I step inside, come to a stop.

She stands at the counter, back to me, wearing a shirt—my shirt. It falls to half-way down her thighs, clings to the swell of her butt. The valley between her arsecheeks is a dark shadow that calls to me. I curl my fingers into fists. Fuck, get a grip on your desires, asshole. I take a step forward. She throws her head back, sways those ample hips from side to side, bumps, grinds. I reach down adjust the thickness that tents my crotch. Jesus H Christ, what is she up to now?

She flicks her head from side to side, holds up her spatula—that same infernal spatula she'd threatened me with the first time I saw her at the cabin. I move toward her. She lowers her chin and screeches. What the fuck? I stare as she croons under her breath, then rotates her body in a figure eight. Huh, is that what they call twerking? I grab my very interested dick, pull on it as she moves her butt in the opposite direction. Sweat beads my forehead. Fuck, she only has to twitch that gorgeous arse and this asshole will come running. Fuck.

I stalk to her. She angles her body, lowers her head and sings into the spatula, the lyrics from a famous Christmas anthem—so famous that even I recognize it.

I shake my head. "Are you singing Last Christmas by Wham!?"

She howls out the next set of lyrics in answer.

I wince. As gorgeous as her pussy is, as sassy as her temperament is, as beautifully sharp as her mind is… Her singing voice…? Well, let's just say I sing better, and I've been asked not to sing.

I close the distance between us, place a hand on her shoulder.

She screams, turns, and brings the spatula down on me.

32

Amelie

The spatula connects with his hand… His injured hand. His shoulders bunch and the color fades from his cheeks. To his credit, he doesn't cry out in pain. His big body goes solid; his chest planes seem to expand and grow bigger as he draws in a breath. Then he takes a step back, another, until the backs of his knees connect with one of the stools at the breakfast bar. He sinks down into it, brings his hand up to his chest and cradles it there. Sweat beads his forehead.

"Ow," he mumbles.

"Bloody apple crumble," I wheeze. The spatula slips from my hand, falls to the floor, bounces once. Gooey chocolate sprays across the floor, dots the edges of his sweats.

"Oh. My," I gasp, "Ohmygod." I take a step forward and my foot slides on the chocolate crepe batter. I stumble, then right myself. "Oh, hell," I cry. "I am so sorry. So sorry. I didn't mean it." I leap forward, reach for his hand.

He jerks back.

I freeze.

"I didn't mean it. You surprised me," I blubber, "Did I hurt you? Ohmigod, omigod, of course, I hurt you. Oh my—"

"Stop," he barks out the command.

I stutter, "I'm sorry, I really am."

"You mean you didn't hurt me on purpose?"

I open and close my mouth. "How could you think that?" I cry. "Do you really think I would—?"

One side of his mouth curls.

I purse my lips together. "You horrible man." I step toward him.

He holds up his good hand, "Stop, before you make it worse."

"Oh." A pressure builds behind my eyes. "Is it bad? Did I break it again?"

"It hadn't healed enough for that to happen." He grunts, "No, you hit the finger in the same place it broke the first time around."

"I didn't." I scowl. I hadn't hit his finger, only his palm, I swear. I stare at his finger in the splint, then back up at his face. "You're so adept at working around that, that I forget sometimes you are injured."

"Is that a compliment for my dexterity?" His lips kick up.

"Something like that." I stare at his features. His color's definitely better than it was a minute ago. "Do you want any painkillers?" I shuffle my weight from foot to foot, "Maybe some of the chocolate cookies I baked and brought here?"

"Haven't you given them to Mother?" He frowns.

I glance away, twist my fingers together. "You were right. It was a stupid idea. I should have ordered something from the shops or stopped on the way here to buy something."

"It was a thoughtful gesture," he replies.

I shoot him a sideways glance. Is he, like, pulling my leg?

He meets my gaze, holds up his hand and winces.

"Oh." My chest tightens. "It's hurting, isn't it? Is it bleeding? Sure I can't get you something for the pain?" I step forward. He widens his stance. I slip in between his legs, glance at his injured palm. "Can you, uh, wiggle the other fingers or something?"

He bends the others, shows me the bird by default.

"Guess you're feeling all right, huh?" I slide back, but he moves his thighs in, traps me in place.

"Oh." I gulp.

"Hmm," he tilts his head, "were you serious about your earlier offer?"

Which one?"

"About making the pain better."

I chew the inside of my cheeks, survey his features, which take on an expression of innocence. As if. I'd bet my last chocolate eclair that he has something up his sleeve.

"Depends," I venture.

"On what?"

"On what you want me to do."

"I'll only tell you if you agree to it."

"I can't agree to it unless you tell me what it's about."

"Trust me." His eyes gleam.

Ha, I draw in a breath. "Famous last words," I mumble.

"I heard that." He holds up his uninjured hand. "If you don't want to do it, you don't need to."

"Really?"

He nods, "I swear on chocolate."

Hmm. I frown, "You don't like chocolate."

"But you do."

"You're supposed to swear on something you hold dear." I huff.

"I swear on you."

My mouth drops open. *Oh, my. Did he say that? He didn't. Should I ask him to repeat it? Nah, ignore it.*

"Fine." I swipe my hair over my head, "What is the thing you want of me? What should I do to make the pain better?"

He holds up his injured finger, "Kiss it."

"That's all?"

"That's all."

"Okay." I draw in a breath, lower my head, and press my lips to his finger. I straighten and he tightens the net formed by his thighs, pulls me closer. My core brushes the prominent tent at his crotch, the one I have been trying to ignore.

"I did what you asked," I say, my voice breathless, "let me go."

"That's not the only place it hurts." He sticks out his lower lip.

"No?" I bite the inside of my cheek.

Weston has the kind of pillowy lower lip made for a pout, but honestly, this is the first time he's pulled that one on me.

Apparently, it takes a rap from a spatula to turn him more amicable. Note to self: next time, aim for his hard head. That might knock some sense into him, hmm?

"No." He shakes his head, "What about the finger between my legs."

I stare at him for half a second, then groan. "Eeyuck, your lines are getting worse."

"And you're getting better at easing my pain."

I shake my head, "So, you want a blow job, before breakfast?"

"Definitely before breakfast, and during and after too."

I squeeze my eyes shut, "I'll pretend you didn't say that."

"You promised," he wheedles. "Come on, Princess, just a kiss. Take the frog out of the well; show it the world."

I laugh, "That was almost clever."

"Right?" He smirks; his chest seems to swell with how pleased he is with himself. This man? I don't know if I should slap him or kiss him. Or both, one after the other.

I frown.

He chuckles, "You hurt me; it's up to you to make it better."

He has a point there.

I drop my gaze to his crotch, then to his face.

His gaze narrows.

I bite down on my lower lip, and those grey eyes lighten, a sure hint that he's aroused. I squeeze my thighs together. So am I. He raises his hand, rubs his thumb over my lower lip, until I release it. "You are not allowed to hurt that; only I have the permission to do that."

"Oh." His words coil around my heart and my blood begins to pound in my veins. That possessiveness in him? It kills me every time. I reach forward, palm him through his pants. He groans. His chest planes seem to harden.

I rub at his length, and I swear, his dick thickens.

"Take it out," he murmurs.

I swallow, slide my fingers down his waistband and curl my fingers around his shaft. The muscles of his belly jump. I push down the waistband; the heavy length of him fills my palm. The vein on the underside throbs, the head swollen and angry. Moisture beads the slit.

"Suck me off," he orders.

I bend my head, lick my tongue around the head. The salty, tangy taste of him fills my mouth. I peer up at him. "I want..." I swallow, " Can I...?"

"What is it?"

I reach around him, scoop up some of the chocolate mixture from the table, rub it across the head of his cock.

"Jesus," he breathes.

I hold his gaze, lower my head again and take him inside my mouth.

"Fucking, fuck." He digs his fingers into my hair, tugs. My scalp hurts. Goosebumps ripple down my spine. I lick the chocolate off his dick and the dark taste of cocoa, edged with his cum, the musky taste of Weston, swirls over my tongue. I swallow; he draws in a breath. He loosens the hold of his thighs around me and I sink to my knees. I grip his thigh for support, squeeze the base of his dick, and his entire body seems to grow rock solid.

"Take me down your throat," he growls.

I bob my head forward, and gag. Saliva drips from the edges of my mouth and my lungs burn. Jesus, he's too big. Will I ever get used to his size?

"Breathe through your nose," he directs.

I swallow, and his fingers dig into my scalp. Shockwaves of lust race across my skin. I moan, take in a breath, then another.

"Eyes on me."

I peer up at him, at those colorless eyes that reflect back what I am — his woman, his slave, his to do with as he wants. And what do I want? Him. All of him. His corrupted tastes, his filthy ways, that tenderness he hides deep inside and reveals to his nieces, his family, to Max. I want that. I want to be at the center of his world, command his attention as he demands mine.

I tilt my head and he slips further down my throat. My chest heaves, my breasts ache, and that empty sensation between my legs intensifies.

His features twist. He brings his hand to my face, rubs away the drool from my chin. He cups my cheek, and something like tenderness glitters in those eyes. He tugs on my hair; I pull back. His dick slips out with a pop. He hauls me up to my feet, peers into my face. "What are you doing to me?" he whispers.

"Whatever it is," I lean in close enough for us to share breath, "I feel the same."

His eyebrows knit. He searches my face again. The raw intensity of his gaze sweeps through my mind, pushes away all other thoughts. He bridges the distance between us, then closes his mouth over mine.

33

Weston

It wasn't supposed to be like this. This sweetness. This feeling of absolute surrender from her that punches me in the gut. My heart begins to pound and the blood thuds at my temples. She parts her lips; I deepen the kiss, swipe my tongue inside her mouth, draw from her taste, suck on her lips... And she gives and gives. A hot sensation coils in my chest.

Without taking my mouth from hers, I bend my knees, grip her under her thighs and lift her up. She wraps her legs around my waist. Her soft core cradles my dick, her breasts thrust up and into my chest. I tilt my head, crush my lips to hers. Her scent fills my senses, her taste goes to my head. I stalk forward and into the bedroom. She winds her arms about my shoulders, tilts her chin up. The softness of her mouth, the heat of her pussy, her pebbled nipples that are imprinted into my skin—all of it sinks into my blood. A pressure builds behind my rib cage. I lower her to the bed, but she doesn't let go.

I lean over her, supporting my weight on my elbows. I press her down into the mattress, thrust my tongue down her throat, drink from her, wanting more…more. I reach down, position my throbbing shaft at the entrance of her pussy.

She moans deep in her throat, digs her heels into my back. The condom. I tear my mouth from hers. "Protection," I mutter.

"I'm on birth control." She stares up, blue eyes darkened to an azure, stormy clouds in their depths. "Come inside me," she whispers, "I want you, Weston."

"Like this?"

"Only like this." She pushes her hips up, her melting core opening, giving, needing.

"Fuck." I kick my hips forward, and slide into her, all the way in.

Her body jerks and the breath leaves her in a rush. I hold her gaze and begin to move, thrusting harder with each shove, plunge, thrust, propelling forward again and again. She grips me with her thighs, buries her fingers in my hair and tugs. I look deeply into her eyes, into the horizon I've seen all this time, the one that had seemed so far away when it was always right here. In front of me. Under me. With me… Next to me. "Come with me," I push into her, impale her, bury myself so deeply that my balls slap against her thighs.

She opens her mouth in a wordless scream; her body shudders and moisture fills her channel and bathes my dick, as I come inside of her. I thrust a few more times, as her body trembles in the aftermath of the climax, then reach down, scoop up the liquid that spills from us. I hold it to her lips. She sucks on it, swallows.

"How do we taste?" I ask.

"Of sin and chocolate," her lips quirk, "of cruelty and togetherness; of lust and secrets." Her voice lowers, "A strength to do what it takes."

"Can you take what I am going to do to you?" I wonder aloud.

"What?" She frowns.

I pull out of her.

She lowers her legs. I lean back on my knees, then stand and step away, over to the side of the bed. "Get up," I jerk my chin at her.

Her forehead creases, but she sits up. Her shirt—my shirt—that she wears is pushed up about her waist and her pussy glistens with the evidence of our combined cum. The sleeve slips down one shoulder, baring the reddened skin of her chest. Skin I'd touched, sucked, marked, fondled…lips I'd worshipped, breasts I'd cupped, nipples I'd pinched. I step back, rake my gaze one last time over the concave of her stomach, the curve of her hips, the creamy expanse of her thighs, the delicate nip of her ankle, her toes, her hitched breath as she swings her legs over and straightens.

"You can go now," I tell her.

"Wait," she straightens her shirt, "what do you mean?"

"Leave," I jerk my chin toward the door.

"W…where?" she stutters, "What just happened."

Everything. "Nothing," I growl.

She takes a step forward, "That… What took place between us… It was different. I was sure you felt something for me. I know that you want me."

"So?" I pull the waistband of my sweats up my waist. "I want many women… Doesn't mean I have to keep them around."

"I am not one of them," she snarls.

"Oh?" I look her up and down, "Just because my dick loves you," I smirk, "because I see your face and my dick gets hard, I hear your voice and my dick gets hard, I know you're in the next room and my dick gets hard… Doesn't mean I feel the same."

"You're not making any sense." She twists her fingers together. "I know you're scared. You've never allowed yourself to open up to another—"

"You think I opened up to you?"

"You did." She steps close and our toes bump, her nipples brush up against me; that chocolate and honey of her scent intensifies. My heart begins to pound and my chest hurts. *Shit. Let go of her; get her out of here. Walk away; don't look back. Release her from that stupid-ass arrangement that never was.*

"You'll get your money. All of it," I snap.

She blinks, "Excuse me?"

"The million a day for six days? It's yours."

"You think this was only about money?"

It had to be. "What else could it be about?"

"Did you think, for even one second, that maybe I wanted to be with you?"

"You wanted to be shut up with me in a cabin with no electricity, over Christmas?"

"Why not?"

"You wanted to spend Christmas getting to know my family?"

"It's the first time I've felt at home anywhere." She sets her jaw.

My guts twist. Shit, this isn't easy. Why do I feel like I am tearing out my heart? Why the hell do I care that she seems close to a break down? You've barely met her... You know everything about her. I know nothing of what she wants... She wants you, that's clear. She needs you as much as you are drawn to her. She senses the connection that binds you together...

And that is the fucking problem. I don't want it. I can do without it. I have enough demons of my own to contend with. I don't need this beautiful, gorgeous angel who swept in and threatens to upset my carefully structured life... Which had, by the way, gone down the shitter since she'd flounced into that cabin and turned my life upside down.

"Too bad; they are not yours."

"Too bad for you." She tips up her chin, "I'm yours. You know it and it scares you."

"You think I am scared?" I laugh.

"I think you are petrified. For the first time, you don't have a plan and it terrifies the hell out of you."

"The only thing that terrifies me is that I'll have to hold you while you have a breakdown, and trust me, Princess, that's not on my list of most-wanted things to do right now."

"I don't believe you." She clenches her fists by her side. "All of this is an act."

"That..." I tilt my head in the direction of the bed, "was an act. Guess I'm good, huh? I take credit."

"For what?"

"I won the bet with myself."

"What bet?"

"Making you fall in love with me... Remember what I told you?"

She squeezes her eyes shut, "That you'd break my heart."

"Have I, Princess?"

She stiffens, opens her eyes, stares straight into mine, "Mine is not the only heart that's breaking; and you know what else?"

I tilt my head.

"You care about me. You're in love with me, but you don't want to admit it. By the time you realize it, it will be too late. You'll come begging for forgiveness, and guess what I am going to do then?"

Sweat beads my palm... *Tell her to leave, to take her chocolate scent, her crazy-ass satchel of baking tools, her penchant for swearing in a vocabulary that consists solely of desserts, and walk out of here. Don't look back at her. Don't indulge her questions. Don't ask her what she means by that tirade.* "What?" I growl, "What the fuck would you do then?"

She reaches behind her, grabs the box of cookies she'd baked and empties it over my head, "Is that answer enough for you?"

Turning, she walks out.

34

———————

Amelie

What the hell had happened there? One second, he'd been inside of me, his cock nestled in my pussy, his lips on mine, my legs tangled about him... The next, he'd ordered me to leave.

If there were a classic case of a man who was running scared that would be Weston Fucking Kincaid. Alphahole extraordinaire. Douchebag of the highest order. Bloody fruitcake, who doesn't know his arse from his head... No. I shake my head. Reprobate snackadoodle who has his head stuck so far up his arse, he has no idea how good the pie is. I sniff. Not even when said pie hits him in the face, and splatters its contents over his beautiful mouth, and he licks it off and — *OMG, what am I thinking?*

I stumble down the stairs, almost miss a step, then right myself, slip on the next one, and come to a halt at the landing. My heart races, my pulse pounds, and a pressure boils behind my eyes. *I will not cry; will not.*

There's a patter of paws on the wooden floor. Max comes bounding out of the open doors of the suite adjacent to the landing.

I bend down, gather him up, then sink down to sit on the step.

"Hey little fella, did you miss me? Did ya now?" I rub his head, hold
him close. A tear runs down my cheek; Max licks it up. He whines,
then pushes his nose into the crook of my neck. I hug his little body
closely as more tears flow down my face. *Shit, stop it, stop it. Not your
fault if he's such an ass, a completely obnoxious man, Mr. Scrooge McFuck...
Gah!* Just because one of my favorite authors had released a book
about a similar a-hole with that name doesn't mean I have to call him
that, huh?

I swallow down the ball of emotion in my throat. I have to get out
of here, return to my life... Spend Christmas alone? My heart begins
to thud. How could he do this? How? A sob catches in my chest. I
glance around, then down at myself. Shit, I am still wearing his shirt
—nothing else. I had left everything behind in that alphahole's room.
No way, am I going back for it.

Max barks, wriggles in my hold. "Oh, sorry little guy, did I crush
you, huh?" I set him down, he darts forward toward the double
doors that lead into the suite. Kirsten bends to pat him. Max brushes
past her and rushes inside.

She straightens, then takes in my appearance.

I flush, "Umm... Uh, it's not like what it seems."

She tilts her head, "Why don't you come in and tell me about it?"

Twenty minutes later, I curl my legs under me, and take a sip of the
fragrant cup of hot chocolate—no, it's never too early in the day for
comfort food—that she'd handed me.

Max places his paw on my borrowed PJ's, and stares up at me. "I
swear he has a sixth sense, huh?"

"Mum, why was Auntie Amelie crying?" Phoenix asks in a loud
whisper.

Kirsten, pats her shoulder, "Because, uh, she had a fight."

"Lover's quarrel, huh?" Skye wanders into the living room, her
specs too big for her face. She has a book in her hand.

"Don't you have homework to do?" Kirsten scolds her.

"I've completed my math assignment."

"What about Latin?"

"I hate Latin."

"Does she have to study Latin?" I ask.

"At her school, yes." Kirsten's forehead furrows, then turns to Skye, "Go on, finish it."

"But… M-o-m," she wails, once more seeming her eleven-year-old self.

"I don't need to study Latin to become a vet."

"You want to become a vet?"

She smiles, "I looove animals." She snaps her fingers; Max perks up, jumps off the sofa and races toward her.

"She and animals." Kirsten shakes her head, "I swear, she is a dog whisperer."

"And a cat one, and a hedgehog one," Skye adds.

"Hedgehog?" Kirsten scowls, "Young lady, if I find any more of those creatures in your room…I'll…"

"Relax, Ma, I was only kidding you," she smirks. Her features resemble her uncle's, aka the alphahole, aka the man who'd fucked me so thoroughly a few seconds ago… I blink. That tightness in my chest returns. I lower my chin, hide my face once again in my mug.

Kirsten draws in a breath, "Back to your studies, with you."

"Whatever." She returns to her room, Max at her heels.

"Can I do my homework too?" Phoenix beams up at her Mom.

"Go on then." Kirsten pulls Phe close, kisses her on the cheek. Phoenix turns to leave, then turns and runs to me. I place my mug back on the table, just in time, for she throws her arms around me.

"Oh," I hug the little girl back, "thanks, baby."

She kisses me on the cheek, then turns and races away.

"Kids," Kirsten sinks back in the arm chair, "they can sense when you're unhappy, you know?"

I nod. "They are both beautiful; congratulations."

"Thanks." She beams. "Their father's the disciplinarian; I spoil them I'm afraid."

"When will he be back?"

"Patrick?" Her face takes on a dreamy look, "Tomorrow, or tonight, if he can. He's on a business trip with our oldest brother."

"Really?"

She frowns, "I take it, Weston didn't mention that they work together?"

I shake my head.

"My father started a media company, that Liam now heads up."

"That's your oldest sibling?"

She nods, "Patrick works with him. Weston… Well, after the incident, he changed. He needed to do something more meaningful with his life."

"Is that why he became a heart surgeon?" I ask, "Or was that to protect his own heart?"

She stares at me.

I flush. "Umm, sorry, didn't mean for it to come out that way, it's just…"

She waves her hand, "No offense taken. I was surprised, is all. I never thought about it like that, but you may be onto something." She pauses, as if to commiserate with me. "I know how obnoxious my brother can be."

"That's putting it mildly." I mutter.

"I assume he's told you about the incident?" she asks.

"Some." I reply, my tone cautious. "He mentioned he and six of his friends were kidnapped and held captive for nearly a month when he was twelve, and during that time, each of them was exposed to some horrific punishment meted out to each of them by the kidnappers. It's why he has a trigger when it comes to clocks and time-keeping devices," I swallow, "I guess."

She nods. "After the cops rescued Weston and the other boys from the kidnappers," she leans forward, "he felt like he had been given a new lease on life. He wanted to make sure he made the most of the opportunity. It's one of the reasons he wanted to become a surgeon." She crinkles her forehead, "Then our father died of an heart attack and that strengthened his resolve."

So, I'd been right about the second part, at least. I meet her gaze, "He seems to think it's because it gives him control over life and death."

"Do you believe him?" she scoffs.

"I am not sure what to make of him," I say honestly.

She looks me up and down, "So you guys had a fight this morning?"

"More than that." I heave out a sigh.

To her credit, she hadn't been taken aback when she'd found me standing by the doorway to her suite. She hadn't asked me any questions either. She'd loaned me her clothes, then handed me the cup of hot chocolate. Hell, she hadn't even been surprised that I'd asked her for cocoa, instead of tea… And that, puts her right at the top of my list.

"What happened between you two?" she asks.

"I…" I glance away, "I think we broke up."

"Fights are normal. They're healthy in a relationship—"

"This is more than that." I jump up and begin to pace. "He told me to leave."

"The room?" her tone sharpens.

"His suite, his life… He told me it was over."

"He told you so, in no uncertain terms?"

Had he? I turn to her. "Yes," I reply.

"I don't believe it," she scowls. "I saw the way he looks at you—"

"How?" I fold my arms around my waist. "How does he look at me?"

"Like he wants to eat you up?"

"Yeah." My cheeks heat. "I mean, we don't have any issues in that, uh, department."

"The kind of chemistry between you two? It could boil water at fifty paces."

I laugh, "I thought I was the only one who made cooking analogies."

"I've been spending too much at home with the kids, ensuring dinner's on the table when my husband arrives from work every evening."

"Do you regret it?"

"Not for a second." She leans back in her chair, reaches for her mug of tea. "I had a corporate career as a lawyer. I enjoyed it, but I wanted more. I needed the entire 360 experience—home, kids… I'll go back to practicing part-time when the kids are older."

"And you'll be fine with that?"

"It's all about balance, Amelie." She smiles, "Once they are old enough to leave home, I am sure I'll go back to practicing full time."

"And you don't see it as a compromise?" I head back to the couch, drop into it.

"For whom?" She chuckles, "I have it all, as far as I can see."

And I have nothing. I twist my fingers together in front of me.

Her features twist, "Hell, I didn't mean it that way. The last thing I want to do is hurt your feelings by rubbing in my..." she circles her hand, "...all this, in your face."

"You're not." I lean forward and touch her knee. "Honestly, you aren't. I appreciate your giving me the time to recover, and for the clothes."

"Anytime." She takes my hand in hers, "I like you, Amelie."

I laugh, "You've known me all of two seconds."

"I go by my gut, and unlike my brother, I actually heed what my instincts tell me."

"Too bad that idiot McDick has no such inclinations." I take a deep breath, "Well, I guess I need to head off."

"Where will you go?"

"I need to call my friend Isla, make arrangements to stay with her. I also need my clothes, which are —"

"Stay here."

"What?" I attempt to withdraw my hand, but she doesn't let go. "I mean it," she says. "Stay with me, as my guest. We have the entire floor, and the guest room is free.

I stare at her, "But —"

"We'd love to have you."

"You don't need to say that..."

"I never say anything I don't mean." Her features take on a haughty look, one so familiar, one I've seen on his face. Shit, staying here, surrounded by his family, where their every action would remind me of the man I need to try to forget? No, just no. Not that I don't like Kirsten, but... To be so near him, and yet, not with him? Gah. I'd have to OD on chocolates to get through the ordeal, and that's definitely not something I can afford, not if I hope to get through the festive season with some semblance of a waistline.

"Thank you," I turn my palm over and clasp hers, "but no thank you."

Her lips droop. She peers into my eyes, then lets out a breath, "There's nothing I can do to convince you, huh?"

I shake my head.

"One night." She lowers her chin. "Stay for dinner tonight, meet Liam and Patrick."

I frown, open my mouth to decline, and she drops her gaze to my pajamas. "You owe me."

"You don't play fair, do you?" *Just like him.*

"It's genetic. Our father ingrained the habit of negotiation at the dining table, I'm afraid."

She rises to her feet.

"Where are you going?" I ask.

"To get your things from Weston's suite."

35

Weston

"You seem nervous, ol' chap," Damian drawls at me from the screen of my phone.

"And you seem full of shit, as usual," I mutter, as I pace in front of the fire in the living room of my mother's home. I'd gone for a run, and when I'd returned, Amelie's clothes and bags had gone from the bedroom. Guess she'd left, after all.

I'd sat on the bed in a daze and wondered if I'd done the right thing.

Yeah, I had. Of course, I had. I didn't need her staying and complicating the situation, aka the state of my feelings for her, further. I'd worked out at the gym after that, pushed myself as much as I could, considering I couldn't do weights yet with my broken finger. Then I had showered and changed into formal clothes for the traditional family dinner at home.

I run my finger around the collar of my shirt. Not that I dislike suits… But hell, if I don't feel more comfortable in scrubs. There is a certain freedom that comes from not having to pretend, when all the power and control is at your fingertips as you perform a surgery, knowing the life of a human depends on you. It is the best adrenaline rush—a responsibility I never take lightly, walking on the edge of a thrill that I crave. One slip up and things would never be the same. *Did I slip up with her?* I scowl. Fuck that. I am not second guessing my actions, no way.

"Fake girlfriend, slash fiancée, slash wife-to-be not helping with your problem then?" Damian smirks.

"What problem?" I growl.

"That you can't get it up, of course."

I frown, "Where do you get your asinine ideas from?"

"The same place you come up with your brainwaves of sharing a cabin with a woman you've met only once before." He chuckles.

"About that," I crack my neck, "it's over."

"Oh, yeah?" Damian tilts his head, "Hold on, I'm adding Arpad to the call."

"Don't..." I begin to protest, when Arpad's face appears in a window. "Man, and I thought I was bad at relationships, this has to be a record, even for you," he snickers.

"Fuck off," I growl.

"So, you think it's over, but it's not really over?" Damian pipes in.

"I am not going to explain myself."

"What are friends for, if you can't use our shoulders to cry on… Or not." Arpad's screen shakes and droplets of water splash the surface.

"Where the fuck are you?"

"On my yacht, enjoying everything life has to offer, unlike you."

"Why the fuck do I take your calls?" I grumble.

"Because you have something on your mind, and need to vent, like a girl?" Damian laughs.

"Because you are heart-broken?" Arpad snickers.

"Okay, bye," I hold my finger over the screen.

"Ooh, someone's antsy. Did we hurt your feelings? Are you upset you're not getting married like Saint and Sinner before you?"

"You look grumpy. Not jerking off either, are you?"

I shake my head, "Fuck that, and fuck you two," *and fuck the woman who put me in this situation, where I am not able to string together two words. Fucking fuck!*

I hear the pattering of paws on the floor, then Max jumps up on the sofa and shoves his face in mine. "Hey," I protest, but he licks my mouth, then turns and peers into the screen.

"Hello, ol' boy," Damian chuckles. "You keeping Uncle Weston company while he fucks up his life?"

"A woman *and* a dog?" Arpad chuckles, "Should I fetch your slippers and dressing gown next ol' chap?"

"Jesus, fuck." I am not sure what I'd intended to accomplish through this conversation, but it wasn't being at the mercy of a mutt and two of my 'friends.'

"At least, I saved the Father from the burden of a virtual wedding." I grouse.

"Speaking of," Arpad drawls, "I'm adding Edward to the call."

No, fuck, no. Why do I insist on calling my 'friends,' knowing I'll be put through the wringer each time?

"Someone mention my name?" Edward's face flickers onto the screen.

"I was just leaving," I grumble.

"You want to hear this." Edward gazes at me with those clear eyes of his which have seen so much and which have yet managed to retain a modicum of innocence. Enough for him to sleep with his thoughts at night, at least.

"How do you manage it?" I snap out.

"You mean, hold down a conversion without losing my wits?"

"That too," I grunt. "How do you always seem so upbeat and energetic?"

"Umm…Maybe because he has no worldly attachments?" Damian offers.

I stare at the Father, who jerks his chin, "I realized the only way out of the aftermath of the incident, was to be true to myself at all times," he says.

"What if the only thing that can soothe my mind is the one thing I must never have?" I mutter.

"Are we talking about someone in particular or a metaphor?"

"What do you think?" I mutter.

Silence stretches across the space. Neither of the other two assholes respond with an off-the-cuff remark. Thank fuck for that. Perhaps it had been the Father I had been waiting for. Guess that's why I'd agreed to this call, which was supposed to be about 7A investments and FOK Media—which stood for Full of Kindness by the way—the companies that the seven of us own.

"I think you're fighting your future," Edward's tone is serious.

"I make my own future," I insist.

He quirks his lips, "You believe that, after everything you've been through?"

"It's because of everything I've been through that I believe it."

Edward tilts his head, "You can't control everything around you."

"Is that why you took the easy way out and gave up the real world for the spiritual one?"

Edward pales. Damian stiffens. Arpad's silent disapproval communicates through the screen.

"Fucking hell." I drag my fingers through my hair. "I didn't mean that Father," I mumble.

"You did," Edward's voice is calm. "I'm glad you are able to speak your mind. In such matters, clear, concise communication is the only way forward."

"What do you mean?" I peer into the screen, trying to discern his features. "Tell me, Father."

"Some of that honesty you displayed earlier... That's what you need to bring to your relationship with her."

"Eh?" I shake my head, "You're making absolutely no sense."

"You know I am." Edward's lips quirk, "Hand on heart, ask yourself what it is that you must do in this situation."

"Haven't I been asking myself that all along? Would I be asking you this question if the answer was at all clear to me?"

"You're the business man here, Weston. Your gut knows what it wants; your heart simply has to fall in line."

"You're not shoddy in the business space yourself." I crack my neck. "You've held your own in all of the business decisions we've made thus far."

"Don't change the topic," Edward admonishes. "What is it that your gut says you should do now?"

"What if it's not clear to me for the first time, huh?"

"Wrong answer," Edward snaps. "You're beginning to piss me off."

I blink. Edward angry? It never happens. That he swore at me? I can count on my fingers the number of times he's done that. "I am not sure what to say," I rasp.

"You don't have to say anything, and you do know what you have to do. Your stubborn-ass head is getting in the way. You're trying to think about this along rational lines, when you know what you have to do."

I laugh, "Have you been spending much time with Saint?" I ask. "You're speaking in riddles."

Edward shakes this head, "Stop deflecting; it won't work." He frowns, "You going to follow your gut and your heart on this? Or are you going to spend the rest of your years regretting the one decision you should have made, which would have changed the course of your life, but you didn't because you were too much of a pussy?"

I stare at him. "I can't believe you said that." I shake my head. "You, of all people, should know I don't shy away from hard decisions."

"But this is much more than that." He tilts his head, "It's, perhaps, not your decision to make. Perhaps this time, you have to allow the circumstances to wash over you, and go with the flow?"

I laugh. *As if I would ever do that?* I haven't come this far in life to bow before events, not if I have my way. "I'm not sure what you're implying but—"

The screen pixelates and my voice echoes back at me. *Huh?* Bloody technology, always fails you when you need it the most. The connection restores.

"Hey man." Damian peers back at me from the screen.

Arpad jerks his chin. "Still here for my sins," he grumbles.

"Where's Edward?" I frown.

"Seems he dropped off?" Damian mutters, "Perhaps he's had enough of you acting like a fool, and decided to cut out?"

"Yeah, well, fuck that." *And fuck him.* My heart begins to race. "Not my decision to make, huh? We'll see." I toss my head.

"You coming out to London for the New Year's party?" Damian asks.

"I'll be there."

"Are you bringing her?"

"That's up to her." I frown. The hair on the back of my neck rises and a tingle runs down my spine. "I need to go, guys."

I hang up and turn. My gaze widens. "What are you doing here?"

36

Amelie

I tip up my chin and march into the room. *What the hell am I doing here? Why had I allowed Kirsten to convince me to stay?* He frowns as I walk past him to the bar, and pour myself some sparkling water. Yeah, I need my wits about me. I'm not going to fuck this up, or give the alphahole the time of the day either.

I glance around the beautifully furnished living room. The painting above the fire place is definitely an original, the settee in the room is made of plush leather and strewn with cushions, giving it a homey look. The wooden floor gleams, no doubt, polished every day by minions. I take in the corners of the room, the other walls—no clocks. Of course, not. Is his family aware of Weston's trigger? Had they done away with all time pieces? Of course, they know about his affliction, right?

Footsteps sound behind me as Weston prowls over, "I thought I told you to leave?"

A ripple runs past my nerve endings. *Don't show how nervous you are. Don't let on how much his nearness affects you.*

I turn, glance around him. "Hey, Kirsten," I wave at his sister.

"Come on over, babe, you gotta see what Phe has drawn for you."

"Coming." I march past him, head high, spine straight, my heart booming in my rib cage. He locks his fingers around my wrist.

I squeak.

"Don't ignore me," he growls under his breath. That harsh edge to his voice? Gah! My nerve endings all flare at once.

I stiffen, glance sideways. "Let go of me," I whisper.

"You don't tell me what to do."

"And you don't get to tell me what to do anymore. You told me to leave, remember?"

"And you disobeyed me."

"You're not my keeper, not even my lover. Any right you had over me, you forfeited right then."

"Have I now?" His fingers tighten on my wrist—and he's using his left hand, which is not his dominant hand, but it might as well be. Is any part of this guy less than 100% assertive? *And why am I going all gooey inside?* Hell, he told me to leave, and just before Christmas. What kind of a monster does that? *And why the hell does my body refuse to behave around him?*

"Yes, you did." I raise my gaze, force myself to see this through, "I'm done with you."

He frowns and something flickers in his gaze. "Amelie, I—"

"Aunteee Amelieee." Phe runs across the room and throws herself at me.

I tug my hand, but Weston still doesn't release it. I half bend, rub the little girl's hair. "Hey, baby, watcha have there for me?"

She holds up the craft paper, showing an outline of a princess that she's colored in, complete with tiara. "Who's this?"

"It's you." She smiles widely. "Princess Amelie."

"Awww." My heart stutters. I tug on my hand again, and this time, Weston releases me. I lower myself to a squat as he takes my drink from my hand. I ignore the gesture, accept the drawing from Phe. "It's beautiful."

"So pretty," Phoenix giggles.

"Yes, you are." I pull the little girl close and kiss her cheek loudly.

She bursts out laughing, then pulls away. I rise to my feet, glance at the drawing. "Aww," I sigh, "it really is pretty."

"You're prettier," Weston's deep rumble surrounds me. I shiver. *Hell, this really was a bad idea.*

I begin to walk away.

"Amelie," he calls out.

Don't stop; don't.

"Your drink."

I wave a hand in the air, "You have it."

I walk toward Kirsten, joining her and the girls. Skye has her nose buried in a book, as usual. She glances up at me, then at the drawing. She snorts under her breath, turns back to her reading.

Kirsten grimaces, then mouths 'sorry.'

I laugh. I remember being far worse at her age. Of course, my parents, being the strict disciplinarians they were, didn't help. It's why I had rebelled every inch of the way. Christmas at home had been quiet, my parents not wanting to change their routine much, even for the festive season. Perhaps there is comfort in everyday chores? More likely, they were so content in each other's company, I'd never fit in with them. Always the third wheel, the outsider looking in. Then they'd retired to Spain; and with that, all expectation of my visiting them for Christmas had been dropped — on both our sides. Our communication had dwindled down to the occasional phone calls, then that had stopped too.

Don't get me wrong, they did their best for me, always provided for me, gave me everything I needed... Except a sense of belonging... The kind of warmth I find here. Max runs into the room, heads straight for me and jumps up.

"Hey boy," I lift him into my arms. "Missed me huh?" He licks my face, and I giggle, "Wow, so much affection, and you saw me what, three minutes ago, huh?"

I glance up and meet Weston's gaze. He raises the glass — the one he had taken from me — and brings it to his lips. He drains the water, then lowers the glass and licks his lips.

I swallow. Shit, what craziness is this, that his every glance is filled with undertones? A crazy sexual tension that will never abate between us. Too bad… He is an alphahole who will never change colors.

"Patrick," Kirsten cries out, then moves forward to greet the man who's just walked in. He opens his arms wide as Phe races for him. He catches the little girl, swings her high and she squeals. "Daddy, you're home," Phe cries.

"I told you I'd be." He kisses her on the cheek, lowers her to the floor, then turning, sweeps his wife into a kiss.

"Ugh," Skye makes a gagging sound, then turns back to her book, which she's reading standing up, by the way.

"Hey, sweetheart, a kiss for your old man?" Patrick grins at her. Skye glances up, sighs, then walks forward and offers her cheek. Patrick hugs her close, and Skye seems to thaw enough to put her arm around him to hug him.

I can't stop the giggle that bounces out of me.

Warmth envelops me, and I don't need to turn round to know that Weston has moved in to stand behind me. "You went against my order."

I snort. "What you going to do about it?" I tip up my chin, "Oh, and I am here because Kirsten asked me to stay. I'll be gone tomorrow, and then we'll never have to meet each other again." I thrust Max at him.

Weston grabs the puppy, mostly because I took him by surprise, no doubt.

Max whines, wriggles around. Weston sets him down and he prances toward the girls.

He straightens, glares at me, "You're still on my turf."

"Whatever." I throw my hands up, pivot and flounce toward the door. Wide shoulders fill the door and a tall man walks in. His features are vaguely familiar. *Huh?*

He glances at me, and his face lights up, "Amelie." He strides toward me.

I blink up, trying to place him. "Hunter?"

"How are you?" He places his hands on my shoulders, then bends to kiss me on each cheek. "This evening just got more exciting," he whispers in my ear.

I chuckle, pat his shoulder, "What are you doing here?"

"Yes, that's what I'd like to know." Weston stalks forward to glare at him. The two men are the same height. Hunter wears a suit that is every bit as well cut as Weston's. His dark hair curls over his collar. He's every bit as handsome as Weston. So why the hell don't I feel the same attraction toward him?

He glances between us, then grins, "I was invited."

"Who the fuck by?" Weston snaps.

"By me."

Another man stalks into the room. I blink. His features, his build, that bored, annoyed perma-dick face... It could be Weston, only it isn't. The creases around his eyes are deeper, his gaze so cold that I shiver. I take a step back and Weston's warmth cocoons me. His big palm rests on my waist and I don't push it off. His touch grounds me in the face of his darker, older sibling walking through the door."

"Liam," Weston drawls, confirming my suspicion.

"Weston," Liam jerks his chin. His gaze rests on me for a second; there's no change in expression on his face, no acknowledgement that he's seen me. And I thought Weston was a jerk? I bite the inside of my cheek. "Hunter's with me," Liam tilt his head. "I am supporting his campaign to run for Prime Minister."

"Thought this was meant to be family only," Weston growls.

Liam barely glances in my direction, "Considering you have your latest piece here, you shouldn't speak, huh?"

I wince. Weston's big body stiffens behind me. Anger thrums from him and he takes a step forward. "Apologize to her," he growls.

I blink. Go figure. Alphahole here, gets all macho and protective when faced with the threat of an enemy. Or perhaps he wants to save face because I'm here as his guest... Except, I'm not.

I turn on him. "I don't need you to fight my battles," I snap, then turn to Liam. "For your information, I am here because Kirsten invited me to stay." I step forward, tip my chin up, "And I don't really care for your impoliteness...and for your apology, even less."

"Liam," a female voice whips through the space.

I look around him and wince. It's Rosie. Of course, it's their mother. That's all I need. What a nightmare. Why did I accept Kirsten's invitation to stay, again?

Phe skips over to me, then slips her hand through mine. I meet her gaze. She tugs on my arm, I bend down, and she whispers, "You're not leaving, are you?"

I draw in a breath, then shake my head. "Not yet," I whisper back.

I straighten as Rosie walks into the room. She glances between her sons, "Everything okay?" There's a warning edge to her voice.

"Yes, Mother," Liam grates out.

She turns to Weston, who hesitates. She tilts her head, and Weston pulls back his shoulders, gives Liam a hard look. "Apologize first," he insists.

I am about to tell him to forget it, when Liam walks over to me. He takes my shoulders then bends to kiss my cheek. "I am sorry about my earlier remark," he says, "I'm afraid Weston tends to get on my nerves. I didn't mean to insult you that way."

He straightens. Weston tugs me closer so I am out of Liam's reach.

Liam looks between us and smirks, then walks around us toward the dining room. *What the hell was that? Apology my foot.* He may have sounded earnest, but that condescending look on his face? Jesus, he is one tough customer.

Rosie turns to Weston, who draws in a breath. He walks over to her, kisses her cheek, "We're good, Mother."

"Good." She pats his cheek. "Let's eat." She walks toward the dining room.

OMG, now that's power, huh? She's got these alphas to heel, and that's a talent she'd have learned early. And how, I mean, seriously, how does she do it? She's the true leader here.

Hunter, Kirsten and Patrick follow. Phe skips forward, with Skye trailing behind.

Weston turns on me and the scowl on his face deepens. He bends his knees, thrusts his face into mine, "I've called the car service. They'll be here after dinner for you. Don't find an excuse to stay back this time, you get me?"

37

Weston

Why the hell is she sitting next to him? I frown across the table as
Hunter leans over to say something to Amelie. She giggles, her
cheeks rosy. From his company? From the wine? From the warmth
in the fireplace, maybe?

I stab my fork into the chestnut and bring it to my mouth. "Why
is she talking to him?" I grumble under my breath.

"Because unlike you, she has manners and knows when to be
polite, especially at family dinners." Kirsten nudges me with her
elbow, "Can't take your eyes off her, huh?"

"Of course, not." I glance down at my plate, "This food is fucking
bland."

"Lost your appetite, huh?" She snickers.

I glower, "Don't try to get a rise out of me."

"I thought I was the only one who could," she replies, "until —"

"Until?"

"Her, of course," she chuckles.

I don't need to look up to know she's glanced across at the
pesky, curvy woman who I'd invited into my life. Holy fuck, what

the hell had I been thinking? "Why is she still here?" I roll my shoulders.

"I can't believe you asked her to leave, and so close to Christmas."

"It's two days to Christmas," I grumble. "Enough time for her to join her family, if she chooses."

"You're a class-A douche," she hisses at me. "Is it because you're in love with her that you're being so terrible to her? Is that why you're going out of your way to insult her, to ensure she'll never look at you again?"

"No, to the first, and as to the second... Well, that's my nature."

"Ha," she snorts. "You can't pull off your mean-ass persona with me, dear brother. You and I are too close for that."

And isn't that the truth. Kirsten is two years younger than me, close enough for us to hang out together. Growing up, I was her protector and she was my shadow, who tagged along with me on all my boyhood adventures. Unlike Liam, who at eight years older than me, was someone I hadn't gotten to know as well. There'd always been a chasm between us, which had only increased after our father had passed on.

I blow out a breath. "I'm not in love with her," I insist again.

"Keep telling yourself lies; that's a specialty of yours, huh?"

"Don't push me on this one," I say through clenched teeth.

Amelie's giggle reaches me. I glance up to find her leaning into Hunter. I clench my hand around my fork, which slips from my fingers and smashes into the plate. The clash rings out and everyone at the table turns to glance at me.

"Sorry, still getting used to using my non-dominant hand for every day stuff," I scowl.

Amelie straightens, glances at me and away. Good. At least, she's heeding the warning.

"Your finger troubling you, much?" my mother asks.

I glance down at my right hand. "The cast comes off next week, then a few more weeks of therapy and I should be back at work by mid-January, at the latest," I reply.

"How did the accident take place?" Liam asks from his position at the foot of the table.

After father passed, Mother assumed the responsibility of running the business, until Liam took over. She still holds veto power on the board and is the head of the family.

"I was forced off the road," I reply.

"Forced off?" Liam frowns.

"No need to concern yourself. I am looking into it, with the Seven."

"The Seven." His lips twitch, "You place too much importance on their friendship."

"At least I have friends, unlike you," I shoot back, then wince. Shit, a few minutes in the company of my family, and hell, if the old insecurities don't come tumbling back.

"I'm focused on my goals, on preserving and growing the family name. I'd do anything for it."

"Including getting married and producing an heir, no doubt?" I scowl.

"If that's what's needed of me, I won't shirk my duties." Liam wipes the edges of his lips with his napkin.

"You're getting married?" Amelie leans forward, her gaze sparkling. "Who's the lucky woman?"

"Someone I haven't met yet," he says coolly.

"So, you don't know her, but you're marrying her?" She frowns.

"Until he does, he doesn't get to take over the family business," Kirsten explains. "Nor, for that matter, can Weston."

"Huh?" Amelie scowls across the table.

I stiffen, nudge Kirsten with my knee. She shuffles away. Fuck! Why do little sisters always have to be such a pain?

"Explain," Amelie insists.

"Until both of my brothers marry, and specifically for Liam, until he produces an heir, they cannot get access to the family business—"

"—Or to their trust funds," my mother completes the sentence. "It's tradition," she elaborates. "Something decreed by my husband's grandfather, and which I hope my sons will honor."

"And Kirsten?" Amelie asks.

"I don't count," she smirks. "Only a woman, after all, and all that."

"And you know your father changed his will to ensure that you inherit your share of the money," Mother retorts.

"I don't get access to the company," she protests.

"Do *you* want access to the company?"

"Guess not," she admits. "Still, it would have been nice if Dad had given me the choice."

"He made sure you'd be taken care of—"

"Not that Kirsten would have lacked for anything, as long as I am here." Patrick folds his arm around her and pulls her close.

Amelie's features grow wistful and she glances from Kirsten to me. I glare at her, she bites down on her lower lip, and damn it, of course, my cock instantly notices.

I hold her gaze. She looks away, raises her glass, "A toast to Kirsten and Patrick." She smiles.

I glance over to my mother, who seems surprised. Then she surprises me, by raising her glass. "A toast." She coughs, rubs at her chest.

"You okay?" I frown.

"Never been better," she smiles, the skin stretching around her mouth. A gleam of sweat glistens on her forehead. She raises her glass in her left hand, her dominant hand, which trembles. All of my senses pop. My visions, tunnels. Even before the glass slips from her fingers, I rise, then rush over to her. I catch her as she sinks into her chair, her breathing ragged, her skin pallid.

"Liam," I snap at my brother, "call an ambulance."

He jumps to his feet so fast, his chair topples over with a crash. He pulls out his phone, walks away as he dials.

I hear the sound of Max barking. Phe begins to cry, then is hushed. More chairs being shoved back, the slap of footsteps on the floor, then Hunter and Patrick crowd me. "Move back," I snap, and they comply.

"Weston," my mother whispers as I lower her to the ground. Sweat beads her upper lip, "Weston." She coughs again.

"Don't talk," I say.

I reach for my mother's wrist to check her pulse and glimpse the steel band attached to her watch—the bloody watch that my father presented to her when they got married; the one she'd put away after the incident, when she'd found out about my trigger. Why the hell is she wearing it? My heart begins to race, the blood thundering at my temples. *I stare at the watch — the hands on the face, the big hand moving fast, so fast, the small hand following pace, the countdown for my life as my kidnapper had hauled me into the small room across the corridor from where I had been imprisoned with the rest, as he'd tied me to the chair, attached the rigged clock to my chest. "Will you survive it this time? Follow the countdown, the ticking of the clock as it edges closer to the end."*

He'd ripped off my blindfold — the light had cast his face in shadow so I hadn't been able to get a good look at him — then left me with only the ticking for company, and I had screamed against the gag, tried to pull free. "If you move, the bomb goes off. If you disturb the clock, it goes off. If you so much as breathe too hard…it goes off. Hell, if you so much as live…it may go off… Will you survive this round?" His voice echoes through my head. I stare at the moving hands of the watch.

"What do you think, Weston?" my kidnapper asks. "Will you live or will you die this round?"

Live or die?

Do I want to die?

What do I have to live for? Why can't someone rescue me and put me out of my misery? If I get out of here, I'll never allow anyone else to control my life…never. Never.

"Weston?"

Never relinquish your power. Never.

"Weston!" Something connects with my cheek. I fall back, glance up into familiar blue eyes. The eyes of an angel. The blue of the ocean, the sky. The only place where I could be safe, where I can soar above it all, away from here, away from these memories, the clocks that tick down to my demise.

"Weston." Those blue eyes blaze at me; silver sparks in their depths. Huh? "You need to help her. Snap out of your shock. Now!" She raises her palm, then slaps me again, and again.

I blink. "Amelie?"

"Thank God," she cries. She pinches my chin, turns my face to where my mother is sprawled on the floor, her hand extended. I press my thumb to her wrist. *There's no pulse.*

"Mother!" I touch her shoulder. "Rosie," I call out her name but she doesn't respond.

Fuck, fuck, fuck. I tilt her head back, lift the tip of her chin and, lean in closer. Her chest doesn't move. I listen over her mouth and nose for breathing sounds, hold my cheek over her nose. Fuck, she's not breathing.

I place the heel of my left hand on the center of her chest, place the heel of the other hand on top of the first hand, interlace my fingers, My injured finger screams in protest—I ignore it. I push down with my arms and hands, using my body weight to compress her chest.

Tick-tock-tick-tock- Push-now-push-now.

My own personal song that has a rhythm that corresponds to the compressions per minute required for the rhythm.

Tick-tock-tick-tock. Push-now-push-now.

Sweat beads my brow; pain sears my arm. I reject it, continue with the momentum.

Tick-tock-tick-tock-push-now-push-now.

I count to 30 compressions, then tilt her head, lift her chin up, pinch her nose. I seal my mouth over hers, blow. Check to make sure that her chest rises. Blow again twice. Then back to chest compressions, count to 30, followed by 2 rescue breaths.

"Weston?"

I focus on my mother's face. *Come on, come on, breathe.*

"Weston, the paramedics are here."

Breathe. Breathe. I continue to push down to the rhythm in my head. *Tick-tock-tick-tock-breathe-now-breathe-now.*

"Weston!" Arms grab my shoulders. I wince; pain radiates from my injured finger; a coldness coils in my gut. I am pulled back. I lower my injured arm to my side, watch as the paramedics take over, blocking out the view of my mother. "It's my fault," I gasp.

"What? No." Amelie's face fills my line of sight. "Weston, it's nobody's fault."

"I froze," I mumble under my breath.

"Weston." Amelie cups my cheek, "Baby, look at me."

"The one time I needed to be in control of my senses, and I lost it. I couldn't move, couldn't breathe… All I could think of was—"

"The incident," she whispers. "Oh, baby, stop torturing yourself."

I raise my gaze to her face, "What's it to you?"

"What?"

"Why are you still here? Didn't I tell you to leave?"

"Weston, man, get a grip on yourself." Hunter touches my shoulder and something inside of me snaps. I rise to my feet, plant my uninjured fist in his face.

He reels back. Fire burns a trail up my arm from the burst skin on my knuckles. "Fuck." That hurt like a bitch, but what-fucking ever. "You keep the fuck away from her, you hear me."

"Man, you have this all wrong." Hunter puts up his hands; blood drips from his cut lip. *Good.*

"Weston," Amelie shoves herself between us, "what's wrong with you?"

"You," I growl. "You're what's wrong." *Fuck you, what the hell are you doing? Making sure you cut all ties with her, huh? You could have accepted her tenderness, her compassion, her softness—that always seems to make you unravel, that makes you weak. She makes me want everything I swore I don't need. Fuck me. And fuck her and,* "Fuck all of you." I stumble back.

She grabs hold of my suit jacket. "Weston, please stop," she sobs.

"Look at you," I snarl, "all empathetic and shit, when really all you want is my money. Admit it."

"No."

"Don't lie, that's why you accepted my deal. Its why you came here, why you're still here. Because you think I'll succumb to your charms? That perhaps I'll settle down and play happy family with you? Well, you can think again. That's not what I want."

"You don't mean it."

"You're right." *Shut the fuck up. you wanker. What the fuck are you saying? Don't do it; don't do it.* "I do want it."

Her chin wobbles, "You do?"

I nod, "Just not with you."

"At least you are being honest." Her features crumple and tears drip from her eyes. She wipes them away, straightens herself, "You may as well admit that you thought up this arrangement, because you wanted to fake a marriage in order to access your trust fund."

As if I need the family money? I am doing fine, more than fine, on my own steam.

I glare at her.

She tips her head back.

I flatten my lips. "Fine," I snap. "That's why I came up with this idea of a fake relationship. I should have known you were all wrong for it."

"Fine." She pulls herself up to her full height, "There's one more thing I need to tell you."

"Oh?"

She nods. "Go fuck yourself."

She brushes past me, walks out of the room, my house, my life… My everything.

My vision tunnels and my heart hammers so fast, I am sure I am having a cardiac as well. *Stop her; stop her.* I step toward her. Liam plants his body in my path.

"Get out of my way," I growl.

"Get ahold of yourself first." Liam grabs my shoulders. I shake him off, raise my fist—the wrong one—the one with my injured finger in a splint. *Fuck.* He swerves; my hand grazes his face. Pain crashes behind my eyes. The next moment something slams into my face, the world tilts, and darkness pulls me under.

38

Weston

"You're a wanker, you ass," Damian frowns down at me.

I tilt my chin up from where I am sprawled out on the examination table.

"Welcome back, Sleeping Beauty," Arpad drawls from the other side.

This scenario is all wrong. As a doctor, I am used to being in there, with the action, inside the OR, where I use my talent, my wits, my instinct, to save lives. Instead, I am sprawled out here…like the loser I am. *Loser, fucking loser.*

I try to sit up, and my entire body protests. I wince. Damian touches my shoulder. "Take it easy, Kincaid," he cautions.

"Fuck off," I mutter. What's wrong with me? I shoved her away. I knew what I was doing, I was aware of it. I had done it while in full possession of my senses. I hadn't been able to stop myself. What should I have said instead? Please stay; don't go. All the shit I threw your way? Those were my issues, not yours. My insecurities, my bloody fallacies about myself. I thought I was invincible, invulnerable, I thought I could control my fate, I thought… I could live without your touch, your kisses, your beautiful cunt…your spirit, your sass, your lips that clung to mine, your heart…your tender heart, your fun-loving attitude, that I admit, sometimes got on my nerves. I mean, can anyone be that chirpy, that happy all the time? What hurts of your own had you been hiding underneath? I'd never bothered to find out… And now, it is too late.

"Too late," I mumble.

"What's that?" Damian lowers his head to my eye level. "The fuck did you say?" he demands.

"It's too fucking late." I drag my fingers through my hair. "I let her go, man."

"Who are you talking about?"

My head whirls; I squeeze my eyes shut to stop it. Run an internal check on my vitals—pain in my right shoulder and my left, my left eye hurts like a bitch, my broken finger is numb and my chest… The band around my chest, that hollow sensation in my abdomen… I straighten, "Mother, how is she? Is she…?" I swallow. *Don't say it; don't think it.* "Is she…?" I swallow down the ball of emotion in my throat. Shit, since when did I become this weak? This unable to take on my share of the burden for my family? This selfish that I am slumped in a corner worrying about myself… My bloody love life, which isn't… It is more than that. Hell. I sit up; my head spins, "Whoa." I slouch down again, "The hell is wrong with me?"

"They had to sedate you."

"What?"

"You had a bit of a breakdown, ol' chap?"

"What?"

"You lost it there," Arpad's somber voice reaches me.

"You're not making any sense, man." I straighten. My shoulder hurts like a bitch—my right shoulder. I glance down at my injured finger; the splint has been replaced by a fresh one.

"Yeah," Damian drawls. "You hit Liam, who decked you. They hauled you into another ambulance, brought you here. You were lucky that you didn't fracture that finger again, though you're going to have to wear that splint for a while longer."

Right!

"And my mother?"

"She's fine," Damian replies.

"She had a—"

"She didn't," He shakes his head.

"What?" I scowl, "She had a cardiac arrest."

"She didn't."

"I don't understand." I scowl.

"She had symptoms resembling a cardiac arrest, but your CPR saved her. But it wasn't a cardiac arrest."

"You are not making any sense."

"She was poisoned."

"What?" I shake my head. "How did that happen?"

"They are trying to find out."

"The food we ate." I rub the back of my neck "The rest of us are fine?"

"Everyone else is, as far as I know," Damian confirms.

"She was targeted," Arpad offers.

"Do they know who did it?" I glance between them. The two men exchange glances.

"What are you thinking?" I growl.

Damian glances down at me, "Who has a vendetta against the Seven?"

"The Mafia," I breathe.

Arpad's features harden; he doesn't comment.

"Fucking asspricks." My stomach churns. Sweat beads my forehead. "They changed our lives… Traumatized us. Hell, I thought I'd gotten over my bloody trigger…but fucking-fuck… I froze when I saw my mother's watch."

"We heard," Damian replies, his tone quiet.

"I couldn't help her." A ball of emotion closes my throat.

"From what we heard, you gave her CPR, which saved her life."

"I didn't do enough." I rake my fingers through my hair.

"Aren't you hearing what we're trying to tell you, asshole? It wasn't your fault."

"Right," I draw in a breath, "I get it." I swing my legs over the side. "I need to go see her,"

Arpad stops me with an arm on my shoulder. "She doesn't want to see you."

"What?"

"No one in your family wants you there."

"Excuse me? Are you joking?"

"Not after how you acted with her..."

"What? You just said my CPR saved her. Why are they pissed at me?"

"Amelie."

"She's not their concern."

"By all accounts, she is now."

"The fuck do you mean?"

"She's in there with them," Arpad adds.

My heart begins to race. *Shit, can I put this right somehow? Have I been given another chance?* If I can get to her and explain my actions... I rise to my feet and the world lurches around me. "Fucking fuck." My legs give way under me and I crash back onto the examination table.

"Man, you're pathetic." Damian glowers down at me. "They don't want to see you. You don't want to go there; it could get ugly."

"They're my family; they'll see me," I insist.

"You sure?"

"I mean, so I was, uh—unreasonable with her."

"You think?"

"Okay, I was an ass. I hurt her—"

"More like broke her heart. What were you thinking? Asking her to leave in front of everyone? A moose would have more sense than you."

"A moose?"

"It's Christmas, and all that," he explains.

"Right." I lurch back up to my feet; my legs seem to hold me this time. I take a step forward, sway. Damian grabs my shoulder. I shake it off, "I can fucking do this on my own."

"Fine, man, whatever." He exchanges a look with Arpad, who shakes his head.

"You bitches have anything to say, you can say it to my face."

"Still crotchety in his old age," Arpad mutters.

"If you cunts can't help me, then you can fuck off," I growl, step toward the exit of the room. By the time I reach the doorway I am panting. I grab the doorframe; sweat beads my forehead. *Shit, the fuck is wrong with me?* My shoulder hurts, but my fractured finger seems to have gone numb, thank fuck. I propel myself forward, make it into the corridor and crash into a nurse. The young woman straightens, shoots me an annoyed glance, then blinks. "Dr Kincaid?"

Thank fuck. She recognizes me from when I'd done my residency in this very hospital. I need all the breaks I can get; so long as I reach her in time.

I glance down at the nurse's badge. "Marcy," I kick my lips up in a smile, "Can you help me?"

She flutters her eyelids and my gag reflex kicks in. *Shit, has to be the drugs I am on. It's no wonder I feel like I am flying. It's also the only reason that I can't tolerate another woman putting the moves on me. Yeah, nothing to do with the fact that a sassy, curvy, pastry chef has entranced me. Sure, keep telling yourself that, fuckhead.* My head spins. I put out my hand to steady myself and Marcy grabs it. *Fuck, this is not right—me touching another woman. The fuck is wrong with you Kincaid?* Eyes on the prize, remember, and right now, I need help in getting to where Amelie…and my mother, and yeah, the entire family is.

I hold onto Marcy's shoulder, "Can you help me?"

39

Amelie

"How dare he do this?" I mumble under my breath. *How dare he tell me that he doesn't want me, doesn't want a future with me? Get over it; get over him.* Every time he's pushed me away, I've returned to him. Like an ant attracted to sugar, like cream on milk, like jelly on the floor — gah, stop. Even my metaphors are beginning to sound pathetic. *Just leave, before he hurts you further. Pulls away at any final shred of self-respect you have left, before he destroys your confidence completely.*

"Did you say something?" Kirsten asks me from her perch on the chair opposite me. We are in the waiting room of the hospital in Durham, where the ambulance had taken Rosie.

I'd seen Liam deck Weston, had seen him crumple to the ground, had lost my shit and run to him, then had ridden with him in the second ambulance to the hospital.

Once the doctors had confirmed that he was going to be okay, I had turned to leave, but Kirsten had stopped me. She'd insisted I stay with them while they waited for the 'all clear' from the surgeon so they could visit with Rosie.

"I think I should leave." I turn to her, "This is a family matter."

"You are family," she insists. "My asshole brother may not see it yet, but he loves you."

"Does he?" I chuckle, but it's completely devoid of humor. "He has a funny way of showing it."

She searches my features; her own soften. She takes my hand in hers, "Sweetheart, I understand how upset you must be with his behavior. I have no words to apologize for god-knows-what-all he's said and done to you. All I can say is, please be patient with him."

"You think I'd be here otherwise?" I swallow. "Only, I'm not sure it's helping."

"Oh, it is, more than you can imagine." She hesitates, "You're the first woman he's brought home. Ever."

"Oh." I swallow, "I... I am...?" My heart begins to beat faster. Does it mean anything? Does it? No.

"That was part of the pretense." I say. "So he could show you all that he intended to settle down. After all, he needs to get married to claim his inheritance, right?"

"Only he doesn't need the money," Kirsten points out. "He's rich enough, not to mention successful enough, in his own right."

"That's true." I admit. "But it doesn't negate that he asked me to pose as his fake girlfriend. Why did he have to boil down the attraction between us to that? Why did he have to turn it into something so...transactional?"

"He can't seem to stop destroying what's dearest to him." Kirsten smiles at me, but it's a sad smile. She holds my hand between her palms.

"Tell me about it," I choke out. "I've tried; I really have. When it comes to him, I seem to have some self-destructive tendencies of my own."

"The chemistry between the two of you..." She fans herself, "Honestly, it's off the charts. I see the way he follows you around with his eyes, like he wants to eat you up."

I redden. "Is it that obvious?"

"You have no idea." Her lips quirk. "It's different, it's special, it's something that's not easy to come by… Maybe once in a lifetime, even."

"You think I don't know that?" I tug on my hand and she releases it. I drag my fingers through my hair. Shit, somewhere during the last few hours, my hair had loosened from the chignon I'd pulled it into. Bet I look a sight, to match how I am feeling inside — beaten, broken, sad… Hell. This isn't why I had left London. This is not what I had bargained for when he'd walked into the cabin naked, swept into my life like a freshly baked baguette which I couldn't keep away from. OMFG, that's it then. That last metaphor… Hell, why does it remind me about certain parts of him which are as beautifully endowed? As thick… As gorgeous to put my mouth on. I rise to my feet.

Kirsten glances up at me. "Where are you going?"

"I… I can't do this." I swallow, "You understand, don't you? If I want to come out of this with even some small part of me intact, I need to go." I turn to leave.

"It's the incident," her voice follows me.

I pause, then turn to her. "So I am told," I say.

"You said he mentioned it to you, but has he told you what they did to him?" she queries.

I shake my head.

"Maybe you should ask him."

"Maybe," I tilt my head, "maybe not." Maybe I've had enough of Weston and his entire family — much as I have come to like them, Kirsten especially, and the kids, and hell, even his mother… She's something — formidable, strong, a true matriarch who holds them together. For good or bad, they are a unit. They fight and hate each other, and when there is a crisis like this, they come together too. They have each other's backs.

Something I've never had. I'm not part of a family; I have my own, but I've never belonged there. Is that why I had wanted to start a company, a business of my own? To create a family, of sorts? Is that what has driven me thus far? Had I sensed that about Weston, and was that one of the reasons I had been attracted to him. That and his gorgeous, beautiful dick, of course, and that caring demeanor of his, which he hides so bloody well. If it had not been for Max, and how he'd taken care of his nieces… Or how he'd been toward his mother, hell, I'd have missed that completely. All in all… It is time to put this behind me, to go home to the future I would build for myself.

I turn, walk toward the exit.

"Amelie," Liam's voice stops me.

I turn to find him striding toward me. "Are you leaving?" He frowns. Those features, so like Weston's, tighten. A lump forms in my throat. Shit, this is not good. Just because he reminds me of the alphahole, who I must try to forget, doesn't mean I need to get all teary.

"Yes," I straighten my spine, "I must go."

"Have you spoken to Weston?" He tilts his head. His dark gaze, so like Weston's yet not, sweeps over my features. No, he's not Weston. He's colder, darker, unfeeling. Weston has that sly hint of humor in his eyes, that hint of wickedness which tempers that mean edge—not that he couldn't be horrible, but always, always there was that playfulness that peeked out, that sentiment that compelled me to tug on it and unravel the man inside… The one I love. "Bloody hell." I bring my hand to my mouth.

"What's wrong?" he asks.

"Nothing." *Everything.*

A shiver runs down my spine. *What have I done? How could I have fallen in love with that…that grumpy ass?* A hollow sensation permeates my legs. I stumble. He grips my shoulder and rights me. "Are you okay?" he asks.

"No, I am not," I whisper.

Weston's voice slices through the air. "Get away from her."

I stiffen. *Don't turn; don't face him, until you have gotten ahold of yourself.*

He sounds so close to me that I draw in a breath.

The hair on the back of my neck rises, and heat invades my back, a sure indication that he's standing not far from me.

I pull away from Liam, who doesn't let go. The hell? I frown up at him, and his gaze widens. His lips quirk. Huh? Is he toying with

Weston? I tilt my head; he subtly shakes his. "About time you decided to make an appearance," he drawls.

"Take your hands off of her," Weston snaps. My nerve endings crackle and I shuffle back, but Liam's hold stops me.

"Or what?" He raises his gaze to meet Weston's. "What are you going to do, little brother?"

"I am going to kill you." Weston's voice is even — no emotion, no sentiment. The hard edge to it ripples over my skin. *Shit, he isn't joking.*

"Let me go," I hiss at Liam, who steps back.

He tilts his head, not breaking eye contact with Weston. "What's got your knickers in a twist, huh?"

"Step aside, Amelie," Weston growls. My heart begins to race. I take in his features, the messed-up hair, those grey eyes, almost colorless, a clear indication that he's in the grip of emotions. When he's like this, he tends to lose control. He doesn't care how much his actions could hurt him, or those around him. He's like a wounded animal, ready to hit out at whoever, whatever seems to be a threat.

"Wes," I whisper.

He raises his fist…his left fist… Shit. If he wounds that…it will take him even longer to heal. What if he wrecks any of the fingers of his intact hand? Already, he's going to be laid up longer than anticipated with his unhealed injury.

"Wes," I grip at his sleeve.

His gaze on Liam, he lowers his chin. "I am going to take you down, motherfucker," he growls.

"Not sure I'd use that adjective considering we are brothers," Liam chuckles.

"How dare you put your hand on her."

"What's it to you? Thought you weren't interested in her." Weston's features harden.

"None of your business," he snarls. A vein throbs at his forehead. "Come within an inch of her and I'll deck you."

"Oh, I'll do better than that." Liam leans in closer, "In fact, I might make a play for her. After all, you've relinquished your claim on —"

Weston swings.

I gasp.

Liam laughs.

I stand on tip-toe, throw my arms around Weston's shoulders… Or as much of him as I can reach, considering how big he is. "Stop it," I snap. "Now."

He blinks, arm raised. Huh? The alphahole stopped in his tracks? Guess Rosie's not the only one who's able to bring them to heel. Maybe I picked up something from her, after all.

"Wes," I lean into him, push my breasts into his chest, dig my fingers into his uninjured shoulder, "look at me, babe."

His big body shudders; his chest planes seem to go rock hard.

"I should fucking thrash him for laying a finger on you."

"But you won't," I declare.

I peer up, to see his throat move as he swallows. The tendons of his beautiful throat flex; the pulse beats at the base of his neck. I reach up and kiss him there, suck on that space where his scent is most profound. Dark edginess, cool pine, warm cloves… My senses cloud with Weston.

"Wes," I tip my chin up, "kiss me."

He glances down, those colorless eyes filled with an emotion… A hint of something that is so very close to… No, not that. He doesn't feel that for me. Oh, he wants me all right, he lusts for me, needs to possess me and claim me, so no one else can, but love… Ha! The alphahole only loves himself. "Kiss me," I insist. "Do it."

He drops his head, closes his mouth over mine. He swipes his tongue in between my lips and drinks from me. He curves his arm around my shoulders, yanks me to him, crushes me to that beautiful, broad, gorgeous chest of his, and kisses me, and kisses me. My head spins; I swear I see stars. He kisses me until my knees tremble, and I hold onto his sleeves, and then I am kissing him back. I open my mouth wider, grind my pelvis into the hard column that tents his pants and I pour myself into that connection between us, where his mouth takes from me and I offer myself up… Completely, wholly, absolutely. His hand comes up to cup my neck, he tilts his head, softens the kiss, until it's his lips on mine, nibbling on my mouth, brushing over mine, tasting of me, inviting me, enticing me, to slide my tongue inside his mouth, to partake of him, to drink from him, to open myself to accept what he is offering—his past, my life, our future together, what I am, what he is, a shared path, for he is mine. And I am his. His, and only his. I tear my mouth from his, so fast that my teeth catch on his lip.

He winces.

I stare at the drop of blood that blooms on his lower lip.

"I'm sorry," I whisper.

"I'm not." His lips curl.

"I am leaving you." I peer into his eyes.

"No." He frowns.

"Yes," I reply, "let go of me."

"What?" He shakes his head. "I can't."

"You can," I thrust out my chin, " and you will."

"No fucking way," he growls.

"Yes, way." My lips tremble and my voice cracks, "Goodbye, Wes."

He looks into my eyes, really looks, and the color fades from his cheeks. "Princess," he whispers. His fingers curve around the nape of my neck. A shiver runs down my back and my sex clenches. Hell, when he does that… Holds me like I am his, promises with his gaze to fuck me like I am his... When he stares at me like I am the only thing in the world that matters… Then I know...

It's time I get away from him. I hadn't meant to fall in love with him... How could I allow myself to feel so much when I was still the woman he'd paid to bring home to meet his family? I don't mean anything to him. I'd been a challenge... Someone to seduce, to buy with his wealth and use as a fuck-toy to pass the time. Hell. The pressure builds at my temples. I am only making this worse on myself. I need time away, time to process everything that has happened. I needed to get away from here.

"Please," I mumble, "let me have this."

His throat bobs and the skin around his eyes creases. Then he lowers his hand.

I step back, walk around him.

"Princess."

I pause.

"This isn't over."

I turn to him, "Yes, it is. You know it is."

His features twist.

I turn, head for the exit.

40

Christmas Day

Weston

I stare into the amber liquid at the bottom of my glass. *Fuck, fucking fuck.* I'd stood back and let her walk away. I hadn't gone after her. I'd held my balls in my hand and allowed her to leave. Am I a man? Can I call myself a male worth his manhood? I hadn't stopped her; I hadn't. *Bloody fuck. Why hadn't I?* For once in my life, I had faltered. I had stood by, and for the second time, let her walk out, and this time, there is no going back. I'd had my chance and I had blown it. I had allowed my emotions to get the better of me.

When she'd stared into my eyes and pleaded with me to allow her to win… I had wanted her to. Not that this is a game, or a war. Okay, so maybe it is a fight between us—this push and pull. This constant thrum of arousal that laces the air, that connects us and makes us want to go head-to-head... Even as I want to yank her to me and kiss her, and suck on those sweet-sugary tits of hers, bury my fingers in her moist pussy, dip my tongue in the crevasse of her belly button, sink to my knees in front of her, thrust my head between her legs and ravish her, please her, make her come.

Hell… Her happiness and her needs, they come first. Her confidence? I never want to shake that. Her sass and fire, her independence? They are a fucking turn on. It's what had challenged me. It's why I had noticed her in the first place. In a world filled with compliance, she had stood out. She had baited me, hated me, pushed me away, and that had only aroused me further.

I'd wanted to...what? Curb her? Tie her to me? I should have known better. A free spirit like Amelie needs to be nurtured, to be allowed to soar as she wants… And I'd be in the background watching, applauding, encouraging, paving her way… Fuck. I shake my head. What am I thinking? What happened to the dominant surgeon who didn't give a fuck about anyone else…except his patients? To be fair, I'd cared for them, but they had been a way to nourish my ego. Fuck. Everything in my life so far has been one long trip to soothe that scared boy inside of me. The one who had never recovered from the incident.

So, I was kidnapped.

I was hurt.

I was…abused. Mentally and emotionally.

Fuck, fuck, fuck. So what? Shit happens; deal with it. How could I have allowed those few days to color my life so completely? Enough to not recognize the only good thing that had come my way. Her.

"Bloody fuck." I drain my glass then hurl it against the wall of the living room. The glass bounces off of the hard surface, hits the floor, bounces again, comes to a rest at my feet. Go figure. *Can't do even one thing properly, can you?* I kick the offending object and it rolls toward the door. A booted foot stops it.

I groan. "Fuck off," I grunt.

"Merry Christmas to you too," Damian's chirpy voice echoes through the drumming in my head.

Fuck.

I turn away, head toward the bar in the corner of the living room.

I grab a glass, reach for the bottle, miss it, swoop down on it. *Finally!* I pour myself a healthy measure of Macallan's. *Fuck that.* I fill the snifter to the top. Set the bottle down on the bar counter with a thwack.

"Careful, ol' chap. That whiskey's older than you."

"So's your nagging," I growl.

"Seen yourself in the mirror lately?" Damian continues.

I frown, "Heard yourself lately?"

"No need to, ol' chap." He smirks. "I rest confident in the power of my good looks."

"Jesus," I swear, "Can you hear yourself?" I wince.

"No sweeter sound in the world, right?" He grins.

I stare up at him. "Did you just say that?"

"What?" He frowns.

"Have you any idea how pompous you sound, you prat?"

"So?" He straightens his arm, tugs on the sleeve of the white button-down that shows below his jacket.

"So?" I raise the shoulders, "So it's bloody off-putting."

Damian frowns. "Who are you, and what have you done to my douchebag wanker of a friend?" he mutters.

"I'll let you know when I find the fuck out." I bring the glass to my lips, take a sip, then grimace. Maybe it wasn't a good idea to substitute alcohol for coffee. I hadn't stopped drinking since I'd dragged my sorry ass home, after seeing my mother in the hospital yesterday.

They'd discharged her this morning, thank fuck. The poison, whatever it was, had vanished from her system. It had left her weak, but she was stable. Thank the bloody gods. I'd lost one parent already; I'm not ready to lose another. I don't want to lose her. "Fuck." I raise the glass, down half of it. Sweat breaks on my brow. My left hand—so far unhurt. Maybe I need to remedy that? Sure, go for it, wipe out the career you've worked so hard to build, huh? Why not, while you're at it, light a flame to everything you've achieved thus far... All of it is nothing, meaningless without her. I slap the glass onto the bar potty it cracks. Huh? The amber liquid bleeds out onto the mahogany counter top.

"You all right?" Damian's voice is concerned.

"Yes. No." I plant my elbows on the bar, in the whiskey which seeps into my sleeves, but whatever. Why the fuck should I care that I smell like a distillery? It's not like she's there to bury her nose in my chest, to rub her cheek into my shoulder, turn her face into my arm pit and coil into me like the feline, sensuous woman she is. "Go away," I moan, then bury my head between my palms. *If I press my hands tightly against my ears, would it block out the sound of her laughter?* I snicker. *Getting delusional now, huh? You've gone mental; admit it.*

"Wes," Damian grips my shoulder, "you've gotta get yourself in hand."

"For what?" I mutter, "I let her leave. Didn't have the balls to go after her either."

"Maybe you aren't ready yet for this relationship."

I stiffen. "The fuck do you mean?"

"She was too good for you, ol' chap."

That she was.

"She's someone who deserves better."

"She deserves the best," I agree.

"And you're all wrong for her."

"Clearly."

"You did the right thing."

Huh? I scowl.

"If you can't make her happy, you should let her go. If she comes back to you—"

"—She won't," I mumble. "She bloody hates me."

"*I* hate you. The world doesn't like you, man, it's normal."

"Thanks," I grumble. "Nice to know I can trust you to have my back."

"Always," I hear the laughter in his voice, turn and shoot him a glance.

His features are schooled into a serious expression, which is seriously weird. Which also means he's trying to rile me.

"The fuck's on your mind?" I growl.

"Me?" He points to himself, "Nothing, man. I'm not the one with a broken heart—"

"I break hearts. I don't get mine broken..." my voice trails off.

He nods. "Sadly, I believe you've crossed over to the dark side."

"What?"

"You remember the thing that had its claws into first Jace, then Sinner, and then Saint?"

"No, I don't." I scowl, and I thought I was delusional?

"I'm afraid you've fallen prey to it as well."

I straighten, lower my chin to my chest, "I have no idea what you're talking about. And it's not because I'm a bit hungover—"

"A bit?" He snorts, "Don't you have to stop drinking before you can be hungover?

I glare at him. "Okay, my head is pounding, and clearly, I've poisoned myself with enough alcohol that I may spontaneously combust at any time—"

"Attaboy." He pats my shoulder, "Tell it like it is. I knew you'd come through."

I shake off his hand, "You're bloody creepy when you go all paternal."

"Me, paternal?" he laughs.

"Stranger things have happened." I roll my shoulders. My stomach copies the motion. "Shit." I wipe the sweat from my upper lip, "I don't think I'm feeling that well."

"Wonder why that is, huh?" Liam stalks in.

"Oh, bloody fuck," I groan. "Thought you'd crawled away under whatever rock you'd been found under."

He shakes his head, "Man, you've gone and done it now."

"What?"

Damian chuckles.

"What?" I ask again.

Liam folds his arms over his chest, "Shit or get off the pot."

"Eloquent, as always." I grimace.

His dark gaze takes in my features, "You look like hell."

"Still better-looking than you."

His forehead crinkles, "Why do I even bother with you, huh?"

"Because you know, at heart, I am the one destined for greatness."

"You've proved that already," he mutters. "You got your way in the end—became a surgeon, saved lives. You make the difference between life and death. You saved mother's life."

He comes forward, grips my shoulder, "Thank you."

Is he for real? "Did you just go all polite as fuck on me?" I scowl.

Liam's features twist, "Guess not even soulless bastards can resist the spirit of Christmas, huh?"

"You mean it, don't you?" I shake my head in disbelief. "You're actually thanking me for the first time ever, that I can remember."

"It is the first time," he confirms. "You can thank your woman for that."

"My woman?"

He nods. "Seeing you fall apart—"

"I didn't fall apart—" I snarl.

"—then give in, for the first time in my living memory, showed me, you have a human side. You're not as obnoxious as you come across."

The headache between my temples intensifies. Should I even bother to make sense of what is happening around here?

Arpad saunters in. "What are you still doing here?" He asks.

"That was my next question," Damian chuckles.

"I don't care either way, by the way," Liam drawls.

I glower. He steps back, then brushes his sleeve, as if to rid himself of all trace of contact. Wanker. Hold on… That's what I was…or had been… Then she'd swept in, and damn, if all those carefully built walls hadn't come collapsing around me like confetti. Did I just think confetti? Does that word even exist in my vocabulary?

Liam turns to leave, then shoots me a look over his shoulder.

"Oh, and Mother said to invite her over when you see her." He stalks off.

"When am I going to see who?" I glower.

"You gonna enlighten him?" Damian smirks.

"Nah, it's inevitable. It's more fun to watch him fight it." Arpad leans his hip against the bar.

Damian glances at me, "Tick-tock, ol' chap."

The blood drains from my face. I stumble, then right myself.

"Fuck." Damian leans forward to grab my shoulder, "I'm sorry, I didn't mean to say it like that. Of all people, I should have remembered about your triggers."

"Fuck that," I growl. "The Mafia; they broke into her bakery."

"When?" Damian straightens.

"She mentioned it to me, when we first met."

"But you weren't connected with her—"

"They'd have seen her at Sinclair's, then at Saint's wedding." I squeeze the bridge of my nose. "If they have been watching us—"

"They may have followed her to the cabin—" Arpad mutters.

"Which was broken into." My heart begins to race. "Fuck. And I let her leave. She's home, alone. If something happens to her..."

"It won't."

"By now, they must realize she means something to me. I brought her to meet my family, after all." Fuck. I'd put her in the path of danger.

"The cops—" Arpad ventures.

"We can't trust them," I growl. "We know they are connected with the Mafia. One leak and—" I don't voice my fears. "Besides, no way am I waiting around here. I need to make sure she is safe."

I stalk past them, toward the door.

"I have to go to her."

"Hold on," Damian calls after me, "You're not planning on driving, are you?"

41

Amelie

"I am such a loser," I cry into the phone as I pace my apartment.

"Wait, hold on, back up," Isla calms me. "Start from the beginning."

I balance the phone, with Isla peering out at me from the screen, on the kitchen table, "Kirsten called me a car—okay a limo. It was a freakin' limo service that she ordered to get me from Durham to London. Can you believe it? That's how these rich folks live, and clearly, I am not one of them."

"Who's Kirsten?" Isla asks.

"The alphahole's sister."

"So, we are back to calling him alphahole, huh?"

"Weston fucking a-hole Kincaid," I growl into the phone. "I never want to hear his name again."

"Urm," Isla clears her throat.

"Don't say it—" I warn her.

"I was only going to say that you just mentioned this name."

"That's what I was afraid of." I wrap the strands of my hair around my palm, "I mean, not that I am complaining about the limo, or anything."

"Of course, not."

"Not after I found the liquor bar in the back of the car."

"I assume you did it justice?" she snickers,

"Yeah," I hiccough. "Oops, sorry." I walk to the kitchen, fill a mug with water—because hell, I always drink water from coffee mugs. That's my little rebellious streak, right there. I sip from the mug, and walk over to the window of my studio apartment. The view is nothing like that from the cabin, or from Weston's mother's home. How funny I'd never been to his place. Where does he even live in London? It's official, I am in love with a man whose neuroses I know better than the basic stuff, you know, like his address, his favorite color. That's me, I do everything upside down, like my life. Fuck me now. I hiccough again. "Sorry again," I mumble.

"The bar in the limo?" Isla reminds me. "I assume you drank of all the whiskey?"

"Nope," I say, all smug. "No whiskey for me. Never touching that stuff, from now on."

"O-k-a-y."

"I sucked down all the champagne because I am celebrating."

"You are?"

"Yeap." I walk back to the shelves in the corner of what passes for my kitchen space, and open the door. Scrounge around. There. I retrieve the boxed wine I'd been gifted with, God knows when. Now is the time to open it. I unscrew it, peel back the plastic seal thingy, then look around for a glass, and fuck it! I tilt it to my mouth, draw from it. The cold liquid hits my gullet and I almost gag. Ugh! Is that vinegar or what? "Argh," I gasp.

"What's wrong?"

"Nothing." I place the boxed vinegar-that-had-once-been-wine back on the shelf and eye it. Do I dare drink more of it, or not? Shit, I can't even decide on the small things in life anymore. My mind is well and truly broken, thanks to that, that... "Idiot." I swear down the phone. "Fucking wanker that he is. A tool. A reprobate. A prick of the first order."

"That, he is," Isla agrees. "So what are you doing back in your apartment?"

"Haven't you heard anything I just told you?" I cry.

"I have, doll, and I think you love that about him."

"Oh." I pull out a chair and sit down with a thump. "That's true, right?"

"So, what made you walk out on him?"

"He was...just insufferable," I snap.

"And?"

"And cock-headed."

"Which is an asset, I assume?"

I hear the smirk in her voice, "Isla, honestly..."

"Admit it, the sex was great."

"Off-the-walls hot," I admit.

"And despite his money, he decided to focus on becoming a doctor."

"True," I admit, reluctantly.

"And he's good with dogs."

"And kids."

"And kids," she agrees. "So?"

"So?"

"What didn't you like about him?"

"Well, I fell in love with him, for one."

"Hmm."

"What?"

"I mean, that was bound to happen. You set yourself up for that, girlfriend, when you agreed to go along with his fake relationship thingy."

"Hello, it was supposed to only be for a few days, and it was contingent on my never sleeping with him."

"That was clever of him, huh?"

"Was it?" I scrunch up my forehead. "You think so?"

"Of course, babe. He used reverse psychology on you. I mean, tell you not to sleep with him and—"

"—and of course, I'd only want to sleep with him." I reach for the wine, swig from it. Grimace. Argh! It's worse than I thought. I set it back with a thump, then jump up and begin to pace.

"And then, he took me home to see his family."

"At Christmas."

"At Christmas." I rake my fingers through my hair. "And he was really cute with his nieces. Hell, the man reads Harry Potter."

She shrieks, "Whaat?"

I wince. "Pipe down," I plead. "You almost burst my eardrum there."

"He reads Harry Potter? How many men do you know who read Harry Potter?"

"He was reading it because he wanted to be able to discuss it with his niece."

"No," she breathes.

"Yes." I hang my head.

"So, he fucks like a god, saves lives like he is God, and reads the kind of books that—"

"—make me want to worship his brain. Yeah," I scowl. When she puts it like that… "I mean, he's not perfect, you know."

"No?"

"He has a beard. I mean, it's unkempt, which is fine if you go in for that sexy just-rolled-out-bed-on-Christmas-morning look."

"Sexy Santa," she snickers.

What I wouldn't give to see him in nothing but a Santa hat.

"Don't call him sexy," I pout.

"But he is," she protests.

"I mean, I can call him sexy, but not you."

She stares at me.

"What?" I frown.

"Nothing." She clears her throat, "What else do you not like about him?"

"He's overbearing, dominant, uh, commands me do stuff, overrides me a lot, hates chocolate —"

"Are you sure?"

"Well, he did eat the chocolate banana muffin batter I made," I offer.

She gives me a perplexed look. "Muffin batter?"

"It's a long story..."

"Okaaay... So, he hates chocolate, but he ate what you made anyway."

"Hmm." And he did say that he was coming around to its taste especially when he licked it off my lips. My cheeks heat. Then he wouldn't let me out of his sight because he wanted to keep me safe. Okay, so I won't tell her that. I bite the inside of my cheek. What else? What else?

"He made his brother apologize to me for being rude."

"Now that's not very gentlemanly is it?" she chuckles.

"Shut up." I wipe my hand across my face. What else? "He did tell me that he wants a future, but not with me."

"You sure? Maybe he was angry or something."

"He was." I hunch my shoulders, "But I can't let that pass, can I? I mean, people speak the truth in the heat of the moment."

"Maybe he wanted to hurt you?"

"And I emptied my box of cookies on his head."

"You did?" She giggles.

"And told him to fuck off."

"Good."

"I should have told him to fuck off more."

"You still can."

"And he doesn't love me."

Isla stares at me, "Did you tell him that you love him?"

"No, of course not."

"Then how can you expect him to reciprocate?"

"Whose side are you on?" I scowl.

"Sweetie, you know I'll always back you up. And I am not saying there is no fault on his side, or that it wasn't wrong of him to have turned your relationship into a barter game of sorts…but—"

"But?"

"It seems there's something between the two of you that's powerful, and if I were in your shoes…"

I tilt my head, "You would…?"

She draws in a breath, "I wouldn't let go of a chance at true happiness that easily. I mean, I'd pursue that guy and sit on him, until he confessed his feelings."

"You would too," I giggle.

"Not that I've been in your shoes."

"Not yet," I smirk.

"Not that I don't want a man or anything…but…"

"But?"

"I'm not in a hurry. The single life's pretty fun too, you know? And as long as I have my book boyfriends…"

"That's what I used to think." I purse my lips, "Then that real life a-hole comes along, and damn, if he doesn't spoil all the book Romeos for me."

"Aww sweetie," she murmurs, "what are you doing there all alone? Why don't you come over to my place?"

I pause.

"I mean, I am only an hour away, if you drive."

"I left my car back at the cabin." Hell, I knew I should have asked the driver to drop me off at the cabin and driven myself here… But yeah, the stupid champagne had gone to my head by then, and I had alternated between giggling and crying. *Why do I always make the wrong decisions, huh?*

"You could call for a taxi?"

The thought of dragging myself out of here and getting dressed and facing her family— Not that I don't like Isla's parents. They're awesome, actually. But to have to put on a face to the world, right now? Nah, no way. I'd rather spend the time baking, and if I happen to eat a lot of what I make? Well, too bad. Life is short, after all. And stressed spelled backwards is desserts, and Mary had a little lamb and the mouse ran up the clock. *Shit, time out. Stop with the nursery rhymes. Stop thinking about anything to do with that asshole, okay?*

"It's fine." I swallow, "I think I'm better off on my own."

"You sure?" She frowns.

"Yeah," I nod. "I'll have a bath and then bake, and I'll feel better then, for sure."

"I don't think you should be on your own now."

"I'll be good." I shake my hair back from my face. "Once I start the baking, I'll lose track of everything."

"But—"

"I'll be fine." I reach for the phone, "I promise."

"You sure?"

I hunch my shoulders, pull my lips up in a smile. "See?" I point at my face, "I'm good."

"Hmm." Isla peers up at me. Someone calls her name and she looks off camera, "I'm coming Mom." She turns back to me, "Gotta go, doll."

"Right."

"Bye."

I blow her a kiss.

She cuts the call. I place the phone down, then glance around the place. Only one way to deal with this. *Fuck the a-hole. Fuck the a-hole. I did fuck him, remember? No, like really fuck him. Gah.* I spring up so fast my chair screeches back on its legs. Oopsie. I bring up my play list on the phone, put it on speaker. Then turn on the oven. What should I bake, huh?

Two hours later, I've pulled the pies out of the oven, left them to cool on the wire mesh. Also, I've chugged down the horrible, almost-vinegary boxed wine, and another bottle of wine. *Gah.* So not a good idea. My stomach rolls and I grab my middle. Argh, maybe a hot bath will help, huh? I march into the bathroom, run the water, toss in a few bath bombs—chocolate, of course. I light the candles, then head back to the kitchen for the wine… Of course, I'm out. Gah! The corner shop should be open and have wine, huh? Should I? Shouldn't I? Fuck that. It's Christmas, after all. I run back to the bathroom, turn off the water, then head over to the shop across the street, pick up one…okay, three bottles of wine, pay the man behind the counter.

"Merry Christmas," he choruses, eyes twinkling.

"And to you." I smile at him, then head back. When I reach home, the door to my apartment is ajar. WTF? My heart begins to race. Is it the same thief who broke into the bakery? Is he back? Gah. I turn to leave. A noise reaches me from the direction of the kitchen. He's in the kitchen. In the kitchen? My pies? No frigging way am I letting him eat them. I made them for myself.

For me. Moi. I deserve that bloody treat after the last few days I've had. I glance around for a weapon. What can I use? I curl my fingers around the bottle of wine, push open the door to my apartment, then creep past the living room. I reach the doorway to the kitchen, pause. His back is to me. His broad shoulders are clad in a black, long-sleeved Henley that clings to the planes of his back which flex, move, ripple with each of his movements. His narrow waist, that tight butt, those powerful thighs outlined in his jeans. He blocks out the sight of the dining table... Where I'd left the pies to cool. His legs are spread apart and the muscles of his triceps flex as he jerks his arm back-forth-back... What the hell? He can't be doing what I think he is. Is he? I take a step forward. He freezes. Shoots me a glance over his shoulder.

"You?" I swallow, "What are you doing?"

42

———

Weston

"What the hell do you think?" I growl at her, hold her gaze. *Don't let her look down; don't allow her to see what the hell you've gotten into here.* Caught with your dick in a pie...and by the woman you're in love with...? Hold the fuck on there. Firstly, that isn't a metaphor—being caught with my dick in a pie, I mean. And I know what you're thinking, and fuck, but I can promise it wasn't inspired by a certain, uh, notorious movie. I mean, I am past the stage of being pimply-faced and ready to shag everything that moves...because I only want to be inside one woman, her... Or, uh! A pie baked by her. Bloody fuck, this is a shit show.

"I... I am not sure what you're doing here?" She takes a step forward, and every muscle in my body solidifies... Except uh, a particular part of me that's throbbing inside the sweet, moist, center of a certain dessert that was baked by her. I mean, can you blame me? Peter had driven me here, and I'd told him to leave, confident that I was spending the night here. Hey a man can hope, right? It is Christmas, after all. I'd walked in here, and the entire place had smelled festive... and of her—that sweet sugary scent of hers mixed with the scent of apple pie, which happens to be my favorite, and all of it had gone to my head... Or rather, to my groin, and she hadn't been around, so I'd done the next logical thing. I'd reached for the pie she'd baked, buried myself in its center. Not that it's a replacement... Far from it, but needs must and all that. It's what she's reduced me to, a man...standing in front of a woman he loves —*no, no, no, not love, never love, in lust —yeah, that's better;* a man in lust, standing in front of his woman with his dick caught in a pie, that she'd baked.

Fuck.

This is all her fucking fault.

I glare at her.

She pales. Her chin wobbles and she bites down on her lower lip, and fuck, if my dick doesn't jump again; inside the goddamn pie I hold with my left hand, in a position that if she came around and saw, it would be very clear what I am up to.

"Don't come closer," I snap. Bloody hell, that's a first —me asking a woman to stay away from me. Not that it matters, of course, because she sidles closer. Bloody woman, can never do what she's told.

"Stop," I growl. "Stay where you are."

She frowns. "My apartment." She huffs, "I can do what I want."

"Wrong."

She blinks. "I rent this flat, you ass."

"Guess who owns the apartment block?"

Her forehead crinkles, then she opens her mouth and shuts it again.

"Well," I smirk, "made the connection yet?"

"You," she swallows, "you own it?"

"Finally." I raise my gaze skywards, "Took you long enough to get that, huh? What's wrong, you eat too much dessert? All that cream gone to your head?" *The fuck?* The connection between my mouth and my brain has well and truly snapped, that I am hurling insults at her... *Shut the fuck up, you wanker.* But fuck, I have to distract her, and what else is a man supposed to do when he's caught with his cock in his hand... Technically, in a warm, soft, juicy, moist confectionary, but you get the picture, huh?

Color sears her cheeks.

"Is that how you got in?"

"I got in because you left the door open." I growl, and my chest tightens, "Do you know how dangerous that is?"

"Did you...did you find out I live here and decide to buy the place?" She frowns.

"Don't flatter yourself," I reply. "It's merely a coincidence, I assure you."

She flattens her lips, "Is it also a coincidence that you're standing like that?" She takes a sideways step; I mirror her movements, in the opposite direction.

"Like what?" I twist my body. Thank fuck for all those gym sessions, not to mention working out with Saint at his horse ranch. My shoulders are wide enough to cover what the rest of my body is up to—I hope?

"Like," she chews the inside of her lip, "like you're holding your...uh.. your..."

"Dick?" I supply. Fuck, yeah. Clearly, she's not going to let go of it, and damned if I am going to be apologetic about being found out. I turn around, allow her to have the full-frontal view. She lowers her gaze to where I hold the plate with the pie in front of my groin...with my dick stuck inside.

She gulps, the sound audible in the silence. Awesome. This is when she tells me to fuck off... Or better still, turns and runs screaming, huh? Instead, she licks her lips. "Why did you stop?" she asks.

"Huh?" I blink, "Excuse me?"

"You heard me." She squeezes her fingers around the bottle of wine, "Why don't you finish what you started?"

"I will, on one condition."

She tilts her head, her gaze locked onto where my dick is sunken into the pie.

"Amelie," I snap.

"What?" She raises her gaze to mine, her pupils blown, her lips parted.

Jesus, I may have just met my match in food kink. Well, figures. She's a baker. I couldn't have picked better.

"Join me," I growl.

"How?" Her forehead crinkles, "How do you mean?"

I glance at the bottle of wine, then back at her.

"No." Her gaze widens.

"Yes."

"No way," she mutters. "I'm not putting that...inside...."

I thrust my hips forward and my cock sinks into the warm, moist, stickiness of the pie. A groan rumbles up my throat.

A whine bleeds from her.

I scowl at her, then at the bottle, "Do it."

"But."

"Now," I snap.

She gulps, pulls the bottle of wine from the brown paper bag. She unscrews it, drops the cap on the floor, then takes a gulp.

"Good girl," I growl.

She draws in a breath, then walks to the table, on the opposite side from me, and places the bottle on it, then hesitates again.

This woman, is she hell bent on killing me? "What is it?" I huff.

She glances toward the doorway, "Uh, I left the door to the apartment ajar when I came in... shouldn't I shut it?"

"Leave it," I order her.

"But—"

My balls ache, my groin hardens, and a snarl rips from me, "I swear, if you don't take off your clothes right now, I'll—"

She unbuttons her coat, tosses it on the chair, then reaches behind to unzip her dress. The material slithers down around her ankles; she steps out of it.

She straightens and the sight of the triangle of pink fabric between her creamy thighs—" Jesus, fuck." The blood drains to my cock, I pull the pie close, and my shaft sinks into the moist center. I stare at the shadow of her flesh outlined against the crotch of her panties, "Take it off," I command. "Don't stop, Amelie."

"Or what?"

I jerk my chin up to her face. Her lips twitch.

"You don't want to tease me."

"Oh?"

I nod, "You have two choices here."

"Do I?"

I allow my mouth to curl, "Either you fuck the bottle and get fucked in the arse by me, or—"

Her chest heaves.

"Or, you fuck the bottle and I fuck you in the cunt, then in the arse."

"Choices, choices," her voice wobbles.

"Take that bloody wine bottle and ride it, Amelie, or I swear, I'll spank you so much you won't be able to sit down for months."

She scoffs, "You exaggerate."

"Do I?" I lower my eyebrows, "Give me a chance to demonstrate just how much I enjoy delivering on my threats." I peel back my lips, "Do it, Amelie. One chance to get my hand on that beautiful curved behind, Princess."

"Jeez," she swipes her hair over her shoulder, "some people have no sense of humor."

"Humor, huh?" I pump my hips forward, impale the bloody apple pie—the hell am I doing? Fucking an inanimate object, when the focus of my obsession is right in front of my eyes.

She shivers, my thigh muscles spasm, and this entire scene is bloody wrong... and so fucking right. "Don't keep me waiting," I grind out.

She swoops down, grabs the wine bottle, brings it to her mouth, then proceeds to close her lips around it, taking it in—as she had my cock, previously. Holy mother of all that's dear to me... That has to be the hottest thing I have ever seen— No, Amelie pulling the bottle out of her mouth, only to lower it between her thighs? That... I swallow. That is bloody erotic. And it shouldn't be. I mean, it is a woman —my woman, turning me on, by easing herself down onto the neck of the bottle. It is not what I expected from her. It's everything I wanted her to do.

My cock lengthens. I grip my fingers around the damned plate of apple pie and follow her movements. In-out-in... She parts her legs, sinks down onto the bottle, the length of which disappears inside her pussy.

My shaft jerks; a pressure coils in my balls.

"Jesus, Princess," I snarl, "you're fucking turning me on."

Her breasts rise and fall, she straightens, lifts her gaze to mine, holds the connection, then impales herself again. She groans and the blue of her irises fades, leaving behind large pupils so black, they seem to take up most of her irises. My throat closes and my heart begins to race. I stare into her eyes, kick my hips forward again. Her movements intensify; so do mine. A bead of sweat trickles down her throat, trails down the shadow between her breasts. My pulse thrums; the blood pumps in my veins. I grip the plate of pie, push into the melting core, again and again. My balls draw up, the pressure in my groin tightens, harder, further, my senses pop, my vision narrows. "Come," I growl.

And she throws her head back, arches her spine, and reveals the slim column of her throat; a shudder grips her body, her thighs clench, a low keening moan spills from her lips, and I can't stop myself. My balls draw up and I come, shooting my load inside the fucking pie. I straighten, slap the plate with the dessert onto the table.

Her legs seem to weaken. She sways, then raises the bottle of wine from between her legs. Her knuckles are white and her hand trembles. She blinks, then licks her lips. She tips up her chin; I crook my finger at her.

She hesitates.

I jerk my chin. She takes a step forward, and another. She closes the distance, pauses in front of me. Tips the bottle of wine to her lips and drinks from it. Her throat moves as she swallows; a drop of red trickles down her chin. I scoop it up, bring it to my mouth and suck on it.

Her gaze follows my actions; her lips part. She holds out the bottle of wine to me. Is she daring me? Does she think she can match me step for step? Does she? I snatch the bottle from her, raise it to my mouth and chug down a mouthful. The complex notes of wood and cherries, chocolate and honey.

I lower the bottle. "Perfect with pie," I declare.

"Isn't it?" Her lips quirk.

She reaches for the serving spade on the table.

"What are you doing?" I growl.

"What do you think?" She cuts off a slice, brings it to her mouth, "Should I eat it?"

The fuck? I glare at the piece of pie, then at her face.

"You wouldn't."

"Wouldn't I?" She tilts her head.

Woman's enjoying it. The thought of her eating the evidence of my arousal? It's a fucking turn on... Hotter than anything I have experienced before.

"Will you?" I lower my chin.

"You daring me?" She raises the slice, "What would you do if I ate this?"

"What do you want me to do?" I counter.

"I want you to—" She glances at the pie, then at my face, "I want you to let me take the lead in bed."

43

Amelie

His forehead crinkles. He glares at my face, and the skin around his eyes tightens. He's considering it. He's actually thinking about it? A dominant man like him... Would he give in to this? Does he want me to eat this...proof of his desire? Does he think I won't? Am I going to do this? I hold his stare. *Say the word; do it.* A bead of sweat slides down my temple. His gaze darts to it, then back to my eyes.

"Do it," his voice is casual, his stance relaxed. *Huh? Does he think I won't? Is he the only one who can get away with playing games?* He's so sure that I won't surprise him, he raises the bottle of wine, swigs from it, then licks his mouth. "Mmm," he smacks his lips together. "Wine and the honey of your cum," he says. "This has to be my favorite drink ever.

I raise the pie to my mouth.

His gaze intensifies.

Bite off a piece.

He freezes.

I chew on it, swallow, his chest rises and falls.

I bite off another piece, chew on it.

His shoulders bunch. His chest planes seem to harden, and he draws himself up to his full height. "Eat it all," he commands.

His rough voice chafes across my nerve endings. My sex clenches. I squeeze my thighs together, stuff the rest of the piece into my mouth.

He curls his lips. "Swallow," he growls, and moisture pools between my legs. Hell, only Weston fucking Kincaid could make that order sound so filthy, so bloody naughty. I gulp down the food in my mouth.

"Open," his voice is rough, his breathing uneven. I part my lips; he raises the bottle of wine to my mouth. "Drink," his voice lowers to a hush. Hell, why do I get the feeling that he's planning something...a scene that's out of my dirtiest fantasies?

Rolling around in the aftermath of my dessert? Check.

Slurping down wine that tastes of my arousal and his mouth? Double check.

Pulling back with suddenness so the wine spills across my chest? You bet.

"Oops," I murmur, glance down at where the wine blots the cloth of my bra. "I think I am going to have to take it off."

"Hmm." He raises the bottle to his lips, drinks from it. "I have a better idea, Princess."

"You do?" I peer up at him from under my eyelashes.

"I do." He nods. He holds up the bottle; my gaze widens. He tilts it, I open my mouth to protest, but already he's poured the wine on my hair.

"What the—" I splutter, "What are you doing?"

"Worshipping you, of course," his voice is sincere, his tone husky.

I take in his features as the liquid drips down my cheeks, my chin, splashes onto my breasts, clings to the cloth that covers my crotch.

"Weston," his name emerges, breathy from my throat. Damn, if I don't sound aroused and turned on—I glance down to where his erect dick—make that two of us. "Weston?" I swallow. What am I asking of him? What do I want from him? "You...you going to deliver on your promise?"

He smirks, "What do you think?"

"I think," I raise a finger to his cheek, drag it down the luxuriant growth of beard on his chin, "you look like Santa Claus."

He stares, then chuckles, "Have you been a naughty girl, Princess?"

"Oh," I shift my weight from foot to foot, "I tried, Santa. I promise, I wanted to be good...but then...I met this man."

"A man, huh?" He leans forward until his chest grazes my breasts, nipples hard, and surely, outlined by the sodden bra, which, if he'd look down, he'd see. But he isn't, because he's staring into my eyes.

He lowers the now empty bottle to the table with a soft thump. "Pray, tell me more about this...encounter of yours," he breathes. The warmth from his body surrounds me; his big, aching, gorgeous shoulders shut out the rest of the world. He bends his knees, thrusts his face into mine, "Don't make me wait." His voice is low, with an edge of that cruelty that is so Weston, which rolls down my spine.

I shiver. "He..." I clear my throat, "He's the most annoying, most obnoxious, most full-of-himself, egoistical —"

His biceps flex; the next instant he grabs my pussy. A whine bleeds from me, "Ah," I stutter, "He's... he's..."

His mouth curls. "He is...?" he prompts me as he begins to massage my core.

"Hard," I mumble. "So hard."

He grinds the heel of his hand against my clit and goosebumps flare on my skin. I shiver, "And sexy, and dominant, and knows just what to do to arouse me to fever pitch, and when he tells me that he'll let me lead in bed, I know that he —"

He digs his finger into my melting channel through the cloth and I groan.

"You were saying — ?" he smirks.

"Was I?" I blink.

"Yep." He nods, "Something about wanting to lead in bed?"

"Yeah," I swallow, "this once."

He fixes his left palm around the nape of my neck, then lifts me up by the hold on my pussy, and plants me on the pie. I squeak, wriggle my hips around, trying to evade the moist filling. He tightens his grip on my pussy. He pushes down with his other hand, and I still.

"Look at me," he growls.

I glance up, trace his features with my gaze—that patrician hooked nose, those clear eyes, the lush dark hair that flows about his shoulders, that pouty lower lip that I want to suck on. I lean up, he holds me in place with his hold on the nape of my neck. His strength is awesome, like really awesome. Why didn't I realize how he could overpower me with minimal resistance?

I reach for his cock, but he clicks his tongue, "So impatient." He snickers.

I scowl. "But I want to touch you."

"Not yet."

"You made a promise."

"And you know what kills me?" He shakes his head, "You actually expect me to keep it too."

"Won't you?" I peer up at him, "Won't you let me take the lead?"

"Nope." He shakes his head.

"But you said—"

"I lied."

Of course, he did. I mean, if he'd allowed me to actually set the pace, I'd have... Thrown myself at him, climbed him, impaled myself on his dick like he'd fucked that pie. The pie... Hell. I wriggle around, and the filling sticks to my behind. "Weston, uh, the filling is getting into all the places it shouldn't," I mumble.

"On the contrary." He grins, "It's filling up exactly the right areas, which I am going to enjoy licking."

"Oh," I gulp; my core clenches. Jesus, is he going to enact the picture he painted right now in my mind?

"Oh, yes." He mocks my strangled exclamation. "And that's only the beginning... Once you are clean, I plan to fill you up with my dick in your pussy, my fingers in your arsehole, and my tongue in your mouth. I am going to make sure every hole in your body bears my imprint. Then I am going to fuck you so hard, you won't know where you begin and where I end, you'll lose sight of what day it is, what time—" he swallows, "what time—" His voice roughens, "What time—"

"What time of day it is," I supply, "whether I am indoors or not, what the weather is like outside, what—"

He releases my pussy, only to plant his big body between my legs, forcing my thighs to widen.

"What ingredients I use in an apple pie—" What the hell am I warbling on about?

He thrusts his dick inside of me, filling me, stretching me, packing me to the brim, with such confidence that I gasp.

"Wes, I... I..."

"Complete the sentence." He glares at my features, "Do it."

"I..." I swallow, "I...want..."

"What?" He brings his free hand to my breast, squeezes it. Sensations radiate outward from the contact. My pussy clenches around his dick and his grin widens. "You were saying?" he prompts, "Something about the apple pie—"

"Fuck the apple pie," I mutter.

"Did that already." He chuckles.

"Sheesh," I grumble, "are you for real?"

"Does this feel real?" He pinches my nipple and I yelp. He bends his head, sucks on it, and I feel the pull deep down in my womb. Everything he does seems to awaken parts of me that had hitherto been happy to exist without communicating with me.

"Weston," I gasp, "you're forgetting something."

He releases my breast, glares up at me, "I am?" He blinks, then his forehead smooths, "I am."

He turns his head, fastens his mouth around my other breast. He sucks on my nipple, curls his tongue around the pebbled bud, bites down with his sharp teeth, and I yell, dig my fingers in his hair and tug.

He grunts and his dick lengthens further inside of me—is that even possible? He continues to lave my nipple, sucking on it, dragging his teeth around the tender flesh, then opens his mouth wider, taking in as much of my breast as he can fit. Heat, lust, pleasure, pain... All of it... None of it... A confluence of emotions whirls inside, tugging at my lower belly, arrowing to my cunt, which clamps tighter around his engorged flesh. Of course, he is pleasuring me, but ultimately, he is the beneficiary. How could someone be so...on target all the time in how he plays my body?

"Weston," I pant, "Please, please, please, please—"

He pulls out of me, raises his head, steps away.

"What the hell?" I blink, "You come back here and fuck me, you hear me?"

"Are you telling me what to do?" His lips quirk.

"You bet I am, you pussy tease, you—" I squeak, for he's grabbed my hips and flipped me over. I am on my arms and knees, butt pushed out in his face. The hell? Then a wetness sinks into my pussy, up my slit, across the valley between my arsecheeks.

"No," I shudder, "Weston, no."

He stops, "No?"

"No," I huff. "I mean, yes. Don't stop, whatever it is that you're doing, don't, oh!" He licks my puckered hole and my entire body trembles. It's filthy, and dirty and it's hot. So bloody hot. "Oh, my God," I breathe. "Oh, my, G-o-d." I yelp, for he swipes his tongue down to my cunt, then licks his way back up to my forbidden hole and back, again and again. My knees tremble and my elbows wobble. I sink down to support my face on my arms. "Wes," I gasp, "oh, you're, I'm—" My entire body seems to shudder. "I'm—"

"Don't you dare come," he growls against my sensitive clit, right before he bites on it. I howl, the sound muffled against my arms. My shoulder shudder, I slide my knees apart, thrust out my arse, giving him more access. He can eat me out like the sweetest of desserts, lick me, suck on me, insert his tongue into my pussy and drink of me. A trembling grips my legs, my back. He begins to fuck my backhole in earnest, shoving his tongue inside, curling it in, before he pulls out and bites on my butt. I huff.

"You taste fucking amazing," he mutters, "like apple pie and my cum."

I chuckle. Now that, would be one hell of a dish to put on the menu of my next pop-up delivery special. He grips my thighs, pushes them further apart. I crack open my eyes, stare down from across the length of my body, to between my legs, to where he swirls his tongue up my inner thigh, licking off the crumbs, then the other side. He meets my gaze, licks his lips, then declares, "I am going in for seconds."

44

Weston

"I am going to fuck you with my tongue." I take in her flushed face, her parted lips, her heaving breasts, "You ready, Princess?"

She blinks. "Do I have a choice?" she moans.

"Nope." I smile in anticipation, smack my lips together. Her breathing grows shallow, she licks her lower lip mirroring my desire, and my cock throbs, reminding me I needed to get on with the program. I'd promised to clean her up, before filling her up again, and I'm a man of my word—when it suits me, of course. I smirk, thrust my face into her pussy and close my mouth around her cunt. She moans, her thighs tremble, and liquid heat streams from her wet channel. I slurp it up, shove my tongue inside her cunt, mirror how I want to fuck her with my shaft—in-out-in— until her entire body shudders, and again.

She groans. "Weston, please..." she whines.

Yeah, I know the feeling. I reach down to grab my cock, pump it once, scoop up some of the pre-cum from the weeping head, then slide my fingers inside her backhole.

"Oh," she wheezes, then pounds her tiny fist into the table, "I'm coming, I'm —"

I tear my mouth from her pussy, grasp her waist and haul her off of the table and onto her feet in front of me. Her legs seem to give way. I hold her up, kick her legs apart, then scoop up her cum and ease it into her backhole.

"Wes..." she moans, "I haven't... I mean... I can't..."

"You can," I growl.

I add a second finger inside of her, and she groans, "It's too much...It's —"

"Not enough." I pull out my fingers, scoop up some of the mushed-up apple and smear it into her puckered hole.

"Oh." She grips the edge of the table, lowers her chin to her chest.

"Relax," I command, then press my palm into the center of her spine. I apply pressure and she bends over, placing her cheek on the table.

"Beautiful." I praise her.

She pushes her hair behind her ear. "Be gentle," she whispers.

"Is that what you want?" I stare at her, "Is that what you truly want, Princess?"

She swallows, then squeezes her eyes shut.

"Tell me," I repeat. "You wanted to take the lead. This is me giving you the choice to direct the proceedings. Do you want it tender or do you want me to take you like you are mine?"

She nods.

"Which one?" I ask.

"Both," she replies. "I want you to take me like I am yours, and I want to take it like you are mine." She cracks her eyelids open. "Please," she whispers.

My heart begins to race, my chest tightens, and something hot twists my heart. *Fuck.* Emotions, feelings, a strange melting sensation that steals up my spine, encircles my ribcage, bears down on my shoulders. I bend over her, until my chest is flush with her back, "You fucking destroy me, you know that?" I press my lips to hers and kiss her. I wrap my fingers around the nape of her neck, tilt my head, ease my tongue inside her mouth, and open myself up to her.

She draws in a breath—my breath, then parts her lips, sucks on my tongue and kisses me back. That melting sensation? It extends to my stomach, my belly, my extremities.

I ease my dick inside her puckered hole.

She groans. I swallow the small sound, bring my hand around to strum her cunt. Good thing it's only my middle finger which is broken. Leaves me plenty of others to play with her clit, slide my forefinger into her pussy, and begin to finger fuck her. She parts her legs, opens her mouth wider. I kiss her in earnest, dance my tongue over hers, allow her to drink from me as I thrust my hips and notch my dick further inside of her. A whine wells up her throat. I drink of it, wind my fingers about her neck, and apply pressure.

Her pulse races at the base of her throat and her chest rises and falls. I slide my thumb inside her pussy, scissor my fingers in her channel. She groans, clenches around my dick, and I fucking see stars. Sweat beads my upper lip, slides down my temple. I dig my heels into the floor, flex my thighs, wait...wait for her to adjust to my size, tear my mouth from hers and kiss her nose, her cheek, her eyelashes, which flutter. "You're perfect, Princess," I whisper, "gorgeous, beautiful, inside and out."

She shudders, opens her mouth, then closes it again. I kiss her on her lips, on her chin, nibble my way up to her earlobe and suck on it.

A moan wheezes from her.

I ease my tongue inside her ear and she trembles. Drag my tongue about the shell of her ear and her entire body bucks. I bite down on her earlobe and she cries out. Her inner muscles give and I slip inside, filling her to the hilt.

A groan erupts from me... Or maybe that was her.

"Jesus." I press my cheek to hers, "You're so tight, so hot...so much everything." My pulse begin to race. "I want you." I mumble half to myself, "I've never needed anything as much as I need you. I have to fuck you, make you mine as completely as I am yours."

She draws in a breath. "Why," she asks, "why do you want me?"

"Because I love you." I snap my eyes open, "Of course, whatever is said in coitus...stays in coitus." I mutter, "I mean, anything said in the heat of passion is—"

"The naked truth?" She stares at me from under hooded eyes. "Will you get out of your own way for bloody once and accept what it is you feel for me?" she snaps.

I glare back at her, but she doesn't back down, "Admit it, alpha-hole, you fucking love me."

"Love to fuck you," I agree.

"You ache for me." Her lips quirk.

"For the rapier-sharp edge of your mind that I love to challenge."

"You can't live without me," her voice is smug.

I scowl. "Adore your pussy." I rotate my fingers inside of her, and color smears her cheeks. "And your arse, which belongs to me, by the way," I inform her, even as I pull out, then thrust inside her with enough impact that her entire body jolts up the table.

"Stop deflecting," she pants.

"Stop talking," I retort.

"Thought you loved my sassy comebacks," she mutters.

"Love your sassy arse." I propel my hips forward, begin to fuck her in earnest.

Her eyes roll back in her head. "Fuck," she groans, "it hurts."

I frown, begin to pull out, "Maybe I should have waited... Should have prepared you better. I could—"

She lowers her chin, trains those blue eyes on me. "Don't you dare," she growls. "You bloody well finish what you fucking started."

Thank fuck. My dick lengthens. I grit my teeth, stay poised at her entrance.

"Another thing I crush on..." I force the words out through gritted teeth, "Who'd have thought your potty mouth would turn me so on?"

"Thought it was all of me? The entire package?" She flutters her eyelashes at me. "Come on, give credit where it's due, Doc. Give me the satisfaction of hearing it from the horse's mouth."

"You calling me a horse?" I arch an eyebrow, then thrust forward and inside of her.

"Oh." She squeezes her eyes shut. "That..." she gulps, "that feels so fucking good."

She bites down on her lower lip, and fuck her, but I can't resist her when she does that. I lower my head, lick her mouth. "Look at me," I order.

She cracks open her eyelids, and those shining baby blues of her stare into my soul.

"Stay with me," I whisper, then propel my hips forward. My balls slap against the underside of her butt, and I sink into her. Her spine arches and her gaze grows frantic. A ripple speeds up her body. Oh, she's close, so close. I tear my mouth from hers. "Come," I growl, and her pussy clenches around my fingers.

Moisture slides out from between her thighs as she shudders. Her eyelids flutter and I click my tongue, "Open your eyes, darlin.'"

She tips her chin up, and I hold her gaze, as I thrust forward. My balls draw up, my cock lengthens, the tension in my groin explodes out, and I come inside of her.

I slump forward, hold my weight up on my elbows, then lower my lips to hers.

"Wow," she whispers against my mouth. "That was something."

"Yeah," I kiss her, "it was."

I pull out of her and she winces. I pull her up, then scoop her into my arms.

"You okay?"

She gazes up at me, her cheeks flushed, her hair stuck to her forehead, her eyes glazed.

"Princess?" I ask again. "Talk to me."

"Hmm." She snuggles into my chest. "Do I have to?" she mumbles, then yawns so loudly her jaws crack.

"I wore you out, huh?" I stalk out of the kitchen.

"Where are you...going?" She yawns again.

"Where's the shower?" I ask.

"Mmmm... That way." She jerks her chin to the side.

I walk down the hallway, reach the bathroom door and shoulder it open.

"I don't think I can stay awake." Her eyelids flutter.

"Just as long as you're awake when I fuck you again."

Okay, maybe not. I prop her up in the shower, turn on the water, soap her up, and wash every inch of her delectable body. She falls asleep in my arms halfway through. That doesn't stop me from slipping my throbbing dick inside of her and taking her. Or again later... When I've dried her and myself off and pulled the covers over her naked body—after I've made sure to close and lock the door to her apartment and ensured all of the windows are safely shut—I slip in beside her, curl my body around hers and try to fall asleep.

Only I can't, because I have a raging hard-on. Her proximity does that to me—turns me on, twists me inside out until I am sure I am one big, seething mass of need. I pull her leg up and over my hip, then guide myself inside of her soft pussy. A sense of peace, of rightness, steals over me. Fuck, this is what I've been missing all along—this melding sensation as I sink into her melting channel, and finish myself off in a few strokes, as I orgasm inside of her and she stirs. I curve my arm around her waist, pull her close and fall asleep with my dick nestled within her warmth.

Twelve o'clock.

Eleven o'clock.

Ten o'clock.

The goddam timer—an old fashioned clock fitted to run backwards—as my kidnapper had informed me, never stops counting down.

Every hour it helpfully rings out the time, so even though I am blindfolded, I have no choice but to follow along in my head.

Nine o'clock

Eight o'clock

Seven o'clock

Every hour brings me closer to the time when my kidnapper is going to come through the door.

Six o'clock

Five o'clock

Four o'clock

Twelve hours, that's how long he'd said he'd be away.

Three o'clock

Two o'clock

One o'clock

The timer passes the twelve-hour mark, and stops. The silence stretches. A beat, another.

My heart begins to race and sweat pools in my armpits. I tug my wrists against my bindings, and pain shoots up my arms. I draw in a breath and the acrid taste of fear fills my mouth. Something is wrong.

Why hasn't the bomb gone off as he'd said it would? Why hasn't my kidnapper returned for that matter? My throat closes, my hands and feet grow cold.

Today, I won't survive the beating. Today, something is different. Today is the day when he finishes it. When he doesn't stop electrocuting me until...my heart gives out.

My heart pounds in my chest, my pulse races, and my stomach coils in knots. The pressure builds at my temples. What's he going to do to me when he gets here?

My head spins and coldness grips my arms and legs... I won't last the day. I have to get through today. Need to focus, focus. Stay still; count down again.

Twelve o'clock.

Eleven o'clock.

Ten o'clock.

My heart beat slows and my pulse steadies. How strange. My biggest nemesis is also the only way I can calm my mind. Stay still, in the moment. You can't give up. Not yet. The door creaks open. I jolt upright. The change in the air indicates he's in the room. Footsteps approach as the door snicks shut. The hair at the back of my neck rises. Fuck. He's here, he's going to hit me...any moment. The floorboard creaks to my right, to the left, behind me. He circles me, comes closer.

"What should I do with you?" he mutters. "Leave you in your filth or put you out of your misery?"

Let me go, I try to say, the words muffled by my gag. Let me the fuck go, you asshole.

"Weston. Weston," he says. "When will you realize that resistance is futile?"

I yank my wrists against my bindings, strain the muscles of my legs. The ropes around my ankles dig into my skin. The ticking of the clock around my chest fills my ears...my mind. It grows louder, ricocheting inside of my head. The fuck is he up to? Why the hell is he not untying me?

He pats my head; I jerk away. The time-bomb around my chest beeps.

"Oops," he laughs, "sorry." He chuckles, "Forgot for a second there that you had to be absolutely still." He shuffles his feet, "Remember what I said about your being let go in twelve hours?"

I nod.

"Guess what? Today is your lucky day."

I stiffen.

"Today is the day I leave you here, with an hour to countdown. When it hits one o'clock... Boom!" He claps his hands together.

My shoulders bunch and the blood pumps in my ears. My heart hammers so loud, I am sure I am going to be sick. Let me out of here. Let me out.

"Sorry, my boy. Some things are best left up to fate, you understand?"

No. What the fuck is he talking about? I lean forward, shake my head. No, don't leave me here, don't.

His footsteps recede.

Stop. Don't go.

"Oh, I forgot to tell you." His voice reaches me from the direction of the doorway.

"If you're lucky, the bomb may not go off."

Bloody piece of shit, he's fucking toying with me. It won't go off. It won't. The door shuts behind him, leaving me with the ticking of the bloody clock. Tick-tock. Tick-tock.

Three o'clock.

Two 'o clock.

So close. An hour to countdown. An hour to my death. Or not? Any moment now. Any moment.

"Weston?" A man's voice calls out, "Weston, you in there?"

The door slams open and I jerk up.

"What the fuck?"

Stay back, don't come close. The bomb — it's going to detonate, it's going to —

"Weston?"

I tug on my bindings, but they don't give. Fuck this, if I'm going to die, I'm not taking another innocent life down with me. The ticking of the bomb seems to get louder... Or is that hammering in my chest? Sweat slithers down my spine. I tug my feet, strain at my restraints. The chair lurches forward. Tick-tock-tick-tock. The timebomb stops. Then —

"*Weston?*"

I snap my eyes open.

"Wes?" Her worried gaze holds mine. Her blonde hair is tangled about her shoulders. I rake my gaze down to her bare breasts, to her belly, to where her thighs grip my waist.

"Wes?" She reaches down to touch my face.

I pull away. "Don't," I clear my throat.

"You going to tell me about what happened when you were kidnapped?" she prods. "Is that what your nightmare was about?"

"What's it to you?" I grind my teeth together so hard that pain shoots up my jaw.

"You have to ask me that, after everything we've been through? After you told me that you love me?"

"About that..." I frown, "I didn't —"

"Shut up," she snaps.

"The fuck?" I growl, "You dare tell me to shut up?"

"Oh, I dare more." She smirks. "I dare to fuck you while you are tied up."

"Tied up?" I frown, then pull at my arms, which are bound above me. I glance up, tug at one leg, then the other. "You bound me to the bed?"

"Close." She smiles, "I bound you to the bed spread-eagled."

45

Amelie

What the hell am I doing? I reach down between us, massage his erect shaft. His chest planes lock and his shoulder muscles ripple. "You think you're going to get away with this?" he growls.

My heart begins to race. My throat closes. The taste of fear coats my tongue and I swallow it down.

"Correction." I allow my lips to curl, "I know I am going to get away with this." I swipe my fingers up his dick to where the swollen head throbs. I squeeze and his hips buck. I drag my thumb across the slit and his body jolts.

"Amelie," he warns.

"Weston," I echo his tone.

I slide my other hand down to cup his balls.

His throat moves as he swallows. "You really, really don't want to do this." His voice lowers to that hush as he speaks, to that edge of meanness which chafes at my nerve endings, that ripples down my belly, then coils in between my legs. Moisture laces my core. His gaze intensifies and his nostrils flare. Hell, as usual, he's so tuned into me, he can sense my arousal.

I squeeze his balls; he grunts. I slide back, lower my head, close my mouth around his shaft. His thigh muscles spasm and his entire body seems to go still. I hold his gaze, bob my head, take him in until his length bumps the back of my throat.

"Fuck." His jaw tics; his shoulder muscles bunch. "You don't know what you are doing," he snarls.

I rise up, so his dick plops out with a wet sound, "On the contrary." I lick the angry head of his cock, "I have a very good idea what I am doing to you."

I swirl my tongue around the rim of the angry throbbing head; he growls.

I drag my teeth across the sensitive skin; his body bucks.

"Oh." I blink. This is fun. It seems I can elicit a response with the smallest action.

I slide my tongue down the length of his shaft; sweat beads his forehead.

"Are you hot?" I ask.

"The fuck do you think?" he snarls.

I giggle. I can't help it, honestly. To see this virile, dominant alphahole laid low by a touch... Mmm. It's sweet revenge. I weigh his balls in my hand, then drag my finger down between his butt-cheeks to tease his backhole.

He grunts, "Fucking fuck." A vein throbs at his temple, his biceps bulge and the veins of his forearms ripple.

Holy shit, he's not going to break free, is he?

He yanks at his bindings which tighten, but hold—Whoa, guess the knock-off Ferragamo scarves are of good quality, after all.

His thigh muscles tense as he pulls on the bindings that circle his ankles. The bed frame creaks, but he stays tied.

The breath rushes out of me. *Gah, that was close.* I lower my face to his groin, begin to give him head. I take him down my throat—gag —*breathe through your nose, breathe through your nose*—I pull back, glance up to find his gaze fixed on me. A vein throbs at his temple; color highlights his cheeks. Wow. He seems aroused and angry—but definitely turned on.

"That all you got, babe?" His lips twist, "Giving up so easily, hmm?"

I frown. Typical of him to turn this into a competition, huh?

I prop my elbows on his hips, swirl my tongue around his cock. "You taste," I frown, "you taste like dark chocolate with a dash of sea salt."

He groans, "Jesus, woman, only you could compare my dick to a dessert."

"It's good," I offer, "I mean, you could do with a trim —"

"The fuck are you talking about?" he scowls.

"I mean the hair on your chin, you dummy." I chuckle, "What did you think?"

"I think when I get loose, I am going to turn you over my knee and spank you."

"Hmm." I dip my head, take him in, swipe my tongue up his cock, then pull back. His balls harden and his shaft lengthens, "Oh," I blink, "that's interesting." I massage that engorged part of him.

"The fuck?" he snarls. "What the hell do you think you're doing?"

"Having my cake and eating it too." I chuckle. My, but I am full of terrible sayings, but hey, if the shoe fits. I raise my shoulders, open my mouth, and take him down my throat again.

"Fuck." His swearing fills the air above me. His cock jumps. Heat seems to leap off of his chest and slam into my shoulders, pinning me in place. I gasp, rise up and position myself above his erect shaft.

He growls low in his throat, the sound a rumble that hints at an inner conflict. He peels back his lips and his teeth glint against his skin. His shoulder muscles seem to broaden, his big body tenses, waiting, waiting...for me to make my move. *Holy shit... This is true power.* Holding the most responsive part of him in my hand...before I sink down and impale myself on his very erect, very hard cock.

"Ah." I throw my head back, breathe in as I adjust to his size. He'd fucked me earlier, but damn, if his every penetration doesn't feel like the first time.

"Ride me," he growls. "Fuck my dick and make yourself come."

His words sink into my blood. I rise up, slam myself down onto his dick. The entire bed creaks. I clench my insides around his shaft, and he groans.

"Amelie," his voice is strained.

I lower my gaze to his face, hold onto his hips for leverage, then I begin to ride him. I raise and lower myself again and again. I don't break the connection between our eyes. His grey eyes reflect back the heat, the tension, the absolute and complete need to own him that grips me. His heart, his soul, his every emotion. I clench my pussy, squeeze my thighs together. "Weston." Only when I hear my voice do I realize I've breathed his name aloud.

"Don't stop," he replies. "Don't you dare stop, until you come."

I swallow, brace myself, then lift up and sink back down at the same moment that he thrusts upward and into me. His cock fills me, stretches me. His gaze burns into me, and I can all but taste his intensity as his big body stiffens, as his shaft jerks inside of me. He pistons his hips upward — fucking me, cramming into me, setting off pin pricks of heat that radiate out from my core, up my spine. The trembling crashes over me, and I gasp, and strain for release. Close, so close.

"Come," he growls, and I shatter. My climax smashes into me. White noise fills my ears, my mind. When I come to, I'm on my back and he's braced over me.

"How?" I frown, "You got free."

"You didn't think your scarves were strong enough to hold me, did you?"

"So, all this time — ?"

He nods, "I pretended to be tied down."

I scowl, "You allowed me to take the lead?"

"This once." He dips his head, kisses me. "Don't expect it to happen again."

"Yeah, yeah," I mutter, "Of course, the Big Bad Alpha Claus isn't going to allow this helpless woman to get away with anything."

"Helpless, my ass!" he scoffs. "You're dangerous, is what you are."

"Why, you flatter me." I flutter my eyelashes.

"And you..." He peers into my face, his features intense, "You..." He swallows, "I love you."

"Oh." A fierce something flares in my chest. Heat sears my cheeks. *Holy shit, am I blushing? No, I am not. Of course, not.*

"Aren't you forgetting something?" he growls.

"Am I?" I tilt my head, "Max is not here, so we don't have to take him for a walk. I showered last night, so I guess I can skip today, and it's Christmas today. Of course, Merry Christmas, Mr. Alpha Claus."

"Merry-fucking-Christmas," he rumbles, "but that's not what I mean."

"No?" I chew the inside of my cheek; my heart flutters in my chest like I'm just about to eat a freshly-baked chocolate croissant. Yum. Only one thing gives me more pleasure. "Umm." I screw up my face, "Let me think... Let me think... Am I forgetting something?" I raise my shoulders, "Nope."

He runs his fingers up my side, "Is that right?"

I giggle. "That's right."

He digs his fingers into my ribcage, and I snort. "Please... Don't —" I gasp.

"My, my, how ticklish you are, little Red."

"All the better to laugh with you, Mr. Claus." I chuckle, then scream, as he tickles my armpits. The laugher wells up my throat. I wriggle around, try to avoid him, but he leans his weight on me.

I howl.

He laughs louder. He holds me captive under him, proceeds to tickle me until I lose my breath. "Stop... No more..." I pant, "Please."

He pauses and his chest heaves. He glares at me, takes in my features. "You're the most beautiful present I have ever received for Christmas," he whispers.

My heart literally melts in my chest. Okay, not literally, but I mean, come on... That was bloody unexpected. I cup his cheek, urge his face closer, "I am still waiting for my gift."

"Oh?"

I nod, "Tell me what happened when you were kidnapped."

He blinks, then his features shutter.

Hell, me and my big mouth. Why did I have to go spoil that

perfect moment? He pulls back, shoves off the bed and glances around the room.

I sit up, "Weston, I'm sorry."

He spots his pants and steps into them. Shit, he's leaving... After all that? He loves me. He'd made love to me. Hell, he'd taken my ass... And damn him... It had taken courage to allow him to do that... I'd enjoyed it...but honestly, it had been a leap of faith to trust him with that... And now...what? He decides to up and leave? And why the hell am I apologizing?

He heads for the door. I jump up on my knees; the bloody sheet is wound around me... How the hell did that happen? "Weston stop right there."

He reaches the exit.

"Stop," I yell. "You can't just leave."

He pauses, then turns to glare at me with that look of superior disdain that I hate.

"Don't tell me what to do," he growls.

Argh! I throw up my hands, "You and your stupid dick-headed ideas."

"Didn't see you complaining earlier when I had you pinned on said dickhead," he snaps back.

"Don't change the topic."

He opens his mouth to speak.

I hold up my hand, "What did I say, to get you all hot under the collar, huh?" I scowl. "What's wrong with my asking you about the incident that clearly impacted you so much you're having nightmares to this day?"

He draws himself up to his full height, which only draws my attention to the width of those beautiful shoulders, those eight—no ten-pack abs—ten pack? I mean, who has a ten pack? Is that even a thing? Apparently, yes, I have the evidence right here in front of me.

He widens his stance, "You can't see it, can you?"

"What?"

"You're so involved in your emotions, your need to find out all my secrets. You have no idea how much it hurts to bring it up, do you?"

"If we are..." I pause. *Say it. Should I say it? Whatever.* I have nothing to lose, except my future... Yeah, fine, if I can't say what's on my mind with him, then this, whatever is between us, is worth nothing. I draw in a breath, "If we are going to have a future, then I need to know about this."

"That's where you are wrong."

My heart begins to race.

Don't say it. Don't say it.

"I said I loved you," he rolls his shoulders, "doesn't mean we have anything keeping us together."

Turning, he leaves.

46

Weston

Nice one. Get right to the heart of it, twist her guts and deliver her a sucker punch. *You're a piece of work, you know that?* Fuck! I stalk out of the apartment block. My bare feet hit the sidewalk. Huh? I'd forgotten to put on my shoes, apparently. I drop my shoes on the concrete, reach for the socks. And, of course, I've forgotten them. I shove my feet into my shoes—take a step forward, the backs of the shoes bite into my heels. Great, I'm sure to get blisters. Good. I deserve that...and more, much more for what I just did. What the fuck happened there? She asked me a simple question and I freaked. Not that I hadn't discussed the goddamn incident with the Seven in the years since—and with the shrink my mother had insisted I see. I'd hated it then...but they'd taken no shit from me. Good for them. I thought I'd dealt with the aftermath of what had happened...but apparently, not.

First, I'd frozen when my mother had collapsed...

Then the realization that I love her—fuck! I stumble, then right myself. I love her.

I've fallen for her.

When had she snuck up under my skin, coiled her scent around my heart, wormed her way into my every waking thought? Somewhere between her walking in on me naked at the cabin and applepie gate, I'd opened myself up to her in a way I had never done before. Her sass, her ability to hold her own against me, the way she fights to hold onto every inch of her dignity, that need inside of her to be dominated in bed, even as she blazes forward, trying to build her business.

She is a smart cookie, my woman. Takes no shit from anyone, and that includes me. It's one of the things I love—the fact that I can be myself with her, secure in the knowledge that she'll give back as good as she gets. Fuck. I drag my fingers through my hair... I left her and haven't stopped thinking about her. How can I already miss her? Her laughter, the way she wrinkles up her nose when she's thinking, how she talks in her sleep... How her features scrunch up before she climaxes, how she draws herself up to her full height, tips up her chin and assumes that haughty ice-princess persona when she is pissed off with me.

How her features had crumpled when I'd told there was nothing keeping us together. I squeeze the bridge of my nose. Why the hell had I said that? Bloody ego of mine. No way, could I stand to share my weakness with her, huh? Would it have been so fucking terrible to tell her what had happened during the time I had been held hostage as a boy? Why the fuck is it so difficult to talk about it still, huh? All the bloody therapy in the world had clearly not helped. Maybe there is a part inside of me that's broken and nothing can fix it—except her. She could have, had I given her a chance. But I'd opted to lash out at her—at the one person who is more important to me than life itself. Fuck. I rake my fingers through my hair, move forward. My foot connects with something on the ground. There's a dull thud. I look down to find coins spilled on the ground, and next to it a steel can is overturned.

"Sorry." I bend, scoop up the money and drop it back into the container.

"Got a cigarette?" a voice asks.

I glance up at the homeless man seated behind the receptacle. He has a Santa hat perched on his head. Had she actually nicknamed me Alpha Claus? I smirk. Talk about being kinky. But hell, if my North Pole hadn't been a snug fit in her stocking. I shake my head. The hell am I thinking?

"Oy," he waves his hand in front of my face, "got a smoke?"

I blink, shake my head, "Huh? Nope, sorry."

"Spare some change instead?" He peruses my features, "You okay there, man?"

"Sure," I mutter, shove my fingers in my pants pocket, come up empty. Search the other pocket and pull out my phone. Huh. "Guess I forgot my wallet." I glance back at her apartment block—okay, technically my block. But fuck, if I am going back there, not after that scene. Best to give her time to cool off, and then what? Beg her forgiveness? Fuck that. If she can't accept me the way I am...then too fucking bad. Her loss. *And yours.* A fine curvy, gorgeous, love-of-my-life-sized loss. "Fuck," I swear aloud.

"You need a drink," Homeless man drawls.

'Yeah."

"Or maybe two," he offers.

I roll my shoulders, "Sounds about right." *Why not?* Liquor seems to be the way forward. Days and weeks and months of pouring myself into liquid amnesia. At least, I am old enough to cope that way... Hadn't had that luxury in my teenage years when my brain had turned to mush after the incident. It wasn't until I had found my calling as a surgeon, that I'd found a goal in life, a way to ground myself and keep moving forward. Until her—she is what makes it all worthwhile. Someone I can take care of, protect, share my fears, my deepest desires... Someone with whom I can build a future. "Bloody fuck," I growl. *Why the hell can't I stop thinking about her?* This is not good at all. "Not good."

"Women, huh?" Homeless man folds his legs under himself to sit cross-legged. I stare at his bare feet. There's something wrong with this picture. I frown. "Your shoes," I say, "what happened to them?"

"Got stolen." He raises his shoulders, "Shit happens." He scratches his jaw—which is cleanshaven? That's what it is. I glance down at his feet again. His toenails are clean and cut short, so I hadn't been mistaken. This guy is finicky about his grooming.

"Take mine." I reach for my shoe, tug it off and offer it to him.

He eyes it warily, then takes it from me and slips it on. "Imagine that; it fits." He chuckles.

I slip off the other one; he shoves his other foot into it.

The shoes do look good on him, actually. I tilt my head, stare up into his features. His eyes are clear...a glitter of intelligence in their depths.

"What happened to you?" he asks.

I frown, "What do you mean?"

He points at my middle finger in its splint.

"That?" I crack my neck, "Someone ran me off the road."

"The world's a dangerous place." He nods. "Gotta take care of what's yours."

I nod. "You're onto something there."

"Thanks for the shoes." He shakes his head and the bells at the end of his Santa hat jingle. "Merry Christmas."

"Sure. Whatfuckingever, man."

I rise to my feet. A man jostles my shoulder as he passes.

"The fuck?" I turn to watch him hurry into her apartment block. I frown. Clearly, this isn't my day. I turn to leave.

"You've got to see what's in front of your eyes," Homeless Guy calls after me.

I pause.

"When we two parted
In silence and tears,
Half broken-hearted
To sever for years," his voice fills the space.

I turn on him.

He holds my gaze.

"Pale grew thy cheek and cold,
Colder thy kiss;
Truly that hour foretold
Sorrow to this," he recites.

"What the fuck was that about?" I growl.

"Byron." He blinks.

My heartbeat ratchets up, "Who the fuck are you talking about?"

"Lord Byron, the poet," he replies. "Who did you think it was?"

I shake my head. Of course, it was the poet. This fucker has no connection to the Byron that the Seven had identified as the head of the Mafia... The ones responsible for kidnapping us and changing our fucking lives. Does he?

"Don't delay." He turns to stare up at the apartment block.

I follow his gaze to the window on the first floor, her apartment. A man's shoulders fill the space.

"The fuck?" I straighten, stare at the window. *There's no one there.* I didn't imagine that. I didn't.

Had she replaced me that quickly? I'd barely left and she'd found someone else to take my place? Someone else to bring her to orgasm, to hold her when she shatters, someone else to gaze into those baby blues of hers and declare his love for her as he holds her in his arms? "How dare she?" I stalk forward, retrace my steps to the apartment block.

47

______

Amelie

What the hell had happened? One second, he'd been tickling me and we'd been laughing together. The next, he'd rolled off me, off my bed, headed out of the apartment—and what the hell was that whole thing about not having a future together? Did he mean it? That that... Dumbass fruitcake. That... Mother-trifle... Argh! I can't even get my insults together.

I stand in the middle of the kitchen surveying the remnants of the apple pie—now crumbled all over the dining table. I fold my arms around my waist, over the shirt I'd slipped on, his shirt... Because Mr Alpha dickhead had marched out leaving it behind. I glance out the window. He had to be cold with that bare chest of his exposed to the elements. No doubt, every woman who passed him would ogle him. No doubt, he'd indulge them too and preen.

I curl my fingers into fists and my fingernails dig into my palms. The hell is wrong with me? Why do I already miss him? Do I want to see him again? Why the hell do I want to spend time with a man who is an obnoxious, full-of-himself prat of the highest order. I lean forward, scoop up a crumb of the apple pie. I suck on my finger and the familiar taste of sweet and savory fills my mouth, interspersed with that edgy, darkness that is him. I stare at my wet finger—

That's what it is. He is the contrast to my forced self-confidence. I mean, I can try to pretend to the world that I have it all under control. I can live by the "fake it 'til I make it" motto, which I had embraced as my own so long ago— Except, I could never fool him.

He'd cut through all that sassiness, all that bravado I present to the world, and known me. He'd seen me for what I am. A woman who wants to be taken, to be possessed, to be taken care of. With him... I trust him to take control. Only with him can I find the strength to surrender completely; and he...? He'd known what I needed even before I had. He'd seen me for the eclair I am. All hard on the outside, but drop me in water and I'll dissolve and impart my sweetness to my surroundings—no wait, that metaphor is all wrong —I mean, hard on the outside, soft on the inside... Well, partially... There is more to me than that. I am more like a sticky toffee pudding —mess with me and I'll screw you up bad... Hell, what am I thinking?

Fact is, there's something between us—something hot and vital and real, something that attracts us to each other even as the contrasts highlight how different we are. I hate him. I love him. I can't live without him. I stiffen. Damn, why the hell did I have to go and fall for the wrong man? At least, he'd confessed he loves me— right before he'd walked out on me. Why the hell can't he let me in on his secrets? Can't he see I want to understand him? That I want to spend my life with him? And he wants it too; he does. Only the alphahole has too much of a bloody ego to see it.

I kick the chair in front of me, which topples over. Pain shoots through my foot. "Ow." I hop around on one foot, then fall against the table, which creaks, put out a hand to right myself, and my fingers brush against the spatula I had used earlier. It hits the kitchen timer, which rolls over. Ah, just what I am looking for.

I snatch up the egg-timer, rotate the dial, and the ticking of the countdown fills the room. I turn toward the oven when the thud of a footstep vibrates behind me. My heart slams into my chest. *Is it him? Is he back?* The dense scent of a man's cologne fills my senses.

I've smelled this scent before; it's someone else. Someone who is in my kitchen, with me. My hackles rise. I grab the spatula on the table, turn as a hand closes over my mouth. I scream but the sound emerges muffled. My heart begins to thud. My throat closes. *Let go of me, let go.* I swipe at his arm with my weapon of choice. His grip over my face tightens. I pull my knee up to kick back at him. He grabs me around my waist.

"Stop struggling or I'll hurt you," he snarls in my ear. His voice is sharp, an edge of desperation heightening his tone. Hell, this man is dangerous. He wouldn't hesitate to follow up on his promise.

I slump in his grasp. He begins to drag me across the kitchen when I hear, "Amelie?" Weston's voice calls out from the direction of the living room, "Where the fuck are you? Who the fuck are you with? Couldn't wait to get me out your hair and invite your lover in, huh?"

His footsteps approach. *OMG, it's him.* I need to get his attention. If I can just manage to get this intruder's hand off of my mouth... I begin to struggle in earnest, hit out with my leg, pull back my elbow, and it connects with his stomach.

He grunts, then begins to drag me toward the cupboard in the corner. No way, no way am I letting him get me in there. I bite down on his hand. He swears but doesn't release me. He yanks on my hair so hard that I see stars. Pain ricochets down my spine and tears of frustration fill my eyes. Dammit, I am not giving in like this. I refuse to be a damsel in distress. Fuck this. I double up my knee then kick back. I connect with his shin, and pain thuds up my leg. The bastard huffs out a breath. His grip loosens. Finally! I wrench my face to the side, then scream.

"Amelie." Weston barges into the room.

The intruder swings around, putting me in in front of him. He swings his arm around my neck, yanks me against him. He's tall and broad; the heat of his body curls over me and my skin crawls. "Let me...go." I cough, swipe at his arm with my spatula. He grabs it, wrenches it from my hold, then throws it at Weston, who steps aside in a move so graceful that I blink. The man can move...and not just in bed. If I get out of this alive, I am going to sit on him, in said bed, and ensure that we not leave that space for weeks.

Weston glances at me, "You okay?" His voice is toneless. His features are hard. Gone is the kinky doctor, the demanding lover, the son who cares for his mother... In its place, is a man far more lethal than the intruder who has me in his grasp.

"Amelie?" Weston snaps, "Answer me."

"Yes." I squeak, then clear my throat. "I am fine."

He turns his gaze to the man who holds me captive.

"What do you want?" he asks. "If it's money, let me get to my wallet—" He takes a step forward.

The man swoops out his hand, grabs a knife from the rack next to the cooking range. He presses its edge to my neck and the blood drains from my face. No, no, no, this can't be happening. My pulse rate ratchets up, my heart hammering so hard in my chest, I am sure it's going to jump out. My head spins. No, I will not faint, no way. I bite down on the inside of my cheek, draw in a breath, then another. The silence stretches. A beat, another.

The ticking of the countdown clock fills the space. Weston's gaze darts to the egg timer—his face pales. A nerve throbs at his temple, beating in tandem with the stupid tick-tock of the timer. Ugh, why did I have to wind it up? Because I could? Because I thought I was alone. Because I was being spiteful... Gah! Death by kitchen timer... Nooo, that's like a terrible B-grade screamer movie. I am not going out this way, not without a fight. I raise my hand and the intruder presses the knife deeper. Pinpricks of pain spark out from the cut and I feel a drop of blood trickling down my throat. The ball of emotion in my chest seems to expand. I try to swallow, but find my mouth is too dry. Hell, do something, anything.

I stare at Weston, at the sweat that glistens on his forehead. *Look at me, look at me,* I urge him in my mind. *Please baby, tear your gaze away from that stupid egg timer—if we get out of this, I promise I'll throw away every single, stupid timer in the house... I'll switch to those silent ones, the newer digital ones even*—I cringe. Okay, so they are not my favorite, but no choice. Needs must, and all that. The intruder grips my arm, urges me to take a step forward.

Weston doesn't move—the muscles of his massive shoulders lock and his chest planes could be hewn out of rock. Everything within him seems riveted by that horrible timer. *OMFG, what the hell am I going to do now?*

The intruder nudges me and I move forward, closer...closer to where Weston stands, rooted to the spot. His jaw tics and the tendons of his throat bulge. His arms are locked into his sides—frozen in the moment that he'd spotted the timer.

How long did I set it for? Ten minutes? Five? Oh God, please let it be for five or less. Why did I have to touch that stupid thing? Can I rewind back this morning...to the time in bed, when he had reached for me and tickled me until I couldn't stop laughing? Had it been just this morning? And why hadn't I thrown my arms and legs around him, clung to him and not let him leave? We could have still been in bed, all toasty and warm, and fucked each other until we'd collapsed again. Yes, that's what I want when this is over—an entire non-stop marathon of make-up sex. *Weston, darling, please hold on, just a few more minutes, just a—* The intruder shoves me forward, I stumble, slip on some of the remnants of the apple pie that are still on the ground. My legs slide out from under me, and I scream.

There's a blur of action. I sense Weston move—he swoops down, grabs the egg-timer, hurls it toward me.

48

Weston

The egg-timer rings as it sails through the air. It grazes the forehead of the intruder — who's wearing a mask. Of course, he is. Motherfucker! And my aim with my left hand sucks! Jesus, and I call myself a surgeon? When I most need precision, I am fucking hampered by the bloody splint. The asshole sways, then the knife slips from his fingers and crashes to the ground.

Amelie lurches forward. She stumbles and my heart slams into my ribcage. I jump forward, reach her as she collapses. I yank her to my side and behind me.

I raise my hand at the bastard, who's still standing. Why the hell is he still standing? I bury my fist in his face. He howls. I swing my fist at him again, he arches back, and I graze his shoulder. He straightens, then swings at me. I raise my left arm, deflect the blow. He comes at me again. I swear, angle my body to protect her. He lands a punch in my shoulder. At least it's the unhurt arm. I grunt, try to weave away. Behind me, Amelie stiffens and wriggles in my grasp. I turn my face — big mistake, asshole lands one in the side of my head. Sparks flare between my eyes. I growl, shake my head.

Amelie snarls, tugs in my grasp. "Let me go," she whispers.

"No," I growl, pull away as the bastard tries to deck me again.

"Unhand me, you macho ass." She pulls away, but I refuse to release her. She buries her teeth in my bicep. *The fuck?*

I grunt, loosen my hold on her, just as the intruder buries his fist in my other shoulder. A growl rips from me; my entire arm throbs...especially the motherfucking middle finger in a splint — "F-u-u-c-k!" I shake my head, focus my attention on the motherfucker. I curl my fist — my bloody left fist — swing at him, land a hit, then again. He grunts, lumbers backward. I head butt him, and he crashes into the counter behind him.

I raise my arm as Amelie yells, "Take that you bastard." She heaves the spatula at the stranger, catches him in the nose. He howls, presses his palm to his face, pushes away, turns and lurches around the dining table. "You bloody prick, you dare break into my apartment?" She grabs the next available weapon — which happens to be the other pie — the one left to cool on the counter behind her. She throws it at the retreating figure, catches him in the shoulder. He grunts, stumbles, steadies himself at the doorframe — asshole's wearing gloves as well.

"You think I am afraid? Huh? You think you can come in here and invade my space... you... you..."

"Dickhead?" I supply.

"No, that's an insult I reserve for you," she cries.

She glances around, reaches for another knife, throws it at him...misses. The blade embeds in the doorframe.

The intruder runs out of the kitchen. The next second, the door to the apartment slams behind him.

"You fucking prick, you horrible, mangy-faced, skiving, conniving, dodgy cocksucker —" She grabs hold of a whisk, hurls it at the door, picks up the pastry brush and throws it, then reaches for a wooden spoon.

I reach for her, "Amelie."

"Randy, ass-whipped... ignominious —" She throws the spoon in the direction of the door, but it only makes it halfway over before hitting the floor. She stumbles forward, reaches for the cookie cutter.

I grab her wrist. She swings at me, her gaze wild, hair flowing about her shoulders.

"Princess, stop," I admonish her. She stabs the rolling pin in my chest, "Ouch." I grunt, press down with my fingers, "He's gone, Buttercup."

"What if he comes back?" she pants.

"He won't," I promise.

"What if he does?" she insists.

I lower her hand, slide the rolling pin from her fingers, "Then, uh, I promise to defend us from him, with—" I raise the rolling pin, "This?" I frown.

She glances at it, then at my face. "That's ridiculous." She giggles.

"It is, huh?" I quirk my lips, then hold up the blasted thing in a defensive gesture, "Well then, am I Westley enough for you?"

"No." She shakes her head, "I prefer you as Weston."

"And I fucking love you, any which way." I peruse her flushed features. "Even armed with deadly kitchen utensils—"

"Baking tools," she corrects me.

"What-fucking-ever." I fling the rolling pin aside, hold out my arms.

She jumps up and into my embrace.

"Fucking hell, Buttercup, you fucking bloody scared me," I say as I scoop her up.

She wraps her legs around my waist. "You stupid oaf, you left me, in the bed, on my own." She hiccoughs.

"Yeah, I am that and more," I agree. "You can call me any bloody insult under the sun and I deserve it all."

"He...he..." She buries her face in my chest, "He held a knife to my throat, oh, my God!" Her entire body shakes, her shoulders treble and my heart, my bloody heart stutters.

"Shh." I brush my cheek against her hair, "Shh, babe, I am here."

"You turned your back on...," she mumbles. "You walked out. How could you do that?" She digs her fingers into my shoulders and I wince.

Fuck, that's how much of a weak motherfucker I have become. I can't even hold up to being mauled by my woman. I reach the table, lower her onto it.

She clings to me. "Don't leave me," she mumbles between gusts of sobbing.

"Don't cry, Princess, please." I hold her close, wrap my arms around her. She doesn't let go, just buries her face in my chest and sobs. I try to pull back, and she only sobs louder.

"Babe," I mutter, "I just want to make sure that you're not hurt."

"You hurt me." She hiccups, "You ass, you broke my heart."

"I am so sorry, Cookie, I truly am."

"Huh?" She leans back in the circle of my arms. "Say that again."

"I am sorry?"

"No after that."

"I truly am?" I frown.

"No, you stupid goof, in between those two phrases."

"What did I say?" I blink.

"A word beginning with C?"

"Cunt?" I smirk.

She slaps my shoulder.

I wince. "Ouch, easy there, darling. I'm afraid he managed to get in a few hits as well."

"You'll survive," she grumbles. "Say it, you idiot, the nickname you just used."

"You mean Caramel?"

"No."

"Candy."

"Noooo," she growls.

"Cherry pie?"

"You are such a tease." She digs her fingers in the shoulder of my hurt arm.

"Hey," I wince, "you're hurting me."

"Good," she huffs, "you deserve it."

"I do," I agree.

She blinks, "Wow, you're actually agreeing that you are a jerkface?"

"Yep."

"And a dickhead?"

"But I am your dickhead, darling Cookie."

"I like that name best." She sniffs, "Especially when you kiss me after saying it."

I survey the skin of throat, which seems unbroken, thank fuck.

"How dare that bastard threaten you with a knife." I trace my thumb over the pulse that flutters at the base of her throat. "When I get my hands on him—"

"You will not go after him," she scolds.

"I must," I reply. "He came after what belongs to me."

"Do I belong to you?" she asks.

"Of course, you do." I run my finger down the hollow between her breasts, around her nipples.

"What are you doing?" Her voice is breathless.

"Uh, taking care of you."

"He didn't hurt me there."

My vision tunnels, "Bastard touched you. I am going to kill him, I—"

She grips the 'V' of the shirt—my shirt, and tugs. The buttons pop and the shirt gapes to reveal the creamy curves of her breasts.

"What are you doing?" I stare at the curves, the nipples that she reveals when she shoves the shirt down her arms.

"Cookie," I breathe, take in the spread in front of my eyes. My throat closes. I stare at the blush that colors her gorgeous skin, her pink nipples that harden into plum-colored pebbles. I bend down, close my mouth around one, and tug. She moans. I bite down and she cries out. I suck on her sweet flesh and she sinks her fingers into my hair. I kiss one breast, then the other, straighten and peer into her face. "You're mine, Princess, my woman."

Her pupils dilate and her breathing grows shallow.

I pull away and she frowns, "Where are you going?"

"To lock the door to the apartment."

"No." She scissors her legs around my waist. "Don't go." She grabs my arms. "Please." Her lips tremble, "Stay with me."

"You're safe, Cookie."

"Only as long as I am with you, Wes." She leans in, drags her tongue around my nipple. I groan. She bites down on the nub with her sharp teeth and I feel it all the way to my cock. My dick lengthens in my pants. The tent at my crotch stabs into her core, still covered by my shirt and her panties.

"Fuck," I growl, "I really should secure the place first."

"You really should check out how wet I am for you."

I reach down between her legs, push aside her panties, and my knuckles graze her melting core.

She pants and I groan, "You're mine, Amelie. Only mine."

I lower my zipper, grab my cock and position it at the entrance to her channel.

"Mine to make love to, to bring to climax over and over again, mine to claim." I kick my hips forward, thrust inside her moist channel. My balls slap against her inner thigh, pressure builds in my groin.

Then the doorbell rings.

49

Amelie

"Expecting someone?" He pulls out of me, the head of his fat dick poised at the entrance to my pussy.

I groan, dig my fingers into his tight flank. "Ignore it!" I plead.

His nostrils flare and the skin pulls tightly across his cheeks. "Sure you're not expecting any lovers? Anyone I need to know about?" He massages the curve of my hip.

I shiver. "You're the only one in my life, Doc," I moan.

"Damn fucking right." He pounds into me again, with such force the entire table shakes. The mixing bowl crashes to the ground, rolls, then comes to a stop.

In the silence that follows I can't stop the giggle that bursts from my throat.

"You think it's funny?" He frowns.

"No," I chuckle.

He pulls out, then sinks back into me. "Yes," I gasp, "yes, it is actually."

"Clearly, I am not doing this right, if you are thinking about something else other than how I am going to tear your pussy apart, how I am going to sink inside you so deep you'll feel like you are splitting in half."

He pumps his hips forward, rams into me, and his balls slap against my inner thigh. *Oh, hell!* A moan spills from my lips. I reach up, wind my arms around him... Well, as much as I can reach, that is. This man is so broad, I reach maybe halfway around his back.

"Wes." I pant... "Please."

"You're fucking killing me, Princess." He bends his knees, loops his arms under my knees, and pulls my legs up and over his shoulders.

Instantly, he slips deeper inside, the crown of his cock hitting that secret part of me — one I didn't even know existed until now. "Oh." I open and close my mouth. "Oh, my," I gasp.

"When I saw that motherfucker with his hands on you, my heart stopped." He growls, "I swear, if you do that to me again, I'll—"

"You'll?"

"I'll chain you to my bed and never let you go until I've fucked every hole in your body over and over again, until I've covered you under layers of apple pie and licked them all off of your skin, off every gorgeous curve, from between your legs, from the tops of your breasts, the slope of your butt, the turn of your ankles, the valley between your arse-cheeks. Then I'll fuck you until I take you to the edge, but I won't let you come. I'll start all over again, this time with chocolate, then cream, then work my way through every ingredient of your dessert repertoire."

"Oh." I blink. My pussy clenches around his dick.

"You like that, hmm?"

"I..." I gulp, "I..."

He smirks, "I am going to fuck you now."

I blink, stare up into those hard features — a flush smears his cheeks, those gray eyes are pools of desire, of lust, of everything I've always wanted and hoped for but never thought possible. I see myself reflected in them — him, me, us... Our future. "Wes," I groan, "don't stop, don't—"

He thrusts forward, impaling me. His shaft fills me, stretches me, his girth imprinting every ridge, every hard inch of him against every millimeter of my sensitive channel. Goosebumps flare on my skin, and pinpricks of pleasure and sparks of heat shoot out from the contact. He slams into me again and I cry out, throw my head back, hold onto him and wait, wait — He begins to fuck me with domination, with precision, with that complete self-assurance that is so Weston. "Oh, my God. Oh, my God. Oh, my God," I chant.

"That's me, baby." He pulls out. "Never forget."

He propels his hips forward, sinks into me, hitting that place inside again and I howl, "Wes, please. I'm, I'm going to —"

"Come with me, Princess," he growls, and I shatter. The climax screams over me, and I cry out again. He kisses me, absorbs the noise I make, as he continues to fuck in and out of me, before sinking into me once more. He tears his mouth from mine. "Look at me," he growls.

I force my eyes to open, meet his gaze as he spills himself inside of me with a grunt, his features contorted into an expression of dominance and ecstasy that is so very Wes. He leans his forehead against mine.

My eyelids flutter shut as I float down from the space he always takes me whenever we make love, where everything is golden and happy and peaceful, save for my heart that hammers. The blood pounds at my temples; it mirrors the thump-thump-thump in his chest.

There's more banging, then the sound of the door to the apartment being pulled open.

"You there, Amelie?" A woman's voice calls out.

I snap my eyes open, "Oh, hell —" I gasp, "It's —"

"Amelie!" The voice sounds closer, "Where are you? My flight got in earlier than expected, I'm — Oh... OH!" There's the sound of a startled exclamation, "Oh, I'm sorry."

I turn my head over my shoulder and heat flushes my face. "Julia," I exclaim.

"Ah..." My friend glances from me to Weston, then back at me, "Umm... I'm so sorry..." She averts her eyes, "Ah, my flight just got in... I came in straight from the airport...uh! Why don't I go get coffees for all of us? I'll be right back."

"Wait, Julia..." I shove at Weston who, of course, doesn't budge an inch.

"It's fine, don't worry." She turns away, waves her hand in the air, "It's all good, honest. I'll, uh, be right back." She scampers off.

I turn to Wes, "Let me go." I slap at his shoulder.

"No," he smirks, "in case you've forgotten, I'm still inside of you."

His dick pulses inside of me and I blink, "You're hard again? How's that possible, you just ah, came..."

"So?" He bends his knees and kisses me, "Merry fucking-Christmas, by the way."

"You can say that again." I throw my arms around him and kiss him back, "Please can we get dressed, before she returns?"

Ten minutes later, I watch him in the mirror in my bedroom. He'd jumped in the shower a few minutes ago, and now he shrugs into the shirt I'd rescued from the kitchen floor.

He does up the buttons—the one's that had survived when I had ripped it off earlier. Gah! Had I actually done that? Around him I seemed to turn into some kind of sex addict. But can you blame me? I stare at the gorgeous planes of his chest being hidden by the fabric. My throat dries. The pleasant ache between my legs intensifies. I'll never get enough of him, never.

He tugs on the lapel of his shirt. "I can keep this off, if you prefer." His lips curl.

"Not a chance." I close the gap between us, then stab my finger into his rock-hard abs, "I don't feel like sharing right now. Besides, this picture-perfect cut physique belongs to me, you get me?"

He chuckles, "My, my, how possessive you sound, little Red?"

"All the better to scratch you with." I drag my fingernail down the demarcation between his pecs. Why the hell can't I keep my hands off of him?

"I can't wait to see you in scrubs," I mutter.

"I am sure I can oblige." He smirks, " kinky doctor-patient games are my specialty."

"And here I thought it was food kink that got you off." I widen my gaze.

"When it comes to you, babe, everything I do takes on another dimension." He runs his big palm down the curve of my waist and slaps my butt.

"Whoa, whoa," I protest. "What's that for?"

"Keeping you warm." He massages my arse, then cups the other cheek with his free hand and squeezes. My sex instantly clenches. He drags me up on my tiptoes, and the tent in his crotch pokes me.

"You're hard," I mumble.

"You're soft." His grip on my backside tightens and my nipples instantly pucker. Moisture pools between my thighs. "This is not the time," I half protest. "Julia will be back any moment."

He groans, "I think I much prefer the cabin. At least, I could have you to myself there."

I chuckle, "I'll always remember it as the place where I walked in on you naked."

"If I had my way, you and I would be naked for a month, on an island in the middle of nowhere."

"Just as long as there is an oven where I can bake." I warn.

"I'd rather see you baking in the sun... Naked, of course."

I shake my head, "Don't you think of anything but sex?"

"Do you?" He chuckles.

"I think you're fast becoming my favorite dessert, Doc Kincaid," I reply.

"You know you are always mine." He laughs and his features light up. His hair is all mussed up, thanks to me — I'd clung to it, when he'd insisted on going down on me, one last time before he'd released me. Seriously, the man is insatiable. The soreness between my legs is testament to that — and the hickeys on my neck, the bitemarks on my breasts — which is why I am wearing this long-sleeved turtle-neck sweater and a fresh pair of jeans. I glance down at his bare feet, "Did you lose your shoes?"

"Gave them to the homeless guy outside the apartment building."

A warm feeling seizes my chest. "You did that?" I ask. "You gave the shoes you were wearing to someone who needed them?"

He raises his shoulders, then widens his stance. "Don't go reading anything into it," he mutters. "It seemed like the thing to do; no big deal."

I scan his features, "I don't know of too many people who'd do that, you know?"

He cracks his neck in a gesture I am beginning to recognize. He does it when he's embarrassed and trying to hide it.

"You're full of shit Dr. Kinky-as-hell-Caid," I say. "You try so hard to come across all dominant and hard-ass, but in reality, you're like... like..."

"Like?"

"A Jammie dodger."

"A Jammie dodger?"

I nod, "One of those cookies which is double-layered, and hard on the outside, but is filled with sweet gooey jam in the center."

"Hmm." His eyes gleam. "You can taste my jam any day, baby."

"Eeyugh," I make a gagging sound, "I left myself open to that, didn't I? Will I never learn?" I groan.

"It's too easy to tease you." He steps closer, "You're the jam to my cookie; the pumpkin to my pie, the chocolate in my toffee."

"Thought you hated chocolate?" I swallow.

He bridges the distance between us, draws me to him, "That's what I thought too." He searches my face, "But then I tasted you and—"

"And?" I whisper.

"I realized it was missing an ingredient."

"Which is?"

He lowers his face to mine. His breath mixes with mine, our eyelashes tangle, our feet bump, he parts his lips, and the doorbell rings again.

"It's Julia," I groan. "I have to get the door."

50

Weston

She twists her body. My grasp loosens and she pulls away, then
pivots and scrambles for the door.

"You," I mutter to the empty room, "it was you that I missed."

*Jesus, fuck, can you hear yourself? Did you just confess that you were
incomplete without her?* Was I? How much do I need her in my life?
Could I go on without her? A future without her would be...bleak,
dull, no patches of color, no scent of complex notes, no flavors that
beckon and open up my senses. Without her... I am less than half the
man I could be... I rub the back of my neck. What the fuck? What
just happened? Why is my heart thumping? The blood pounds at my
temples and my shoulder muscles knot.

Without her... There is no future... There is no me... Bloody hell.
I rotate my head, dig my fingers into my hair and tug on it. I can't
leave here without her, no way. I don't know what the future holds,
but if I don't keep her close... I'll never have a chance of finding out
either. As long as she is with me... I stand a chance, at having everything I didn't even know I had wanted... She makes me chuckle,
lightens the load I've carried alone for so long. I want her by my side,

in my house, in my bed. My ring on her finger, her hand in mine, her body writhing under me as I bury myself inside of her, as I try to tame her, hold her down and fuck her, as I open myself up to her and claim her. I am going to chain her to my side in a way that she'll never leave. I have to do it. Have to get her to see things my way. That her future is mine, that I am her future, that she is my... Everything.

The band around my chest tightens and a ball of emotions fills my throat. A pressure builds behind my eyes, fuck... This...this thing that tears me apart inside and twists my guts, that buries its weight in my stomach, knots my insides and coils in my chest...dries up my throat and hardens my balls. It has to be... It has to be...fucking love. I grab my hair and tug on it. I'd said it out loud earlier, but I'd shrugged it off as something you say in the heat of the moment. But this...this gasping for breath, this sensation of my heart having been scooped out of my body, this nervousness inside of me that grows and grows, even as a desperation tightens my skin, my shoulders, my spine... All of it points to the fact that I am a fucking goner. I am in love... Bloody fuck, I am... And there's nothing I can do about it. My heart begins to pound so hard against my rib cage, I am sure I must be having a cardiac... Except I know I am not... It's the emotional shock causing my palms to sweat. My thigh muscles bunch. I lower my hand, not surprised to find that my fingers are shaking. I stalk out of the bedroom into the tiny living room space.

She faces Julia, who offers her a coffee from the takeaway tray. "I don't want to impose," she mutters.

Amelie curls both of her palms around the paper cup. "It's no imposition," she says.

"No, it isn't," I agree.

Both women turn to me.

Amelie frowns.

Julia tilts her head. "We haven't met, I'm Julia," she says.

I walk forward, halt next to Amelie, "I'm Amelie's boyfriend." Yep, I am well and truly pussy whipped. Since when had my identity become secondary to my position in her life, eh?

Amelie draws in a breath.

Julia smiles. "Good to meet you, Amelie's boyfriend." She holds out the tray of coffee.

"Thank you." I accept one of the cups, swig from it. Damn, but why couldn't it contain a shot of whiskey, at the very least? I suck down more of the coffee.

"You two been dating long?" she asks.

"Yes," I reply.

"No." Amelie shoots me a glance, her gaze narrowed.

"Long enough for me to ask her to move in with me." I smile.

Julia looks between us. "Congratulations." She holds out a hand. Amelie ignores it.

"You... you..." She gapes at me.

"You're coming with me." I say simply.

"I'm not," she splutters, tries to pull away.

I tug her closer, tuck her into my side, and tiny thing that she is, she fits right there, plastered against me.

"Come on babe," I plead, "I can't leave you here, not after the break-in."

"Break in?" Julia exclaims.

"Yeah," I reply, without taking my gaze from Amelie's face. "Someone broke into the apartment earlier today."

"It...it was the same man who forced his way into my bakery." Amelie swallows.

"He was wearing a mask," I remind her. "How can you be sure?"

"I'm sure." She nods. "I... uh, recognized the scent of his cologne."

"You did, huh?" Something hot stabs at my chest. Whoa, what the fuck? Why the hell am I all twisted up inside because she smelled another man's aftershave? This is bloody ridiculous. "That settles it," I growl. "You're not staying here a second longer. You're coming with me."

Her gaze narrows, "I don't think so."

"Yes, you are," I snap.

Her features pinch and she sets her jaw. Fuck, I can't let her go all obstinate on me. Not that I don't mind whipping it out of her, but well, we have company—not that it would stop me, but Julia is her girlfriend, and the one thing I've learned from the rest of the Seven hooking up, is that, you did not show down your woman in front of her friends.

My woman. Mine. I draw her even closer.

She tilts her chin up, "What are you doing?"

"Convincing you." I lower my head, press my mouth to hers, keep the kiss soft, coaxing. I nibble on her lower lip, and when she gasps, I swipe my tongue inside her mouth, just a quick in and out, enough to remind her what is in store if she comes with me, enough to communicate that I need her, want her. A whine tumbles from her lips. My dick instantly lengthens. I tighten my hold on her shoulders, lessen the intensity of the kiss, pull back, brush her lips with mine one more time. "See, that's all settled."

"Oh." Her eyelids flutter, "Wes—"

"Don't say no." I peer into her face, "Come home with me."

She holds my gaze, her chin wobbles, then she nods. "Okay."

Okay! The breath I'd not been aware of holding wheezes out. *What the bloody fuck? Had I been nervous as I'd waited for her reply? Had I actually given her a choice?* And if she had refused? Would I have left...? No, I'd have parked myself here and ensured there was security around the clock. Not that I have anything against this flat... Except there is no telling if the intruder will be back. Besides, I want her in my space, in my bed. I have to be inside of her again.

I stare at her, and her pupils dilate. She licks her lower lip, and her breathing goes ragged.

"Right, get what you need," I say.

She turns, then gasps, "Oh, my God, Jules. I can't leave you here."

"What rubbish." Julia looks between us. "I'll be fine."

"No way, am I letting you stay here. What if the intruder returns?"

"I'll lock the door from the inside," she insists.

"It's not safe," Amelie shuffles her feet, "I don't feel comfortable leaving you here."

I frown. I can't allow her to stay on, but I don't want Julia to come with us either, not when I want Amelie to myself... No way, am I sharing her with anyone else... Not yet... Not for a while, which means... There is only one way out. "I have an idea."

51

Amelie

"Holy fuck." I stare out of the window at the view of Tower Bridge from the window of Weston's penthouse.

He'd informed me that I was on his guest list, so I could come and go as I please. Also, my fingerprints had been added to the fancy-ass security thingy on the front door to the apartment. So I had to simply touch my palm to the lock pad provided and—wowza!—the door would open to let me in. Oh, he'd let me try it and it had worked on the way in. Woo. That is some fancy shit. The kind of security only the seriously well off could afford.

Don't get me wrong, I knew he was loaded...and talented, and over-the-top dominant...but this... All this luxury that surrounds me... It's too much. When we were at the cabin, London had seemed so far away. It had been easy to forget about daily life, my debts, my growing business, the fact that he is so bloody out of my league. And at my apartment... Well, that had been my turf. I had felt more in control maybe... Which is a laugh, considering it has been broken into. It is also the place where he told me he loves me.

"Did you mean what you said?"

I hear the words and curse myself. *Why the hell can't you filter your thoughts, bitch? Why is it so important to know what he feels for you?* He wants me. He was taking no argument about leaving me behind at the apartment either. So, he lusts after my body... I mean, that's good, right? It's a start. The fact that he finds me attractive? Heat sears my back, then his big arm wraps me around my waist. He pulls me back and flush against his big chest. Instantly, I feel tiny and cherished and taken care of. Big mistake. He is going to lure me in, fuck me senseless, keep me in a sex-induced haze, and when I wake up from it, I will regret every little piece of me I had shared with him.

"Do you actually want to know the answer to your question?"

Of course, he knows what I was referring to... And yeah, I definitely want to know the answer.

"No."

I shake my head.

"Liar," He pulls me close so my back is plastered against his perfect chest. Heat from his body cocoons me, sinks into my blood.

My toes curl. My thighs clench. *Get your mind out of the gutter, you slut.* "Umm," I hesitate. "It was nice of you to have a security system put in my flat, and on such short notice."

Yeah, he'd made one phone call and in half an hour, his security consultant had arrived, armed with an array of devices. She'd checked out the place, then rigged it with enough alarms and sensors to satisfy his exacting demands. It had taken less than two hours from start to finish, during which time, Julia and Weston had gotten along well. I'd watched from the sidelines as he'd charmed her, put my friend at ease, so that by the time it was time to leave, she was completely convinced that this was the right move for me. Well, apparently, he saves that hard-headed, demanding alphahole side of his for me... Not that I am complaining. It is part of his appeal — I admit, that firm hand of his is a bloody turn on for me. If only I could always live in this sex-haze of a bubble, huh?

He wraps both of his arms around my shoulders, enveloping me in that gorgeous scent of his. "You're deflecting, babe." He bends to nibble on the shell of my ear.

I shiver.

"Didn't think you were such a coward." He blows in my ear, and I shiver. Bloody hell, with him, every part of me turns into an erogenous zone. Bet I've sprouted nerve endings where none existed before... *All the better to sense you with, Mr. Wolf.*

He spreads his fingers over my stomach. The width of his palm is so wide that the tip of his thumb brushes the underside of my breast. My nipple instantly pebbles. *Stupid, stupid, that I am so responsive to him.*

I pull away from him. Of course, he doesn't let me budge, not a millimeter. Against his strength, I am helpless. His force of will, his confidence... How is it possible that he always seems to know what he wants? Unlike me. My entire life is a two steps forward, one back kind of scenario. "Let me go," I mumble.

"Not a chance," he growls. The edge of his voice shivers down my spine, sinks into my center.

"Wes," I plead, "you're making this very hard."

"I'll make it simple." He releases me, only to flip me around. "Look at me."

I stare at his chest, the smattering of hair that peppers the dent between his perfect abs. We'd walked in and I had headed for the view and lost my composure. Now, when I lean in and press my nose into his skin and inhale, notes of sweetness mixed in with his darker scent fills my senses. "You smell like us," I whisper, draw in another breath, then bend and lick him. "You taste like honey and chocolate bomb overlaid with cinnamon and cloves and a dash of vanilla." Yum!

A groan rumbles up his chest.

"Woman you've got to stop comparing me to desserts."

"Oh?" I glance up at him, "Shall I compare thee to a summer's day instead?"

"Shakespeare?" He tilts his head.

I stare up at that perfect visage, that strong jaw, the mean upper lip that hints at the dominance inside that drew me to him...those thick eyebrows, the eyelashes that fringe his keen gaze. Everything about him is right, more than right. He is the complete package—he fits me; body, mind and soul, and damn it... This is all wrong. I can never have him, could never keep him. What do I have that could hold his attention? Why does he have to understand me so well? Tears knock against the back of my eyes.

"What's wrong?" He frowns.

"I don't belong here."

"You belong with me."

"I don't want you."

"You do."

"I can't do...this."

"What?"

"Whatever this is." I wave my hand in the air, "Playing house...or rather playing mansion—or whatever it is the other half calls it."

"Is that what you think this is?" He seems perplexed.

"Isn't it?"

"Maybe," he concedes. "Maybe not." He releases me, then steps back. He'd changed clothes, and now his tailored slacks mold his thighs and cling to that spectacular butt as he paces the floor in his Italian shoes—how many of them does he have in his closet, huh?

He drags his fingers through his hair, drawing my attention to how his biceps bulge against his button-down shirt. My mouth waters. *Whoa down girl, haven't you feasted on his delectable body enough?* And that's the problem. I'd prefer to lick his sculpted abs—and uh, other parts of him—over chocolate. Shit, I am so screwed.

"I am not sure what this is between us," he concedes.

"You're not?" I blink. The alphahole is always bloody sure of himself. He rolls his shoulders now, then cracks his neck, then pivots to face me, with his eyebrows knitted into a look I can only describe as confusion. This is a first.

"I'm not," he confirms my suspicion. "When I walked in and realized you were in danger, when he held that knife to your neck, something changed."

"It did?"

"I thought I'd failed you. If something had happened to you, I could have never forgiven myself."

"You're not my keeper," I mutter. "I've taken care of myself for so long."

"And look where that has gotten you." He scowls.

"What?" I blink, "Did you just say what I think you did?"

"Look," He holds up his hands, "I'm not saying you haven't tried your best, but I could make things much easier for you with my money, my contacts."

I swallow and something hot stabs at my chest. My throat closes and my eyes burn. Why the hell had I thought anything had changed? Because he'd chased that goddam burglar from my apartment? No, hold on, I'd played a part in that too. Because he'd ensured that my friend would be safe in my apartment? That was because he wanted me close, where he could keep an eye on me, take care of me, control me. That's what this is about.

He wants me here so I can be his little fuck toy. He'd have his way with me... Oh, yeah, I'd enjoy every second of it too.. And then what? He'd throw me away? Well, he'd have paid me for my time...

And I don't want it. I'd rather live in debt for the rest of my life, than be obligated to him.

Not that it wasn't part of the arrangement. I mean, I'd gone into it with my eyes open, not realizing I was giving him what he needed —a way to manipulate me.

Whatever the future might hold for us, whatever there could be between us... As long as the money stands between us...the money I had accepted...it would always be a relationship which would be measured, a connection which had a number attached to it... It's too finite. Too tangible. Too...restrictive. Something that goes against how I had lived my life, the future I wanted for myself. I want him, all right, but not at the cost of my self-respect.

If I stay, and accept the money, and allow him to treat me like one of his other women, someone whose bond is tainted by the materialistic aspects of life... We don't stand a chance. Not the way I want.

"This...is all wrong," I say.

He closes the distance between us, "I don't agree."

"I don't want your money."

He stares, "Excuse me?"

"I don't like how it makes everything too easy."

"Are you kidding me?" He scowls. "That's what it is meant for—to pave the way, to achieve dreams, to help you get what you want."

"I can do it on my own." I tip up my chin. "I will achieve my goals, on my own merit."

"What are you saying?" He glowers, "You're not making any sense to me."

"For the first time since I met you, I am making sense to myself."

His gaze widens, "So you admit that I affect you?"

I throw up my hands, "That has never been in dispute. I mean, come on, it's clear we can't keep our hands off of each other. Put us in a room and we'll end up in bed. Hell, I hear your voice on the phone and I'm wet."

"You are, huh?" He smirks and his shoulder muscles seem to broaden.

"OMG!" I slap my forehead, "Of course, you'd choose to focus on the more obvious. Of everything I said, is that the only thing you heard?"

"You want me; I want you. We're good together." He raises his shoulders, "What else is there?"

"Everything." I swallow, "And nothing." I peer into his face, "After all that we've been through, you still don't get it, do you?"

"Is this about the money?" He scowls, "Because if that's the case, I'll double what I am paying you."

"Money?" A chill spreads across my skin. "You think it's about the money?"

"I'll triple it."

"Triple?" I stare, "You'll triple the money?" *Is he for real? Isn't he hearing anything I am trying to communicate to him? And I thought he got me?*

"That's eighteen million pounds in your bank account on New Year's Day."

I cough. That's a bloody hell of a lot of money. I'd never see that in this lifetime, for sure. If I accepted it, I'd never be able to live with myself. I'd hate myself every day for the rest of my life. Besides, what's the difference between one million and eighteen million, huh? Other than the zeroes? That's the thing with money. The more you have of it, the less it does for you. Nope, I may have been blinded by what the money could have done for me—could still do for me, but not anymore.

"I'll throw in this penthouse," he growls. "Hell, say the word and I'll sign it over to you."

I open my mouth, then purse my lips together, "Good bye, Weston."

I brush past him, spot my suitcases by the door of the living room. He'd had his driver deliver my suitcases to this address. Sneaky bastard had planned it all along... How did I miss it? How come I didn't see through him? I was an acquisition for him. A possession. Hell, he even dropped the 'L' word in the height of passion, hoping it would convince me to give in to him. Well, fuck him, and his money and his bloody view—which is spectacular, I've never seen that view of London in real life before and will probably never do so again. Tears prick the backs of my eyes. *Get out before you bawl your eyes out over that ass.*

I ignore my luggage; it will only delay me, and I don't want that. I have Peter's contact details; I'll ask him to deliver it home. I'm sure Weston won't stop him, will he? I hesitate. Too bad. I'll have to risk it then. I am not stopping here for one second more. I grab my chef's satchel from the coffee table, tuck my handbag into my side, then head for the door.

"Don't you want to check out the kitchen?" He calls out.

I pause. "What?"

"The kitchen," he says, "it's to your right."

I stare straight ahead. Focus my gaze on the double doors to this blasted, beautiful penthouse. *Get out of here, get out of here.* I take a step forward.

"It has a never-before-used double oven that you have to see."

"It does?"

"You bet." He walks past me, heads toward what I assume is the kitchen. "And all the ingredients you'd need to bake apple pies..."

I swallow.

"Macaroons," he drawls.

I tighten my grip on my bag.

"Triple chocolate cake," he adds.

I turn to him, "Nothing I can't do in my kitchen."

"With this view?" He jerks his chin toward the kitchen, "Not to mention, the complete range of baking tools that you'll need to whip up your specialties."

"You know how I feel about your flaunting your wealth in my face, right?"

"Who said anything about money? This is simply a fully-equipped kitchen, crying out for the right chef to inaugurate it and give it purpose."

I frown. *How the hell does he know exactly how to get to me?* I mean, his words... They are like coffee in the morning, like oats for granola bars, like custard for fruit salad, argh! Stop it...your comparisons suck. Besides, I don't plan to stay. I'll take a peek, check out the kitchen... I mean, it's only a few minutes more, right?

52

Weston

She glances at the big-ass oven — the sleek, professional one, perfect for a baker to use at home, the one I'd had installed yesterday... Whew! She hates my money, but fuck, if it doesn't have its advantages. I've never given the money a second thought, to be fair. Perhaps, it's what comes from being born into wealth... And my career as a heart surgeon? Let's just say, it pays well. And I had invested with the Seven. We had chosen our ventures carefully, especially FOK media which had been a passion project and an investment, which is already paying dividends. So, fuck if I am going to apologize for the money that was mine by birth and which I had helped multiply through my hard work. I get where she's coming from though. She wants to strike out on her own... And I am not stopping her. I'm simply removing obstacles from her way, giving her the best chance of success. Doesn't she realize that? Why can't she accept the fact that everything that is mine is hers? If I could serve up the world on a platter to her, I'd do it. I stiffen. Do I think that? All that emo shit that I'd been sure was not for me...? Clearly, I'm rolling in that shit, thanks to Ms. Chocolate Cookie... Hell, I've even accepted the presence of chocolate in my life, and Christmas, and all that shit that has never mattered before? I want it all...with her. That's it. I need help—need to figure out how to solve this conundrum that I have worked myself into.

I pull out my phone, pace the floor of my bedroom, as I dial Damian's number.

"Motherfucker!" he says as his greeting.

"Merry fucking Christmas to you too, asshole," I reply.

"Yeah, yeah, same to you with knobs on." He yawns, "What are you doing on the phone with me? I thought you'd be shacked up with your bride in the penthouse."

"Jesus, I'm not married man. Far from it."

"Why aren't you?"

"What the fuck are you talking about?"

"Straight question, man." He yawns again. "Why don't you put a ring on her finger, put the two of you out of your misery, and let the rest of us get some sleep, huh?"

"Whoa, whoa." I cough. "You're not mincing any words here. What's up? You got a woman there you're eager to get back to?"

"What do you think?" He chuckles.

Yeah, he's with someone.

"Look I need your advice," I mutter.

"I gave it to you already. Don't expect me to make your decisions for you."

"Christ," I mutter, "what's prompted this level of candidness."

"Maybe it's the Christmas spirit, bro." I hear him move around. "Maybe I am tired of watching you screw up over and over again." His footsteps thud on the wooden floor, then the rustle of clothes reaches me. "Hold on." I hear the sound of muffled voices, then he comes back on the call. "So, where were we?"

"You sent her away, huh?" I ask.

"Bros before hoes and all that... " he replies, "Also, she's not the one, so..." I sense him raise his shoulders.

"How do you know that she isn't?"

"When you know, you know," he says, "and you do know, you just don't want to accept it."

"You're full of platitudes," I grumble.

"And you're full of shit," he retorts. "Why the hell don't you have a conversation with her?"

"I've tried, believe me."

"Have you, though?"

"What?"

"Told her how you feel. Have you done that?"

"I told her I love her."

There's silence, then he says, "How did you say it?

"What do you mean?"

"I mean, did you say it like you meant it?"

"Of course," *I think...* "only she didn't say it back."

"She didn't?"

"Nope." I begin to pace, "Maybe she doesn't feel the same way. I mean, I'm not the easiest when it comes to matters of the heart."

He bursts out laughing, "Says the heart surgeon."

"Har, har." I continue, "It's because I am so intimately conversant with that particular organ that I am wary of it."

"Have you thought of the possibility that maybe she doesn't love you?"

"What do you think, I'm stupid?"

"Do I need to answer that question?"

"Don't bother." My stomach ties itself in knots. "She probably doesn't, man, and that's fine. Perhaps in time, she'll develop feelings for me."

"Who are you and what have you done to Dr Asshole Kincaid?"

Heat flushes my neck, "Fuck off, man. If you have something to say, say it."

"You're pussy-whipped."

"You have no idea." I squeeze the bridge of my nose, "It's why I offered to triple the money I'd agreed to pay her —"

"What?" he explodes. "You did what?"

"You heard me," I mumble. A hollow feeling coils in my chest. I squeeze the bridge of my nose, "Fuck, I shouldn't have done that, huh?"

"The opposite, man. You need to take the money out of the equation."

"What do you mean?"

"Change the tone of the relationship."

"How?"

"Replace it with something...that means more to you than money... Offer that up to her... Something that you'd never have imagined giving to anyone else, or giving up for someone else." He pauses, "It could also be something that's ingrained in you... perhaps a habit which you'd change for her?"

I blink. "That...that's profound, bro."

"Sometimes I surprise myself." He laughs. "It's easier to be objective when it comes to other's problems, know what I mean?"

"Yeah," I blow out a breath. "I have to do this, right?"

"You bet," he replies, "it's time you left behind the boy who was kidnapped for good."

53

"Q: What do you call a lamb covered in chocolate?
A: Candy Baa."
-From Amelie's diary

Amelie

I slide the tray of chocolate cookies out of the oven. Yeah, I've been here for a half hour already. What can I say? I'm a sucker. And it doesn't take me much time to mix up the cookie batter. Not when all of the ingredients, and more, are available... And the oven...? Whoa!

I rake my gaze over the sparkling steel surface of the top of the range oven... The man has his faults, but he hadn't compromised when it came to the kitchen. I turn to glance out of the window; the evening light of the city pours in through the large panes. I can see the Thames and the bridge. OMG, Tower Bridge gleams as it picks up the rays from the setting sun. The entire scene is almost surreal, and beautiful, and completely not what I am used to.

But you could...you could stay here, bake in this kitchen every day, sleep in his bed every night, have him fuck you and bring you to orgasm. Hell, bet he'd even proclaim his love again and probably mean it this time... You could have everything you've dreamed of... So why the hell are you holding out? That fucking independent spirit of mine... Why the hell do I have to be this adamant?

It had seemed all right to take his money earlier... But that was before I realized I want more, want him to want me for who I am. A cakehead, who has to figure out things her own way, without help or interference... At least, he'd left me alone to get on with the baking. *Where is he anyway? Why hasn't he checked in on me yet?*

I place the cookies on the cooling trays I'd found.

I had been on the verge of leaving and he'd managed to stall me. Clever man—he knows me too well. I smile at the thought, until I realize it's not true. If he really knew me, he'd know what I want from him. He wouldn't be trying to buy me. Suddenly, I want to cry. I need to get out of here.

I walk toward the door, then pause. I wonder what else he has in this big-ass place? Should I explore? Shouldn't I leave instead? I pause... But the cookies. Okay, I'll stay until the cookies have cooled.

I set the alarm on my phone, pocket it, then creep out of the kitchen. I head for the living room; he's not there. Turn and walk into the next room. It's a playroom, filled with toys. Bet Phe spends a lot of time in here.

I walk into the next room—a study filled with books where an eleven-year-old pre-teen would love to spend time. Yep, this is Skye's. I guess his family comes over to visit often. Does he babysit his nieces? Of course, he does.

I head into the adjacent room. The scent of cigar smoke and something else—his scent, those heavy testosterone notes tease my nostrils. This is his space, a study, more of a man-cave, complete with volumes of medical journals on the shelves.

I peruse the titles, glance down. Huh? He has an entire shelf filled with the Harry Potter books. So, he liked to read them for pleasure? Aww. A warmth trickles through my chest. I stiffen. No, you cannot allow yourself to soften. Damn it, maybe this hadn't been such a good idea.

I'd hoped to find something that would incriminate him, allow me to nurture my need to have a low opinion of him. Instead, all signs confirm that this is a man who loves his family, who has the kind of quirks I enjoy. And yeah, he is a surgeon, and he does save lives. I hunch my shoulders. The man is bloody complex and too attractive, and I don't stand a chance. This had been a bad idea. Speaking of, where the hell is the Doc? Had he been so confident that I would stay, that he'd left? Had he done it to give me some down time? To cool off maybe, and come to my senses? Typical male manipulation. I huff. He knew if he left me alone in his space, I'd investigate it. I reach the doors to his bedroom, hesitate. Go on, do it. A quick peek, that's all it is.

I shove open the doors, enter a room which I swear is as big as my apartment. My feet sink into the carpet that stretches out toward a massive king-sized bed in the center. To one side, sliding doors open onto a terrace, beyond which is the inevitable spectacular view of Tower Bridge. And at the far end? That has to be a walk-in closet. I march toward it, push open the doors and peek in. It's filled with an array of his pants, shirts, ties, suits, scrubs, his designer shoes. No watches, of course. I know, now, why he doesn't keep those accessories. Also, one entire side of the closet is cleared out. For what? Did someone else just move out? Or had he been so sure that I'd move in with him? Presumptuous, much?

As I near the kitchen, the scent of freshly baked cookies teases my nostrils. My mouth waters and my belly grumbles. I hasten my pace, head for the oven. Ha, life's so much better when you have cookies in your hand. And really, I should have left, but procrastibaking is my specialty. You know, when you have a million things to do, but you put it on the back burner and prefer to bake? I snort, then brush my hand over the apron that I'd pulled on. It's a designer piece, that much I can tell. Who makes designer aprons? More to the point, who buys them? Weston fucking Kincaid does, that's who.

I lean over the cookies, inhale the heady perfume. OMG, almost as good as fucking... Well, that's what I used to think. Then I'd met Weston and okay...baking is my second favorite pasttime now, the first being, riding his monster dick, licking the frosting off of his penis... Stop, stop. Enough already. Change of topic, focus on something else. I reach for a cookie and bring it to my mouth.

"Is that for me?"

His voice sounds so close, I squeak. The cookie slips from my fingers. He swoops down catches it.

"Good save," I mutter as he straightens and turns to me.

He glances at the piece of cookie in between his fingers, then raises it and holds it to my lips.

"Open." His gaze is fixed on my face. He peruses my features, searching... searching for... What? My compliance? That I'll throw myself at his feet and ask him to fuck me? That I'll reveal my feelings? Tell him how I've fallen for him, that I want a future with him? Have I allowed him to distract me because I don't want to leave? Because I already miss him—his large body that pins me down and allows me to be weak... Secure in the knowledge that he'll catch me. He'll take care of me... I know that...but I want more. I part my lips and he pops the cookie in. I bite down. The soft texture melts in my mouth. I lick my lips. He lowers his gaze to my mouth, watches me with that intensity that's so Weston. I chew, swallow, open my mouth. He feeds me more of the cookie. I chew, swallow again. This time, his breath catches. The tendons of his throat move, his shoulders bunch. "Amelie," his voice is harsh and soft at the same time.

"Don't." I should turn away. This is where I walk away and never look back. Write off the past few days, count this Christmas as a lost cause, then go home to my apartment—now secure, thanks to him—and bake until I can't see straight. Then swallow down enough wine that I don't remember much of the immediate future. Go through the motions in life... Move on... Pick myself up again and plod forward, one freaking step at a time.

He holds up the last piece of the cookie.

I shake my head, "You have it."

He glances at it then pops it into his mouth. He chews on it and that's when it sinks in.

"It has chocolate," I mutter.

He raises his shoulders, "So?"

"Thought you didn't like it?"

"Told you I was coming around to it." He bends his knees and peers into my face, "In fact, it's fast becoming my second favorite dessert to eat."

My heart stutters. One stupid bit of praise from him and my heart literally seems to melt, like the chocolate in those stupid cookies.

Don't ask him. Don't.

"What's the first?" I mumble.

"What do you think?" His lips curve.

My cheeks heat. My belly flutters. *Don't blush. Don't let him see how much that compliment pleases me.* I swipe my hair over my shoulder. "Don't think that you can get back in my good graces by praising my cooking."

"Baking" he corrects me.

"Right." I drag my fingers through my hair. *Why the hell do I get the feeling that everything is out of my control, right now?* "It's time I left."

I brush past him.

"Stop," he calls out, then softly adds, "Don't leave, Cookie."

I hunch my shoulders, keep my gaze trained on the door. *You don't want this, don't want him like this. You are a big girl; you can move forward on your own. You don't need any alphahole to jerk you around and think he can buy you with money.*

"Princess," his coaxing voice follows me, "I'll let you take the lead."

54

Weston

What the fuck? Did I actually say that? And I meant it, too. Anything to make her stay.

Why can't you tell her how much she means to you? Well, I am about to show her that. And isn't showing better than telling, and all that fucking emo stuff that women believe in?

She pauses at the door, hesitates.

"I mean it." I keep my voice firm. "You can do what you want with me, and I won't stop you. I'll let you take the lead in bed."

She turns to glance at me, "You will?"

"Yep." I jerk my chin.

"Right now?"

"The deal's valid for the next ten seconds."

"Deal, huh?" She frowns.

Fuck, seems I can't change my vocabulary that easily. Go on, you can do this, for her sake. Tone it down, asshole. Keep it easy; don't show how much you need her to retrace her steps, and return to you. And once she does... I'm never letting her go. I am going to find a way to tie her to me. Yep, I have to. Don't fuck this up! I loosen my shoulders, force my muscles to relax. "Okay, not a deal then, an open invitation."

"Invitation?" She chews on her lower lip. Damn her, why does she have to seem so enticing? I force my attention off of my throbbing groin, narrow my gaze on her.

"Anything you need, babe." I hold up my hands in what I hope comes across as an unthreatening gesture, "You name it, you can have it."

She frowns, "What's the catch?"

"No catch."

"I don't believe it."

"Better believe it." I allow my lips to curve.

She stares at my face.

"What?"

"Did you actually smile without smirking?"

"I don't smirk..." I protest.

She arches an eyebrow.

"Okay, maybe sometimes," I concede.

"All the time," she grumbles. "I've never known you not to smirk, not that it isn't hot in a mean kind of way—"

"Aha, so you do find it hot?" My mouth curls.

"I rest my case," she snaps.

Bloody fuck, what the hell does she want me to do? Change my personality overnight? It's taken thirty-three odd years to cultivate this dickface persona. But for her... I'd give that up too... Only with her, that is. To the rest of the world, I'd still be the asshole surgeon with the bad attitude... But for her... I'd do anything.

Does that include letting go of control...for a tiny window in time...allowing her to have her way with me? My balls tighten; my skin crawls. Giving up choice? Not something I'd ever imagined doing...not before her. Only for her.

She is my woman and she'll get her satisfaction when, where and how she needs it. Everyone else will deal...and that includes me. Fuck. I wipe the smile off my face. "Better?"

She raises her shoulders. "Maybe," she takes another step forward, "maybe not."

"I know something that will make it better." I begin to smirk again.

She scowls.

I grimace, school all expression from my face. Best to keep my mouth shut, lock my muscles, dig my feet into the floor. I stay still... Wait... Wait for her to come to me, to tip her head back and meet my gaze.

"Anything, huh?" She drags a finger down my chest, down to my waistband, in the direction of where my cock tents the crotch of my pants.

Blood rush to my groin; pinpricks of heat follow in the path of her touch. "Anything," I growl.

She unbuckles my belt, and my dick thrusts against its restraints. Fuck, at this rate, I am going to come in my pants and she's barely touched me yet. My fingers tingle. I raise my hand.

She glances at it, then at me, "You promised," she reminds me.

I curl my fingers into a fist, then raise my hands and lock them behind my neck, "Indeed." I keep my gaze trained on her face.

Her pupils dilate and color pinks her cheeks. She lowers the zipper, then shoves my pants and my boxers down in one sweep.

The breath catches in my chest as I kick aside my clothes.

She reaches down and winds her fingers around my throbbing dick. My groin hardens, my balls tighten, and I grip my hands together. *Don't release them. Don't reach for her. Don't push her down onto her knees. Don't ask her to take you inside that gorgeous mouth and don't ask her to suck you off... Don't.* She reaches for her shirt and whips it off.

I stare. "What are you doing?"

"What do you think?" She pulls off her bra, then shoves off her boots, and wriggles out of her jeans and panties. Her full tits jiggle as she straightens. She runs her hand down her stomach, to where her pink pussy glistens. She strums her lower lips and my cock jumps in response.

"Huh?" She stares down at her crotch, then drags her fingers up to the swollen bud of her clit. My dick lengthens, I bunch my shoulders, and my balls grow impossibly hard.

"Jesus," I snarl.

"You shouldn't swear using his name on Christmas Day."

"If you don't get on with what you have in mind, I am going to—"

"Going to?" She flutters her eyelashes, "What will you do?"

I narrow my gaze. Why that sassy, little sex kitten. Apparently, giving Princess Buttercup a long leash means she thinks she can run away with it, huh? I glare at her. She pales, but doesn't break the eye contact. "Well," she asks, "shall I continue?"

"Do it," I growl.

"Hmm." She pushes a finger into her cheek, "You don't seem like you're having a good time."

"Doesn't matter." I dig my fingers into the palm of my hand, draw in a breath, count down the time.

Twelve o'clock.

Eleven o'clock.

Ten—

"What are you doing?" she frowns.

"Counting down the time in my mind.

"Why would you do that?"

"It's a technique that helps me find equilibrium."

"And yet clocks trigger you?"

"They used to."

"But not anymore?" She nods, "You didn't flinch when the egg timer rang in my kitchen."

"I may have been too busy saving someone's arse to notice." I mutter.

"You mean someone's gorgeous arse, right?" She wrinkles her nose at me. Fucking adorable. My heart stutters... It bloody stutters. Damian was right, I am pussy-whipped... And I want to whip her pussy too, every chance I get.

"Someone's curvy, beautiful, egg-shaped bottom, to be precise," I reply.

"My butt isn't egg-shaped."

"Wanna bet?" I drawl. "It's as smooth, and as curvy as that blasted egg timer you have—which, by the way, is a hideous piece of kitchenware, with no aesthetic sense."

"Are you saying my butt is ugly?"

"You are not butt-ugly, no," I clarify. "But if you don't get on with your seduction routine — I promise the marks I'll leave on your backside will not be pretty."

"You promised that I could lead," she scoffs.

"But you're not," I snap. "You're talking your mouth off, when you could be putting said orifice to much better use."

She throws up her hands, "Are you going to let me do this my way or not?"

"Fine, fine." I crack my neck. "What fucking ever. Take your time, dawdle, say whatever comes into your mind, while I suffer in silence."

"Hardly suffering and it's not like you've stopped speaking either."

True. I scowl, "You seem to bring out the worst in me, Buttercup."

"As do you." She chuckles, then glances around her before heading to the refrigerator. She pulls out a bottle of milk, then shuts the door and walks toward me.

"Anything, huh?" She asks.

I glance at the white liquid in the bottle, then up to her face, "Anything."

She holds up the bottle, tilts it over my chest.

55

Amelie

What the hell am I doing? I should have left an hour ago. Yet, here I am
—first seduced by his kitchen, and now, by the man himself, who
stands in front of me, naked as the day he was born, cock thrust up
and out at me. OMFG, his dick... I've seen it up close, I've had it
down my throat, inside my pussy, my arsehole... And yet, I swear as
the milk pours down his chest, pools in the nest of hair at his groin,
and drips down from his balls... I've never seen something this...
erotic. This hot. This...gorgeous...almost as orgasmic as the sight of a
triple chocolate cake lathered in freshly whipped cream.

A moan wells up my throat and my breathing goes ragged. I
empty the rest of the milk on him, place the bottle on the island, then
lean in and trace a path between the demarcation of his pecs, down
his concave stomach. I dip my tongue inside his belly button; his abs
ripple. Holy fuck. This... This is too much fun. The way his body
responds to my touch? Wow... That's power. All six-feet four-inches
of alpha hunk, at my mercy. Mine to do with as I want. Mine to
tease, mine to hold and squeeze. Mine to climb up and wrap myself
around him, if I want.

I bring my palm up and weigh his balls; a groan rips out of him. Every muscle in his body solidifies. I drag my tongue along the hair that arrows down to his shaft. His dick jumps and his thigh muscles spasm. I circle around to the underside then trace the path to its logical end, the tip of his dick. I close my mouth around him and he swears, "Fucking fuck, you're killing me, Princess."

I haven't even started.

I straighten, then turn and march back to the refrigerator. The hair on the back of my neck rises, and I know he's stalking me, watching my every move, waiting for me to push him to the edge, and I will...but first, I want to have some fun. He'd teased me and taunted me and I am going to return the favor.

I pull open the refrigerator. Oh, yeah! I straighten, pivot with the bowl of Jell-o—who'd made it? A housekeeper? Does he have a housekeeper? Of course he does. He's rich, remember? Filthy rich. Well, fuck that. I'm rich too, when it comes to talent. I can bake like a goddess and I can tease like a slut.

I bump my hip against the refrigerator door to shut it, then run a finger around the rim of the bowl. His gaze narrows and his nostrils flare. He glances at the quivering gelatin, then up at my face. He tilts his head, a warning look in his eyes. A shiver runs down my spine. Oh, he's going to get back at me for this, I'm sure... But whatever... I'm not going to stop, not when I am having so much fun. I amble over to him, wriggle my hips when I stop in front of him. His chest rises and falls. I dip a couple of fingers into the gelatin, scoop some of it out, and hold it up to his mouth. "Open," I command.

"Lick or suck, Princess?" he growls.

"Whatever you please," I breathe. A bead of sweat runs down his temple. Moisture beads my upper lip. Hell, is the heating on in here, or what? He lowers his head, closes his mouth around my fingertips. I feel the tug all the way down to my cunt. A moan spills from my lips. His mouth curves, he licks his tongue about my fingertips, swallows, then nips on my fingers. Moisture oozes between my legs. Oh, shit. I'm as turned on as he is. This was supposed to be his punishment... Ha! How stupid of me. The only person who will come out at the losing end of this bargain is me. I turn, place the bowl of Jell-o on the island, then grab my panties and pull them on.

"What are you doing?"

I don't reply, shrug into my jeans, find my bra and pull it on.

"Princess?"

"Shut up," I mutter, "I know what you're doing."

"Oh?"

I nod. "You're trying to lure me into staying."

"Am I?" he growls.

I snatch up my blouse, shrug into it. "Yes, you are." Tears knock at the back of my eyes, and honestly... I don't know why. I mean, why the hell should I feel like the entire world is ending? I could stay; he wants me to stay... But that would be empty, wouldn't it? I'd still be only a possession to him, something he had bought.

"Amelie, talk to me." He frowns. "What the hell is going on in that pretty head of yours?"

"Nothing, asshole." I toss my hair over my shoulders. "You can take your...your penthouse and fancy kitchen and oven, and all your privileged-as-hell shit, and stuff it where the sun don't shine."

"Princess..." he takes a step forward; I hold up my hand.

"Don't you dare," I snarl. "Don't you fucking say anything. Don't try to stop me. At least this once, would you stick to your word, and stay right there, until I am gone? This once, can you allow me to leave with a modicum of self-respect?"

He stares at me, his features wearing an expression of frustration. "Amelie, please."

I flip him my middle finger, then grab my phone, snatch up my chef's satchel and my hand bag from where I had placed them on the kitchen island and march out.

56

Weston

I squeeze my eyes shut. The woman I love walked out. I hadn't had
the balls to tell her how much I cared for her; all I'd been worried
about was emptying said balls into her. I lower my arms to my sides.

I should have stopped her; should have hauled her over my
shoulder and marched into the bedroom, where I'd have thrown her
on her back and thrust into her, kept her pinned down until she
forgot all about leaving me... About the money, and her business and
my bloody ego, which, as per usual, stood in the way. Jesus, couldn't
I have said something...anything to stop her from leaving?

Woulda. Coulda. Shoulda. Since when had I begun to overanalyze my reactions, huh? Gone are the days when I'd forge ahead,
not caring who I offended. Hell, I had never cared about how my
actions affected those around me.

Apparently, she affects me in more ways than I care to admit.
Not the least of which is how my groin knots, my cock thickening as
I yearn to be inside of her. I grab my shaft and squeeze, swipe it from
root to head with practiced skill. Only, it's not doing it for me at all. I
need something more, something warmer, moister, something that

would clasp me the way her cunt had when I had thrust into her and taken her.

I glance around, take in the empty milk bottle, the bowl of Jell-o —my cock jerks, bombarded by images of how she'd scooped up the gelatin and offered it to me, her lips parted, tongue caught in concentration between her teeth.

The princess had challenged me. *Me.* The alphahole who has never allowed *any* woman to take the lead... I'd handed it to her, and she had left me. I hunch my shoulders, reach for the Jell-o, scoop up some from the center. Hmm, this has possibilities, huh? Except... I tilt my head. The damn Jell-o is too bouncy and it's bound to fall apart. No, I need something else. I plop the Jell-o back, glance around, and spot the basket of fruits in the center of the island... Hmm... I reach for a peach, glare at it. Apparently, doing it to the apple pie had not been enough. Here I am, searching for more substitutes for her pussy. The last time, I'd resorted to such desperate measures, I'd been...fifteen? And horny as fuck. Nothing has changed...

Except, now I know how it feels to make love to my woman. Jesus, the fuck is wrong with me? Getting soppy and sentimental over her? Thankfully, I still have my balls... Time I put them to good use, huh? I stare at the peach, what if I were to scoop out some of the pulp in the center along with the stone? Hmm... This won't do at all... One more thing that has changed since I was fifteen... My bloody cock is twice the size it had been... Okay, three times if you measure the length of the hardon that I'm sporting. Fuck.

I toss the peach aside, reach for the watermelon. Desperate times and all that... I glare at it, pump my cock again. Am I going to do this? Fuck a bloody watermelon? Would it be cheating on her if I did? A fruit is an inanimate object, right? As in, it doesn't have feelings, in the technical sense of the word, so it can't reciprocate sentiments... So, it does not constitute being unfaithful if I stick my dick in it, does it? I frown down at the offending fruit, massage its curved circumference. It's smooth...too smooth... Too cold... Nothing like the living flesh of her butt, the slight indentation of the dimple in the center of one arsecheek, that I had caressed before I'd cupped her backside and squeezed, then hauled her up so she could wind those gorgeous legs around my waist, before I'd pushed her up against the nearest hard surface and —

Fuck. Stop this line of thinking, you prick. It should be her heart you're focusing on. Her needs. The fact that she had thrown my money back at me... Hell, no one had done that before. But she isn't like anyone else I've ever encountered. Amelie...with her sass and her wit, and her habit of swearing by using names of desserts. Jesus, she is more delectable than any creation I've ever sampled. And I had let her leave. Again... I...

If I had stopped her, she'd have never forgiven me. She'd pleaded with me to let her leave...and I had... I'd stood there and watched her flounce out. What do they say? Something about, if you love someone let them go. If they return, they belong to you... And if they don't...?

Fuck that. No way, am I going to stand around here while she...*figures out her feelings*... I take a step forward, then stop. Wow, even my thoughts are dismissive of her feelings. And if I go after her...? I'd coerce her, bulldoze over her feelings, her choices... Hell, I'd ensure that she comes around to my way of thinking...and that... Fuck... This is not the time for my alphaholish, caveman-ish behavior. I mean, that's what I am. No excuses but... I hadn't become a surgeon without knowing when it was time to pull back.

I can't lose her.

I have to be strategic.

Have to trust...hope that she'll come back. And she will. She has to. I snatch up my phone from the corner of the island, dial my banker's number. When he comes on the line, I tell him to cease all further payments to her accounts. I am not surprised when he informs me that the money I'd sent through earlier had been returned electronically by her already. Yeah... Buttercup knows how to get a move on me.

I toss my phone aside, roll my shoulders. She'll return to me; she has to. The connection between us is too strong. She wouldn't ignore it... Would she? Nah! She'll get my message, get what I've been trying to communicate to her... Which is...that I can't live without her. She'll figure it out. She is smart, switched on. The love of my life has a razor-sharp mind. Surely, she'll glean what I was trying to communicate with her. Meanwhile... I glance toward the liquor cabinet. Only one thing a man can do when forced to bide his time. I stalk toward the bar, grab a bottle of whiskey and twist it open. I raise it to my lips.

57

Amelie

"Past pleasure doubles present pain,
To sorrow adds regret,
Regret and hope are both in vain,
I ask but to — forget."

I take in the words scrawled on the board held by the homeless man.
I'd ridden the elevator down, and walked out of the apartment
building.

Every step I'd taken had echoed the thumping of my heart. I am
doing this. Really doing this. I am leaving him. Good thing I had
gone online and returned the money already. A few days ago, I'd
checked my bank account and the zeroes in my account had brought
home exactly how much I stood to gain from this relationship. I
could pay off my debts, expand my business, ensure my parents are
taken care of for the rest of their lives... And he'd always take me for

granted. He'd known that I could be bought. Next time we came to an impasse... He'd know how to get his way. Throw more money my way...

And no, it's not only the money that binds us. There is so much more—emotions and conflicts and a buzzing physical attraction that shows no sign of abating. There is so much there to build on... But the money...would always be a barrier... Unless he looks past it. Unless I take a risk, and leave him... Give him space to figure out his shit, while I do the same thing. I'd pushed forward, and had almost stumbled across the outstretched legs of the homeless guy.

"Excuse me," I mutter and step around him... Which is when I spot his shoes: tailormade, Italian leather, spotless, and polished to within an inch of its life. They seem familiar. Huh? I stare at them. Where have I seen them before?

"Pretty fancy, huh?" Homeless guy chortles, "Think these will impress the ladies?"

I glance up at his face. "I am sure they'd have an impact," I say. "Where did you get them?"

He frowns, "You mean, what's a man like me doing with shoes like these?"

My cheeks heat. Hell, that hadn't come out polite at all, had it? "I meant, uh... They seem familiar. Someone I know had a similar pair."

"Boyfriend?" He asks.

"He's...ah, currently no friend," I mutter.

"Ach!" he cackles, "Had a fall out with your man, huh?"

"Maybe, probably." I raise my shoulders, "He's an arrogant so-and-so. Know what I mean? He thinks he can buy anything."

"Not you, obviously." He nods.

"Exactly... See?" I flick my hair over my shoulder, "And he claims to love me."

"Do you?" he shoots back.

"Huh?" I frown, "Do I what?"

"Do you love him?"

"Yes," I reply. "Wait, I mean... No... I mean, yes...but..."

"No buts." He tilts his head up, pulls his legs up to sit cross-legged, "You gotta tell him that."

"I do?" I scowl.

"Absolutely," he jerks his chin, "better to take the risk and be sorry than to be a coward and—"

"Regret it," I complete his statement. "Yeah... Well..." I glance away. A pressure builds behind my eyes and my heart begins to race. What the hell is wrong with me? This constant back and forth... This not knowing my own mind... It's bloody tiring. So much easier to plan out a menu and bake. Even though the outcome of a dish is not completely in my hands, at least I can control the environment... Decide the ingredients. And if I change something, hell, I know the risks of what I'm doing. But with him...? I can't predict a thing. Not my reaction to him, not his ability to throw me off guard... Well, except for that sizzling attraction between us that throbs and ties us together. For better or for worse—that is one thing I can count on. The one ingredient that would never fail to liven up the dish... I mean, the relationship... I mean... I blink, turn to him. "I should, right?" I ask.

He lowers his board to the ground, then glances toward the apartment. "Go on, then."

I take in his features, those intelligent eyes undeniable, despite his unkempt whiskers.

"Who are you?" I frown. "What are you doing here?"

"All the world's a stage and we are but actors," he chuckles.

"First Byron, then Shakespeare?" I stare at him. "You have a thing for poets?"

"Or for pompous wankers who churned out pretentious shit."

"Sounds like someone I know," I mumble.

"Don't we all?" He rises to his feet, sketches an exaggerated bow, "Don't delay, young lady." He snatches his hat with the change inside and slams it on his dreadlocks. "Goodbye." He hauls the board over his shoulder and walks off.

"Bye." I turn, retrace my steps toward the apartment. What a strange man. He was well educated, no doubt about it. And his accent... I could have sworn he sounded almost posh. And when he'd smiled...his teeth were perfect. Which is bloody odd in England. I mean, when was the last time I'd met anyone with even teeth... Other than the alphahole... And the Seven...who had clearly spent a fortune on the dentist. But normal people like me... Hell... We can't afford that kind of dental work. So how had the homeless guy swung that, huh? I turn to call out, but the sidewalk is empty. Geez, he must have doubled his speed to get away from me or something. I shake my head. The shoes did fit him though. Chalk it up as one more good deed for Dr Grumpy McDick. He has his redeeming points... A lot of them, actually.

Too bad it isn't enough... Is it? I shake my head. *Stop overthinking this. Just march back for the last time and tell him how you feel.* As easy as baking banana bread, which would be done in double-quick time in his oven. Fine, fine... Don't think about his kitchen, or his equipment... No, definitely don't think about the tool he hides in his pants either. *Get on with it; don't back out, bitch.* I stomp inside the apartment, and head for the elevator door, which glides open. Shit, even the elements are working with me on this.

I reach the penthouse, push the door open and walk in. I cross the living room, pause only to place my satchel and handbag on the center table, then peek into the kitchen. There's no one there. Hmm. I pivot, head for the bedroom, when I spot movement. I pivot head toward the sliding doors at the far end of the living room, pulling them aside. I step outside and onto the terrace, walk another few steps and spot the hot tub... This one's sunken into the decking with steps leading down, and at the other end of it...is him. I'm drawn to him like chocolate to a clean surface... know what I mean? I pause at the tub.

He's sprawled in the water that froths around his waist, the bubbles covering the bottom half of his body. Not that I have any doubt about the state of his undress. He leans back, raises a bottle of whiskey. His biceps bulge and his shoulders flex. He brings the bottle to his mouth, swigs from it. The tendons of his throat move as he swallows.

I am instantly wet.

He raises his other hand, places a cigar between his lips. I rake my gaze over his features, watch him watch me with unblinking eyes, as I take another step forward. I reach the edge of the tub. The water writhes below me. My heartbeat writhes in my chest.

He glares at me from under hooded eyelids. He lowers the cigar, blows out a cloud of cigar smoke. The scent of cloves and spices, of darkness and lust, passion and fucking... Hell... I'll always associate the scent of cigar smoke with wild, out-of-my-head desire.

He doesn't move, doesn't say a word.

I shuffle closer, my toe brushing against something smooth. There's a plop as it falls in. I glance down to find an egg timer floating on the surface.

I bend my knees, reach over and scoop it up.

He glances down at the object, then up at my face. His lips twist, he swallows and opens his mouth, and I'm sure he's going to say something. Instead, he takes another swig from the bottle of whiskey. The skin across his knuckles stretches white... Huh? I peer across the distance and at his features... Lines radiate from the corners of his eyes, and the hollows under his cheekbones seem more pronounced. Why had I not noticed that before?

He keeps his gaze focused on my face, the skin around his mouth tightening. That's it—something's on his mind. But what? Why would the most confident man I have ever met seem unsure of himself.

"Why are you so on edge?" I laugh nervously. "I'd think you were going to pop a marriage proposal or something," I mutter, "if I didn't know you better."

His face pales. My gaze widens. I take in the way he holds onto the whiskey bottle. The skin of his knuckles stretch white. Then the bottle slips from his grasp, hits the decking and rolls away... "Fuck." He swears, then straightens. His lips twist. An expression I can't fathom grips his features.

"Holy shit." I gasp, "Is that what you are going to do...? I gulp. "No way. You aren't, are you?"

Again, he glares at the stupid egg timer I am holding. What the hell? I stare down at the curved object, raise it, fiddle around with it. I twist it and it comes apart in my hands, revealing something shiny, something with a perfectly-cut sapphire that winks back at me.

My throat dries. My heart begins to thud. "What...what is this?" I squeak.

"A fucking gummy bear," he growls, "what do you think it is?"

"I... I..." I glance at the ring, then back at him, then at the ring again.

"How... how long have you been planning this?"

"Since I met you?" He tilts his head, "Strike that. From before I met you. The ring was my grandmother's."

"Oh!"

"You mean oh, yes, don't you?" he drawls.

"Wait, wait." I draw in a breath. *Stay calm, don't lose it now.* Need time to think, just a bloody second here. I tip up my chin, train my gaze on him, "How did you rig the timer to accommodate it, considering I was gone for less than half an hour?"

He yawns.

"Of course. You repair clocks, so you could adjust a stupid egg timer, huh?" I pout.

"Not apologizing for the fact that I pulled off an almost-miracle, babe." He thrusts out his chest, "Besides it is Christmas."

"Wow," I stare. "Seems you're getting into the spirit of the season, after all?"

"As you are coming around to the idea of our wedding."

"Yes." I nod.

"So, it's settled then." He grins.

"What?" I shake my head. "No, no, no, I didn't mean it that way. I mean, not yet... I mean... What the hell!" I exclaim. "This can't be happening."

"It is." He shakes out his palm — the one with which he'd gripped the whiskey bottle.

"Did you hurt your good hand? I ask.

"I've been hurting in other places since I met you," he grumbles.

"Anyone ever tell you, you have the manners of an oaf?" I scowl.

"Only you, babe." He rises to his feet — the water pours off of those sculpted abs, his concave stomach, drips off of that spectacular cock. *Oh, my God!* I swallow, take a step back, stumble, drop the ring, let go of the pieces that formerly constituted the egg timer, swoop down, catch the ring. I straighten the ring, slip it onto my left ring finger. I blink, open my eyes in surprise. "It fits."

"Of course, it does," he snaps.

"Presumptuous, much?" I huff, turn my hand this way and that. The heart of the ring glows with silver sparks. Wow. My pulse thuds at my temples; my stomach bottoms out. OMFG, does this mean, what I think it does?

"You're marrying me," he growls. "What's so presumptuous about that?"

"I haven't said yes."

He looks at my hand then back at my face. "You're wearing the ring. Are you saying no?"

"You haven't asked...you...you...ass!" I yell.

He blows out a breath, stalks his way across the length of the sunken pool to where I stand. He glances into my eyes. Despite the fact that I am standing on a higher level, we are at the same height... That's how fucking big my alphahole is. I gulp; he frowns. His chest rises and falls, then he reaches out and takes my left hand.

58

Weston

"I won't take no for an answer," I tell her.

She scowls, tugs at her hand. I hold on. *Fuck, get a grip, asshole. Stop thinking about yourself. Get rid of the fear that she'll refuse you and leave...* Nope, not this time. I'm not going to fuck this up, nope. I've conducted quadruple bypass surgeries... This...this should be a cake-walk... Not.

I shake my head, bring my other hand up, and enclose her slim palm between my much larger ones.

I clear my throat. She glances at me, and suddenly, my scalp feels too tight. My heart hammers and my muscles tense. I rotate my shoulders, bend my knee and press it into the side of the pool.

"Amelie," I peer up into her face, "will you be the chocolate to my whiskey, the caramel to my bourbon — ?"

She blinks.

"—the spice to my tea, the fruit filling to my pie —"

Her lower lip trembles... *Huh? Is that a good sign?*

"—the butterscotch to my toffee," I raise one eyebrow, "the cookie to my coffee?"

She giggles, then slaps a hand over her mouth.

I allow a smirk to curl my lips, lower my head and brush my mouth over her knuckles, "Well?" I tilt my head up at her, "Amelie, will you marry me?"

"Not good enough," she replies.

"What?" I blink.

"You can do better than that."

"What the fuck?" I growl.

She shakes her hair from her face, "Go on, Mr, Alphahole. Why should I marry you?"

"Because I'll make you happy?"

"So can others."

"Because you can cook in that bloody kitchen with the oven I had installed specifically for you?"

"You...you did?" Her gaze widens. Damn, if I don't see heart-shaped little icons in place of her irises.

"It was nothing," I mumble. Why the hell had that popped out? Hadn't meant to blurt that out.

She looks away, then back at me. "What else?" she asks, her voice an octave lower than earlier. That's good. I am on the right track... *Go on, motherfucker, lay it out. It's now or never, you loser.*

"Because every time I see you, I can't see a way around fucking you, giving it to you until you're a whimpering gooey mess in my arms?"

"Oh!" She trembles. "Keep going," she says, her voice breathy.

I turn her palm face up in mine, bend and lick the skin between her fingers.

She shudders.

I drag my tongue down to her fingertip and kiss it.

"Because we're going to fuck right now in this pool, then on the decking, in the living room, in my bed, on the bloody kitchen island...on every surface in my home, and when the sun comes up tomorrow, we'll know every nook," kiss, "cranny," kiss, "crevasse of each other's bodies."

She makes a humming sound deep in her throat.

"You like that hmm?" I smirk.

"Much better," She agrees. "You're getting the hang of it, Mr. Alpha Claus, but it's not enough."

"You're right," I agree.

"I am?" She frowns.

"I haven't told you yet, how I'm going to walk you places, my Buttercup, up the aisle, into each day of our future lives...ease you into bed every night, wake you up with my tongue inside your melting pussy every morn—"

She chokes out a laugh, "And you were doing so well."

"Right?" I grimace, "I can't help myself, my sweet Cookie. When I see you, I lose sight of myself. When I scent you, I ache to be inside of you. And when I see you in pain," I swallow, "I want to turn the world upside down until I soothe it all away."

"Oh," she stutters, "that...that was romantic."

"I'm not done yet."

"No?"

"Not even remotely." I allow my lips to curve, mirror the happiness that filters through her gaze, "I'll take care of you, I'll love you, shield you from the elements, ease obstructions from your path—"

She frowns.

"Because that would be my prerogative." I declare.

"If that's not what I want?"

"We could discuss it," I say slowly.

"We could?"

"Perhaps."

Her forehead creases and she tugs on her hand again. My heart rate gallops. "I won't do anything you don't want me to," I add.

"Hmm."

"I promise." I hold up my right palm, "We can fight over it, then kiss and have hot make-up sex."

"As long as you don't steamroll me into agreeing." She frowns.

"As long as we agree to disagree," I say at the same time.

She huffs.

I twine my fingers through hers, "Come on, babe. Allow me to help; it's what I do best."

"I want to build my business on my own merit, you know?"

"And I understand and completely get that...but if I can pave the way so you spend your time on the actual creation and less on fighting through roadblocks?"

She shuffles her feet, then glances at me. "For every pound you spend on paying off my debts, you'll also put one toward a scholarship for someone less privileged who wants to study baking at a school of their choice."

"Done," I blow out a breath. "You can manage this each year through FOK media, a division of 7A investments that was set up for exactly such causes."

She blinks. "You agree?"

I straighten my shoulders, "If that makes you happy..."

"This makes me happy." She sinks down onto the decking, sticks her legs into the hot tub and, parts her legs. Finally, fuck! I move into the 'V' between her thighs.

"You make me fucking happy," I hold her gaze, peer into those baby blues which mean more to me than life itself. "It was a time bomb," I say. "They wrapped a timebomb around me and left me in a locked room for days."

Her chin wobbles, her face pales. "The kidnappers?" she whispers. "They did that?"

I nod. "If I so much as moved or breathed wrong it could go off, so they said."

"What...what happened next?"

"My kidnapper... I couldn't see his face because I was blindfolded... Which didn't help, because I could imagine the moving hands of the clock in my mind." I swallow; my fingers tremble.

She grips my hand, and warmth chases away the ice that had crept into my veins. I focus on her beautiful face, those flushed features. "He kept coming in and torturing me, sometimes beating on my legs, sometimes hooking me up to electricity. Each session was timed, it lasted precisely an hour, all of which was counted down precisely by the clock." I chuckle, the sound harsh. "The torture went on for days I thought, but it was really only for forty-eight hours, so I found out later."

She gasps, "Oh, Wes." She places her palm over my chest, "Baby, I'm so sorry."

I focus on her gaze, the silverly sparks in her eyes. "That last time..."I force out the words, "he said he'd be back in twelve hours. I counted down the time, past the twelve hour mark. He was late. I knew then, he was going to kill me. He came in and started raging at me, told me he was going to kill me. He hooked me up to the electrodes. I sensed him move away to start the electricity. I knew there was no way I was going to survive that session. I prayed that my heart would give out before the pain got too bad. He switched on the electricity, and left."

"Wes, no." She throws her arms about me, "Oh my God, that's terrible." She presses her cheek into my chest and moisture dampens my skin. She's weeping, for me? Something inside of me dissolves. I fit my knuckle under her chin, tip up her head.

"The cops arrived within minutes of that... They broke through, switched off the electricity, had their best bomb disposal expert dismantle the one around my chest. Turns out, it was a hoax all along."

"What?" She gasps, "I mean it's a good thing, but still... That bastard."

"Yeah." I cup her cheek, "I escaped with no outward scars... I was lucky, unlike some of the Seven."

"It's why you guys are so close."

"Close? Ha!" I smirk, "The only person I want to be close to is you, baby."

I lower my head, brush my lips over hers. "You're welcome, by the way," I whisper.

"For what?"

"For the three words you were going to tell me earlier, but didn't, and which you are going to reward me with now."

"Reward you?" She pouts.

"Yep." I reach down, lower the zipper on her jeans. She grips my shoulders, rises up, and I yank down the pants and panties, ease them over her hips, then step back and pull them off of those gorgeous legs. I stare at the pink flesh between those beautiful thighs. "For the orgasms I am going to bring you to in the next hour."

"So sure of yourself. If you think you can trick me into—"

I step between her legs, hook her knees over my arms, pull them up and over my shoulders, then notch my dick against her pussy, "Into?"

"Saying that I want you—"

I lunge forward, impale her in one motion. She stutters, then her pussy clamps around my dick.

"Say it," I growl.

"I... I need you," she gasps.

I pull out of her, stay poised at the entrance to her channel. "Look at me," I pant.

She raises her head, sears me with those beautiful blue eyes.

"Princess," I lower my head to hers, share my breath with hers, brush my lips over hers "I want to hear you scream out those three words." I kick my hips forward, sink into her.

She curves her spine, throws her head back, "I love you," she yells. "Love you, love you... Only you."

My vision tunnels; blood beats at my temples. I haul her to me, kiss her hard. Then, I begin to fuck her in earnest—thrust into her, bury myself in her sweet pussy again and again. Bring my arms around her, pull her to me as, with a last ferocious drive of my hips, I sink inside of her. "Come," I growl.

59

Amelie

His command slices through my mind. His voice echoes in my subconscious. Heat from his body slams into me, sinks into my blood. Everything in me snaps tight, then I shatter. Moisture gushes out from between my thighs as the climax sweeps me up, higher and higher. I throw my head back and scream, *I love you, I love you.* Or maybe I just chant that in my head.

Black specks flicker at the edges of my vision. Above me, his shoulders draw back, his chest muscles harden, his body shudders, his cock thickens inside of me, then with a harsh groan, he comes inside of me. I slump against his chest, am half aware that he hauls me up in his arms, steps out of the hot tub and carries me inside. I must have snoozed, for when I open my eyes next, I am tucked into his side in his bed. I rub my cheek into his hair-roughened chest. "I would have told you anyway," I mumble.

"Hmm?" He rubs lazy circles over my upper arm.

I glance up to find him sprawled against the sheets, eyes closed. He has one hand flung behind his neck. A slight smile curves his lips. So, this is how it is to see the brute relax... In his den, surrounded by his possessions, in the arms of his woman. *His woman.* I reach up, cup his cheek.

"I love you," I whisper.

He smirks. "I know."

I hit his shoulder.

He laughs, cracks open his eyelids, "I adore you, Princess."

"Oh." I open and close my mouth, shake my head.

"What?" he grunts.

"Nothing."

"Say it," he drawls, "I promise I won't bite."

I purse my lips, scan his relaxed features, "I can't get used to this emo version of you."

He sighs, "No pleasing some people."

"Not that I don't want you to be nice to me and all that," I explain.

"Actually, I think you don't." He grins, then lowers his gaze to my breasts.

"What's that supposed to mean?"

"It means." He flips me over onto my back and my breath hitches. His eyes gleam and his big shoulders seem to swell further, if that is even possible. He glances up at the headboard, then back at me.

"Don't you dare," I huff.

"You challenging me?"

"Maybe," I mumble as a frisson of heat runs up my spine.

He glances around, then rolls off of the bed. I lower my arms. He turns to me, points his finger, and says, "Stay."

"Bossy," I grumble.

"You ain't seen nothin' yet."

He stalks over to the walk in closet. I hear him rummaging around, then silence. A few seconds later he walks out.

I gasp. "Oh my."

"Like it?" He stands there in his scrubs. The green material molds to his torso, outlines the cut abs of his chest, tents at his crotch—ha! so what's new?—and clings to his powerful thighs.

"You look—"

"Hot?"

"I was going to say yummy."

"Is everything a food reference to you?" He laughs.

"Is everything about getting the last word with you?"

He tilts his head, "Except with you."

"Oh?"

"You know it's true, babe. After all, I let you get away with chocolate."

"Someone had to change your mind about the devil's food." I chuckle.

"So you decided to feed it to the devil himself?"

"Are you the devil?"

"Where you are concerned, I am your lover and your protector, your lord and master, your to-be husband."

I curl the fingers of my left hand around the ring, "I haven't said yes to marrying you yet."

"Oh, you are about to." He raises his hand, and I spot the black ties he holds in his grasp.

"What...what's that for?"

He grins at me and his eyes glint. He stalks around the bed, then places his knee on the bed, throws his leg over my waist and straddles me.

"Wes." I draw in a breath.

"Trust me, Cookie." He leans over and ties my wrists to the headboard. Then rolls off of the bed and walks away again. What the hell?

He returns holding an egg timer in his hand.

"How many of those things do you have?"

"Enough." He grins. "Since you seem to have a penchant for the blasted thing, I figured I'd buy enough to see us through the rest of our lives together."

My heart stutters. OMG, did he use all the words that I've wanted to hear from him? "You're awfully confident." I tip up my chin.

"Nothing I can't deliver on, Princess." He winds up the egg timer. The ticking down of the timer fills the room.

"Doesn't that sound trigger you?" I ask.

"I'm changing it's association in my head." He places the timer on the side table, then climbs onto the bed and straddles me. "Close your eyes." he raises the second necktie he holds in his hand.

"B... but." My heart begins to race. My mouth dries. I can't stop the trembling that runs up my spine. "Wes."

"Trust me." He leans in and kisses me, a hard reassuring kiss, that sinks into my blood. I am instantly wet and he hasn't even started.

He peers in my features, "Okay?"

"Okay."

He leans over and wraps the tie around my eyes. Darkness engulfs me. My senses pop. The ticking of the timer heats my blood. "W...Wes?" I whine.

"I'm here." He cups my cheek, then his lips meet mine again. He licks my mouth, then whispers. "I forgot to tell you one thing."

"What?"

"You won't come until the timer rings."

60

Weston

"Not fair," she gasps, craning her neck toward me.

"All's fair in bed." I lower my head and kiss her breast. She moans; the sound travels down my spine and my guts churn. My heart begins to race. I cup her other breast and my fingers tremble.

The ticking of the clock grows louder; my stomach hollows out. Maybe this had not been a good idea. I close my mouth around her nipple and bite down.

She gasps.

My groin hardens.

I drag my mouth down her stomach, to her belly button, flick my tongue in and out of the indentation.

She moans. Her thighs tremble. I grip the curve of her waist, nibble kisses to the apex between her legs. I blow on her pussy and her body bucks, "Weston," she pleads.

The sound of her voice slices through the noise in my head. This time it is about her. Not about what the bastard did to me. Not about how he'd tied the ticking timebomb to my chest and left me. I hook my arms under her knees, pull her legs over my shoulders.

I smooth my hands down her trembling thighs, and cup her pussy, "Mine," I growl, "only mine." I lower my head, swipe my tongue up her lower lips.

She whines.

I curve my tongue around the swollen bud of her clit; she shivers. Slide my hand down to squeeze her arse cheek.

Her entire body shudders.

I slide my finger inside her backhole; she bucks.

I insert my tongue inside her channel, ease it in and out of her. Bring my free hand to her clit and pinch it.

"Oh, hell, oh, hell." She digs the heels of her feet into my back, thrusts her pelvis up and into my face. The sweet scent of her tugs at my nostrils, the warmth of her juices coats my tongue. My belly clenches and my dick lengthens as the ticking of the clock counts down in the background.

I need more, more.

"Wes?"

The tick-tock of the clock grows louder. My fingers clench; a bead of sweat slides down my back. I drag my mouth up and to her face and kiss her deeply. She opens her mouth to me, and I thrust my tongue inside. I drink from her, that addicting, honeyed essence of her, mixed with the taste of her cum. My belly trembles, I dig my knees into bed, ease a finger inside her channel and bear down.

"Weston," she screams, "Oh, my God, Wes."

More, I need more. I need her warmth, her happy-go-lucky nature, her sass and fire. I need all of her, subsumed into me. I need her to ground me. I release her lips, then reach up and tear the blindfold from her.

She blinks, then her gaze narrows on me.

"What's wrong?" she asks. "Wes?"

"Nothing." I mumble.

"Something is."

"I need..." I frown.

"Me, take me, Wes." Her chest heaves, "Please, baby, come inside me."

Her blue eyes gaze into mine, the silver sparks in their depths similar to the sapphire I'd bought her... Except she is here, vital, real... Nothing else in my past, or my future, matters. Only her.

I loosen the drawstring on my pants, then grasp my dick, and notch it against her wet opening.

"Amelie." I brush my lips over hers. "I love you," I say. "I love it when you smile at me. I love it even more when I am the reason for your smile."

Those sappy words? Yep, that's me. Alphahole extraordinaire felled by a woman who is the sassiest, brightest, most special woman I have ever met.

"Oh, Wes," she sighs, "I love you too."

I slide inside her; she trembles. I stay there, allowing her to adjust to my size. I ease my tongue inside her mouth, tangle my tongue with hers, bring my other hand up to untie her bindings. She wraps her arms about my shoulders, pulls me closer. I prop myself on one elbow to keep my weight off of her. I hold her gaze, keep the connection, as I pull out of her, then thrust back in. Her pussy clenches around me. She digs her fingers into the back of my scalp, tugs on my hair. My cock jerks, thickens, and I begin to fuck her in earnest. In and out of her, as I slide a finger inside her backhole.

She groans and I swallow the sound, continue to kiss her, as I kick my hips forward, impale her to the bed. My balls harden, a pressure building in my groin. I don't stop. I thrust into her, again and again. She arches her spine, pushes up to meet me. Locks her ankles around me, flattens her breasts against my chest planes, strains against me, consumes me.

The ticking of the clock fades. I tear my mouth from hers, "I'll never get enough of you. Not until every inch of you is married to every inch of me, and not even then. Not until I've broken you completely, and myself. Until every part of you bears the imprint of me, every cell in your body recognizes that you are mine. Mine. Only mine, you get me?"

She nods. "Only yours," she whispers. "Always yours, love you Wes—"

I kick my hips forward and bury myself inside her with such force that the entire bed shakes. The headboard slams into the wall;

somewhere something crashes to the floor. The timer rings as I growl, "Come with me, Princess."

Her mouth opens in a silent cry. She holds my gaze as she shatters, as her body trembles under me, as my orgasm takes hold and I come inside of her.

Her chest heaves, sweat beads her upper lip, and I bend down and lick it up. "Yum." I smack my lips. "How the hell do you manage to taste so sweet?"

"How the hell do you manage to turn sex into an orgy each and every time, my love?"

"Hmm." I bump my neck to hers. "Love it when you talk dirty to me, babe."

"Love it when you—" She blinks. "Did you hear that?"

I frown, "What?"

"Did somebody call your name?"

I angle my head, "Don't hear anything."

I reach down to kiss her again, when, "Weston, where the fuck are you, arsehole?" Damian's voice reaches me from the direction of the doorway.

I groan, "The fuck?"

She giggles, "Looks like your friends decided to pay you a visit on Christmas day?"

"Something I can do without." I grouse.

"Weston... Hey...oops. Sorry, man," Damian apologizes.

I turn, glare at where Damian stands in the doorway, face averted.

"I didn't see anything. I promise."

"Fuck off," I growl.

"A bit too late, old chap."

"Where the fuck is the wanker?" Another voice—Arpad's calls out.

"If he thinks he can spend Christmas on his own, he's got another think coming. What's he up to— Oh hell, did we interrupt something?" *Is that Edward?*

I grab a pillow, throw it in the direction of the doorway. "Back the fuck off, you tossers."

"Sorry."

"Didn't mean any harm."

"You ah —finish what you started. We'll be at your bar."

The voices fade.

"Close the fucking door behind you," I call out.

The door slams shut.

This is what happens when your friends have unrestricted access to your apartment, something I intend to rectify at the first opportunity. I draw in a breath, glance down at my fiancée, "Where were we, babe?"

"We need to get out there." She stabs a finger in my chest.

I lower my head to hers, "In good time."

61

____

Amelie

I walk into Weston's living room just as the doorbell rings.

Weston—who's changed into slacks and shirt— opens it as Saint, Sinclair and Jace walk in carrying a massive Christmas tree wrapped in a net. Weston leads them to the far corner of the room, where they cut off the net and proceed to set it up.

Weston turns to me, crooks a finger. I frown; he smirks. I

mentally throw up my hands, walk over to join him. He wraps his arm around me tugs me into his side.

"Did you plan this?" I ask.

"What?" He grins.

"All this." I jerk my chin toward the Christmas tree currently being set up by his three friends, then to the bar where the other three are having an argument about the latest cricket scores.

The doorbell rings again, then the door is pushed open, and Isla walks in, followed by Sienna—Jace's wife, who pushes a pram with their newborn son.

Victoria follows her.

She smooths her hands down the green dress, as always, looking like she's stepped off a catwalk. She pauses halfway into the room, when Saint looks up. He closes the distance between them and pulls her into a kiss. His large hand covers her stomach protectively. Yep, these two are next in line to have a baby.

"Oh! How romantic." Isla waves a hand in front of her face. She turns to me and her face cracks into a big smile. "Well then, did you two make up your differences?"

"What differences?" Weston smirks, pulling me in for a kiss.

She chuckles, then her gaze widens, "Oh wow!" She gasps, then walks over to us, "Is that what I think it is?" She stares down at my hand.

I hold out my palm. She grabs my fingers and squeezes. "Ouch," I gripe.

"That's one big-ass ring, you bitch." She leans back, glowers at me, "You were holding out on me?"

"Relax," I assure her, "It happened only a few hours ago. He proposed—"

She squeals so loudly that everyone else in the room turns to us.

"Omigod, omigod." She claps her hands, " This is awesome! Another wedding to plan."

"Ah...no." I shake my head.

"What do you mean?" she asks.

"No way, am I going in for the whole song and dance of a society wedding."

"But Amelie," she whines, "you only get married once."

"Which is why it's going to be something low key, and romantic... Something with a specially-crafted menu of desserts."

Weston, bends his head. "Will it have cock pops?" he whispers.

"Chocolate cockups," I correct him.

"What-fucking-ever," He grumbles, "as long as you bake them only for us, and only you eat them."

"Possessive, hmm?"

"Just don't want anyone else's mouth on my penis, except yours."

"You got a deal." I grin.

"What did I miss?" Summer flounces in, hair flowing around her. She's in a festive onesie with glitter threaded through almost every inch of it.

"Woman, you're too bright for me." Sinclair prowls toward her. He makes a grab for her, but she evades him and giggles. He swoops down, hauls her close and she melts into his arms. They kiss, until her phone begins to ring. She tries to pull free, but he doesn't let her go. "Sinner," she mumbles against his mouth, "I need to get this."

"Fuck it," he responds.

"It may be Karma. I've been hoping that she'd call."

He releases her lips, but holds her in the circle of his arms.

She pulls out her phone from her bag, "Hello?" she says. Her face brightens. "Karma!" she exclaims. "Where have you been? I was beginning to get worried."

She listens for a second, raises her gaze to Sinner.

He frowns down at her. *Everything okay?* He mouths.

She raises her shoulders. "You sure, you're fine?" she asks, then listens to the reply. "So you won't be home for the New Year either?"

Her lips curve down. "Aww honey, I miss you." She listens some more. "Well if that's what you want..." She tips up her chin, a worried set to her features. "Right, okay. Well I'll see you soon, I hope. You take care, sweetheart, oh! And Merry Christmas." She cuts the call.

"How is Karma?" I call out to her. "When is she coming back?"

Summer turns to me, "She sounded... Fine... I guess." Her forehead furrows. "She's staying on in Sicily for a while longer."

"Ooh." Isla rubs her hands together, "That's so romantic. Maybe her new boyfriend doesn't want to let go of her, huh?"

"Maybe," Summer says slowly. "I wish she'd come home. I want to meet him, you know? Make sure he's treating her right."

"I'm sure she's fine, babe." Sinclair kisses the top of her head. "He's probably being possessive, that's all."

She snorts, "You should know."

"You bet." Sinclair smirks, "Once you find the woman of your dreams, you never let her out of your sight, or out of your bed. You make sure you keep her satisfied enough that she never wants to leave your side; you—"

"Enough." She turns in his arms, slaps a hand on his mouth, "Honestly Sin, you have no filter."

"Not when it comes to you, I don't." He grins down at her.

"But when it comes to you, I know exactly what turns you on."

His eyes gleam, "And what's that?"

"You're all about the chase, my love."

"Am I now?" His lips curl.

"Yep." She tips up her head, "Like now—"

She yanks back in his grasp. His grasp loosens, and she pivots and takes off toward the inner rooms.

"What the—" He seems startled. "You come back here Summer, and finish what you started," he growls.

"Not happening." She laughs, "You going soft, Sin? Worried you've lost the edge? Bet you can't catch me." She disappears around the corner.

His jaw drops, "Why you little..." He takes off in hot pursuit.

There's another knock on the front door; it swings open, then Julia walks in. She glances around the room, then spots me. Her face brightens.

"Jules." I wave at her, "What are you doing here?"

"I invited her." Weston brushes his lips over my hair. Seems Dr. Alpha Claus can't keep his hands off of me, huh? I snuggle into his side. "Thanks," I say. "And by that, I assume you knew this little get together was happening?"

"I had an inkling."

"Is that my Christmas gift?" Damian draws abreast. I look up to find his gaze arrested by Julia.

"She's my friend," I warn him.

He tilts his head, a considering expression on his features. "She's hot," He declares.

"She's off-limits to you, douche," Weston glowers at him.

"Shouldn't the woman have a say in that?" Damian interrupts.

"As long as Amelie gives you the go ahead..." Weston raises his shoulders.

Damian turns to me, "Well?" He smiles, "What do you say?"

"Do you promise to treat her right?" I scan his features. "Promise you won't hurt her."

"I promise to treat her however she wants me to." He smirks.

"Hmm." I frown. "Julia doesn't suffer fools gladly."

"And, rock stars?" His grin widens, "what does she think of them?

"Why don't you ask me directly?" Julia's voice interrupts us.

Damian pivots to face her, "Better still, how about I show you...?"

TO FIND OUT WHAT HAPPENS NEXT READ DAMIAN AND JULIA'S STORY IN MARRYING THE BILLIONAIRE SINGLE DAD. THIS BOOK ALSO FEATURES WESTON AND AMELIE'S WEDDING.

READ AN EXCERPT FROM MARRYING THE BILLIONAIRE SINGLE DAD - DAMIAN AND JULIA'S STORY.

Julia

"Show me huh?" I tilt my chin up, "You ain't got nothin' that I haven't seen before."

"Don't bet on it." The too-full-of-himself asshole stares down that patrician nose at me. His blue gaze narrows and those cerulean eyes seem to bore into my soul. A shiver runs up my spine. This man? His presence is potent. He leans in close and the heat of his body slams into my chest. My thighs clench and moisture leaks from my core. Damn him. Why the hell am I so turned on by this stranger? I'd accepted Weston's invitation to come over and spend Christmas with him and Amelie. I'd expected for some of his friends to be here.

What I hadn't counted on was this overconfident, dominant, macho male to capture my attention from the moment I'd walked through the door. The kind who'd simply declare his intent, stake his claim and take what was his, politeness be damned. Am I his?

The hell am I thinking?

I don't know him, want nothing to do with an over-the-top, possessive male like him. Nope. He'd tear apart my carefully ordered life, the one I've spent way too long building up brick by brick. I've gotten here by sheer grit and hard work and no rich prick is going to turn that upside down.

"I don't bet." I school my features into a mask of indifference. "I prefer certainties, a path to my goal, one I never veer from."

"Is that a challenge?" His eyes twinkle. He curls his lips and that smirk... OMFG... that upper lip of his seems to thin further. Combined with that puffy lower lip, that square jaw, the tendons of his gorgeous throat that stand out in relief and highlight the hollow at the base of his throat... Hell... He's lethal, all right. And too hand-some to be real. Guys like him exist on the cover of magazines, in online memes that I drool over in secret. Nah, he exists in a different world, a rarefied space I have no intention of being part of.

"Take it any way you like." I raise a shoulder. "I don't care."

There is an indrawn breath. I turn to find Amelie staring at me with huge eyes. She shakes her head, moves toward me, only her fiancé pulls her back. He whispers in her ear. She blinks and her cheeks turn pink. He turns her around and they walk off, leaving me alone with this reprobate of the first order... aka this big growly male who glares at me with... Something like intent in his eyes.

The hair on the back of my neck rises. My stomach trembles. "Ah... I... I guess best I circulate among the guests. Uh! Don't want to seem impolite or anything, know what I mean?" The hell am I blathering on about? "Good to have met you." Not.

I turn to leave, take a step forward, another. Okay... Maybe this is going to be fine. I'll just sidle out of here and— Warm fingers encircle my wrist. I am pulled around, and hauled up against the massive chest of said douche canoe... My breasts plastered against those ripped abs, which I had noticed outlined against his sweatshirt.

I gulp and my knees tremble... They bloody tremble. "Let go of me."
I demand.

"No."

"What?" I narrow my gaze on that sinful-as-fuck face. "You
release me right now or else —"

"Or else?" He peels back his lips and his teeth sparkle against the
tan of his sculpted features. At my silence, he continues, "You were
saying —"

"That this is a misunderstanding. I am not interested in you."

"Neither am I in you."

"Doesn't seem that way from where I am, buster," I snap.

"So much anger under that tightly-controlled exterior. I wonder
how it would be to peel back the mask you wear to the world, to
unveil the heat and passion that lurks under the surface, to show you
how it could be if the right man were to touch you in your secret
places, the ones you think you have hidden away," his voice lowers to
a hush, "but which I can see, feel, touch, suck..."

My sex clenches. I swear my panties self-combust. A whine
bleeds from my lips. I purse my mouth, stare at him. "I don't care for
self-obsessed, insufferable, prats. You've got the wrong woman."

"I don't think so."

He lowers his head until our eyelashes tangle. Until I am pressed
to him from toe to chest. My nipples tighten to push up against that
unforgiving wall of his torso. Something hard stabs into the cradle of
my core. I draw in a sharp breath.

"See what you do to me, Juliet?"

"Julia," I stutter. "My name is Julia."

"I prefer to call you lover, and you're welcome."

"I'm not and... For what?" I frown.

"Not yet," he corrects me, "and... for the kiss." He smirks.

"What kiss?" I scowl, "And you have some ego presuming —"

He swoops down and closes his mouth over mine.

*To find out what happens next read Damian and Julia's
story in Marrying the Billionaire Single Dad. This book also
features Weston and Amelie's wedding.*

Scan this QR code to find the book

How to scan a QR code?

1. Open the camera app on your phone or tablet.

2. Point the camera at the QR code.

3. Tap the banner that appears on your phone or tablet.

4. Follow the instructions on the screen to finish signing in.

READ AN EXCERPT FROM KARMA AND MICHAEL BYRON'S STORY IN MAFIA KING

Karma

"Morn came and went—and came, and brought no day…"

Tears prick the backs of my eyes. Goddamn Byron. Always creeps up on me when I am at my weakest. Not that I am a poetry addict, by any measure, but words are my jam.

The one consolation I have, that when everything else in the world is wrong, I can turn to them, and they'll be there—friendly steady, waiting with open arms. And this particular poem had laced my blood and crawled into my gut when I'd first read it. Darkness had folded into me like an insidious snake that raises its head when I least expect it. Like now. I'd managed to give my bodyguard the slip and veered off my usual running route to reach *Waterlow Park*.

I look out on the still-sleeping city of London, from the grassy slope of the expanse. Somewhere out there, the Mafia is hunting me, apparently.

I purse my lips, close my eyes. Silence. The rustle of the wind between the leaves. The faint tinkle of the water from the nearby spring.

I could be the last person on this planet, alone, unsung, bound for the grave.

Ugh! Stop. Right there. I drag the back of my hand across my nose. Try it again, focus, get the words out, one after the other, like the steps of my sorry life.

"*Morn came and went — and came, and brought no day…*" My voice breaks. "Bloody, asinine, hell." I dig my fingers into the grass and grab a handful and fling it out. *Again. From the top.* I open my eyes, focus on a spot in the distance.

"Morn came and went — and came, and…."

"…brought no day."

I whip my head around. His profile fills my line of sight. Dark hair combed back by a ruthless hand that brooks no opposition.

My throat dries.

Hooked nose, thin upper lip, a fleshy lower lip, that hints at hidden desires. Heat. Lust. The sensuous scrape of that whiskered jaw over my innermost places. Across my inner thigh, reaching toward that core of me that throbs, clenches, melts to feel the stab of his tongue, the thrust of his hardness as he impales me, takes me, makes me his.

"*And men forgot their passions in the dread*
Of this their desolation; and all hearts
Were chill'd into a selfish prayer for light.."

Sweat beads my palm; the hairs on my nape rise. "Who are you?"

He stares ahead, his lips moving,

"*Forests were set on fire — but hour by hour*
They fell and faded — and the crackling trunks
Extinguish'd with a crash — and all was black."

I swallow, squeeze my thighs together. Moisture gathers in my core. How can I be wet by the mere cadence of this stranger's voice?

I spring up to my feet.

"Sit down."

His voice is unhurried, lazy even, his spine erect. The cut of his black jacket stretches across the width of his massive shoulders. His hair… I was mistaken. There are strands of dark gold woven between the darkness that pours down to brush the nape of his neck. My fingers tingle. My scalp itches.

I take in a breath and my lungs burn.

This man, he's sucked all the oxygen in this open space, as if he owns it, the master of all he surveys. The master of me. My death. My life. A shiver ladders its way up my spine. *Get away, get away now, while you still can.*

I take a step back.

"I won't ask again."

Ask. Command. Force me to do as he wants. He'll have me on my back, bent over, on the side, over him, under him, he'll surround me, overwhelm me, pin me down with the force of his personality. His charisma, his larger-than-life essence that will crush everything else out of me and I… I'll love it.

"No."

"Yes."

A fact. A statement of intent, spoken aloud. So true. So real. Too real. Too much. Too fast. All of my nightmares…my dreams come to life. Everything I've wanted is here in front of me. I'll die a thousand deaths before he'll be done with me… And then, will I be reborn? For him. For me. For myself. I live first and foremost to be the woman I am…am meant to be.

"You want to run?"

No.

No.

I nod my head

He turns his head and all of the breath leaves my lungs. Blue eyes —cerulean, dark like the morning skies, deep like the nighttime, hidden corners, secrets that I don't dare uncover. He'll destroy me, have my heart, and break it so casually.

My throat burns. A boiling sensation squeezes my chest.

"Go then, my beauty, fly. You have until I count to five. If I catch you, you are mine."

"If you don't?"

"Then I'll come after you, stalk your every living moment, possess your nightmares, and steal you away in the dead of midnight, and then..."

I draw in a shuddering breath; liquid heat drips from between my legs. "Then?" I whisper.

"Then, I'll ensure you'll never belong to anyone else, you'll never see the light of day again, for your every breath, your every waking second, your thoughts, your actions...and all of your words, every single last one, will belong to me." He peels back his lips, and his teeth glint in the first rays of the morning light. "Only me." He straightens to his feet, and rises, and rises.

He is massive. A beast. A monster who always gets his way. My guts churn. My toes curl. Something primal inside of me insists I hold my own. I cannot give in to him. Cannot let him win whatever this is. I need to stake my claim in some form. *Say something. Anything. Show him you're not afraid of him.*

"Why?" I tilt my head back, all the way back. "Why are you doing this?"

He tilts his head, his ears almost canine in the way they are silhouetted against his profile.

"Is it because you can? Is it a...a..." I blink, "a debt of some kind?"

He stills.

"My father. This is about how he betrayed the Mafia, right? You're one of them?"

All expression is wiped clean of his face, and I know then I am right. My past... Why does it always catch up with me? *You can run, but you can never hide.*

"Tick-tock, Beauty." He angles his body and his shoulders shut out the sight of the sun, the dawn skies, the horizon, the city in the distance, the whisper of the grass, the trees, the rustle of the leaves... All of it fades, and leaves me and him. Us. *Run.*

"Five," he jerks his chin, straightens the cuffs of his sleeves.

My knees wobble.

"Four."

My heart hammers in my chest. I should go. Leave. But my feet are welded to this earth. This piece of land where we first met. What am I, but a speck in the larger scheme of things? To be hurt. To be forgotten. To be brought to the edge of climax and taken without an ounce of retribution. To be punished... By him.

"Three." He thrusts out his chest, widens his stance, every muscle in his body relaxed. "Two."

I swallow. The pulse beats at my temples. My blood thrums. "One."

Michael

"Go."

She pivots and races down the slope. The fabric of her dress streams behind her, scarlet in the blue morning. Her scent, lushly feminine with silver moonflowers, clings to my nose, then recedes. I reach forward, thrust out my chin, sniff the air, but there's only the green scent of dawn. She stumbles and I jump forward. Pause when she straightens. *Wait. Wait. Give her a lead. Let her think she has almost escaped, that she's gotten the better of me... As if.* I clench my fists at my sides, force myself to relax. *Wait. Wait.* She reaches the bottom of the incline, turns. I surge forward. One foot in front of the other, my heels dig into the grassy surface as mud flies up, clinging to the edges of my £4000 Italian pants. Like I care? Plenty more where that came from. An entire walk-in closet full of tailor-made clothes, to suit every occasion, with every possible accessory needed by a man in my position to impress... Everything, except the one thing that I have coveted from the first time I had laid eyes on her. Sitting there on the grassy slope, unshed tears in her eyes, and reciting... Byron? For hell's sake. Of all the poet's in the world, she had to choose the Lord of Darkness.

I huff. All a ploy. Clearly, she'd known I was sitting near her... No, not possible. I had walked toward her and she hadn't stirred, hadn't been aware. Yeah, I am that good. I've been known to slice a man from ear to ear while he was awake and fully aware. Alive one second, dead the next. That's how it is in my world. You want it, you take it. And I... I want her.

I increase my pace, eat up the distance between myself and the girl… That's all she is. A slip of a thing, a slim blur of motion. Beauty in hiding. A diamond in the rough, waiting for me to get my hands on her, polish her, show her what it means to be…dead. She is dead. That's why I am here.

Her skirts flash behind her, exposing a creamy length of thigh. My groin hardens; my legs wobble. I lurch over a bump in the ground. *The hell?* I right myself, leap forward, inching closer, closer. She reaches a curve in the path, disappears out of sight. My heart hammers in my chest. I will not lose her, will not. *Here, Beauty, come to Daddy.* The wind whistles past my ears. I pump my legs, lengthen my strides, turn the corner. There's no one there, huh?

My heart hammers, the blood pounds at my wrists and my temples, and adrenaline thrums through my veins. I slow down, come to a stop. Scan the clearing.

The hairs on my forearms prickle. She's here. Not far. Where? *Where is she?* I prowl across, to the edge of the clearing, under the tree with its spreading branches. *When I get my hands on you, Beauty, I'll spread your legs like the pages of a poem. Dip into your honeyed sweetness, like a quill into an inkwell; drag my aching shaft across that melting, weeping entrance.* My balls throb. My groin tightens. The crack of a branch above shivers across my stretched nerve endings. Instinctively, I swoop forward, hold out my arms. A blur of red, dark blonde hair, skirt swept up in a gust of breeze. She drops into my arms and I close my grasp around the trembling, squirming mass of precious humanity. I cradle her close to my chest, heart beating thud-thud-thud, overwhelming any other thought.

Mine. All mine. The hell is wrong with me? She wriggles her little body, and her curves slide across my forearms. My shoulders bunch and my fingers tingle. She kicks out with her legs and arches her back. Her breasts thrust up, the nipples outlined against the fabric of her jogging vest. *She'd dared come out dressed like that…? In that scrap of fabric that barely covered her luscious flesh?*

"Let me go." She whips her head toward me, her hair flowing around her shoulders, across her face. She blows it out of the way, "You monster, get away from me."

Anger drums at the backs of my eyes; desire tugs at my groin. The scent of her is sheer torture, something that I had dreamed of in the wee hours of twilight when dusk turned into night. She's not real. Not the woman I think she is. She is my downfall. My sweet poison. The bitter medicine I must imbibe to cure the ills that plague my company.

"Fine." I lower my arms and she hits the ground butt first.

"How dare you?" she huffs out a breath, her hair messily arranged across her face.

I shove my hands into the pockets of my fitted pants, knees slightly bent, legs apart. Tip my chin down and watch her as she sprawls at my feet.

"You...dropped me?" She makes a sound deep in her throat. So damn adorable.

"Your wish is my command," I quirk my lips.

"You don't mean it."

"You're right." I lean my weight forward on the balls of my feet and she flinches.

"What...what do you want?"

"You."

She pales. "You want to...rob me? I have nothing of value. I'm not carrying anything...except." She reaches for her pocket.

"Don't," I growl.

"It's only my phone."

"So you say, hmm?"

"You can..." she swallows, "you can trust me."

I chuckle.

"I mean, it's not like I can deck you with a phone or anything, right?"

I glare at her and she swallows, "Fine... You... You take it."

Interesting.

"Hands behind your neck."

She hesitates.

"Now."

She instantly folds her arms at the elbows, cradles the back of her head with her palms.

I lean down and every muscle in her body tenses. Good. She's wary. She should be. She should have been alert enough to have run as soon as she sensed my presence. But she hadn't. And I'd delayed what was meant to happen long enough.

I pull the gun from my pocket, hold it to her temple. "Goodbye, Beauty."

To find out what happens next read Karma and Michael Byron's story in Mafia King

Scan the QR code to get your book

How to scan a QR code?

1. Open the camera app on your phone or tablet.

2. Point the camera at the QR code.

3. Tap the banner that appears on your phone or tablet.

4. Follow the instructions on the screen to finish signing in.

AMELIE'S RECIPES

Amelie's Chocolate Pancakes

Prep:
5 mins

Cook:
8 mins

Total:
13 mins

Servings:
4

. . .

Yield:

  8 pancakes

Ingredients:

  •1 ¼ cups all-purpose flour

  •¼ cup unsweetened cocoa powder

  •3 tablespoons white sugar

  •¼ teaspoon salt

  •2 eggs, at room temperature

  •1 ¼ cups milk

  •½ teaspoon vanilla

Method:

1.Add milk, water, eggs, flour, cocoa powder, and sugar to a blender in the order listed. Cover securely, then turn the blender on and process until completely smooth.

2.Heat a crepe pan or large round pan over medium high heat. Spray with non-stick spray, and add just about 1/3-1/2 cup of batter. Tilt it quickly but carefully, evenly distributing the batter over the pan.

3.Cook for about 1 minute until the bottom is dry and cooked, then flip and cook another 30-60 seconds until the second side is cooked. Exact cook time will depend on the temperature of your pan.

4.Repeat until all batter has been used and serve with fruit and whipped cream as desired.

5.Leftovers can be store in the refrigerator for 3-4 days and reheat perfectly!

Amelie's tip: If you want a bigger chocolate flavor, drizzle them with chocolate sauce.

Amelie's Double Chocolate Chip Cookies

Prep:
15 mins

. . .

Cook:
10 mins

Total:
25 mins

Servings:
40

Yield:
40 cookies

Ingredients:
- 1 cup butter, softened
- 1 cup white sugar
- 1 cup brown sugar
- 2 eggs
- 1 teaspoon vanilla extract
- 2 cups all-purpose flour
- 1 teaspoon baking soda
- 1 teaspoon salt
- 1 cup unsweetened cocoa powder
- 3 cups chocolate chips

Method:
1. Preheat the oven to 375 degrees F (190 degrees C). Grease cookie sheets.

2. In a medium bowl, cream together the butter, white sugar and brown sugar until smooth. Beat in the eggs one at a time, then stir in

the vanilla. Sift in the flour, baking soda, salt and cocoa powder; mix well. Stir in the chocolate chips.

3. Roll tablespoonfuls of dough into balls and place them one inch apart onto the prepared cookie sheets.

4.Bake for 8 to 10 minutes in the preheated oven. Allow cookies to cool on baking sheet for 2 minutes before removing to a wire rack to cool completely.

Amelie's tip: Whisk coffee grounds or espresso powder into the flour and you'll score amazing mocha notes.

*Or you can fold in your favorite snack food (hehehe — you know what mine is right? *smirk*)*

Amelie's Banana Chocolate Muffins

Prep:
15 mins

Cook:
25 mins

Additional:
10 mins

Total:
50 mins

Servings:
18

Yield:
12 muffins

. . .

Ingredients:
- cooking spray
- 1 cup brown sugar
- 6 tablespoons butter, softened
- 6 tablespoons ground flax seed
- 1 teaspoon vanilla extract
- 2 eggs
- 2 cups all-purpose flour
- 1 teaspoon salt
- 1 teaspoon baking soda
- 3 ripe bananas, mashed
- 1 cup chocolate chips
- 1/2 cup chopped walnuts (optional)

Method:
1. Preheat oven to 350 degrees F (175 degrees C).
2. Spray muffin cups with cooking spray or line with paper liners.
3. Beat sugar, butter, flax seed, vanilla, and eggs together in a bowl until smooth and creamy.
4. Sift flour, salt, and baking soda together in a separate bowl. Mix creamed sugar mixture, into the flour mixture until fully incorporated and batter is stiff. Beat bananas into batter with an electric mixer on low.
5. Fold chocolate chips and walnuts into batter; spoon into the prepared muffin cups, filling each cup 3/4 full.
5. Bake in the preheated oven until a toothpick inserted in the center of a muffin comes out clean, about 25 minutes. Cool in the tins for 10 minutes before removing to cool completely on a wire rack.

Amelie's tip: Good when promptly served with vanilla ice cream; even better with dark chocolate ice-cream, yum!

Amelie's extra special Apple Pie

Prep:
25 mins

Cook:
45 mins

Total:
1 hour 10 mins

Servings:
8

Yield:
1 - 9 inch pie

Ingredients:
- 1 ½ cups all-purpose flour
- ½ cup vegetable oil
- 2 tablespoons cold milk
- 2 teaspoons brown sugar
- 1 teaspoon salt
- 6 Fuji apples, cored and sliced
- ¾ cup white sugar
- 3 tablespoons all-purpose flour
- ¾ teaspoon ground cinnamon
- ½ teaspoon ground nutmeg
- ½ cup all-purpose flour
- 1 cup brown sugar
- ½ cup butter

· · ·

Method

1. Preheat oven to 350 degrees F (175 degrees C).

2. To Make Crust: In a large bowl, mix together 1 ½ flour, oil, milk, 1 ½ teaspoons sugar and salt until evenly blended. Pat mixture into a 9-inch pie pan, spreading the dough evenly over the bottom and up the sides. Crimp edges of the dough around the perimeter.

3. To Make Filling: Mix 3/4th cup sugar with cinnamon, nutmeg, and 3 tablespoons flour. Sprinkle over apples and toss to coat. Spread evenly in unbaked pie shell.

4. To Make Topping: Using a pastry cutter, mix together ½ cup flour, ½ cup sugar and butter until evenly distributed and crumbly in texture. Sprinkle over apples.

5. Put pie in the oven on a cookie sheet to catch the juices that may spill over. Bake 45 minutes.

Amelie's tip: When I am baking at home, I often take a shortcut and use a frozen pie crust. Why not huh? Keep it simple.

ABOUT THE AUTHOR

Hello, I'm L. Steele.

I write romance stories with strong powerful men who meet their match in sassy, curvy, spitfire women.

I love to push myself with each book on both the spice and the angst so I can deliver well rounded, multidimensional characters.

I enjoy trading trivia with my husband, watching lots and lots of movies, and walking nature trails. I live in London.

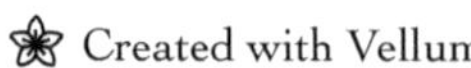 Created with Vellum